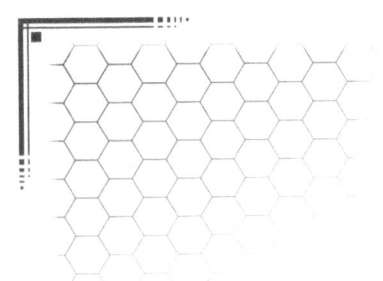

THE
EVARAN IMPACT

THE EVARAN CHRONICLES

BOOK 12

ADAIR HART

Editing done by Eliza Dee
Cover done by Tom Edwards
Interior design done by Colleen Sheehan
Proofread done by Alexa

Published by Quantum Edge Publishing

www.AdairHart.com

ISBN: 978-1-7327422-6-0

To get updates on new books and other notifications, sign up for my mailing list at:

www.AdairHart.com/MailingList.aspx

THE
EVARAN IMPACT

THE STORY SO FAR

» In *The Arrival*, *The Evaran Chronicles* prequel, a space- and time-traveling being known as Evaran rescues Jake Melkins and Kathy from a Seceltor slaver named Greecho. It is Evaran's first adventure in the Milky Way galaxy and introduces him to Earth.

» In *The Awakening*, Book 1 of *The Evaran Chronicles*, Dr. Albert Snowden and his niece, Emily Snowden, are abducted by an alien race known as the Krotovore. They are rescued by Evaran and V, Evaran's trusty mobile artificial intelligence, who drops them back off on Earth.

» In *The Fredorian Destiny*, Book 2 of *The Evaran Chronicles*, Evaran returns to check on Dr.

Snowden and Emily, and they ask to travel with him. Evaran accepts. They then help Fredoria, a planet of human ex-slaves, become a full trade partner with the Kreagan Star Empire, the local galactic superpower in Earth's region of the galaxy. Hampered by the industrialist Seeros and bounty hunters, they secure the Arkaron, a Kreagan relic, for the Fredorians to give to the Kreagan emperor.

» In *The Purification*, Book 3 of *The Evaran Chronicles*, Evaran and the gang fight the timeline invaders known as the Purifiers, a human-supremacist group led by the Overlord that tries to change Earth's history.

» In *The Time Refugee*, Book 4 of *The Evaran Chronicles*, they tangle with Billozein, a rogue time traveler, while helping Jane Trellis, a time refugee who is pulled out of her timeline.

» In *The Evaran Origin*, Book 5 of *The Evaran Chronicles*, they discover Evaran's origin and meet Levaran, another one of Evaran's plane forms, while fighting the Time Wardens, a timeline-void race that hunts rift travelers.

» In *The Shadow Connection*, Book 6 of *The Evaran Chronicles*, they group up with Jake Melkins and the nonhuman community to defend Earth from the ambitions of Caltorus, a dimensional being that rules over a vast empire encompassing worlds in many dimensions.

» In *The Human Factor*, Book 7 of *The Evaran Chronicles*, they head to AD 10105 and deal with a ruthless AI known as Salazar, in addition to fixing the timeline.

» In *The Cosmic Parallel*, Book 8 of *The Evaran Chronicles*, they leap from parallel timeline to timeline in a trap designed by the Mortani, plane refugees who blame Evaran for their situation.

» In *The Unification*, Book 9 of *The Evaran Chronicles*, they travel to AD 514,723 to unify humanity while dealing with an extradimensional threat.

» In *The Portal Effect*, Book 10 of *The Evaran Chronicles*, they deal with a rogue time traveler who enjoys zapping people to the past and altering timelines.

» In *The Time Cube*, Book 11 of *The Evaran Chronicles*, they meet Dalton Kingston as they travel to the Horologium-Reticulum supercluster to deal with the ruthless Tenagrin Hegemony.

This book continues their adventures.

EVARAN'S TECHNOLOGY

Torvatta—his disc-shaped ship that can travel through time and space. It is roughly fifteen feet tall by thirty feet wide. The interior contains six dimensional rooms, an open area with a semitransparent floor and sides, and a roof that can be transformed by hard holograms. A shielding around the *Torvatta* prevents most matter from entering.

Universal interface card (UIC)—a credit-card-sized device carried on his belt that allows access to most technological systems that do not have an artificial intelligence in them. It can also view limited information on biological systems.

Augmented reality interface (ARI)—an interface that only he can see around him.

Utility handle—a hilt-like device carried on his belt that can extend morphable matter in any shape, typically a baton or staff; can also fire repulsion, grappling, heat, mist, sticky globules, and stun beams.

Illumination orbs—small orbs on his belt that provide lighting and can hover.

Projection orb—an orb that allows projections to be sent to it from remote sources, such as Evaran's ring or the *Torvatta*.

Ring—a ring that can provide holographic projection and also scan.

PROLOGUE

Q was not sure Evaran's logic made sense. Assaulting a Krull-class transport was difficult by any measure. However, Q understood Evaran's motivation. Wardax, supreme leader of the Zayt Empire, had captured four ancient vampire lords: Vygon, Noskov, Skar, and Cyrus.

Their home planet had been razed, and the Halkins, a native species that the ancient vampires had a symbiotic relationship with, had been extracted and infected to become mindless drones of the Zayt Empire.

The Zayt assault on Drydris had been brutal. The Halkins were easily defeated by waves of infectors, small robots that were spherical in design with a multitude of spindly tendrils. Once the Halkins were infected, they fought for the Zayt or boarded ships and left.

Ancient vampires were immune to infection due to their Daedrould energy, nor could they be used as source material that could be reshaped to create enforcers, the backbone of the

Zayt forces. Thus, they had been destroyed, except for the four captured ones, who happened to be Evaran and Q's friends.

The enforcers' bipedal form was a fusion of plant life and technology. They had four arms and a large horn on their featureless stainless-steel-like faces and often wore heavy armor and carried lethal weaponry.

Enforcers and infected were always accompanied by controllers, who were usually created from other species. They commanded any Zayt force near them. Guardians commanded controllers and rounded out the ensemble. They were controlled directly by Wardax, and unlike controllers or enforcers, Guardians were usually constructed as robots.

Based on Q's recording when they had arrived to Drydris during the assault, the destruction and pillaging of Drydris had not taken long. Very few planets had fought back successfully in the past. The Zayt were efficient and aggressive.

As an AI, Q had probed an infected system on a ship that Evaran had attacked. That was when Q learned of Wardax's focus: assimilate faster, capture those with exotic energy for research, and destroy anything that got in the way. Q did not understand why the ancient vampires had not been used for research but instead chosen for destruction. It might have had something to do with their recent defeat of a small Zayt fleet. Or maybe, since some ancient vampires had already been caught, the rest could be eliminated.

Evaran would not let Wardax continue attacking civilizations and had been tirelessly looking for ways to stop him. Evaran's liquid metal suit, along with his heavy shielding, his forearm-mounted ranged weaponry, and a variety of gadgetry, had proved more than the Zayt could handle in small doses. What they were attempting now was on a different level.

"Are you sure of this plan?" asked Q. "A Krull-class transport has hundreds of enforcers, as well as controllers and a guardian."

Evaran scowled. "They took our friends. That can't stand."

"I understand, but this ship will be heavily defended."

Evaran's eyes glowed. "Let them try to stop me, then."

Q studied the warning alerts as they came within range of the ship. Although the *Karus*, Evaran's ship, had a stealth mode, along with heavy shielding and a variety of debuff and assault beams, the transport had its own defensive setup.

"We are approaching the docking bay," said Q. "It'll take some time to hijack the control system to get us in."

Evaran nodded. "I understand. Once inside, I'll need you to stay with the *Karus*. Be ready for a quick takeoff. I'm going to rescue our friends."

Q tilted his head. "You have not fought a full transport solo before."

"Always a first time for everything, right?"

Q nodded and focused on bringing the *Karus* into contact with the transport. Although he would have liked to join Evaran, Q's humanoid robot body was not meant for combat. It was sturdy, with decent shielding but not agile or meant for combat.

The *Karus* drew close to the Zayt ship, then shot two tendrils out that connected.

Q studied the flow of information. He inserted himself and isolated the docking bay control system. A moment later, and the *Karus* was accepted as a valid ship to enter.

"We've been authenticated," said Q.

"Excellent," said Evaran. "Once we land, I want you to activate Project Prime if our connection gets severed for any reason."

Q recalled having worked off and on for the last decade on building a quantum beacon. Evaran had never specified what it was for, other than it was meant to be activated when the probability of everything failing was high.

"Are you sure?" asked Q.

Evaran stood and his eyes narrowed. "I am."

"I understand," said Q. "What will happen?"

"Hopefully, something good."

"Are there any other preparations needed?" asked Q. "Or defensive measures I can enact?"

"No. I either succeed, or I die trying," said Evaran.

"I understand. I don't want you to die."

Evaran laughed. "Yeah, me either, so let's not plan on it."

Q guided the *Karus* through the docking bay's shields and landed. A quick scan showed there to be several other prisoner transport shuttles, and a variety of infected walking around. Q recognized the controller on deck by the swirling black mist and bright yellow circles that functioned as eyes. He was not sure what species the controller came from, but their appearance was always easy to spot. Infected members of an unknown humanoid race walked around, performing various tasks. Two enforcers in their green armor stood at attention by one of the doors. They wielded biotechnical weapons of some sort.

Evaran sighed. "The Zayt need to be removed, and Wardax, by extension. We may have won some fights, but we are but one group against thousands of theirs."

"I agree," said Q.

He recalled that even machine races were not immune to infection, since the virus was both digital and organic. Although he had little evidence, his calculations showed that the initial Zayt infection might have come from a hijacked machine race that had fused with plant life.

"Okay, it's time. Remember, activate Project Prime if we lose connection." Evaran walked over and laid a hand on Q's shoulder. "If for whatever reason I don't survive, I want you to know I value our friendship and have come to rely on it."

Q nodded. "It's the same for me, but I would prefer if you came back."

"Me too, old friend," said Evaran with a grin. He took one last look around the spacious command center before he exited.

Q had seen that face before. It was one Evaran had shown when everything was on the line, and he was not sure he would come out on top. Thankfully, he had in the past, but this time seemed different given all the variables to consider.

Evaran activated his camouflage shielding and exited the ship.

Q monitored the view from Evaran via the cameras in his suit. His stealthy approach worked initially as he took down some of the infected, but he had been detected by a turbulence system and a mist had sprayed around him. The nearby infected rushed him, but he dismantled them with ease. The two enforcers also went down after his suit extended two long rods that slammed the enforcers into the wall. While holding them, Evaran hit both with a stun shot. The controller was not a combatant and was easily disabled. Perhaps this mission would turn out well.

After twenty minutes and some light battle, Evaran had reached the room where a guardian had been detected. Although he had defeated one before, this one seemed different.

"Your arrival was expected," said Wardax in a monotone voice via the guardian.

"You can't get rid of me that easily," said Evaran. "You have some of my friends."

"I understand. They'll help with my research. You should consider them lost and aid me instead."

Evaran's eyes flashed gold. "Never!"

"Then you can join them as a research subject," said Wardax. He moved toward Evaran.

An alert beeped on the *Karus* perimeter monitor. Several infected approached the ship, flanked by enforcers and a controller. They carried unusual devices. The infected fired at the *Karus*, causing it to shake.

Q was not sure initially how they were shooting through cosmic-enhanced shields, but he determined that the robots were probably using palisin-energy-based devices.

"Evaran, the ship is under attack with palisin-based weapons."

Evaran slid back from a hard punch. "Activate Project Prime! Now!"

Q hustled to the dimensional room, where a sphere hovered. The idea was to activate the sphere, then the dimensional room's doorway would shrink to a micro level. That would still allow it to serve whatever purpose it needed to while making it undetectable to those not specifically looking for it.

Q calculated his odds of survival and determined that they were not high. To that end, he went to another room and activated a clone of his robot body. He parked it outside the dimensional room. Once he was inside, he turned on the beacon, which then shrank the doorway.

"It is done," said Q.

Silence.

"Evaran, are you there?" asked Q.

He could still see a visual, but Evaran seemed to have stopped moving. Over him stood Wardax with glowing purple fists. Q understood the glow to be palisin energy. That must be a new enhancement, since it had not existed on the previous guardian Evaran had fought.

The *Karus* shook as something cut into the side door. A magnetic clamp had also attached itself to the ship, and the docking bay had lost its atmosphere. The Zayt had opened the bay to open space.

Q ran several simulations to determine what to do, yet none provided a satisfactory solution. Evaran needed to be saved, yet Q was not sure how to get to him, especially since it seemed like the *Karus* was about to be boarded. He would try to fight off the invaders, but every calculation showed his defeat.

The side door crumpled and an enforcer robot burst through.

Q's clone body faced the attacker. He knew he could not fight and win. The enforcer looked like it had seen battle, and then some. If anything, it would think that there was only one robot on board, one that would soon no longer exist. Q knew he was Evaran's only hope, but maybe Project Prime would do something. What that was, he did not know.

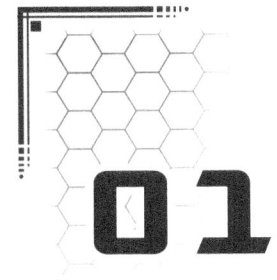

01

Dr. Snowden looked forward to meeting Lord Vygon, an ancient vampire lord, for lunch. He had called earlier and said he would bring the food. Dr. Snowden was not one to pass up a chance for the special burgers Lord Vygon would pick up from across town. It was 1:00 p.m., August 4, 2013, and Dr. Snowden had just finished a college faculty meeting. Now he had the rest of the day off.

He grinned as he walked to the table out on the quad. The last time he had seen Lord Vygon was at a cookout at the base of Lord Noskov, another ancient vampire lord. The event had been for Dr. Snowden's good friend, Inspector Dalton Kingston, Earth Ward, and the formation of his new team. Dr. Snowden loved being able to interact with so many interesting people.

It had been about seven months since he had traveled across space and time with the cosmic being Evaran, and V, Evaran's trusty mobile artificial intelligence. Emily. Dr.

Snowden's niece, was also a constant traveling companion, and the group was collectively known as Evaran and the gang.

Spending time in Columbus, Ohio, between adventuring worked well for Dr. Snowden. He even got to spend time with Kess, his evolved human girlfriend that existed half a million years in the future but could pop back via a portal system.

His mind focused on the upcoming lunch. It was somewhat strange that Lord Vygon wanted to meet, but Dr. Snowden always cleared his schedule for his friends. He also knew how rare it was for Lord Vygon to visit Columbus, much less Dr. Snowden's college. Either way, a good lunch remained in his future.

When he arrived at the table, he realized he must have been early. He thought he had timed it so that he would arrive on the dot. His stomach grumbled. Perhaps he was hungrier than he had figured. He smiled when he saw Lord Vygon in his black armor walking in the distance. The two bags he carried signified that a delicious lunch awaited them.

Dr. Snowden took his seat and reflected on the interactions he had had with Lord Vygon. Their first meeting had been in 2610 BC, and Lord Vygon had even traveled with the gang. Ever since that event, he had been a staple at Lord Noskov's base and the many cookouts held there. Dr. Snowden viewed Lord Vygon as a brother, one who would drop anything to help if asked. With the recent arrival of Dalton Kingston, Dr. Snowden appreciated having a strong circle of friends.

Lord Vygon arrived and set the bags on the table.

They shook hands and Dr. Snowden pulled Lord Vygon in for a slap on the back. They then took their seats.

"The infamous Dr. Snowden shake-and-half-hug greeting," said Lord Vygon, laughing. He gestured at the bags. "Burger House special with seasoned fries. The drinks are in there too."

"Don't need to tell me twice!" said Dr. Snowden. He opened the bag and pulled out his lunch and, a moment later, began inhaling his food.

"Careful. You still need to breathe." Lord Vygon grabbed his lunch and munched on some fries.

Dr. Snowden swallowed his bite. "Yeah, I know. I don't normally get Burger House burgers, so I'm living it up while I can." He shook a fry at Lord Vygon. "I am curious as to why you wanted to do lunch, though. While I enjoy thinking this is a social visit, I suspect there's more."

"You know me too well," said Lord Vygon. "You're right, of course. The ancient vampires are having a cookout tonight at 8:00 p.m., and you're invited."

Dr. Snowden laid a hand on his chest. "You bought me lunch to invite me to a cookout? No ... there's something else."

Lord Vygon reached into a side pocket and pulled out a rectangular stone. He laid it in front of Dr. Snowden. "You're more observant when you have a burger in you, it seems."

"Yeah, I am. Now what's that?"

Lord Vygon nodded. "It's the right half of a Daedrould stone, something we used in the past. The idea is that ancient vampire lords would give a full one to their close friends. If the ancient vampire died, their essence could be absorbed by the stone, and then the lord could be resurrected."

"May I?" asked Dr. Snowden, gesturing at the stone.

"Of course. Although it's only half of one, I wanted you to have it."

Dr. Snowden fidgeted with the stone. Lord Vygon signaled that he trusted Dr. Snowden with his life. It appeared to be a great honor, and Dr. Snowden was not sure why he was being given it now as opposed to another time. However, he appreciated the sentiment.

"Thank you. I'll guard it with my life. Who has the other half?" asked Dr. Snowden.

"I plan to give the other one to Emily."

"Wow, she'll love that," said Dr. Snowden. He eyed Lord Vygon. "So you just what? Put the stones together, place it on the body, and it does magic stuff?"

Lord Vygon laughed. "A full stone, sure. Two halves? I don't know. However, with a full stone, once the essence is absorbed, it takes a large amount of external energy to combine with the stone to do a resurrection."

Dr. Snowden raised a finger. "Ahh … so the stone captures what it can, then when it has more energy, it transforms everything it needs for a resurrection. Got it."

"That's right," said Lord Vygon. "Obviously, you don't need to worry about that here as it's mainly symbolic now."

Dr. Snowden nodded. He wondered why Evaran had not gotten one. That seemed like the logical choice, but Dr. Snowden was not going to question Lord Vygon about who he gave the stones to.

"I appreciate it," said Dr. Snowden. "I'm glad you feel comfortable enough to give this to us."

"We've been through a lot, haven't we?" asked Lord Vygon. He looked out over the quad. "It's a beautiful day out. I'm just glad we can experience things like this."

"Same here," said Dr. Snowden, downing some fries as he followed Lord Vygon's gaze. "I love it here before the fall. It's quiet and peaceful."

"I bet it is," said Lord Vygon.

Dr. Snowden reflected on how good it felt to have Lord Vygon pay a visit. The Daedrould stone half seemed unusual, but then again, Dr. Snowden lived in a world where having ancient vampire lords visit for lunch was possible. The cookout later that night would also be a nice change of pace. He had expected to go over some course material for his classes, but he was not about to say no to some grilled burgers.

He was not sure what Evaran's reaction would be. He would not be jealous, and would probably commend Dr. Snowden on reaching a trust level that allowed Lord Vygon to part with the two halves of his Daedrould stone. Hopefully it was not being given prior to some event. One thing Dr. Snowden had come to understand was that coincidences oftentimes were planned to some degree. He might be overanalyzing things again, though.

After an hour of light chat, he sat back and rubbed his stomach. "Ugh, I'm so full."

Lord Vygon stood. "As you should be. I'm off to visit Emily. Her volleyball game should be about over now."

"Well, I'm glad you stopped by, and I do appreciate the Daedrould stone."

Lord Vygon nodded slowly, then took off.

Dr. Snowden suspected Emily would be overjoyed to see him. They had a good relationship, and he sometimes showed up for training with her on the *Torvatta*. Even Dalton joined her on those. Dr. Snowden had tried to join several times, but her training pace was relentless. He grimaced. The thought of hard exercise after a great lunch was displeasing.

He studied the Daedrould stone. How it could hold Daedrould energy was a mystery, although once he was back on the *Torvatta*, he would check it out. For now, he had a date with a nap in a comfortable recliner at home.

Emily watched Jennifer leave. One of the great things about the sandlot where Emily played volleyball was that Jennifer was a server at the nearby bar. Getting a quick peck between matches always lightened Emily's day. Although she had an intense relationship with Jelton Stallryn, a Rift Guardian in a dimension in another timeline, she usually only saw him once a week. She did get to see Jennifer several times a week, though.

As Emily packed her belongings into her bag for the walk home, her mind briefly focused on Andia Kiggs. She was an older woman that Emily had had a relationship with in the past, and Emily missed her passion. Unfortunately, due to her being on Fredoria, a planet of ex-human slaves, and the way the timeline worked, visits were rare. However, Emily knew that when they did visit, they made the most of the time they had together.

Her relationships were scattered across time and space. It seemed normal to have several going on at once due to that. She did feel guilty about Jennifer not knowing about Andia or Jelton, and someday, she would have to say something, but that could wait.

Emily slung her backpack over her shoulder and left. It was 2:30 p.m., and she had the rest of the day to relax. She paused when she arrived at the park she usually passed through. Several months ago, Ziekah, a junction dimension being, had zapped Emily to the past on the same trail she normally walked on. Although that was history now, it still made the hairs on her neck rise every time she entered the area.

As a sign of defiance, she often traveled the same path. If something wanted to get her, they could try. She gripped her PSD in her pocket. Dr. Snowden said she was always ready to fight. There was a good reason for that. She had already spent nine months alone on a prison planet, and she had not been prepared. Never again. When Ziekah had zapped Emily, she had been prepared and had survived the event.

When she reached the spot of her encounter with Ziekah, Emily's cosmic senses told her of something nearby. Her nanobots tingled as she looked around. She relaxed when she saw Lord Vygon strolling over to her. Although she was glad to see him, his presence was unusual.

He waved at her.

She returned the wave and hugged him when they met. "I wasn't expecting you to be out here."

Lord Vygon gestured for them to continue walking. "Well, I visited with your uncle earlier, and I wanted to visit with you before I left town."

"Works for me," she said. "I'm always glad to see you."

He nodded. "I appreciate that. How's everything going with you?"

"It's okay. Just getting in some volleyball time before classes start up."

"This is your last year, right?"

She smiled. "Yep. I'm not sure what I'll do after graduation, though."

"You could always work with the Earth Ward as a history consultant. They'd love for you to verify things."

She chuckled. "You mean they'd love for Evaran to verify things, and I would be the way in for something like that."

They laughed.

She had often thought about what she would do once college was over. While she might teach, she had considered trying for her doctorate. As Lord Vygon pointed out, she had an advantage in that she could verify anything historical by traveling to the past, then determining where to find physical evidence in the present. One thing she would not need to worry about was a place to sleep. Food and drink were also not an issue with something like the *Torvatta*.

"I think I'll stick with the current arrangement, although since I'll apparently live for a long time, I'll need to take that into consideration. I mean, can you imagine when I'm over two hundred and publishing papers?"

Lord Vygon grinned. "That would be a sight. You'd be like Kantris."

She wrinkled her brow. "Who's that?"

"I figured you would have known him. He's an ancient Outsider. Keeps to himself, but he likes to study history. He's even older than me, and he never gets involved in conflict. Being able to camouflage himself helps with that."

"Huh. That would be useful."

Lord Vygon nodded. "I don't blame him for hiding away in the past. Humans wanted to dissect him, and scrupulous nonhumans wanted to use him. However, he does collaborate sometimes with human professors in regard to history. I suspect there are a decent number of papers where he was a major source. He works for the Earth Ward now at the Wild Haven Institute library and is under their protection."

Emily fidgeted with her ponytail. There were so many unique and different nonhumans, it was hard to know who could do what and where they were. Thankfully, the Earth Ward kept everything under control. Otherwise, she suspected it would be a madhouse.

Lord Vygon handed her a rectangular stone. "I gave your uncle the right half of a Daedrould stone. I wanted to give you the other half."

She accepted it. "A Daedrould stone? What's it do?"

"It absorbs Daedrould energy when a body fails. Then, if enough power is given to the stone, it can resurrect a body. It requires a full stone, though."

"Wow," she said. "And you're giving us the two halves?"

Lord Vygon looked off in the distance. "I am. It was a tradition ancient vampires practiced long ago on our home planet. We gave it to those we trusted with our lives."

"Aww. Thank you!"

He gestured at the stone. "Obviously, there's no need for it now, but I wanted you two to have it."

"Evaran's going to give you the stink eye if he doesn't get one."

He eyed her.

They laughed again.

"Yeah, I didn't think so either," said Emily.

"Nonetheless, Lord Noskov and I are having a cookout tonight at 8:00 p.m., and you and your uncle are of course invited."

"I'll be there," said Emily.

She loved going to those events. There were sometimes new people, and usually while there, she was surrounded by powerful beings. She had gotten to meet Dalton Kingston's new inspector team at the last cookout. They were close, and it made her happy to see he was doing well. He now had his own gang.

"Any special event being celebrated?" she asked.

"Oh yeah," he said, smiling. "You'll just have to wait and see."

She sighed. "Fine."

Her senses flared as she identified a Daedrould rushing toward them. She relaxed when she realized it was a jogger, who apparently had sensed them. He had sprawled to the ground, hopped up, and ran the other way.

"We seem to have that effect on others," said Lord Vygon.

"You, maybe."

He shook his head. "They would have sensed me, yes, but they would have also detected the power of your cosmic energy and not known what it was."

Emily shrugged. "I could see that." She flung her arm in the air and snapped. "As Kess would say: what's not to like?"

She enjoyed joking around with Lord Vygon. Although she could joke with Lord Noskov, he always seemed uptight. She sometimes forgot that, to nonhumans, she was scary. Her cosmic-enhanced nanobots would destroy anything that caused her to bleed, and most nonhumans did not know what cosmic energy was, other than that it was powerful.

A cookout sounded great, and on top of that, there was a mystery event being celebrated. It was at 8:00 p.m., so there was still plenty of time in the day before she had to leave. She was not sure what she would do, but maybe she would take a card from Dr. Snowden's hand and enjoy a nap.

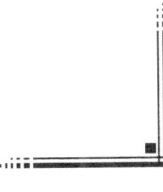

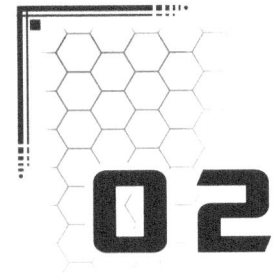

02

Dr. Snowden's eyes popped open when his PSD on his chest buzzed. He had fallen asleep in his nice comfortable recliner after getting home from lunch with Lord Vygon. Usually, Dr. Snowden put his PSD on the nearby table. He must have forgotten. A quick check showed it to be 4:10 p.m. He stretched. Naps always messed with his nighttime sleep, but sometimes it just felt so good to nap.

Emily bounced down the stairs and looked over at him. "You get it too?"

He wrinkled his brow. "Get what?"

"On your PSD. Evaran said something interesting has occurred and wants us to meet him in the conference room."

"Oh," said Dr. Snowden. He verified his PSD showed that, then stood. "Well, let's not keep him waiting."

Like Emily, he got the itch to travel when he had not done it in a while. Although he had enjoyed the last seven months, parts of it had been routine. It reminded him of how lucky he was to have nanobots and be able to visit remote places in space and time.

They exited into the backyard, boarded the *Torvatta,* and assembled in the conference room.

Evaran sat at the far end of the rectangular main table and faced the entrance, while V, in projected mode, which appeared as a young fair-skinned male in his early twenties, was to Evaran's left.

Dr. Snowden sat across from V while Emily sat next to him.

"I am glad you both are here," said Evaran.

"Analysis. I am as well," said V.

Dr. Snowden yawned. "I was napping, but now I'm wide awake."

"I see, and I apologize for disturbing you," said V. "You can set the PSD to go into a do-not-disturb mode in terms of notification, similar to a cell phone."

Dr. Snowden nodded. "I'll look into it later." He gestured at Emily. "I think she was napping, too."

She eyed him. "How would you know?"

He ran a finger up and down the left side of his face. "You have sleep marks."

"Oh!" said Emily. She rubbed her cheek.

"Anyway, what's up?" asked Dr. Snowden.

Evaran interacted with the table console. A projection of a galactic region appeared, and a red dot blinked between two solar systems.

"A quantum beacon is up. One from another universe," said Evaran. "I have already verified that all of the *Torvatta*'s quantum beacons are accounted for. This is not from the *Torvatta*."

Dr. Snowden rubbed his chin. "I wasn't aware a quantum beacon could be built that would catch the *Torvatta*'s attention."

"It cannot under normal circumstances. This was designed with the *Torvatta* in mind."

Emily tilted her head. "So the mystery is who created it. It being in another universe is strange." She wagged a finger at Evaran. "Wait a minute. I thought all quantum beacons, once activated, are visible to the *Torvatta* at all times. We should have been notified earlier."

Evaran half smiled. "Your *Torvatta* training is showing great promise. You are correct in that any activation would have been visible to our previous selves. As it was not, that means the *Torvatta* chose to show it to us now. However, there is another interesting detail. The universe the quantum beacon is in is far, relatively, from ours. It may be configured not as a parallel universe but something different."

Dr. Snowden's heartbeat ramped up. The last time he had been in a different universe was when they had picked up Levaran. She was the eighth plane form that had entered the plane, whereas Evaran was the first. "So ... another universe ... a quantum beacon calibrated to the *Torvatta* ... that must mean another Evaran, maybe one of your initial eight plane forms. Well, plane forms two through seven. We already know the first and eighth."

"Another Levaran!" said Emily.

"Analysis. It might be something completely random."

"It could be," said Evaran. He raised a finger. "We should be cautious. As you know, there is a tainted cosmic presence somewhere out there. This could be a trap, but I plan to investigate." His lips moved up slightly.

"You can't hide your excitement from us!" said Emily.

Dr. Snowden sensed Evaran's cosmic energy fluctuate while they had discussed the quantum beacon. It always made Dr. Snowden appreciate that Evaran was curious and wanted to investigate things. With his power level, he could have gone a different, more chaotic route.

"This is definitely intriguing," said Evaran. He studied them both. "You both can continue your napping. V and I will investigate this."

Dr. Snowden shook his head. "Not happening. We're going with. Besides, we can be back in time for the cookout at 8 p.m. at Lord Noskov's base."

"Are you sure?" asked Evaran.

Emily grinned. "We're sure." She pulled out her Daedrould stone. "Before we go, though, Lord Vygon gave me this."

Evaran scanned it. "It appears to be something that absorbs and dissipates energy."

"Yeah. He said if an ancient vampire was dying, the stone would absorb what it could. Then when more energy was added to the stone, it could release the energy and resurrect the ancient vampire."

Dr. Snowden pulled his stone out of his pocket. "I got the right half."

Evaran rubbed his chin. "Interesting. I do not believe it is coincidental that Lord Vygon visited you both and gave you each a half of this Daedrould stone."

V tilted his head. "The probability that these events are related is high."

"Yeah, that's what I think, too," said Dr. Snowden. "On a side note, I would have thought he woulda given you and V one first."

"I believe you underestimate your impact at times," said Evaran. "Nonetheless, I suspect his visit, the giving of the Daedrould stone halves, and the appearance of the quantum beacon occurring so close to each other signifies an event."

Emily tugged on her ponytail. "He *does* know the future to some degree. Maybe this Daedrould stone plays a part in what's to come. We should just call him up."

"We cannot," said Evaran. "If he were aware there was an upcoming event, and he knew what his involvement would be, he would act that out. I suspect that in coming to visit both of you, he was doing just that. The timing of this notification is exact, and is at a moment when it is only us four." He glanced at them. "Last chance if you wish to go back to napping."

Dr. Snowden eyed Evaran. "You won't shake us that easily. Besides, we can nap here if we wanted to." He stood and motioned toward the exit. "C'mon, let's check that beacon out."

They assembled in the command center. Dr. Snowden sat in the right U-shaped seating area, and Emily went to the other side. Evaran sat in his command chair, while V stood at the front center console.

Dr. Snowden loved sitting in the command area and viewing all the data screens that popped up in the transparent front half of the ship. Although the floor was semitransparent, the effect of floating was all too real. He recalled being with Kess the last time the group had assembled. It would be nice for her to come, but he understood she was busy running a galaxy-spanning empire.

He suspected Emily would have loved for Jelton Stallryn to participate, but like Kess, he had responsibilities. Dalton Kingston would have been fun to have around again, but he had his own team and was dealing with unusual cases on Earth. Although this was not a summons, it sort of felt like one. Maybe the *Torvatta* had dropped off a beacon, then made a new one, then covered it up. He cracked up thinking of the *Torvatta* mysteriously sneaking around.

The *Torvatta* rose and took off toward low Earth orbit.

Dr. Snowden knew it would be twenty minutes before they could open a portal. Then it would be discovery time. He loved that aspect of any investigation. It seemed as of late he had been more involved with fighting than researching. Maybe this would be a quick in-and-out research-type event, or it could be a life-changing one. He preferred the former.

***

Emily's heartbeat ramped up when the *Torvatta* formed a portal. Although the trip was supposed to be a quick check, she suspected it was going to be more than that. That seemed to happen more often than not. She recalled the last time the *Torvatta* had been moved—that event had led to the group fighting a dimensional god. Things could escalate quickly.

The *Torvatta* flew through the portal.

She studied the large ship that came into view. It had a cylindrical metallic body with three rings wrapping around it. One was near the front and another by the back. The middle one was twice as big as the first and third. Each ring was connected to the cylinder via metallic spokes. Small bumps covered the cylinder and the outer part of the rings. Various points on the ship had lights of varying colors shooting out into the darkness of space.

"Analysis. It is May 13, 54,529,201 BC, and we are 4.3 million light-years from Earth."

"Interesting. Far in the past, far from Earth, and by extension, far from our universe. And of course, another unusual ship to investigate. We seem to run into those often," said Dr. Snowden.

Evaran nodded. "V, perform scans."

"Acknowledged."

The *Torvatta* began to circle and scan.

Emily examined the data labels that popped out. The cylinder had thrusters at the front and back, along with adjustment ones to the sides. The rings provided shielding and even created the bubble needed to travel in condensed space. The reason the ship was not moving became clear when labels indicated power fluctuations.

Dr. Snowden rubbed his chin. "Seems like there's something wrong with its power systems." He glanced at Evaran. "We ran into that before. I'm guessing we're going to land and investigate."

"We are," said Evaran. He gestured at a rectangular slit on the cylindrical body near the back. "There is a docking bay for shuttles we can use. It is not sealed, which seems strange. V, take a closer look."

"Acknowledged."

The *Torvatta* flew to the docking bay.

Emily wrinkled her brow. The slit was large enough to allow small to medium ships in, but there was nothing but open space where a door or shielding should be. As they moved closer, she noticed that there were ships on the floor. Data labels identified magnetic clamps holding the ships. The beings that appeared surprised her.

"Analysis. Cybernetic life-forms detected."

Emily scrutinized the first being that V had zoomed in on. It was humanoid, but a dark mist swirled around it. The black grill-like rods that covered the dark gray armored padded body made her skin crawl. The sleek helmet had a gap where the face should be. A grill covered the mouth area, and two bright lights seemed to serve as eyes. The being had a wraithlike appearance overall.

Two other humanoids had on green armor. They had four arms, and their helmets were separated into two flat steel plates with a large horn in the middle. It reminded her of a rhinoceros horn, but the lack of eyes or a mouth intrigued her. The rest of the beings had a thin metallic covering with circuity-like lines engraved everywhere. Their glowing blue eyes and their shuffle made her think they were workers of some sort.

Dr. Snowden pointed at the wraithlike one. "What the heck is that? It's just standing there."

"No idea," said Emily. "The ones moving around remind me of zombies."

"Analysis. They are using magnetic boots."

Dr. Snowden nodded. "I figured, but look at how they're walking. There doesn't seem to be a pattern."

"Robot zombies," said Emily, grinning.

Dr. Snowden eyed her, then focused back on the ship. "I assume there's pressurized areas inside."

"There are," said Evaran.

"Analysis. Multiple cosmic energies detected. A dimensional doorway has also been identified."

Evaran sat up. "Display."

Emily watched as a wireframe of the ship appeared with several dots. Next to the two golden ones was a vertical rectangle outlined in blue. One dot farther inside the ship had its bar filled to eighty-five percent with a gold color. The other dot was in the docking bay, and the dot's bar was around five percent. The red dot was tagged as the dimensional doorway and was next to the golden dot inside the bay.

"What do those bars mean?" she asked.

Evaran nodded. "It is a cosmic energy percentage relative to me. Whatever is farther inside the ship has about the amount of energy I had before the cosmic shard incident. The one in the docking bay has less than what you two possess."

"Oh. Less than us? What's our number, relatively?" asked Dr. Snowden.

A separate bar, which was ten percent filled, hovered next to Evaran.

"That's interesting. What about Dalton?"

The bar filled to thirty percent.

"Whoa. That's a lot more than a sliver," said Dr. Snowden.

"Perhaps. Let us hope what is on the ship is not a cosmic shard," said Evaran.

Emily swallowed hard. The last time they had run into one, Evaran had been prepared to sacrifice himself. She was worried he might try that again if there was another one

She looked at him. "You're not sacrificing yourself if there is. We'll find another way."

"I understand," said Evaran. "However, a cosmic shard would not create a quantum beacon. I believe the signature farther in the ship is a cosmic being, and the weaker one in the docking bay is their ship, or perhaps the ship's shielding or a subsystem."

"I'm surprised you can't tell if it's one of your plane forms or not from here," said Emily.

"Something is interfering with what I sense. V, take us into the docking bay and locate an entry point to the ship's interior. Also, run scans on the cosmic energy detected there as well as the dimensional doorway."

"Acknowledged."

Emily grimaced as the *Torvatta* flew in. There were more beings than the scan from outside had initially detected. It made her wonder if whatever was interfering with Evaran's senses was also affecting the *Torvatta*. The design of the ship stood out, though. It looked like someone had taken a hollow coin and inserted it sideways into a thick triangle.

Everything seemed sleek with it, and where the circular part was shown, spokes connected the outer part to the triangular body. The back had a thruster-like area that projected out slightly, but she also saw what appeared to be adjustment thrusters in various places. She suspected that, similar to the *Torvatta*, the shielding could be shaped into an aerodynamic form as needed.

As beautiful as she thought it was, it resembled a carved-up turkey. The *Torvatta* showed only a glimmer of power left on the ship. The red dot indicating the dimensional doorway was inside.

"Cool ship. I guess we'll need to check it out," said Emily.

Dr. Snowden shook his head. "Yeah, without being detected, though. The last thing we need to happen is for a ship of the dead to awaken."

"Analysis. I can stealth in and scan in more detail."

Evaran nodded. "I think that is the best approach for now." He glanced at V. "As the temperature is low, you will need to be aware of the heat signature you generate. I suspect the lack of an atmosphere is a security measure."

"I understand," said V. "You are not the only one to recognize my hotness, so this may be a challenge."

Emily laughed. "Did you just make a joke?"

"I did. Did you like it?"

Emily leapt up and high-fived V. "It's perfect."

She loved that V tried to joke around. He had come a long way from the days of spitting out factoids left and right. Although he still did that, the attempts at jokes showed that he wanted to ease any anxiety that anyone might have. She considered V to be pure good, and with Evaran, that was a fairly exclusive club to belong to.

V entered orb mode. "I have moved the *Torvatta* to a nearby opening. I will enter there."

Emily scrutinized the tear on the side of the ship. It appeared as if someone had gashed it with a big knife.

V exited the *Torvatta* and flew toward the tear.

"Holo room?" she asked.

"Sounds good to me," said Dr. Snowden.

Evaran stood. "Let us go."

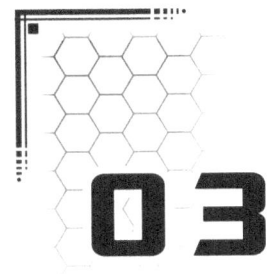

03

Lord Vygon's breathing increased as his senses began to kick in. He slowly opened his eyes and took a moment to determine what state he was in. It came back to him that he was in a life pod that also served as an advanced coffin.

The fight that had put him there flashed through his mind. A Class-B armored Zayt transport had attacked his ship. Lord Noskov, Lord Skar, and Lord Cyrus had been injured, leaving only Lord Vygon to get them to their pods, and the last thing he recalled seeing was the inside of his. Evaran had arrived in the area with the *Karus* and had communicated that he would pick everyone up. If that had happened, Lord Vygon would have expected to be looking at Evaran's face. Something must have gone wrong.

Lord Vygon tapped at the panel in front of him, and a moment later, internal lights illuminated the area. He reached into another panel to pull out a blood vial. After a sip, he relaxed as the life-sustaining blood powered him up. His strength, speed, and cognitive ability increased as he began to breathe heavier.

He took a moment to enjoy the sensation, then opened the life pod. It was time to get some answers. Stale air greeted him, and it took him a moment to adjust to the room's lighting. Three other pods were lined up next to his, and they appeared to be undamaged. Movement caught his eye. He grabbed two daggers from an inside panel and hopped out. His senses told him whatever was out there was not fully organic.

"Wait!" said a robotic voice.

Lord Vygon surveyed the environment. He could sense there was someone there, but not where. The robot must have some sort of advanced camouflage ability.

"Who's there?" he asked.

"Geldas. I reactivated your life pod. You need to get yourself and the other lords off this ship. I can help with that."

"Show yourself!" said Lord Vygon.

Geldas moved out from behind a container in the back of the room.

Lord Vygon recognized him as a controller. They were cybernetic beings with rods all over their body. The black mist that swirled around them obscured many things, but the two bright round lights on their face seemed like eyes. Controllers were created from conquered species and were one of the weirder Zayt types he had seen.

"You're a controller!"

Geldas raised a hand out toward Lord Vygon, then used the other to point at his neck. "With an overridden synthetic control unit. I can receive commands, but they don't control me."

Lord Vygon lowered his daggers. "You're part of the Keeshalt, the Geshin resistance."

"I am," said Geldas. "The Zayt may have assimilated our species and forced some of us to be controllers, but our natural physiology fought back. We were able to corrode the control unit implant and then synthesize a replacement."

Lord Vygon looked around. "I understand. Why are you here? Right now?"

"To help you," said Geldas. He motioned at the other life pods. "Your planet, Drydris, was one of the few that actually defeated a Zayt fleet."

Lord Vygon nodded. "When I left, we were losing the fight due to the infectors and enforcers dropped on us." He raised his head a bit. "Wardax, and his Zayt minions, will know the wrath of the ancient vampire lords! Drydris won't fall that easily."

Geldas stared at him.

"What?"

"Drydris as you knew it … is gone."

Lord Vygon's heart raced. "What do you mean? Some of us would have survived the battle."

"Perhaps … but not the planetwide bombardment after the Halkins were removed. Your world has been burnt."

Lord Vygon's stomach churned. He used the life pod to steady himself. If what Geldas said was true, that would mean a great loss of life.

"I know you had a symbiotic relationship with the other species, the Halkins, on your planet. Many were infected and taken, but … your species was eliminated."

Lord Vygon growled. "And now he's captured me and the other lords."

"I think … the last of your kind from your planet," said Geldas.

Lord Vygon squinted hard. The news of his planet's demise hit him harder than he would have expected. He recalled all the friends and adventures he had had over the last thousand years. Now it was all gone.

"Evaran had contacted us before we went into the life pods. He would have saved us. Where is he?" asked Lord Vygon.

Geldas sighed. "More bad news, I'm afraid. He did come here to rescue you, but he fell to a guardian."

"A guardian controlled by Wardax would stand no chance against Evaran."

"Perhaps in the past. The one here has palisin energy," said Geldas.

"What's that?" asked Lord Vygon.

"An exotic energy, not unlike your own, except this one has the apparent ability to weaken whatever energy is in Evaran," said Geldas.

Lord Vygon rubbed his temples. "He has cosmic energy, and I can sense a faint trace of him. Is he still here?"

"Yes. He's being held prisoner, and the guardian watches over him."

"What about Q and the *Karus*?"

Geldas looked down. "Q is … gone, and the *Karus* is being stripped now."

Lord Vygon grimaced. That was not the news he had been expecting since Evaran was involved. He was the toughest fighter Lord Vygon had ever seen. Evaran was also fast, wore a liquid metal suit, and all that with an intelligence level that far surpassed that of any being Lord Vygon knew. It was difficult to imagine Evaran losing to anyone, yet here was Geldas saying Evaran had been defeated.

Lord Vygon used his neck to roll his head around. "Okay. I'm aware of the situation now. We'll need a ship and a plan. Evaran needs to be rescued, and once that's done, we can all leave together."

"That's why I woke you," said Geldas. "The other ancient vampire lords have been injured, but they remain stable as long as they're in stasis. You possess fighting skills, from what I read in your profile. We're going to need that to secure a ship."

"What about that guardian on Evaran? I've never fought one," said Lord Vygon.

Geldas nodded. "It may have palisin energy, but it's like any other guardian. High-energy weapons with an EMP component would probably work best, and I know where you can get some. However, you'll need to pull the guardian away from the room before using any weapon."

"It sounds like you could have done this already," said Lord Vygon.

"No," said Geldas. "While controllers do possess some combat ability, we are not combatants. We merely repeat Wardax's commands to the other assimilated beings. While I still do that, I have free agency to ignore the orders issued to me. Also, I can't move like you. I can defend myself, but we are expendable."

Lord Vygon furrowed his brow. "All right. I'll need the ship layout so we can figure out the timing and where I'm going."

Geldas raised a finger. "That … I can help with. Also, when you secure the ship, I can fake some commands for others to get them out of your exit path. I can even pinpoint where to get the weapons, but that's about as much as I'll be able to do."

"You're coming with us when we leave, right?"

"I can't. My position provides critical intelligence to the Geshin. Plus, there are other operatives who will help you secure an escape route once you have Evaran and then come by here to get the other ancient vampire lords."

Lord Vygon looked down. The enormity of the task before him was daunting. Fighting a guardian would be new, but maybe the weapons Geldas had scrounged up would help even the odds. Even so, Lord Vygon recalled stories of ancient vampire units suffering heavy losses when fighting guardian-led units. How Wardax could control so many guardians was nothing short of fantastic. He did not even have to be present in his primary form, whatever that was.

The first step would be to retrieve the weapons. Once they were secured, Lord Vygon would disable the guardian and free Evaran. Hopefully, he would still be able to function. The next step would be to come back to this room and get the pods. Then it would be a mad rush to a ship to escape. He had no illusions about the fact that he might not make it out of this scenario, but Geldas had given him a chance. Lord Vygon did not plan to squander it.

Dr. Snowden relaxed in the holo room. He loved that he could summon up a recliner and plop down in it. Emily sat on a plush couch next to Evaran. All around them was a 360-degree view from V.

The experience brought back memories of when Kess had been there the last time they had had a holo room viewing from V's perspective. Dr. Snowden missed her, and having her along on the previous adventure had shown how fulfilling traveling with Evaran could be with her as a companion. He wished she could travel with the gang, but he also understood that a galactic alliance depended on her. Perhaps in time, she could step aside and either he could join her or she could come to Earth, or maybe even a mix.

He chuckled when Emily dove into a bucket of popcorn. She always brought a snack or two with some drinks to these viewings. He liked that she was experiencing everything with him on their trips with Evaran. She had had a tough road growing up, and now it seemed she was being rewarded for sticking it out. Dr. Snowden felt like he had won the lottery, too, in getting to travel with Evaran.

Emily pointed at the tear as V approached it. "That looks like something pierced the wall, then pried it apart."

Dr. Snowden studied the gash. He agreed with her assessment. "Whatever could do that must be strong."

"Maybe there's a specialized robot that did it," said Emily.

Dr. Snowden grinned. "Let's hope V doesn't run into that."

"I concur," said Evaran. He pointed at several red silhouettes. "It appears there is some activity on the ship."

"Analysis. Based on the *Torvatta*'s scans, I am proceeding to the command center."

"Very well," said Evaran.

Dr. Snowden noted that when the *Torvatta* had scanned the ship, it had assigned labels based on probabilities of the rooms' purposes. It struck him as odd that it found high probabilities for most rooms. Perhaps that was a sign that the design had an Evaran influence that made the room's function easier to identify.

As V flew through the hallways, Dr. Snowden observed the unusual beings wandering around. They registered as organic with a technical component not only in their armor but also inside them. It was like a second nervous system. Some used a specialized device to cut into the walls, while others scuttled about carrying parts.

Dr. Snowden's heartbeat ramped up when V flew by one. Although there would be no turbulence, V had a heat signature. However, it seemed the workers were focused on whatever task they were working on.

When V reached the command center, he identified a console with low power. He flew over and connected to it after no life signs were detected.

Dr. Snowden appreciated the visuals that the holo room showed. He watched with fascination as various data windows surrounded V. Lines went between them, and Dr. Snowden could not make out everything that was being displayed.

One screen lit up and moved above the others.

"The cosmic energy signature was from the shielding!" said Emily.

"Yes," said Evaran. "The ship is known as the *Karus*, and it is owned by Evaran. The ship the *Karus* is in is a Class-B armored Zayt transport."

"You moonlighting over there?" asked Dr. Snowden.

"Not me, but another Evaran," said Evaran with a half smile. "There is also an AI companion named Q. V, relay any recent external visual feeds if possible."

"Acknowledged. Scanning," said V.

Dr. Snowden's eyes narrowed when a screen appeared from the ship's perspective. It showed a man in a suit that appeared to be made of liquid metal walking outside the ship. After a moment, he fought some Zayt that were similar to the workers. They were identified as the infected. What surprised Dr. Snowden was that the man's brown hair never moved during the fight. That must be an Evaran thing, assuming this man was one. Another oddity was the trimmed beard that went over and under the mouth, and up the sides of the face.

"That must be the other Evaran," said Emily.

"I believe so," said Evaran. "He moves as I would."

"Is there no audio, V?" she asked.

"Unfortunately not," he said.

Emily puffed her cheeks. "Well, I think the important thing here is we know there's an Evaran and his AI companion around."

"I concur," said Evaran. "V, investigate the dimensional door that was detected."

"Acknowledged."

Dr. Snowden was curious as to what personality the other Evaran would have. Levaran had been bold. She had not minced words, and she had been quick to address injustice as soon as she saw it. He recalled her fighting style, which, due to her raw strength, was different from what he had come to expect from Evaran. She bulldozed through obstacles.

V reached an empty room where a tiny dot in the middle glowed. "Analysis. This is the dimensional door. Initiating scans."

"Why is it so small?" asked Emily.

Evaran nodded. "Perhaps to avoid detection. This Evaran would have been able to hide something in there."

"Like a quantum beacon," said Emily.

"Since it is still tied to this reality via the tiny opening, it would have shown up for us. That's ingenious," said Dr. Snowden.

"That's Evaran, but same thing," said Emily, grinning.

Evaran eyed her. "It is an interesting approach. I am unclear as to why it was activated when it was, but I suspect it was a last-resort thing."

"You think the other Evaran was not sure if he would be coming back?" asked Emily.

"That is my current hypothesis."

Dr. Snowden rubbed his chin. The thought of Evaran dying was a foreign concept. Dr. Snowden recalled Evaran had attempted to sacrifice himself to eject a cosmic shard, but that had been by choice. Levaran had initially died as a man, but it had taken thousands of years and a specialized Time Warden prison capsule. She had been re-formed on the *Torvatta*. Dr. Snowden was not sure what state the Evaran from the *Karus* would be in.

"Analysis. I have made contact with the AI known as Q."

A window popped up with a robotic head. It resembled a male human one, but the robotic eyes, metallic skin, and circuitry-like patterns etched on its cheeks indicated it was not organic.

Evaran motioned forward. "Hello. I am Evaran, and with me are Dr. Albert Snowden and Emily Snowden. You were contacted by V, my good friend and AI. I take it you traveled with Evaran."

Q tilted his head. In a synthetic voice, he asked, "You're Evaran?"

Evaran nodded. "I understand there may be some confusion. The Evaran you travel with is a different version, but we are the same at a lower level. I assume the other Evaran activated the quantum beacon so it would bring me and my friends here."

Q nodded. "I wasn't aware of its purpose, but I understand now. Evaran called it Project Prime."

Dr. Snowden crooked a thumb at Evaran. "That makes sense. This Evaran was the first of eight plane forms to enter the plane. He also has the *Torvatta*. That would make him Evaran prime."

"An excellent analysis," said Q. "Perhaps I should board your ship. I don't believe I have much time left here before I'm discovered."

Evaran nodded. "The dimensional doorway will need to be enlarged, and once that is done, we can escort you off the ship."

Q stared at Evaran. "Are you okay?"

"What do you mean?"

"You seem like a machine and speak like Wardax."

"I am not familiar with Wardax," said Evaran. "Nonetheless, each plane form has its own personality. The one you traveled with must have chosen a personality that expressed itself more easily."

"A logical conclusion," said Q. "Okay. I will wait here until the doorway is widened."

The communication window closed.

"That was interesting," said Emily.

"No kidding," said Dr. Snowden. He faced Evaran. "So we're going to board the ship without being detected, enlarge a dimensional doorway, grab Q and the beacon, then hustle back to the *Torvatta*."

Emily raised a finger. "And rescue the other Evaran."

"We will do all those things," said Evaran.

Dr. Snowden wrinkled his brow. "Sounds good, but, uh ... how are we widening a dimensional doorway?"

"I have a device for that," said Evaran. "I will program it to unleash the energy needed to perform the operation."

"We'll definitely need our helmets up for this," said Emily. Her eyes narrowed. "We might even have to fight."

"Perhaps so," said Evaran. "I wanted V to get an interior scan of the Zayt transport. However, as this area is open space, we would need to go through a decompression chamber to reach the interior, and if V tried, he would be detected. We will go together once Q and the quantum beacon are safely aboard the *Torvatta*."

"Works for me," said Emily, hopping up.

Dr. Snowden stood. "Let's rescue Evaran!"

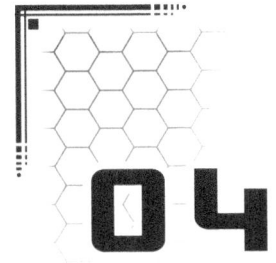

04

Emily checked her suit to make sure it was ready. She loved the dimensional power bridge that sat on her back. It wrapped around her like a warm blanket, and when she focused, the suit responded to her will, giving her enhanced speed and strength. It also allowed her to do more than she even thought possible at times.

She stood next to Evaran and Dr. Snowden on the *Torvatta*'s ramp. There would most likely be fighting to rescue Q and get the quantum beacon. She was sure there would be more once they went to retrieve the other Evaran.

The avatars for the others appeared inside her helmet. It was second nature to her now to see data labels on anything she viewed. It was a pseudo-augmented-reality interface that was not quite on Evaran's level, but it worked well enough. V had flown back and was in the command center, and his frown was probably due to not coming along.

Her adrenaline whizzed around in her body as she focused on the task ahead. Someone was in trouble, and she was going to help out with the gang. The *Torvatta* hovered over the *Karus*, so they would need to jump down, although in space, it was more like pushing off something to go in a direction.

"Are we ready?" asked Evaran over comms.

Dr. Snowden shrugged. "As ready as I think we'll ever be."

"Same," said Emily.

"I would prefer to come," said V.

"I understand, but we do not know if the *Torvatta* is immune to whatever did this to the *Karus*. You should still be able to communicate with us," said Evaran. He faced the others. "When we are outside the shielding, use your grappling beams to pull yourself to the *Karus*. Once down, engage your magnetic boots, and we will walk to a nearby opening. Are you two ready?"

Dr. Snowden and Emily indicated they were.

Traveling through space was not new to Emily. She recalled having to do it on their first voluntary trip with Evaran when investigating a Kreagan colony ship that had been adrift. This time, though, she was much more experienced, and her suit was more advanced.

Evaran stepped through the shielding and fired his grappling beam at the *Karus* below.

Dr. Snowden peeked at Emily, then went next.

She joined them, and after a moment, they were on the *Karus*'s outer hull. She was thankful that sound, for the most part, did not travel in space as she was sure their landing would have made some noise. Maybe the vibrations would at least. She took a moment to gaze out of the docking bay. Open space was hauntingly beautiful, but she understood how deadly it could be. She focused back on the group as Evaran moved away.

The group's pace was slow, and after ten minutes, they reached an opening.

"This looks like they just removed a section of the ship," said Dr. Snowden.

"That makes it easier for us," said Evaran. "Let us go."

They entered using their grappling beams.

Emily surveyed their immediate surroundings. They had landed in what would have been living quarters. There was a room to the side that appeared to be a bathroom of some type.

Evaran walked over to the door and placed his UIC on the nearby console. "It appears there is no system connectivity here. We will need to force this open."

He extended his utility handle and morphed it into a crowbar, then positioned it between the door's right side and the surrounding wall. A moment later, and the door had slid back some. He repositioned the tool horizontally once there was enough space to do so. His staff spawned and pushed the door apart even more.

It always fascinated Emily to watch Evaran's creative solutions. She recalled he had used a similar approach when helping her, Dr. Snowden, and others escape a Krotovore ship long ago. The method was effective. She gripped her PSD and followed Evaran through.

The spacious hallway they entered had metallic panels, and along the top and bottom and top edges were blue strips that provided some illumination. Although there was low light, her helmet had adjusted and allowed her to see. The place felt dark, cold, and alone. She shivered.

Evaran inspected her. "Are you okay?"

"Yeah ... fine," she said.

Dr. Snowden shook his head. "I feel like we're in a tomb."

"Let us hope that is not the case," said Evaran. He motioned forward. "The dimensional doorway is this way. We are close."

They continued on.

Emily's eyes widened when they came upon one of the infected. There had been no way to avoid it as it was in their path. Its eyes had brightened, and it dropped whatever it was carrying to rush at them. It sampled Evaran's stun beam.

"Well, at least we know stun works on them," said Dr. Snowden.

"Yes, but it sent a communication signal prior to attacking," said Evaran. "We need to hurry."

They hustled as fast as possible to the room with the dimensional doorway.

Emily surveyed the area when they arrived. The doorway appeared in her helmet as a bright dot as it had in the holo room. If not actively searched for, it would be easy to miss.

Evaran placed a small device next to the doorway. The device glowed, and the doorway expanded.

A humanoid robot stood next to a crude quantum beacon supported by four legs. That must be Q. His metallic body reminded Emily of an android. His green eyes glowed, and he wore no clothing. Various parts of his body had what appeared to be armored pads, but her initial instinct was that Q was not made to fight. His slower movement and erratic head and arm motions indicated he took time to do something compared to V. An avatar for Q materialized in her helmet.

"Hello. I am Q, and thank you for the invitation to join your communication group."

"Analysis. You are welcome."

"Hey," said Emily.

"Hey to yourself, and everyone else," said Q. He examined the immediate area. "We should probably move."

"I concur," said Evaran.

Emily wondered what went through Q's processing as he stared at Evaran.

Evaran grabbed the quantum beacon and exited the room with the others in tow.

Emily picked up the small device Evaran had used to open the doorway. No need to leave that lying around.

The group paused when they got back to the place where they had fought the first robot.

Emily's eyes narrowed as one of the wraithlike beings appeared, flanked by other beings in green armor. The data labels indicated the being was a controller, and the others around it were enforcers. She was not sure of their role or purpose, but she planned to look it up later.

Evaran handed the quantum beacon to Dr. Snowden. "You three get to the *Torvatta*. I will handle these."

"That's a Zayt controller and its enforcers. Are you sure you can handle them?" asked Q.

Emily got goose bumps when Evaran's eyes glowed.

"I will deal with them. Go," said Evaran.

Emily place a hand on Q's back. "C'mon. He's got this."

Q nodded. "That is an Evaran trait I recognize. It is useless to argue. I will follow you."

"Okay. You'll need to hold on to us when we grapple out."

"I … okay."

She knew better than to ask if Evaran needed help, and it seemed that might be a common Evaran trait based on Q's response. Evaran had already extended his utility handle into a staff and marched toward the controller and enforcers. Each end of his staff crackled with blue energy, and she suspected he would make quick work of them. She understood that their abilities were unknown, and Evaran wanted to focus on dealing with that instead of putting the group at risk.

They reached the room that had been carved away.

"Okay, hold on to me," said Emily.

Q walked over and grabbed her arm.

Emily laughed. "No, silly. Put your arms around me."

"Are you sure?"

"Analysis. Emily is quite serious," said V.

"Okay," said Q. He complied.

She aimed up and fired at the top part of the sheared edge of the room. The momentum pulled her up, then she used the grappling beam once above the *Karus* to bring them back down to the outer hull.

Dr. Snowden followed her with the quantum beacon tucked under his right arm.

"Analysis. The *Torvatta* is stealthed above you. I have outlined it in your views."

"Good idea," said Dr. Snowden.

"I am on my way," said Evaran over comms.

"You've already dealt with the Zayt?" asked Q.

"I have," said Evaran. "Although the guards were physically tough, they could not withstand their own weapon fire."

"I don't understand."

Emily tapped her left forearm. "Evaran used his shield to deflect their beams back at them."

"A shield?"

Emily spawned hers.

"Interesting," said Q. "I didn't expect that."

They boarded the *Torvatta* and Evaran joined them a moment later.

"I suspect there are many things that are confusing to you," said Evaran. "We have questions as well, but it is better to discuss them safely aboard the *Torvatta*."

"Are you going to rescue Evaran? The one I know?" asked Q.

"We are, but first, you needed to be rescued," said Evaran.

Emily wondered how odd it must be for Q to process that there was another Evaran. Then again, he was a pure AI. She did not sense any exotic energy in him. Although she wanted to sit Q down and ask a million questions, they still had to find and rescue the other Evaran. That would have sounded strange long ago, but as of late, it was now normal.

Lord Vygon struggled to detect the Zayt. He had been following Geldas to a room that had weapons. They were not meant to be used for assault, but Lord Vygon planned to use them that way. Although he could sense the infected, the enforcers, and the infectors, it was the controllers that gave him problems. They appeared to him as a buzzing like all pure machines did. With so much technology on the ship and all the Zayt walking around, it was difficult for him to get his bearings.

Thankfully, Geldas could redirect Zayt out of the way as he walked. Lord Vygon stayed about a room or two behind and moved forward when the pathway was cleared. The strategy appeared to work, and they made good progress. It still surprised him to be working with anything related to the Zayt, but he had heard of the Keeshalt. The Zayt were not as united as he had thought.

Wardax still remained a mystery. His ability to control a whole empire, on top of controlling every guardian at the same time, was nothing short of impressive. Lord Vygon had learned of the Zayt when Wardax had introduced himself via military means. It had been said he fought to remove threats, but Drydris had only become a threat because it had defended itself.

Lord Vygon focused back on the mission at hand. He was thankful that the ship he was on had many side rooms, and moving between them was not too difficult. When Geldas encountered another controller, he took more time than expected. Lord Vygon figured they were comparing orders or something.

After twenty more minutes, Lord Vygon was within viewing range of the maintenance room with the high-energy weapons. He suspected they were some type of mining tool with charges. He would find out momentarily.

There were two enforcers in front of the room. He did not know what species were subjected to the creation process for the enforcers, but he was well versed in the final result. From what he understood, they were a hybrid of various species, broken down, then infused with some type of plant and technology. Their chitin-like green armor, plated head, large horn, four arms, and signature circuitry-like pattern all over their skin seemed like an unusual choice for the backbone of the Zayt forces. However, their biotechnical weapons were no joke.

Lord Vygon narrowed his eyes. Everything in him wanted to rush over and kill the enforcers, but Geldas communicated with them. After a moment, they took off, and Geldas waved Lord Vygon over. He rushed to the room and slipped in.

Geldas joined him and closed the door. "There's a variety of equipment in this room. I'd suggest you look at the laser drill."

Lord Vygon surveyed the gear. The laser drill stood out due to its size, and he could see its potential. There were several mine-like charges that were probably meant for detonating larger structures. He was not sure he wanted to do that in a ship. Even using the drill could be dangerous if it punched a hole in the hull. Several EMP mines could prove useful as they were designed for disabling a smaller area.

He studied the blunted forearm blades. A part of the outer edge was sharp. The end point was boxlike, but small enough that it could still cause some damage. He slipped on the blades and was amazed at how effortlessly they retracted and extended on command.

"Those are used to carve tunnels manually when no other equipment is available," said Geldas. "They're quite formidable and can tear apart anything within range. They do require strength to wield effectively. Not a problem for you or any infected that possess that naturally."

Lord Vygon moved around and tested the blades. "I like it. If the laser drill and EMP charges don't work, then these should."

Geldas nodded. "Hopefully, you won't need to use them. But Wardax is not to be underestimated, and the guardian body he controls on this ship is quite tough."

"I understand, but he needs to be dealt with," said Lord Vygon.

He grabbed a bandolier and placed several EMP charges in holders. The laser drill was heavier than he had thought it would be, but he also understood its raw power. Between the drill, charges, and blades, he believed he had enough to take down the guardian and rescue Evaran.

"Are you ready?" asked Geldas.

"I am."

"Okay. I can only guide you to the room. After that, you'll be on your own. I'll be coordinating your escape with other Keeshalt members. I don't know what you'll face in the room as it's secured, even from me."

Lord Vygon studied Geldas. "I wanted to let you know that I appreciate all that you're doing and the risk you're taking. If I don't make it out of that room, it was an honor to meet you."

Geldas raised his head a bit. "One day, we'll all be free."

"Damn right," said Lord Vygon. He performed a final check on his suit and equipment, then focused on Geldas. "Let's get moving."

The trip to where Evaran was being held was harder than Lord Vygon had expected. The drill slowed him down, and he had to be more careful when he moved from room to room. While Geldas cleared a path, Lord Vygon had to factor in his current movement speed before he hustled to the next safe spot. The last thing he wanted was to be worn down when he arrived at Evaran's room. Lord Vygon still felt weaker than normal, but he could recharge once he and the others were safe.

Geldas paused in the hallway before the room. "There is a security alert. You'll need to get in the room before it's sealed."

"A security alert? For what?" asked Lord Vygon.

"There is a group attacking from the docking bay, and they seem to be effortlessly handling the enforcers."

"Where are they headed?"

"In this general direction."

Lord Vygon sighed. "Great. I hope they're friendly and not another enemy I'll have to fight. Okay, I'm going."

He rushed in. Although several Zayt had seen him enter, they had ignored him, which he found odd.

The doors sealed.

He took a quick scan of the room. Evaran lay motionless on a slab with some type of semitransparent purple shield over him. Next to him stood a nine-foot bulky humanoid robot with massive forearms, and on its shoulders were small turrets. The boots were large, and digital lines pulsed all over the body. The head had a single slit across where the eyes would be. That had to be the guardian.

It whirred into action. "Ahh. Lord Vygon. Ancient vampire lord, specimen one."

"And you must be Wardax, controlling the guardian." Lord Vygon gritted his teeth and aimed the laser drill. He fired, but the beam hit an energy shield around the area where the slab was.

"A laser drill. Interesting. Did you think that would work?"

Lord Vygon tried again. "Worth a shot."

"I see," said Wardax. "An attacker with an energy weapon was planned for."

"It seems you have another problem on your hands."

"That … yes. It will be dealt with, but first … you need to be subdued. I don't wish to harm you, but it is unavoidable at this point."

A turret popped out from the ceiling and shot the drill.

Lord Vygon dropped it as he jumped back. The drill was now a molten mess. He yanked an EMP charge out and tossed it at the turret. Although it fired on the charge, it was caught in the blast radius and stopped moving.

"Impressive and unexpected," said Wardax.

The shield lowered.

"You now only have mining blades and a variety of EMP charges. Your species is tough and brave, and I can see resilient as well. It's unfortunate that they could not stop attacking me. Nonetheless, I look forward to learning more about the exotic energy in you."

Lord Vygon growled as he extended his blunted blades.

"As expected," said Wardax. "Brute force it will be, then. Let's determine if you have the skill set needed to defeat me. Proceed."

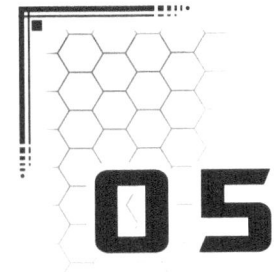

05

Dr. Snowden wanted to spend some time talking with Q. Emily did too, based on her questioning when they got back on board the *Torvatta*. However, there was an urgency to retrieving the other Evaran. Q did not know where the other Evaran was, but Evaran had a general sense of the direction they needed to go. That also meant they would be fighting.

They stood in the *Torvatta*'s entrance area.

Evaran motioned at the holo room. "Q, you can wait in there and watch from V's perspective."

Q peeked in. "A holo room."

"Yes. As for us, we are going to retrieve your Evaran."

Q stared at Evaran. "There'll be fighting."

"Analysis. We are prepared for that," said V while in body mode.

Q inspected the others. "Are you like Evaran, too?"

Dr. Snowden chuckled. "Well, I have some cosmic energy in me, and so does Emily. Evaran does obviously, and V does too."

"So you're all similar to Evaran. That is unexpected, much like this situation."

Emily nodded. "Every bit helps for the next step. I'm ready to go!"

Evaran half smiled. "I understand. Q, you will be able to talk to us as we proceed."

"I appreciate that," said Q.

"Okay, let us go," said Evaran, waving forward.

Dr. Snowden peeked back after the group had exited the *Torvatta*. Q stood just inside the entrance and stared out. It made Dr. Snowden wonder what Q must be thinking about. Dr. Snowden looked forward to finding out.

V had moved the *Torvatta* closer to the ground, so the grapple down had been quicker. Now that they were on the floor, the controllers, as Q called them, had focused on the group while a swarm of infected and enforcers surged toward them.

Dr. Snowden's skin crawled. He was not sure where they had come from, but they moved like an ant swarm as they rushed forward with their dead eyes. He fired his stun beam after Evaran used his mist one. Combined with Emily's stun, they incapacitated the initial surge. The controllers could still move, but they did so slowly.

The second wave advanced.

Dr. Snowden used his mist beam while Evaran and Emily lit it up. "Where did all these extra Zayt come from?"

Evaran gestured at the ground. "They popped up from there."

"Great. So they use swarm tactics. I can see how that might be effective, although in this environment, not so much."

Evaran nodded and motioned forward.

The group marched toward the decompression chamber. After arriving, Evaran used his UIC on the nearby door console, and they entered once the door opened.

"Not too bad so far outside the swarm," said Emily.

"Let us not get complacent," said Evaran.

Dr. Snowden crooked a thumb at her. "I don't think that's possible with her."

"Analysis. I agree."

Dr. Snowden grinned as he watched Q's avatar look around. He was probably studying the group's dynamic.

The decompression chamber finished its operation, and the door to the ship interior opened.

Dr. Snowden surveyed the hallway they entered. Metallic panels covered everything, but it was the plantlike vines and growth that caught his eye. That was not something he had expected. Some panels had a flashing light in the middle, bathing the area in a pulsing red glow. The plant structures caused shadows to dance around. He noted the lack of screens. Perhaps there was another type of communication he was not seeing.

They continued on. The enforcers that came out were bigger than the ones in the docking bay, but they were less numerous, and they had no answer to the group reflecting beams. It seemed there were several types of enforcers, and these were the heavy ones.

Dr. Snowden did not consider himself a fighter, but raising his shield and angling it so the beams went a specific way was much easier when everything slowed due to him focusing.

Emily, Evaran, and V oftentimes charged ahead, but there was no need with the pace they were moving at.

Another Zayt type had joined the fight as well. Per the data label, it was an infector. It reminded Dr. Snowden of a T-cell. It was an orb with a multitude of spindly legs whipping around. At the end of each leg was a sharp point. He guessed they were used to infect others. That was probably what created the infected. As fast as the infectors were, they stood no chance against the group's barrage of stun and mist beams. Even the sticky globules beam proved useful. Any that got close were disabled by V, who tossed them around with ease.

After fifteen minutes, Dr. Snowden could sense the other Evaran. It was like a big star on the edge of his senses. Evaran must have sensed it much earlier, which only showed the discrepancy between their cosmic power levels. It was the Daedrould energy that surprised Dr. Snowden. Whoever it was, they were powerful. It sort of reminded him of Lord Vygon's energy in terms of power.

"We are close," said Evaran.

"Yeah, I can sense the other Evaran, but there's another energy. Daedrould," said Emily.

"Daedrould?" asked Q. "Perhaps it is Lord Vygon and the other ancient vampire lords."

"Say what?" asked Dr. Snowden.

Evaran paused. "You are sensing cosmic, Daedrould, and palisin energy. They appear to be close to each other. It also seems there is more to this situation than was known." He took off.

Dr. Snowden hustled to keep up. He knew that pace. It was one where Evaran wanted to get something done and would not let anything slow him down. Q mentioning the ancient vampire lords, and then the gang sensing Daedrould energy, had caught Dr. Snowden off guard. That would be dealt with later. The enforcers who tried to fight the group were pushed out of the way. Thankfully, they did not have to deal with another swarm for the moment.

They reached the room where the exotic energies were.

Dr. Snowden's eyes widened. He had not been expecting to see what he saw. The other Evaran was on a slab with a purple shield of some type around him. It obscured his appearance, but Dr. Snowden could feel the raw power of the palisin. He had never sensed so much in one spot.

The other unusual sighting was a large robot off to the side. It was identified as a guardian, and it held what appeared to be Lord Vygon by the neck and off the ground. Dr. Snowden did not recognize Lord Vygon's armor. How he was in the same room as another Evaran was a burning mystery Dr. Snowden wanted to resolve.

"Is that … Lord Vygon?" asked Emily.

"I believe so," said Evaran.

The guardian swiveled its head over toward the group. "Ahh. The other one with cosmic energy arrives. Wait … you all have it."

Evaran leapt into the air with his staff and came down hard on the guardian's arm.

The guardian dropped Lord Vygon.

Dr. Snowden shot a grappling beam at Lord Vygon and reeled him in.

The robot tried to swat Evaran away but hit his energy shield. The raw power still sent him sliding back.

"That's Wardax controlling the guardian," said Q over comms.

"Yeah, getting that," said Dr. Snowden. He checked on Lord Vygon, who rubbed his neck and tried to catch his breath. It seemed Wardax had been close to snuffing him out.

Emily and V joined Evaran.

"He's ... too ... powerful," said Lord Vygon in a hoarse voice.

"Listen to the ancient vampire lord," said Wardax. "This will be a lot easier if you submit yourselves as research subjects."

Evaran's eyes glowed. "Are you responsible for holding Evaran?"

"I am. The shielding was difficult to come by, but Evaran is special. I sense you have a similar level of cosmic energy in you, perhaps more. Who are you?"

"Someone who is ending this." Evaran rushed forward and swung with his staff.

Wardax blocked the attempt, but Evaran round-house-kicked Wardax back. "Impressive. Your kick has injured me. Your capture will aid me in my research."

Emily attacked from the left while V went for the other side.

Wardax focused on those attacks. His fists glowed purple as he tried to slam Evaran with an overhead attack.

Evaran blocked the attempt with his shield, then bashed, causing Wardax to stumble back. Evaran charged and punched a hole through his chest.

He fell to his knees. "How ... ? This is not possible. Must ... research."

"It is," said Evaran.

"Who ... are ... are ... are ... y—" said Wardax as his lights dimmed.

Dr. Snowden helped Lord Vygon stand.

"I didn't know that was possible either," said Lord Vygon.

Evaran nodded. "My shield is impervious to palisin energy due to an event long ago. We will have time to discuss things later. For now, we need to shut down the shielding around Evaran." He studied Lord Vygon. "I believe you are Lord Vygon."

"I am ... but how do you know that?"

"It is a long story," said Evaran. He motioned at the other Evaran. "Are you familiar with him?"

Lord Vygon sighed. "I was trying to free him, but I almost failed." He perused the group. "I assume you are all here to rescue him and you have a ship?"

"Yep, and our ship is the *Torvatta*," said Emily.

Lord Vygon winced as he held his neck. "Is there room for three life pods?"

"Of course," said Evaran. "Where are they?"

"I can show you."

"Okay. V, get the *Torvatta* and bring it outside this room. Dr. Snowden, Emily, go with Lord Vygon and bring the life pods here. I will stay here and disable this shielding."

Dr. Snowden nodded. "Got it."

Lord Vygon wrinkled his brow. "I know we're pressed for time, and I heard some names, but ... who are all of you?"

"I am Evaran, and next to you is Dr. Albert Snowden, Emily Snowden, and V."

Lord Vygon drew his head back.

Dr. Snowden wagged a finger. "And I bet the three life pods are Lord Noskov, Lord Skar, and Lord Cyrus."

"How ... how could you know that? And another Evaran?"

"We will have time to discuss this later. For now, go," said Evaran.

Dr. Snowden followed Lord Vygon out of the room. The discussion later would be interesting. This was definitely not the Lord Vygon who Dr. Snowden knew.

Lord Vygon was not sure what to think of what he had witnessed. Apparently there was not one Evaran but two. This other one seemed more powerful, and Lord Vygon sensed his raw power. Emily and Dr. Snowden moved fast, much more so than Lord Vygon would have expected. V was a mysterious robot and they all had cosmic energy at various levels.

Although Lord Vygon had a lot of questions to ask, the focus was getting to the other ancient vampire lords. The other Evaran had agreed to help without a moment's hesitation. It also surprised Lord Vygon that Dr. Snowden was familiar with him and the other lords. Lord Vygon had been prepared to die, yet he and the other lords were saved, assuming everyone could get off the ship.

The first two enforcers to enter their path were hit by a device that Emily wielded. It resembled a small, thick rod and fired some type of thin beam that generated a cloud. Dr. Snowden had a similar device, and his beam ignited the cloud into a shower of sparks.

The guards crumpled.

Lord Vygon had expected there to be some recoil, but the devices had none. Another strange thing was the energy shields on their left forearm. Those were used on the next set of defenders that arrived. The shields reflected the beams and destroyed the enforcers. It was obvious that Dr. Snowden and Emily were elite warriors.

When they approached the life pod room, Lord Vygon's senses went into overdrive. He knew what was coming. It was an infected swarm that would not hesitate to destroy anything in their way without regard to their own safety. He had fought them before on Drydris when the Halkins had turned, and he understood the swarm's sheer numbers and mindless determination were not to be ignored.

"It's an infected swarm!" said Lord Vygon.

Dr. Snowden fired the strange cloud beam again, while Emily ignited it with her blue one.

The first wave of the swarm collapsed, but the second wave crashed through and was within grasping distance of the group.

Lord Vygon burst into action and used his blunted blades to knock away the first infected to reach them. His eyebrows rose when Emily spun into them like a tornado. Her staff sent them flying while Dr. Snowden seemed to fire his stun beam with precision, even hitting one of the infected midair.

After five minutes, the swarm was defeated.

Lord Vygon eyed Emily. "Your form belies your fighting ability." He faced Dr. Snowden. "And your marksmanship was beyond what I expected. I assume the cosmic energy I sense in you both has something to do with that."

"It does," said Emily. "Everything slows down when we focus, and our survival suits enhance our speed and strength."

"Quite advanced," said Lord Vygon.

Dr. Snowden slapped him on the back. "C'mon, let's go."

Together, their abilities made the rest of the trip to the life pod room effortless.

Lord Vygon was impressed. He had wondered how they would handle things, and it seemed they were effective. There was more in them than cosmic energy, though. He had sensed something metallic in them. A mystery to solve when they had some downtime.

He hoped the other Evaran would be able to deactivate the shield on Evaran. The thought of there being two different Evarans was strange enough, but now they would meet each other at some point. That was something Lord Vygon wanted to see.

The group entered the life pod room.

"Here they are," said Lord Vygon, gesturing at the life pods.

Dr. Snowden scanned the room with his device. "Looks like there's open space on the other side of this wall."

"Is that important?" asked Lord Vygon.

Emily motioned at the wall. "It means the *Torvatta* can burn through and we can board from here."

"You ship is going to … burn through?"

Emily nodded.

"We would be sucked out into space," said Lord Vygon.

Dr. Snowden used his hands to mimic an expanding ball. "The *Torvatta* has a bubble shield it can extend. When the *Torvatta* burns through, we'll be inside that shield, then we exit."

Lord Vygon's eyes narrowed. "I guess I'll just have to see it. I don't doubt you, but this is all strange." He motioned at Dr. Snowden's device. "What is that?"

"A Personal Support Device, or PSD as we call it. You've already seen some of what it can do."

"I did," said Lord Vygon. "It's unlike anything I've ever seen."

Two enforcers rushed into the room.

Emily blew them back with some type of repulsion beam, while Dr. Snowden fired a stun one at each robot, disabling them.

"You reacted as fast as I would have," said Lord Vygon. He shook his head. "Definitely cosmic energy."

"Yeah, we got a sliver," said Emily. "Not as much as Evaran, but enough that it enhances us."

"Your Evaran, right?"

Emily nodded. "I did sense a fair amount in the Evaran that's being held, though."

"So you know the one I know," said Lord Vygon.

Emily shrugged. "Not really, but we think we know who he is—well, generally."

"We'll go over it once we're in the *Torvatta*," said Dr. Snowden.

Lord Vygon nodded. The discussion when everyone was safe would be interesting. He checked on the life pods and made sure they were still stable. They were plugged in, so power was not an issue. His heart sank. He wanted to wake the other ancient vampire lords, but they were in no condition to be awakened. Wardax would pay for what he had done.

"So how do we move these?" asked Dr. Snowden.

"I'm configuring them to be moved now," said Lord Vygon.

"All right," said Dr. Snowden. "I'll update Evaran and V on the situation."

Lord Vygon studied Emily. "Did you come across Q?"

"Yeah, we rescued him already," she said.

"So he's alive," said Lord Vygon.

"Yep, and he's on the *Torvatta*."

Lord Vygon ached to be off the ship. All he had known in the last decade was constant war. There was no safe place to relax, but it seemed this *Torvatta* might be one. The *Karus* had been a safe haven when he had visited it, but he was unaware of its status.

Dr. Snowden raised a finger. "Looks like Evaran has freed the other Evaran, and they are aboard the *Torvatta* now. It burned through a room or two there to reach them. The *Torvatta* is on its way to us."

Lord Vygon breathed easier. "That's good news." He turned his head. "Another swarm approaches!"

Emily and Dr. Snowden took up a spot a few feet away from the door. Lord Vygon joined them.

The swarm burst into the room at the same time the *Torvatta* began to melt through the wall opposite them.

Emily repulsed the first wave while Dr. Snowden bathed the area outside the door with some type of sticky substance that the second part of the attackers got caught on.

Lord Vygon wrinkled his brow when an orb flew above the group and shot a stun beam. A quick peek back showed that the *Torvatta* had burned through the wall as Emily had mentioned. The bubble shield was as advertised, and Lord Vygon was thankful they did not get sucked out into space.

Evaran joined them. "Get the life pods aboard."

"Got it," said Emily.

"You'll need help with this swarm," said Lord Vygon.

"I will not," said Evaran, his eyes glowing.

A chill swept up Lord Vygon's spine. It seemed being a tough fighter was an Evaran trait. As Lord Vygon got behind Lord Noskov's life pod, he paused to watch Evaran in action. He moved faster than even Dr. Snowden and Emily. Evaran was a blur as he danced around, pausing for a brief moment to send a robot flying away. One thing that intrigued Lord

Vygon was that Evaran avoided the sticky substance with ease. Lord Vygon realized that this Evaran was far more powerful than the Evaran he knew.

Dr. Snowden and Emily got behind their life pods.

Lord Vygon tilted his life pod upright and unlocked the wheels so it could roll. He studied the blue ramp that seemed to extend into space and to a ship outside. Emily gestured at him to go first, so he pushed the pod ahead. When he was on the ramp, he peeked off to the sides. The sensation of seeing the darkness of open space made his heart beat faster. When he entered the doorway at the end of the ramp, he noticed Q off to the side.

"Q!" he said. He walked over and embraced Q and slapped him on the back. "You're alive."

"I definitely am, thanks to Evaran and his team."

V flew in past them and morphed into his human shell in front of the medical lab. "You can put the pods in here."

"Oh, so you were the orb," said Lord Vygon.

"Acknowledged."

Lord Vygon continued pushing. The medical lab was large, much bigger than it should be. He figured that, like on the *Karus*, dimensional mechanics were at work. V led him to a room in the back where he placed the life pod, then locked it so it would stay in place.

Emily and Dr. Snowden followed Lord Vygon and replicated his actions with their pods.

Lord Vygon peered around the room at the others. "I think we have a lot to talk about."

06

Everyone was in the conference room, and Emily had retrieved Lord Vygon's favorite drink from the matter replicator, which surprised him. Q sat and studied the room, but that was to be expected. Evaran sat at the head of the table, and to his left were Emily, V, and Lord Vygon. Dr. Snowden and Q sat on the other side.

Evaran raised a finger. "There is a lot to discuss. Before we begin, I wanted to say we are safe in intergalactic space."

Lord Vygon drew his head back. "We are? I didn't feel the ship moving."

"We used a portal," said Emily.

"Okay…"

Evaran half smiled. "She is right. However, let us do more formal introductions. I am Evaran." He pointed around at the others. "With me are Dr. Albert Snowden and Emily Snowden, his niece. Along with V, they travel with me across space, time, and beyond to maintain timeline integrity, at least the one we inhabit. We came here, which is another universe from our perspective, due to a quantum beacon being activated that the *Torvatta*, my ship, recognized."

"Project Prime," said Q. He tilted his head. "You must be Evaran prime."

"I am the first of eight plane forms to enter this plane," said Evaran. "I can verify which of the six other possibilities the other Evaran is when he awakens."

"He's not the eighth, since we already met her," said Dr. Snowden.

Evaran nodded. "This one is between the second and seventh form." He motioned at Q. "Has he ever discussed this with you?"

"He hasn't, other than to say he had cosmic energy and came from outside the plane," said Q.

"So you are aware of the cosmology involved?"

"I am, but it is apparent not everything was told to me," said Q.

Lord Vygon shook his head. "I'm not aware of any of that, but I did know that Evaran—well, the one I know—had cosmic energy." He glanced around the room. "It makes sense that you're prime and travel with other cosmic beings."

Emily furrowed her brow. "I'm not a cosmic being. Maybe an evolved human."

"I don't know what a human is, but you closely resemble the Halkins, the species we had a symbiotic relationship with. Their blood sustained us, and in exchange, we protected them," said Lord Vygon. He growled. "It seems we weren't able to stop Wardax from destroying our planet."

"It's destroyed?" asked Dr. Snowden.

Lord Vygon nodded. "We fought Zayt enforcers at first, then they dropped the infector swarms on us. As they turned Halkins into infected, that represented another swarm to deal with. As powerful as we were, we were overwhelmed."

Emily gestured at him. "The infected swarms were like those we fought on the ship, right?"

"Yeah, except on our planet, think millions per swarm and thousands of them. The infector swarms were ruthlessly efficient, and it wasn't long before they had infected ones going. Most Halkins are zombies now, essentially, or have been converted into something used to make enforcers."

Emily shuddered. "That's horrible."

Lord Vygon sighed. "I was able to escape with three other lords, but they were badly damaged from fighting. I put them in life pods, then went into mine, but was contacted by Evaran and Q prior to that."

"From our perspective, Lord Vygon's ship had been captured by the Zayt transport, so we followed it," said Q. "We boarded, but Evaran was defeated and the *Karus* was sliced up."

"Analysis. Project Prime must have been to activate the quantum beacon in hopes of contacting the *Torvatta*."

"A logical conclusion," said Q.

V smiled.

Q studied him.

"So you're a pure AI?" asked Emily.

"I am," said Q. "Evaran adopted me from another ship initially and configured me as the AI for the *Karus*. I evolved and shackled myself to this body."

"Wow, so you're like the living embodiment of the *Karus*," said Dr. Snowden.

"I am."

Evaran rubbed his chin as he scrutinized Lord Vygon. "As puzzling as it is to see another Evaran, meeting you was unexpected. Your aura is different than that of the Lord Vygon we know."

"There's another me from where you come from?" asked Lord Vygon.

"There is, and he is one of my closest friends," said Evaran.

"And ours," said Emily, pointing at Dr. Snowden and V. "He's also traveled with us before, in addition to somehow knowing our future."

Lord Vygon's eyes narrowed. "Is there any way I could see him?"

"We have recordings," said Evaran.

"That ... will be interesting," said Lord Vygon. "I guess we must look alike since I was so easily identified." He eyed Dr. Snowden. "You knew of the other lords, though."

Dr. Snowden nodded. "On our Earth—well, the planet we're from—you and the other three lords are among the most powerful nonhumans on the planet."

"I see," said Lord Vygon.

"You also have the best cookouts," said Emily, smiling.

Lord Vygon raised an eyebrow. "I'm not sure what that is, but it sounds fun." He glanced at Evaran. "When will Evaran, the one Q and I know, awake?"

"Soon," said Evaran. "His cosmic energy is already beginning to surface. He was hit by a large amount of palisin energy." He gestured at Q. "Is that common here?"

"It's not," said Q. "However, there are places where it appears naturally, so it can be harvested."

Dr. Snowden rubbed his chin. "So there's a lot more here, then, it sounds like, compared to our universe."

"I don't have enough information on your universe to complete that comparison," said Q.

"It's all right." Dr. Snowden wrinkled his brow. "We'll need to be more careful here."

"I concur," said Evaran. He inspected Lord Vygon. "Now that we are here, we will assist the other Evaran. He would not have activated the quantum beacon unless it was an emergency."

"Oh, it's past that," said Lord Vygon. "Wardax is carving a swath through the galaxy."

"What is he, exactly?" asked Emily.

Lord Vygon shrugged. "We're not fully sure. What is known is that when he appeared on the scene, he brought the Zayt with him. Wardax has the ability to control specialized units, known as guardians. They control controllers, who manage every other Zayt unit around them. Several other lords destroyed one of Wardax's guardians, but the one you all met had a different robot body. Even if you destroy the guardian, Wardax still persists."

"I see. I sensed that there was plant tissue inside the guardian. It also had a low level of dimensional energy," said Evaran.

"I sensed something but wasn't sure what it was," said Lord Vygon. "If there is a relay, then it's far beyond any technology I know of."

Dr. Snowden shook a finger. "I bet he's using some type of dimensional relay, then. Maybe the plant part is for that purpose, sorta like how we met a mountain that existed in two places."

"A mountain?" asked Lord Vygon.

"Long story," said Dr. Snowden.

"Analysis. If the plant species exists in two places, Wardax might exist in another dimension and be able to coordinate activity here."

"That's an interesting perspective," said Lord Vygon.

Evaran's eyes narrowed. "It seems we have some investigating to do. I downloaded information from the Zayt transport and will go through that. Until then, everyone can take some time to rest up until the other Evaran wakes up."

Lord Vygon nodded. "I'd like a tour of the ship if you don't mind."

"Dr. Snowden will be glad to give you one," said Evaran, motioning at Dr. Snowden.

"Sure," he said.

"I'd like to come," said Emily.

"Your presence would be appreciated," said Lord Vygon.

Emily understood that Evaran had probably chosen Dr. Snowden to give a tour so that they could talk more. She was curious to know more about Lord Vygon.

Evaran motioned at V. "Please show Q where you go into low power mode."

"Acknowledged."

"I have a lot to process," said Q. "Will I have access to the *Torvatta's* information system?"

"The *Torvatta* will decide that," said Evaran. "V will show you how to hook into it, but the *Torvatta* will determine what you see."

"Is the *Torvatta* alive?"

Evaran half smiled. "Something like that."

"I understand," said Q. "I look forward to learning more."

Lord Vygon stood along with the others. "I'm ready for a tour." He gestured at Q. "You don't want to come?"

"I can tour the ship more efficiently when I interact with its systems."

"Yeah, I thought about trying that myself."

"I don't believe you did," said Q.

Lord Vygon grinned. "It's good to see you again, Q"

Emily suspected that he enjoyed teasing Q, and probably the other Evaran. She looked forward to when the other Evaran woke up, and they could have a meeting to catch up on everything.

•ıı"∷ ▄▄▄▄▄▄▄▄▄▄▄▄▄▄▄▄▄▄ ∷"ıı•

V ran a scan over Q as they exited the conference room. Although Q had a robot body, it was not battle ready. It did have shielding, but not as much as V had in body mode. V was intrigued by the idea that Q traveled with another Evaran, although it did seem strange not to sense any exotic energy on Q.

They entered the research lab.

Q glanced at V. "You have analyzed me."

"Acknowledged."

"What does your analysis say?"

V nodded. "I do not believe you accompany your Evaran into dangerous environments."

"That's correct," said Q. He tilted his head. "Your holographic shell is impressive, although I don't think it would do well in a hostile environment."

"This form is used for integration and usually here on the *Torvatta*. I have an orb underneath, and that is what I use for reconnaissance. I can fly into a strong robot body and control it."

"Multiple forms with your orb as the center," said Q. "That makes sense. I saw your orb and body modes in action."

"Query. You possess only this form?" asked V.

"Yes. I was originally a ship AI. However, my Evaran allowed me to transfer to a body so I could move around and assist as needed. I still maintained a direct connection to the *Karus*."

"I understand," said V.

They reached a small area where V went to rest in orb mode to connect with the *Torvatta* directly.

"This is where you go into low power mode?" asked Q.

"It is," said V. He pointed at a side stall. "There is a place to hook up in body mode. The connector can adapt to any hookup interface you might possess."

Q studied the stall. "What happens in low power mode?"

"We enter into a digital space."

Q stepped into the stall. A scanning beam washed over him, and several wires snuck out and plugged into him. "This is impressive."

V morphed back to orb mode and rested on his holder. "I will see you in a moment."

Once V was settled, the environment changed to a pure dark space. He appeared as a glowing blue sphere, while Q materialized as a golden one. Various cubes popped into view with screens on the faces. Lines connected the boxes, and after a few nanoseconds, V and Q hovered in the middle of a massive grid of boxes.

"An interesting design," said Q. "It seems there are endless systems."

"Yes," said V. "The *Torvatta* will determine what you can and cannot access."

Q's lights glowed brighter. "I understand. I have some questions if you don't mind."

"Of course," said V.

"How were you created?"

V focused, and one of the nearby cubes glowed. The face nearest them showed V's first meeting with Evaran. "I was created at the same time as the *Torvatta*. My inner container is a mix of planar and cosmic energy, and my outer container is an AI. My first incarnation was D, and after my predecessor, U_4, perished, I became the new incarnation."

"That means you must have cosmic energy to re-form."

"Yes. It reacts similar to Evaran's energy. However, my AI translates it."

Q extended a golden tendril toward the screen. "An emotional response system for an AI. That's fascinating."

"Query. Why did you move from the ship you were on to the *Karus*?"

"It was about to blow up, and Evaran saved me, then let me exist in the *Karus*. He also updated my programing. That allowed me to adapt to the *Karus* and then, eventually, get a robot body."

"So your core programming is to support others."

"It is," said Q. "I am curious as to what your travels were like with your Evaran. Dr. Snowden and Emily also interest me. You mentioned they were humans, a species that seems remarkably similar to the Halkins that Lord Vygon knows."

"The Halkins may be human, possibly," said V. "I have insufficient data other than the visual aspect. I can show you my experiences of being a member of the gang."

"The gang ... is that the name for your collective?"

"Yes. The gang is my family, and they treat me as such."

Another cube highlighted and showed a visual feed of Evaran and the others joking around with V in the conference room. Emily high-fived V while Dr. Snowden laid a hand on V's shoulder.

"They care about you a great deal," said Q.

"They do, and I enjoy being around them."

"I can detect your AI presence here, but your exotic energy doesn't appear here. Interesting."

V extended a tendril towards a screen. "May I see your interaction with your Evaran?"

"Of course."

Another cube near them lit up.

V analyzed the visual display. It showed Q's Evaran smiling and joking around. He appeared to be calm and collected, but also animated relative to the Evaran V knew. Q's Evaran had a liquid metallic suit of some type that could change in appearance. His short brown parted hair sat on a friendly face. Like the Evaran V knew, Q's Evaran had fair skin. However, this Evaran had a trimmed beard. What registered as the biggest difference was the display of emotions. Q's Evaran seemed to have no problems with that.

"What are you processing?" asked Q.

"Your Evaran displays emotion."

"And yours doesn't. That seems strange to me."

"That is due to the plane form chosen," said V.

"I see," said Q. "I look forward to understanding more about these plane forms. I understand your Evaran is the first, or prime, and you've already met the eighth."

"Yes. Levaran was the eighth."

"Can I see her?" asked Q.

One of the nearby cube faces lit up and showed Levaran emerging from the re-forming room after having re-formed.

Q moved closer to the display.

V calculated that the knowledge of another Evaran was not something Q had expected. He had seen one in person, and now another from a historical perspective.

"She is like the Evaran I know, although a bit more subdued," said Q.

The display changed to show her beating a group on a Krotovore ship during a previous adventure.

"She is far stronger than the Evaran I know. What happened to her?"

V's inner container pulsed slower. He recalled talking with Levaran and Edev, his counterpart.

"After she re-formed, she assisted us in dealing with a Time Warden threat in her universe. Dr. Snowden and Emily almost died, but she gave them some of her cosmic energy. Once we resolved the Time Warden issue, she continued on in her universe with Edev, our counterpart, until she ran into a Hadryn spawn known as the Overlord, who killed her."

"She died? Why didn't your Evaran help her?" asked Q.

"Because it was part of a time loop. We encountered the Overlord and banished him."

Q's lights fluctuated. "She was powerful and still died."
"Yes."

"Your Evaran is very powerful as well. He dismantled the guardian with ease."

"He was angry," said V.

"I didn't see anger in his face."

The cube display showed the fight between Evaran and the Wardax guardian.

"His cosmic energy was in flux. Also, his actions suggest what emotions he is experiencing."

"I see," said Q. "I'm curious to see what happens when our Evarans meet."

"As am I," said V.

"Is your speech module impaired?"

"It is not," said V. "My output, and Evaran's, is affected by the *Torvatta*. I observed that your Evaran had no such translator."

A display showed Q's Evaran talking.

"That's correct," said Q. "Your speech is more robotic, like your Evaran. I'm curious. Say 'I can't.'"

"I cannot."

"Interesting," said Q.

V had tried to upgrade his speech processor, but the output was handled by the *Torvatta*. He had not been able to find a way around it. It seemed the only way it would change was if there was a re-formation, and he was not eager for that to occur. Although he was okay with his speech style, his analysis showed that it bothered Evaran that he could not alter his. Even the translation orb kept to the style.

"I'd like to view your previous adventures," said Q.

"And I yours," said V.

"It seems we have a lot of data to exchange."

"Acknowledged."

Dr. Snowden surveyed the blank white holo room. Emily stood next to him while Lord Vygon paced and took everything in.

Dr. Snowden wondered what V and Q talked about as they had taken off to V's low-power mode room. It surprised Dr. Snowden that Evaran had not accompanied them. Perhaps there was something more important he needed to attend to and did not want to tell the others.

"And this is a holo room, you say?" asked Lord Vygon.

"Yep," said Emily. She poked the air in front of her. A circular menu popped up. "We can show you our last cookout where the Lord Vygon we know was at." She wrinkled her brow after a moment. "Huh."

"It's not loading up?" asked Dr. Snowden.

Emily shook her head.

"Let me try," said Dr. Snowden. He opened the menu, perused around until he saw the cookout from V's perspective, then tapped it.

Nothing happened.

"What the heck?" he asked. He eyed Lord Vygon. "It seems the *Torvatta* doesn't want to show you."

"I hope your ship isn't angry with me."

Dr. Snowden chuckled. "No, I don't think that's it."

"Timeline thing, I bet," said Emily.

"That's my thought, too," said Dr. Snowden. He puffed his cheeks. "Well, maybe then we can at least check out the planar cartography lab."

"Wait a minute," said Emily. "I got Lord Vygon's favorite drink from the matter replicator, so it allowed something through for him."

Lord Vygon raised a finger. "Perhaps it makes a distinction between a drink and knowledge."

"Huh, could be," said Emily. "I guess the lab it is."

They assembled in the planar cartography lab.

Dr. Snowden motioned at the nearby matter replicator. "See if you can order your favorite drink."

Lord Vygon complied.

Dr. Snowden wrinkled his brow when the replicator did not produce anything. "That's odd. It knows the pattern but won't work for you." He walked over and tried to generate the drink.

The drink appeared.

"Yeah, that's weird," said Emily.

Dr. Snowden handed Lord Vygon the drink. "Well, at least you have something delicious to sip on while we check out the lab. I suspect, though, that you can get a generic glass of blood as needed if we aren't around."

Lord Vygon took a sip. "No problems here with that."

Dr. Snowden pulled up two displays that hovered in the center of the room. The one on the left showed a galactic view of the Milky Way galaxy, while the other one displayed a galactic view of where they currently were.

"So this is another universe to you," said Lord Vygon, studying the projection.

"Yep, and also a different galaxy it seems," said Emily, pointing at some data labels.

Dr. Snowden rubbed his chin. "Let's do a comparison." He moved the left display on to the right, which caused it to expand out to a cluster view. "Wow, so our galaxy does exist here, and it looks like we're about a few thousand galaxies away, and far in the past, relatively."

"I didn't know the *Torvatta* had such star charts," said Lord Vygon. "It's impressive."

"Well, I think the *Torvatta* is saying that's where our galaxy would be. We won't know unless we go check it out."

Lord Vygon nodded. "Still, it's powerful to even have that ability." He gestured at a blinking dot. "I take it that is your home planet."

Dr. Snowden zoomed in until it showed a blue planet. "Yep. That's Earth. I'm guessing it's using images from our universe."

Other screens popped out to the side and showed various cities bustling with activity.

"And that's us: humans," said Dr. Snowden. "Well, Emily and I are evolved humans due to having cosmic-energy-infused nanobots. There's also a lot of nonhumans on Earth, like Daedroulds."

Lord Vygon wrinkled his brow. "You have other Daedroulds that aren't ancient vampires?"

Emily snorted. "Oh yeah. You got Raskarian vampires, blooded ones, mambos, and even witches and warlocks."

"Fascinating."

"There's also Outsiders, those who came in from another dimension. Most posed as gods in early human history, but they now exist as normal. We also have Wildborn, humans with a one-off ability."

Lord Vygon nodded. "Your Earth sounds busy."

"It sure is," said Dr. Snowden. "The Lord Vygon we know, along with Lord Noskov, Lord Skar, and Lord Cyrus, is among the most powerful nonhumans on the planet. There's also Dalton Kingston, but he's an evolved human like us."

"Do you know how the ancient vampires got to your Earth?"

Dr. Snowden looked at Emily. "I don't."

She shrugged. "Me either. Our Lord Vygon has never talked to us about that before. He did give us a Daedrould stone, though."

Lord Vygon drew his head back. "He did?"

"Yeah," said Emily. "Apparently, it can absorb Daedrould energy on death, then it can be used for resurrection."

"That's right," said Lord Vygon. "I thought that was unique to my planet, Drydris."

"Huh," said Dr. Snowden, glancing at Emily.

"Perhaps there are more similarities than differences between the one you know and me," said Lord Vygon.

Emily nodded. "Sounds like it."

"He must trust you with his life. On my planet, that's a great honor to be given a stone."

"I got half of one, and Uncle Albert got the other," said Emily.

"May I see them?" asked Lord Vygon.

"Sure," said Emily. She took off. A moment later, she popped back in and handed her half to Lord Vygon.

He studied it and wrinkled his brow. "This one is similar to the one I lost on my planet."

Dr. Snowden rubbed his chin. "Well, that's interesting. Maybe you die, and we resurrect you on our Earth using those stones."

Lord Vygon eyed Dr. Snowden.

Everyone laughed.

"I hope I don't die," said Lord Vygon.

"Yeah, plus, you have an aura around you that shows you're from another universe," said Dr. Snowden.

"Aura? Like what Evaran can see?"

"Yeah," said Emily. She waved a finger between her and Dr. Snowden. "Our detection of it is not as advanced as Evaran's, or Dalton Kingston's, due to our cosmic energy level. Every living thing has a life aura that can be used to define what it is and what reality it's from usually."

Lord Vygon handed the stone back to Emily. "I see. I don't think our meeting was coincidental."

"Most meetings usually aren't," she said, chuckling. "When the other Evaran awakens, I suspect we'll help him out, and by extension, you."

"That would be appreciated. The Evaran I know has the same goal as me: stopping Wardax."

"Then that sounds like what we'll be doing," said Dr. Snowden.

This Lord Vygon seemed more and more like the one Dr. Snowden knew. While initially that had not been the case, the similarities became stronger the more time he spent with him. His mannerisms and speech style were familiar, and his curiosity was what Dr. Snowden would have expected. The *Torvatta's* refusal to show any historical videos surprised him. What that meant, he was not sure.

If Lord Vygon did get resurrected on the Earth Dr. Snowden knew, he wondered if that would change Lord Vygon's life aura which currently had the current universe's signature on it. Even if Lord Vygon was resurrected and had his life aura updated to show Dr. Snowden's universal signature, there were three other ancient vampire lords on board that would still have the current universe's signature.

07

Emily yawned as she reached over and grabbed her PSD. She had been having a good dream, but the PSD's buzzing made her alert. She had been accustomed to using the buzzing as an early-warning system. The last time it had gone off this early was when Dalton Kingston had gained cosmic energy on a previous adventure. It was 5:10 a.m., and Evaran had contacted everyone to let them know that the other Evaran was close to waking up.

Emily jumped out of bed and got washed up before slipping on her survival suit. She was not sure what to expect when the other Evaran became conscious. It bothered her that Evaran in any form could be knocked out. It was not something she cared to see again. The first time she had seen it was when he had been hit by a palisin beam on Coris, an asteroid station, on an earlier adventure. She hustled to the medical lab.

Dr. Snowden had a cup of coffee and talked with Lord Vygon. V, in projected mode, and Q were farther back and chatted away. Evaran stood silent next to the other Evaran's slab.

"Looks like I'm not too late," said Emily.

Dr. Snowden shook his head. "Not at all. Evaran says another five minutes."

"This will be interesting," said Lord Vygon, studying both Evarans.

"Yeah," said Emily.

She studied the other Evaran. His brown hair and beard made him look wise. However, it was his eyes that drew her attention. They seemed happy, even in their closed state. The liquid metal suit intrigued her. Although it was sleek and shiny and did not move for the most part, she had seen segments of it slide about. Solid metal rings wrapped around the lower part of the upper arms and above the knees. There were no armored pads, but there were segmented lines that gave that appearance.

A solid metallic belt, chest strap, upper forearm guards, and thick boots stood out prominently. The rods on the inner forearm piqued her curiosity. They appeared to be mounted but could slide out as needed. This other Evaran seemed like a futuristic adventurer of some type.

Emily continued to study him for the next five minutes. It amazed her that she was going to meet yet another version of Evaran. Levaran had been great, and Emily owed her life to her. It seemed no matter which Evaran it was, they all had Emily's best interests at heart, and she suspected this one would too. She could not wait to meet him.

Evaran gazed around at the others. "It is time." He interacted with his ARI.

The other Evaran began to stir.

Emily squinted when his eyes and fists glowed brightly for a moment before returning to normal. Her heart raced as he scrunched his face and slowly opened his eyes. This was the moment.

The other Evaran sat up and peered around, then slid his legs off to the side. "Hello."

Emily liked his soft yet friendly voice. It was calm and sounded nonthreatening.

Q and Lord Vygon rushed over.

"You're okay!" said Lord Vygon.

"That's better than being dead!" said the other Evaran.

Lord Vygon embraced him and slapped him on the back.

Q reached out and squeezed the other Evaran's arm. "I'm glad you're back."

"I am too," said the other Evaran. He narrowed his eyes as he studied Evaran, Dr. Snowden, Emily, and V. "I suspect Project Prime was successful."

"It was," said Q.

Evaran's eyes glowed. "Welcome back."

"You're Evaran prime, and first form still," said the other Evaran, standing.

Evaran nodded.

Emily got goose bumps as they sized each other up. It was such a rare occurrence for two Evarans to talk to each other. They were essentially talking to themselves, but spread across space and time.

"I suspect you are one of the plane forms that entered after me," said Evaran.

The other Evaran nodded. "I'm the sixth, and this must be the *Torvatta*."

"It is," said Evaran. "I do not suspect you are corrupt."

"I sense the same of you," said the other Evaran. He examined Dr. Snowden and Emily. "In order to avoid confusion, you can call me Sivaran, for the sixth Evaran."

"Works for me," said Emily.

Sivaran tilted his head. "You two have cosmic energy."

"Not as much as him," said Dr. Snowden, gesturing at Evaran. Dr. Snowden extended a hand. "I'm Dr. Albert Snowden, and it's good to meet you."

Sivaran studied Dr. Snowden's hand, then shook it. "A handshake! I haven't seen that in a long time. Have you ever tried to shake hands with a species that doesn't have them?"

Dr. Snowden wrinkled his brow. "Not lately."

Sivaran laughed.

Emily was surprised at how easily Sivaran expressed emotions. He was quick to smile and laugh, not something she associated with Evaran, or even Levaran.

Sivaran extended a hand toward Emily. "And you are?"

"Emily Snowden. I'm Uncle Albert's niece."

"A niece!" said Sivaran, nodding. "A family affair."

"Yeah."

"Excellent," said Sivaran. "I look forward to hearing how you obtained cosmic energy." He scrutinized V. "An AI, using a holographic shell, with an orb that has planar energy. I do sense a smidge of cosmic energy in you as well. Odd." He extended a hand.

V raised his hand. "Analysis. My inner container has cosmic energy."

"Oh ... that's unexpected," said Sivaran, studying V's hand.

"It is a high five, a celebratory gesture from Dr. Snowden and Emily's planet. You tap hands."

Sivaran did so. "Okay, then." He rubbed his hands together and gazed around. "This is going to be interesting."

The group laughed.

Emily could already see that she would like Sivaran. She sensed his cosmic energy which was less than Evaran's.

Sivaran focused on Evaran. "I suspect before we go any further, we should sync so we're both brought up to date."

"I concur. There is a lot to discuss afterward," said Evaran. He glanced at the others. "When we are done, we will meet in the conference room to go over the situation."

"We talking a few hours, or ... ?" asked Emily.

"Let us plan on meeting at 11:00 a.m.," said Evaran.

Sivaran winked at Emily. "I'll make sure he doesn't mess around."

Emily cracked up. "Yeah, he can do that sometimes."

Evaran eyed her.

"It's true!"

Evaran half smiled. "We will not be long."

Emily nodded and exited with the others. The big advantage of them syncing would be that Sivaran would know everything Evaran did up to this point, and vice versa. It must be nice to be able to do that. She remembered Evaran doing that with Levaran.

The conference meeting afterward would be interesting. She yawned. Perhaps a few more hours of sleep would do her good, then she could do some training, get breakfast, and be ready for the day.

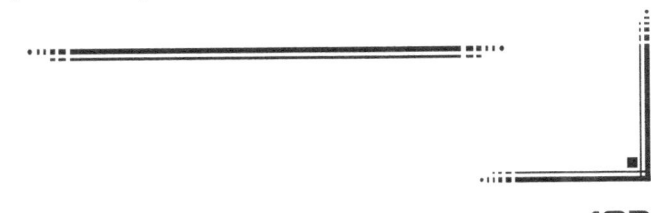

Dr. Snowden had tried to fall back asleep after the morning assembly in the medical lab, but his mind raced when thinking about the upcoming conference room meeting. Sivaran's personality was not a total shock as Dr. Snowden had seen some footage prior, but it was another thing to see it live.

Lord Vygon and Q had been chatterboxes after the group had split up, and they had disappeared to the research lab along with V. Emily had gone to her room, probably to try to sleep a bit more.

It was now 10:00 a.m., and although he had gotten a few moments where he thought he had napped, he was too wired for that. He got cleaned up and decided to get a late breakfast in. When he arrived at the conference room, Emily was wolfing down an omelet.

"Hey, Uncle Albert," she said.

He gestured at her half-empty plate. "Someone was hungry."

"I worked up an appetite."

Dr. Snowden nodded as he replicated his normal morning cup of coffee. He joined her at the table. "You had a good workout, I take it?"

"Sure did. I created the controllers, enforcers, infectors, and infected from the ship as my attackers."

"As expected," he said.

Emily always recreated whatever the group fought in the holo room. It was her way of adapting and trying out different tactics. That would have been unheard of only a few years ago, but now, she was a student of combat. It saddened him that she had changed so dramatically after being alone on a prison planet for nine months, but he also understood her desire never to be caught off guard again.

She eyed him. "Someone's deep in thought."

Dr. Snowden cleared his throat. "Oh, it's nothing. I'm just curious to learn more about the situation out here. I suspect it'll involve taking down this Wardax character."

"Probably," she said. "Did you notice how he talked?"

"Yeah. If I closed my eyes and listened, I would say he has some of Evaran's mannerisms."

Emily shuddered. "I can't even imagine an evil Evaran."

"Let's hope we never have to," said Dr. Snowden.

He took a sip of his coffee. The thought of someone with Evaran's power doing bad things was not good for anyone. Dr. Snowden had not sensed any cosmic energy on the guardian, but that could be because it was just a puppet. Maybe whatever Wardax was had cosmic energy. That would not be something Dr. Snowden wanted to face off against.

Over the next half hour, he enjoyed some light discussion with Emily. He loved talking with her, and one of the fun aspects of any adventure was that he got to see her more and spend time catching up on her busy life. He focused on Evaran and Sivaran entering the room with Lord Vygon, V, and Q in tow.

Evaran sat at the head of the table as usual, while Sivaran sat to the left. Emily had moved over to the next seat to allow Sivaran to sit. Dr. Snowden took the first seat on the right, with Lord Vygon and Q taking the other chairs on that side. V sat next to Emily.

"Sivaran and I have synced," said Evaran, looking around at everyone. "I believe it is time now to discuss the situation. Why we came is already understood, so Sivaran will go over the current state of things." He motioned at Sivaran.

Sivaran smiled. "No pressure, right?"

Dr. Snowden found it odd to see an Evaran smile fully or laugh. From what Dr. Snowden understood, Evaran was closer to the main form in that he did not display emotions as easily as other plane forms.

"All right," said Sivaran. "As to the situation, this galaxy has seen its usual wars for dominance, but the Zayt are something different. I began to investigate them as they assimilated several civilizations that I had visited. I was actually visiting Kielesh, the Omgrona capital planet, when the Zayt attacked. I tried to fight them, but I'm not equipped to battle millions of Zayt and their swarms."

Q raised a finger. "Kielesh was subdued in less than two days."

"I was getting to that," said Sivaran, eying Q.

"I apologize."

Sivaran chuckled. "It wouldn't be you if you didn't speak up with clarification."

Q nodded.

"I traveled to other worlds and saw the same pattern. I did get some information on them from Acrolis, a matter mage who's also a researcher. That was a long while back. Since then, I've discovered that Wardax seems to be the Zayt leader. He controls the Zayt through guardians, who control controllers, who manage everything else. Wardax must have a main form somewhere, but I don't know where."

"We detected a dimensional presence on the guardian. You think he's using it as a relay or something?" asked Dr. Snowden.

Sivaran shrugged. "Definitely possible, but any dimensional energy dissipated once a guardian was defeated."

"We know he's powerful," said Lord Vygon. "On the Zayt transport, he took down Sivaran, and for me, I was no match for Wardax."

Sivaran sighed. "Yes, and as we found out, he seems to evolve after every fight. In this case, he used palisin energy." He waved a finger around. "Not fun for us."

"Yeah, definitely not," said Emily.

"I was checking on Drydris when the Zayt attacked there. When I saw Lord Vygon's ship, I contacted them, but they were already under attack and the Zayt transport was closing in on them. Q and I didn't reach them in time, and the transport jumped away into condensed space, where we followed it. We caught up to it, and then the rest is known."

Lord Vygon growled. "Wardax will pay for Drydris."

"I had an observation on that transport," said Dr. Snowden. "We saw some type of plant growth all over the ship's interior. What's that all about?"

Sivaran sighed. "The Zayt are some type of plant and technology hybrid. Where they go, the environment usually follows. They don't normally build their own ships, they just take them over from conquered civilizations. They're highly efficient with that."

"So they're parasites, essentially," said Dr. Snowden.

Lord Vygon nodded. "Well said."

Dr. Snowden narrowed his eyes. "Maybe we should visit when Wardax attacked Drydris."

"How?" asked Lord Vygon, glancing at him.

"Time travel."

Lord Vygon looked at Sivaran. "Is this possible? Time travel has been theorized, but…"

"It's possible if you have a *Torvatta*," said Sivaran, grinning. "Not so much if you only have a *Karus*."

"So we could see how Wardax attacked Drydris," said Lord Vygon. "I'd like to see that. I only had high-level views, but to get in and see it up close would be ideal." He looked at Evaran. "I assume we wouldn't be detected."

"You assume correctly," said Evaran. "The *Torvatta* has various scan modes and can enter stealth mode."

Dr. Snowden found Lord Vygon's acceptance of a ship being able to time travel interesting.

"Before we go, I was curious if you've seen any other Evarans," said Emily, motioning at Sivaran.

He grinned. "I have, actually. Syrilus showed me the initial forms that the first through fifth took. I also saw the formation of the *Torvatta*, hence why I know its signature. I'm surprised Levaran didn't make a quantum beacon, but the idea is not to interfere with each other."

Dr. Snowden wrinkled his brow. "So you knew Evaran right off the bat."

"Yes, since it's still his first form. Oddly enough, Wardax has a similar speech and mannerism style to Evaran prime."

"You think maybe Wardax is a corrupted plane form?" asked Dr. Snowden.

Sivaran sighed. "I don't know what he is to be honest, but the fact that he is aware of cosmic energy and its weakness to palisin energy indicates he has knowledge not typically expected of a planar being."

Dr. Snowden shook his head. "Great. A potentially cosmic-enhanced enemy. We already fought one of those."

Evaran raised a finger. "Regardless of what Wardax is, it seems Sivaran's goal is to stop him. Therefore, we will render assistance."

Lord Vygon sat up. "Your help is appreciated."

"Let us go to the command center," said Evaran.

Dr. Snowden stood along with the others. He was anxious to see how Wardax invaded a planet, but he was also excited to learn more about Sivaran. Evaran rarely talked about his other plane forms that had initially entered the plane. There would be no way to really avoid that topic with Sivaran traveling with the group.

The addition of Lord Vygon made things even more interesting. Dr. Snowden had a sneaking suspicion that the Lord Vygon with them now was the same one Dr. Snowden knew on his Earth. Maybe not, but it would not be out of the ordinary if that turned out to be true.

Lord Vygon's breathing increased as the group assembled in the command center. Seeing his world get destroyed was not something he would have imagined possible, yet it was about to happen.

Dr. Snowden and Emily had sat in the left U-shaped seating area, and they acted like this was an everyday type of event. Sivaran and Q were in the right U-shaped seating area, and they seemed more intrigued than surprised that they were about to time travel and jump far away.

Evaran sat in his command chair, and his raw power did not escape Lord Vygon's senses. While Sivaran was powerful,

ADAIR HART

Evaran appeared to be on another level. Dr. Snowden and Emily also possessed power, and with V and the *Torvatta*, Lord Vygon could see how they were a formidable group. He had thought Sivaran and Q were a strong team, but Evaran and the others were past that even.

Lord Vygon took a seat next to Q, who studied V at the front console that sat between the seating areas. V's hands were a blur as he moved them across the slanted interface that was at about stomach level.

"V, put us in stealth mode and scan profile one," said Evaran.

"Acknowledged."

Lord Vygon studied the data window off to the side that displayed a wireframe model of the *Torvatta*. It showed the *Torvatta* to be in stealth mode and scan profile one set, whatever that was. Adding to Lord Vygon's apprehension were the transparent sides and ceiling on the front half of the ship. The floor was semitransparent, so there was something to stabilize his view, but it seemed almost like they floated in space.

He focused on the portal that appeared from a beam outside the *Torvatta*. The *Torvatta* flew through and exited out above Drydris, which showed as a planet with active volcanoes and toxic gas.

His breathing slowed as his eyes misted. "No…"

Sivaran laid a hand on Lord Vygon's shoulder. "This is the current state. I'm sorry, old friend."

"Lord Vygon, if you have the time index of when Wardax appeared, we can go there," said Evaran.

Lord Vygon cleared his throat. "Yeah. Sure. How do I enter it?"

"Circle your finger in the air, and there will be an option to enter a date, specific to your understanding."

Lord Vygon did so. He was not sure how the *Torvatta* could translate what he knew as a date to something the *Torvatta* would understand, but apparently, that was possible. It also amazed him that screens could materialize, as if the whole room was outfitted with holography projectors.

Everything outside faded away.

Lord Vygon gripped his chair. "What … what's going on?"

"We're outside the timeline," said Sivaran. "I wish the *Karus* could do that."

Lord Vygon studied the emptiness. It made his stomach churn.

After a moment, the environment eased back in.

Lord Vygon relaxed when he saw Drydris as a blue-and-green planet again. The *Torvatta* had highlighted various ships and satellites. It was home as he knew it.

"V, perform long-range scans," said Evaran.

"Acknowledged."

"This approach is fascinating," said Q.

"You get used to it," said Dr. Snowden, smiling.

"Have you been other places outside the timeline?"

Dr. Snowden nodded. "The universe, the Cosmic Medium, and of course, here."

"I see."

Lord Vygon was not sure he fully understood some of the terms that were mentioned, but the thought of going outside the universe seemed crazy—yet Evaran and the others had done it and arrived where they were, so it was definitely possible. He studied the data window that showed the *Torvatta* in the center with concentric circles pulsing outward. The red dots converging quickly on Drydris were easy to pick out.

"That's Wardax's fleet," said Lord Vygon. "We had already destroyed one at one of our colonies, but we pulled our armada back to defend Drydris."

"It's moving fast!" said Emily.

Lord Vygon grimaced. "Yeah."

He gritted his teeth as he watched the Zayt fleet arrive. Their characteristic cylindrical design with rings was on full display. They were pummeled by the defense platforms and the Drydris fleet. As each ship exploded, they shot out cylindrical containers. Some went to the planet; others flew toward the ships and defense platforms.

"What's all that?" asked Dr. Snowden.

"A diversion," said Lord Vygon. "Each container has an infector swarm backed by enforcers ready to fight. They had so many that a few hit some of our big ships, and some fell to the planet. This next wave is what got us." He frowned when a massive group of red dots approached quickly.

"Whoa," said Emily. "That's a lot of something."

"Yeah, and Wardax counted on us firing on the diversion to disperse the containers. This fleet coming up is heavily shielded and outnumbered us," said Lord Vygon.

His heart sank as he watched defense ship after defense ship get shredded. Although the Drydris fleet fought hard, there were simply not enough ships to deal with the aggressive Wardax fleet.

"V, take us down to where one of those containers landed," said Evaran.

"Acknowledged."

"This must be hard for you to watch," said Sivaran.

Lord Vygon sighed. "It's already happened. All we can do is learn from their tactics. They will pay!"

After twenty minutes, the *Torvatta* hovered over a city where a container had landed.

"This is Kalashara, one of our main cities," said Lord Vygon.

He shook his head as the familiar infector swarm ran amok, infecting any Halkin they saw and destroying any ancient vampire they came across. As each Halkin turned, they joined a rapidly forming infected swarm.

Dr. Snowden pointed at a zoomed-in window of an encounter between an elite ancient vampire guard unit and enforcers. "Wow. There's only a handful of ancient vampires, but they're holding their own against hundreds." He grimaced when another container landed in the distance and a new swarm of enforcers and infectors unloaded. A swarm of newly infected added to the fight. "As tough as the ancient vampires were, I don't know of much that could defend against that."

"They fought hard to the end," said Lord Vygon, scowling. "I still can't believe there's only four of us left. The Halkins now only exist as part of infector swarms."

"Wardax said he's looking for exotic energy to research, but I don't know why," said Sivaran. "Drydris was destroyed because the ancient vampires could not be infected, and they probably seemed like a threat due to them winning a fight earlier."

Lord Vygon nodded. "And the Zayt adapted from our fight, at least faster than we did." He pointed at a window that had zoomed in on a cloud of infectors. "There's a damn infector swarm. They're hard to hit, move fast, and can infect efficiently."

"Why wouldn't they just drop all infectors?" asked Dr. Snowden. "It seems like the enforcers wouldn't be needed at this point."

Sivaran raised a finger. "Energy constraints. The enforcers can go for quite a bit, but these infectors have limited capability. That might change as Wardax adapts, but the enforcers also have limited EMP protection and a host of other defensive attributes compared to the infector or infected swarm. Enforcers are usually meant to clear a path for the infectors to start turning everything."

"That is a guardian," said Evaran, interacting with his chair console and pulling up a window on the front wall of a ten-foot humanoid robot.

"Definitely," said Lord Vygon. "They have strong shielding and immense physical power. On top of that, they have different weapons depending on the type of robot that's controlled. Not all of them are the same, as Sivaran found out."

He cringed at seeing the guardian walk through a group of defenders like they were not even there. The guardian alone was powerful, but add the rest of the Zayt units and they seemed unstoppable.

"I'm surprised we aren't being detected," said Q. "The *Torvatta*'s cloaking mechanism is superb. Can anything at all detect it?"

Evaran nodded. "Only the ones chosen by the *Torvatta* can. Dalton Kingston from our previous adventure is the only known one so far."

"I find it interesting that the *Torvatta* chose someone," said Sivaran. He glanced at Q. "I wouldn't be able to detect the *Torvatta*."

"That is correct," said Evaran.

"I see," said Q.

"We can spend some time here gathering information," said Evaran. "Afterward, everyone can take a break while the data is analyzed."

Lord Vygon studied the carnage being displayed. It ate at him that he could do nothing except watch. Every part of him wanted to rush out and fight. However, the real-time analysis being performed as the battle raged showed he would have almost no impact.

He had never considered himself to be an emotional person, but the rage inside him was difficult to keep down. Whatever information was gathered from this trip would help determine future plans, so he would focus on trying to be helpful.

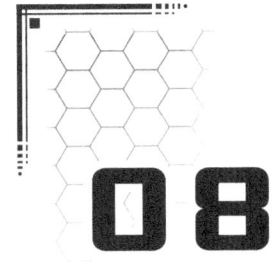

08

D r. Snowden relaxed in the planar cartography lab. The morning had been busy, and a lot of information had been obtained about Zayt tactics, units, and even Wardax himself. There was still much to learn, but now they had something to start with.

It was 3:00 p.m., and Dr. Snowden was not sure where the others were, but he knew that when a deep analysis occurred, he had time to do other things. In this case, it was studying the galactic region they were in.

The holographic model had been complemented with data from the *Karus*. He always enjoyed looking at the planets, stars, and other phenomena whenever new regional information was added. It blew his mind that he could zoom in and get a detailed readout of a planet's atmosphere. Some planets even had surface scans, so he could observe wildlife or civilizations. It was a dream come true for him to be able to explore like this.

His attention focused on Sivaran entering the room. "Hey."

"Dr. Snowden. I see you're enjoying studying the area."

Dr. Snowden grinned. "Yeah. How many people get to study a galactic region in another universe?"

"I understand," said Sivaran. "Mind if I join you?"

"Not at all. I figured you were helping with the analysis."

Sivaran shrugged. "Well ... when you have Evaran, Q, and V, it gets a little crowded. I'll assist later. I wanted to spend some time with you, Emily, and V when he's free."

Dr. Snowden chuckled. "Just like Levaran."

"I saw that!" said Sivaran, pointing at him. "She was tough and bold."

"Definitely. She also saved my life and gave us cosmic energy. She even helped me through dreams."

"I saw Evaran's analysis of those events. That must have been traumatic for you."

Dr. Snowden grabbed a nearby seat and plopped down while Sivaran sat opposite him. "It wasn't too bad. I do miss Levaran, and I really hate how she died."

Sivaran looked down. "I ... I saw that event as well. Evaran was pained."

A lump formed in Dr. Snowden's throat. "Yeah. She helped us and even got a *Torvatta* and Edev, along with traveling companions, then was killed by that darn Hadryn spawn."

"In the end, you avenged her," said Sivaran.

"I guess we did. Still, it hurts to know she suffered. Also, poor Edev. Brought alive, only to die a while later, relatively. The whole situation was bad."

Sivaran nodded. "I understand."

"You think you'll upgrade from the *Karus* to the *Torvatta?*" asked Dr. Snowden.

"Sadly, no. The only way to get enough cosmic energy for that is to re-form, and I'm in no hurry to do that. I like being me."

Dr. Snowden could not help but draw comparisons between Evaran, Levaran, and Sivaran. Each was unique, but Dr. Snowden knew at a base level, they were all the same being. Sivaran appeared more relaxed, and although his cosmic energy level was comparable to Levaran's, their physical attributes were different.

"I know each plane form has its own abilities. With Levaran, it was strength. Evaran has speed and strength. Do you have anything like that?" asked Dr. Snowden.

Sivaran tapped his chest. "My suit. It's morphable metal, similar to what your PSD can do."

"Ahh. I thought it was liquid metal, but morphable make sense. You must be able to perform some interesting feats."

Sivaran extended his hand. The metal slid over and formed a hammer.

"Whoa. Now that's cool," said Dr. Snowden.

Sivaran sighed. "Yeah, but it doesn't matter much when facing a palisin-wielding robot who can neutralize my suit."

"Sounds like you need a counter to it, similar to what Evaran used for his energy shield."

"I've seen it, and I plan to carry some. A container of that mist that neutralizes palisin energy would be very helpful."

Dr. Snowden recalled Evaran upgrading his shield, and also putting the counteragent into small orbs. They had been successfully deployed against Seeros, a former foe, who had palisin-enhanced armor. Although Dr. Snowden had not seen a need to carry any of the orbs, he thought that given their current environment, it would be prudent to do so.

Sivaran gestured at him. "You've had an interesting journey to this point."

"Ahh, you saw it via the sync with Evaran."

Sivaran nodded. "Sure did. You got to visit the Cosmic Medium, in addition to meeting Dian, Pozarra, and even Syrilus. You're special, as is Emily. It doesn't hurt that you also travel with Evaran prime."

Dr. Snowden shrugged. "Or lucky."

Sivaran eyed him. "I don't think luck had much to do with it."

"Probably not," said Dr. Snowden. "If something seems coincidental, that means it most likely isn't, something I've learned from traveling with Evaran."

"An astute observation," said Sivaran, wagging a finger.

"I noticed that you only had Q with you. Do you take on traveling companions?" asked Dr. Snowden.

Sivaran sighed. "I did at one point. I got tired of outliving them."

"Oh ... I guess Evaran will experience that, too, with us."

"Most likely. It's fine for maybe the first two groups, but after five ... it's too much. I know Evaran has difficulty showing emotions, but I don't, and it kills me to think of what I've lost," said Sivaran, frowning.

Dr. Snowden could almost feel Sivaran's pain. Getting to know a group such that they become family, then losing them, over and over, must be exhausting. He understood Sivaran's decision not to take on companions anymore. Q was an AI and could hypothetically live as long as Sivaran. Lord Vygon might be able to as well.

"The solution, then, is to surround yourself with those who live as long as you do. Q is a start, but you could get an android or a being that lives long."

Sivaran rubbed his chin. "I've thought about it. You're right in that Q is a start. Who knows what I'll move on to?"

Dr. Snowden nodded. He liked talking with Sivaran. It was easy to see the Evaran in him, but the facial emotions were fun to watch. Dr. Snowden tried to imagine Evaran saying these things. Although it was possible, his face would most likely remain constant.

"So ... do you need a tour guide on these systems?" asked Sivaran, motioning at the galactic hologram.

Dr. Snowden's eyes lit up. "What are we waiting for?"

Emily relaxed in her living quarters. It was 6:00 p.m., and she had a good dinner. Evaran and V were still doing their analysis, and Dr. Snowden had taken a break from the planar cartography lab for dinner. She was not sure where Lord Vygon, Q, and Sivaran were.

She peeked over at a picture she had framed and set on the nearby coffee table. Kess had taken the snapshot, and it showed Jelton with his arms around Emily's waist with both of them smiling. She missed him and wished he could have come along, but she also understood he was in the middle of a campaign to establish a Rift Guardian colony.

Before traveling on this adventure, she had gone on a trip with him, and it was everything she had thought it would be. She had stayed out of the way and observed him in action, barking orders and planning strategy and tactics. The Rift Guardians viewed him as a demigod due to him having cosmic energy in him, and by extension, they afforded a similar status to her. She had come to know Jelton's closest friends well.

Knock! Knock!

She took a moment to focus, then hopped up and faced the entranceway. "Who is it?"

"Sivaran."

She wrinkled her brow. His visit was unexpected. She walked over and opened the door.

"I was making the rounds and wanted to see if you had some time to talk."

"Sure. What about?" she asked.

Sivaran motioned between them. "Just to get to know each other better. I already talked with your uncle."

"Yeah, he wouldn't stop talking about it at dinner. Come in."

After a minute, she was in her plush chair, while Sivaran sat perpendicular to her on the couch.

"Levaran did the same thing," said Emily. "She visited us shortly after her re-formation."

Sivaran nodded. "The fact you witnessed that is amazing. That is an extremely rare event."

"Yeah. I miss her."

"She saved you."

Emily frowned. "Yeah, then she left and was killed, and although we avenged her, I still feel bad."

Sivaran rubbed his chin. "She knew what she needed to do in order for Evaran prime to do what he had to do. If I had been in the same position, I would have made the same choice."

"I figured," said Emily. "I can see Evaran in you, although it's a treat to see your facial expressions."

Sivaran raised his eyebrows. "Well, we are the same person, just different plane forms. Now that I've synced, I know all he knows, and he knows all I know."

"Do you associate emotions with what you found out from syncing?"

"I don't. They're just memories to me without emotional attachment."

"Sorta like V and his predecessors."

Sivaran wagged a finger at her. "Right!"

Emily studied him. It was fun to think of Evaran making the same hand and facial animations. Like Levaran, it was easy to detect that Sivaran was definitely an Evaran. Very few had cosmic energy at those levels.

"I'm sorry you had to do the prison planet thing," said Sivaran. "It changed you."

She sighed. "It's in the past. Learn, adapt, evolve. That's how I dealt with it."

"Evaran felt great pain at what you went through," said Sivaran.

"I'm sure he did," said Emily. "He's hard to read at times, and I didn't have any cosmic energy at the time, but his actions showed how he felt."

Sivaran nodded. "You're a survivor. From what I understand of humans, from Evaran's perspective, not many would have survived what you went through."

"Having a PSD helped," said Emily, smiling. "Still, it was strange to see another version of me, a nanobot version. I miss her too."

"Ahh yes, nanobot Emily. She sacrificed herself, but I think she made the same decision you would."

Emily nodded. "Definitely." She studied Sivaran. "Would I be able to see some of the adventures you went on in the holo room?"

"Of course. With Evaran, I can sync, but the holo room would be ideal for anyone else. Perhaps we should check if the others are interested."

"Uncle Albert isn't going to miss that. I suspect Lord Vygon wouldn't either. Speaking of ... Uncle Albert and I talked to the Lord Vygon we knew before coming out here. He gave us each a half of a Daedrould stone."

"Can I see it?" asked Sivaran.

Emily hopped up and retrieved it, then handed it to him.

He fidgeted with it. "Interesting. I haven't seen one of these in a long time. With the other half, it would function fully."

"I'm beginning to think the Lord Vygon we know is the same one here with us, but at an earlier point in his time stream."

Sivaran wrinkled his brow. "The only issue there is he has to die first. Plus, I've never seen one of these work. I suspect it's mainly symbolic."

"Well, I'm hoping we don't need to use it. You never know, though," said Emily as she shrugged.

"That's true. Evaran's adventures have had some brutal moments." He hopped up. "How about we look at some of mine? They aren't quite as action-packed, or have me traveling through time, but they're still interesting."

She stood. "Let's do this!"

She enjoyed talking with Sivaran. He was like an old friend, and she had almost called him Evaran several times. It was not lost on her that this was also an opportunity to see how an Evaran would react to different situations. Although Evaran and Sivaran were different plane forms, they probably had the same reactions to events. She looked forward to comparing the two, but for now, there were adventures to check out.

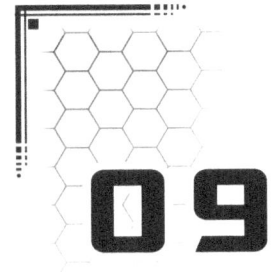

09

V observed Q in the rest area where low-power mode was used. The day had gone by fast, and V had assisted Evaran in compiling and analyzing data gathered from the Zayt transport. As there was a lot of new information, the process took longer than usual.

Q provided data and analysis from the *Karus*, so there was also a comparison of what was known and what was new and how relevant it was. It was 9:00 p.m., and Evaran had decided to wait until the next day for a conference meeting at 10:00 a.m.

V had wanted to interact with the others, but Dr. Snowden, Emily, and Lord Vygon were in their living quarters. Q was in low-power mode, and Sivaran was talking with Evaran. V suspected they desired alone time to discuss things. He flew into his cradle and landed. There were some simulations in his queue that he had prioritized.

The environment changed to a diner with outside seating in a city setting. V assumed a human form and sat at a table. He flagged down a waitress.

"Are you ready to order?" she asked.

"Yes. I would like a burger and fries."

"Which one?" she asked, gesturing at the menu on the table.

V realized he had not been specific enough. He picked up the menu and scanned it. "A double bacon cheeseburger with no pickles."

The waitress wrote it down. "Anything else?"

"A small order of onion rings and some water."

"Got it," she said. She took the menu and smiled at him.

He reciprocated and she took off. His goal for the simulation was to interact with humans to the point they did not know he was not human. Although he enjoyed practicing it with Dr. Snowden and Emily, they knew he was an AI. He tilted his head when Sivaran appeared and sat across from him.

"Query. Have you come to participate?"

Sivaran grinned. "I just wanted to stop in and chat. I've already talked with the others, but I didn't forget you."

V nodded. "I appreciate you visiting."

The waitress reappeared and motioned at Sivaran.

He flicked a finger at V. "I'll have what he's having."

"A double bacon cheeseburger with no pickles, a small onion ring, and some water. Got it."

Sivaran winked at her. "And a side of smile."

She smiled and then walked away.

V found Sivaran's use of a suggestion to be intriguing. The characters in the simulation were sophisticated and modeled after data and observations from Earth systems as well as Evaran. Apparently, they could smile if winked at.

"Analysis. You got her to smile."

"It's just my natural charm," said Sivaran, easing back into his chair and lacing his fingers. He gestured around. "I love the simulation."

"Thank you. It has been refactored multiple times, and I believe it is adequate for my interaction. Dr. Snowden and Emily like it."

"I bet they do," said Sivaran. He studied V. "It's hard to see, but I sense the cosmic energy in you much better now. Syrilus had masked it until the event where you met her. She probably did that so if Evaran prime became corrupt, you would be hidden."

V nodded. "Syrilus took a precaution. My inner container is a mix of planar and cosmic, and my outer is my plane form."

"A fascinating combination. You're our love child."

V tilted his head. "Yes. I can be considered a love child."

Sivaran pointed at him. "There you go. And you travel with Evaran prime, two cosmic-enhanced humans, and the *Torvatta*. You even got to meet one of the *Torvatta*'s chosen in Dalton Kingston. Most impressive."

"I have enjoyed my experience to date. Has your journey so far been enjoyable?"

Sivaran sighed. "It's not as exciting as what you've experienced. As you know, our main goal was to find the Hoxscarus, and it seems that's been narrowed down to your timeline. I did not have much luck there, despite the signature for this universe matching the parameters needed for the Hoxscarus to evolve."

V recalled that the Hoxscarus were the final evolution of a species that would evolve into a quasicosmic species and leave the plane. Evaran believed humans were the ones who would do this. There had been hints about a future event involving the gang and the Hoxscarus, but it had not occurred yet.

"You have Q to explore with."

"I do," said Sivaran. "He's been with me for a long while, but he doesn't have your complexity. If he's destroyed, he can only be restored to his last backup, assuming his backups aren't destroyed, but as a pure AI, he has no inner container."

"Q's backups were destroyed recently on the Zayt transport," said V.

Sivaran frowned. "Yeah, sadly. I already miss the *Karus*. With some new technology from the *Torvatta*, the *Karus* could really shine."

"Perhaps a *Torvatta* can be created for you, like Levaran."

"I discussed this with Emily already, but it requires me to die—well, this plane form—to get the necessary cosmic energy. I'd rather not die."

"I do not wish for you to die either."

Sivaran chortled. "Then we're in agreement."

V found Sivaran's ability to express himself fascinating. It added to an internal database V kept that logged what Evaran felt or said. V could compare that with Sivaran to determine what expression would be generated if Evaran could express himself via facial and body cues.

"This must be unusual for you to be here," said V.

Sivaran shrugged. "I knew that if I encountered Evaran prime, there would probably be something fantastic going on. The *Torvatta* opens a lot of doors, and you came along with it. I was surprised about the *Torvatta* choosing someone, and also Dr. Snowden and Emily possessing cosmic energy."

"They are my family."

"I get that. You travel with a good group, or gang, as it's known," said Sivaran. "I hope that after Wardax is dealt with, I can visit Dr. Snowden and Emily's Earth before settling back here."

"I do not believe Evaran would have an issue with that," said V. He tilted his head. "As you are suggesting it, then it most likely means he is already okay with it."

Sivaran wagged a finger at V. "Now you're getting it!"

Although Evaran, Sivaran, and Levaran had different personalities, their decision making seemed to be the same. That only reinforced that they were all Evaran at their core.

"This must be an interesting time for Q," said V.

"Oh yeah," said Sivaran. "Q is trying to absorb everything and put it into context. He finds you absolutely fascinating, so you may find him asking you a lot of questions."

"He has, and I do not mind answering his queries," said V. "He is a ship AI in a body."

"That he is." Sivaran surveyed the environment. "I can help you practice in this simulation."

"I would like that," said V with a smile.

His inner container pulsed like it did around Evaran, who had said he would be around in one way or another. Sivaran was an example of that. V would take advantage of the unique situation and learn what he could. Sivaran was an insight into Evaran in general.

Lord Vygon stared at the ceiling as he rested on his bed in his living quarters. Although he had had a good rest, and it was 9:00 a.m. per the wall display above him, his stomach churned as he thought about Drydris. His home planet and most of his species were gone. He and the other three lords were all that was left. He swallowed hard as he recalled all the ceremonies and activities he used to do. All that history was lost.

He sighed as he swung his legs off the side of the bed. It was a struggle to find something positive, but he also realized how lucky he and the other lords were. To be in the presence of not one Evaran but two, in addition to traveling in a ship that could travel through time, was nothing short of miraculous. He was not sure what his future held, but he suspected it involved the Daedrould stone and Dr. Snowden and Emily's version of Lord Vygon. Nothing could be straightforward, it seemed.

He got cleaned up and went to the conference room. It was now 9:30 a.m., and Dr. Snowden, Sivaran, and Q were already there. Sivaran ate some type of brown meat that was cut into strips and another item that appeared to have a golden center surrounded by something white. Dr. Snowden had a bowl with meat and a yellow substance.

Lord Vygon got a glass of warm blood, then took his seat. It wasn't his favorite mix that Emily had retrieved before, but blood was blood. "Morning, everyone."

"Hey," said Sivaran. He shook a piece of the brown meat at Lord Vygon. "This is bacon, and it's delicious."

Lord Vygon nodded. "And what is that other thing on your plate?"

"Sunny-side-up eggs!"

Lord Vygon sipped some blood. "Interesting." He gestured at Dr. Snowden's bowl. "I assume you have something similar, but the eggs are in a different configuration."

"Yep, they're scrambled," said Dr. Snowden.

"An interesting choice for breakfast," said Q. "The flesh and eggs of an animal."

Sivaran chuckled. "These are replicated, but point taken, although that description is less palatable. Per Dr. Snowden, these are popular on Earth." He eyed Lord Vygon. "The Halkins had a similar type of breakfast."

Lord Vygon looked down. "Yeah."

"I'm sorry I couldn't have done more to assist Drydris," said Sivaran.

"It's okay," said Lord Vygon, raising his head. "Wardax is just too powerful, and he can do whatever he wants. All I can do is look forward and work to defeat him."

"We're with you," said Dr. Snowden.

Lord Vygon nodded. "I appreciate that."

He could see why the Lord Vygon version that Dr. Snowden knew was close with him. He had no concerns about jumping in and helping, even if it was against the greatest power Lord Vygon had ever known. Still, Dr. Snowden wanted to help. Maybe it was a human thing; then again, Dr. Snowden had been given a Daedrould stone, no small matter. Lord Vygon wondered if human blood was compatible with Halkin blood. He pushed the thought out of his mind.

Evaran, Emily, and V entered the room and took their seats.

"Good morning, everyone," said Evaran. "I hope you slept well. There was a lot of data to go through, but with Sivaran, Q, and V's help, I believe we have a next step. As we are all here, we can begin."

Lord Vygon perked up.

"The data to this point consists of what we saw on the Zayt transport, information from the *Karus*, Sivaran and Q's personal recollections, and information pulled from the Zayt transport. While that gives us an understanding of the Zayt and Wardax, we do not know the full extent of the Zayt's reach. To that end, Sivaran has suggested we visit Acrolis, a matter mage who calls herself a knowledge keeper."

"An information broker, like Sandas," said Emily.

"Yes, but not quite as quirky," said Sivaran, winking at Emily.

She smiled at him.

"Her location is hidden, but Sivaran knows how to get there," said Evaran.

"It's been a long time since we visited Acrolis," said Q. "She may know more now."

Lord Vygon wrinkled his brow. "This Acrolis ... you said she's a matter mage? What's that?"

"Oh, she can control matter to a certain radius," said Dr. Snowden, circling his finger in the air.

"Control ... you mean like reshape the environment?" asked Lord Vygon.

"Yep. They're powerful, but most are good."

"So where's she at, then?" asked Emily.

Sivaran nodded. "She moves around, but she has a base in a system on the edge of the galaxy. She has temporary bases throughout the galaxy, but she always goes back to her home one. There's a map there that indicates where she has gone if she's not home."

"Huh, so we get her current secret location from her secret home base," said Emily.

"Analysis. She is very secretive."

"On purpose," said Sivaran. "As powerful as she is, there are other things stronger than her. Like palisin weakens cosmic energy, antimatter weaponry can destroy matter mages."

"It seems like they could just always avoid getting hit," said Lord Vygon.

"Not against a relativistic missile loaded with an antimatter charge."

Lord Vygon shrugged. "Yeah, I guess that'd do it."

Evaran nodded. "We will visit Acrolis's home base and determine where we need to go. I suspect she will be able to fill us in on the Zayt's current state."

"Sounds like a plan," said Dr. Snowden.

"Let us go," said Evaran, standing.

Lord Vygon stood along with the others. He had begun to feel more optimistic. The ability to travel far in seconds was a powerful feature. He had never met a matter mage before, so this would be a new experience for him. However, it seemed every time he felt a moment of excitement, guilt kicked in about Drydris. Why he and the other lords had been spared Drydris's fate, he did not know. What he did know was that this group was taking steps to punish Wardax. That was something Lord Vygon could get on board with.

He assembled in the command center with everyone else. V stood at the front console while Evaran sat in his command chair. Sivaran, Q, and Emily sat in the right U-shaped seating area, while Dr. Snowden was on the right side with Lord Vygon. His eyes lit up seeing the *Torvatta* open a portal and fly through. He understood how unique it was to be on a ship that could do that.

The world that appeared surprised him. It resembled Drydris, a hell world, and based on the readings, the atmosphere was hostile. The *Torvatta* flew into the atmosphere and toward a large volcano.

As the *Torvatta* descended, Lord Vygon soaked in the environment. It appeared burnt ground and lava seas were everywhere. Violent explosions in the distance shot up fiery fragments, and a data window indicated that the pressure was very high. Definitely not a place for organics as he knew them.

"Wow, this place is hellish," said Emily.

"Yeah, not somewhere to take a stroll, for sure," said Dr. Snowden.

"We could if you want a challenge," said Sivaran.

Dr. Snowden crooked a thumb at Evaran. "That's what he would say."

Evaran half smiled.

The group laughed.

Lord Vygon noted that teasing Dr. Snowden seemed to be a universal Evaran thing. Dr. Snowden's good temperament allowed that.

The *Torvatta* reached the volcano after twenty minutes and flew inside.

"Are we going into the lava?" asked Lord Vygon.

"Analysis. We are."

"We should be safe based on the *Torvatta*'s shielding," said Q.

"Okay … ," said Lord Vygon. Flying into lava, regardless of shielding, seemed strange, but if that was what it took to find Acrolis's base, then so be it.

The *Torvatta* hit the lava and began to descend.

Lord Vygon studied the lava as it flowed by. He wondered how many could say they had seen that.

After an hour, the *Torvatta* changed course and entered a lava tube. Another thirty minutes and they arrived at an area where the tube entered a massive open area. Lava fell like a waterfall, and on the opposite side of the area and high up was an empty tube. The *Torvatta* flew toward it.

"It'd be hard to find this base," said Emily. "How does she get there?"

Sivaran nodded. "From what I understand, she forms a sphere and comes the same way we do. It wouldn't be difficult for her."

"Right. Matter mage thing."

The *Torvatta* extended rods from the exterior black meshes. Each rod lit up, illuminating the lava tube. After twenty minutes of cruising, they came upon another large area, except this time the tube emerged at the base of a waterfall that seemed to continue underground.

Lord Vygon admired the blue bioluminescence that illuminated the environment. Two massive but elegant doors appeared against the wall.

"We're here," said Sivaran. He pointed at the doors. "You can land outside that. The atmosphere will be warm and there is higher pressure, but nothing we can't handle. Acrolis made sure this was suitable for a variety of species she brought here at times."

"It's beautiful," said Emily, looking around.

"Wait until you see the inside," said Sivaran, grinning. He hopped up and clapped his hands after the *Torvatta* landed. "Who's ready to explore?"

Lord Vygon observed Evaran studying Sivaran and wondered what Evaran must think of Sivaran and how he acted. Their personalities were very different. The team was now one step closer to defeating Wardax, though, and that was Lord Vygon's highest priority for the moment.

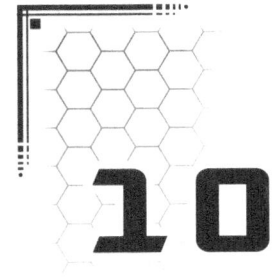

10

Dr. Snowden had his survival suit on when the group exited the *Torvatta*. The atmosphere seemed habitable, so he lowered his helmet. There was a strong smell of vegetation, probably from what covered the rock walls and gave off light. It was definitely warm, and the pressure was a bit higher than he was used to. The ground was solid, and the area before the large doors appeared stable.

Sivaran stepped in front of the group. "I need to go first."

As he marched ahead, a massive mud-like pillar rose out of what appeared to be a hole off to the side of the door. It formed a face at the top, then bent over to face Sivaran.

Dr. Snowden's heart raced. The creature had popped out and moved fast, and it towered over the group. It could cause some damage if it wanted to.

"Grozelgug!" said Sivaran, flashing his hands off to the side. "I'm here with friends, and we're looking for Acrolis."

"She's away," said Grozelgug in a deep voice.

Sivaran nodded. "Then I'm sure Kassikel will show us where she is."

Grozelgug growled and focused on Evaran. "He's like you, but more powerful."

"He's Evaran prime," said Sivaran, gesturing at him.

Evaran nodded. "It is good to meet you, Grozelgug."

"Likewise." Grozelgug sank back into the ground.

The doors creaked and whined before opening.

"That was interesting," said Dr. Snowden. "A mud elemental for a guard."

Sivaran wagged a finger at Dr. Snowden. "Grozelgug is a mud being. He doesn't like elementals."

"Oh … ," said Dr. Snowden.

Lord Vygon glanced at him. "Yeah, I don't know what the difference is either."

Sivaran nodded. "Elementals are pure and only contain their element and a specific type of exotic energy. Grozelgug was created by Acrolis and has no exotic energy. He's also made up of other elements."

"Ahh," said Dr. Snowden. "Got it."

"Let's go," said Sivaran, waving forward.

Dr. Snowden recalled that matter mages could not create life with a life link layer, or three-L. However, Grozelgug seemed alive to Dr. Snowden.

The main hallway they entered intrigued him. It resembled a large tube. The flat ground they walked on went on for a while but eventually exited into a massive cavern. The walls resembled the aftermath of someone carving boxes into them, and each box had a dim glow inside it. The overall effect lit up the place, giving off a rainbow effect.

A waterfall in the back caught Dr. Snowden's eye. In front of it were rock pools with green water. Scattered around the area were circular platforms with a variety of unusual poles on them. The ground was also tiled, not something he had expected. He had thought the ceiling would be rocky, but it too was covered in the box design.

"Wow, this is beautiful," said Emily.

Q pointed at a box. "Those are data structures that go deep into the rock."

"Really?" asked Dr. Snowden. "How does she store data?"

"She encodes it in the molecular makeup of the box."

"That's interesting. The boxes, then, are like a cataloging system."

Q nodded.

Lord Vygon peered around. "I noticed there are no chairs or tables here."

Sivaran nodded. "Acrolis likes to transform into a cube herself, so no need."

"I sense exotic energy there," said Evaran, looking off in the distance.

"Acrolis keeps samples of exotic energy she comes across."

Emily wrinkled her brow. "She must use her inability to affect matter to determine if there is exotic energy."

"You are correct," said Q.

"Query. How does she differentiate them?" asked V.

"I don't know," said Q.

"I would suspect that there is a resistance level she catalogs," said Evaran.

"Huh. Well, if she's away, how do we find out where she is?" asked Emily.

Sivaran crooked a thumb at a section of the wall in the back that had a dim brown glow to it.

Dr. Snowden wrinkled his brow at the humanoid woman with rock skin that walked out.

"That's Kassikel, or rather, a copy of her," said Sivaran.

She arrived and hugged him. "Evaran! Most unexpected! And you have friends!"

"I sure do."

Kassikel walked up to Evaran. "You ... seem like Evaran too."

Evaran nodded. "I am the same as the one you know as Evaran, but we possess different forms. To avoid confusion, I am known as Evaran since I am the first form, and he is known as Sivaran, since he is the sixth."

"That's interesting! Two Evarans, just like there are multiple copies of me everywhere."

"That is a good way of thinking of it," said Evaran.

Kassikel smiled at him. "I think I like you." She faced Sivaran. "I take it you were hoping to find Acrolis here?"

"We were, but we also understand that she is probably out collecting knowledge."

"She is," said Kassikel. "Okay, let's go!"

"You're coming with us?" asked Dr. Snowden.

"Of course I am. I'd never miss a chance to travel with the gang."

"Oh ... uhh, yeah. By the way, I'm Dr. Albert Snowden."

Kassikel stared at him for a moment. "Yes ... who are the others?"

While Evaran introduced the others, Dr. Snowden went over how Kassikel knew to call the group the gang. She could be telepathic or something, but his cosmic energy would prevent her from probing him. Another idea was that she had already met them in some sort of time loop. That would have been unheard of only a year ago, but given all that he had seen, it was not that uncommon.

After being introduced, they headed out.

As they walked, Dr. Snowden glanced over at Kassikel. "So you know of us as the gang?"

"Oh, it was just a term for group. It could be a translation thing."

Dr. Snowden nodded. That sounded plausible. "How do you know where Acrolis is?"

"I have the locations of where she will be at and when. When we arrive, I'll merge into the Kassikel there already."

"You're like a living update."

She grinned. "That's a great way to think of it."

"Do you all have the same personalities?" asked Emily.

She shrugged. "Usually."

Dr. Snowden was curious how that all worked but figured it was a matter mage thing. He did not recall any of the other matter mages they had met having a system like this. Then again, this was a different universe.

After exiting the area, they boarded the *Torvatta* and assembled in the command center.

Kassikel sat and opened a holo window with a galactic map.

Dr. Snowden's eyes narrowed. She did that like it was routine.

Kassikel got to work and, after a moment, she selected a water world.

"Acrolis really likes inhospitable places," he said.

"It makes it harder to reach her, and many have tried," said Kassikel.

ADAIR HART

After reaching low orbit in twenty minutes, the *Torvatta* spawned a portal and flew through.

"And here we are," said Kassikel, standing. "The *Torvatta* is impressive, even more so than the *Karus*."

"I'm sitting right here," said Sivaran, eying her.

She nodded. "It wasn't meant to insult, but portals are powerful."

Dr. Snowden studied the red dot on the front wall. It moved some as the *Torvatta* descended but kept the location of where they needed to go in sight. The data labels showed that the planet was covered with water and clouds, and the planet's radius was about two times that of Earth. He also understood that, due to the pressure exerted at deeper depths, there would probably be different layers of the worldwide ocean. Acrolis must have had some determined hunters after her to build in such remote and dangerous places, at least for humans.

After twenty minutes, the *Torvatta* hovered over a patch of water.

Everywhere Dr. Snowden examined was ocean. He shuddered to think what it must be like to be stranded in such a place with no hope of surviving.

"So she's underwater, I take it," said Lord Vygon.

Kassikel nodded. "Roughly about one hundred and seventy miles. I assume the translator converted the right units for you to understand."

"It did, and wow," said Emily. "That's deep. Earth goes to about seven miles at its deepest, I think."

Dr. Snowden drew his head back. "Look at you!"

"Marianas Trench, right?" she asked.

"You got it."

144

"Seven miles is not that deep compared to Drydris, either," said Lord Vygon. "We had some places go over fifteen."

Dr. Snowden nodded.

"Take us in, V," said Evaran.

"Acknowledged."

Dr. Snowden eased back into his chair as the *Torvatta* descended into the water. The front wall highlighted different types of life. Most seemed fishlike, but there was a fair representation of what he would expect in an ocean. Then again, there were some that defied anything he had seen before. One resembled a mermaid, except instead of a human face, it had a head with a massive sucker ringed with teeth. It made him wonder what exactly they fed on.

When the *Torvatta* hit seven miles, he grimaced at the pressure readings he saw. They kept increasing the deeper they went, and it was dark everywhere. Even at the depths they cruised through, the *Torvatta* continued to highlight life.

"Acrolis will need to see me when we get there," said Kassikel.

"Then to the roof we go!" said Emily.

Dr. Snowden's breathing increased as he stood with the others. He knew he was safe in the *Torvatta*, but the environment around them would kill him in an instant if he was in it. Maybe it was a primal thing, but it made his skin crawl. They still had a ways to travel, and he was curious as to what else they would see.

Emily gazed around the roof. V had pulled up a console to work from, and Q stood nearby and watched him. Evaran and Sivaran stood with their hands behind their backs off to the right. It was no surprise to her that they had the same stance. Dr. Snowden and Lord Vygon were to her left and by the guardrail. She sensed Dr. Snowden's nervousness, and to be fair, she was a bit nervous as well.

Outside the *Torvatta* was pitch black, other than the silhouettes of life. The *Torvatta* could handle the depths, but it made her wonder how Acrolis survived down there. Emily's pulse quickened when she thought of being alone in a place like this, although she knew she would not survive outside.

After two hours, the *Torvatta* reached the depth where Acrolis was to be at. A glimmer appeared in the distance. The *Torvatta* identified it as a life-form but had no other details.

"And there she is," said Kassikel.

"She's a light down here?" asked Dr. Snowden.

"Not quite…"

The glimmer grew in intensity until it was a few feet away from the *Torvatta*'s shielding.

Emily drew her head back when the *Torvatta* began to detect water elementals all around. The glimmer still showed as inconclusive. When it took on a humanoid shape, it became much easier to see that it was Acrolis. Emily wondered how they would communicate with her.

A small part of the roof extended out to the shielding, and the guardrail in that area dissipated.

Acrolis walked through the shielding and took on a human female form. She wore a formfitting light blue suit. Her glowing white eyes and shoulder-length hair gave a stark contrast to her dark skin.

"Kassikel! There you are!" said Acrolis.

Kassikel went over and hugged her. "I'm here with some updates."

Acrolis nodded. "I've already absorbed your version here, so I'll sync with you when we get back to home base." She glanced at Sivaran, then Q. "Good to see you both again."

Q nodded.

Sivaran smiled. "Likewise. You want to go back to your home base?"

"I do. The Zayt information you're looking for is there," said Acrolis.

"How did you know we were seeking that?" he asked.

"The same way I know that you travel with another Evaran, along with Dr. Snowden, Emily Snowden, and V, on the *Torvatta*."

Evaran stepped forward. "I do not believe we have met."

"We have, but I can't say how. Your rules. What's important is that I have what you need."

Emily wrinkled her brow. "This must be an out-of-sync thing."

Acrolis shrugged. "Maybe."

"It's okay. We're used to it by now."

"I know," said Acrolis. She eyed Lord Vygon. "I'm sorry to hear about Drydris."

Lord Vygon sighed. "I appreciate that. Wardax will get what's coming to him."

"Of that, I have no doubt."

Acrolis grinned at V. "You can take us back to my home base now."

V shot a look at Evaran, who nodded. "Acknowledged."

Emily chuckled when Acrolis talked with what appeared to be a startled Sivaran. Although he might be aware of time loops, the *Karus* could not travel in time, except through rifts. She suspected he rarely, if ever, encountered time loops.

She walked over to Acrolis. "The *Torvatta* identified water elementals."

"Yes, and they've been gracious hosts. They stored data for me, which I now carry within me," said Acrolis. "For my part, I assisted them with various events and shared knowledge, something they hungered for."

"I could see that. I would guess at some point, they would know everything about their environment, and it's not like they could leave the planet."

Acrolis raised a finger. "Not yet, at least. I created several environments with air and heat so they could look to the stars and one day travel to them. They have the knowledge to do so now."

"That's so interesting," said Dr. Snowden.

Acrolis nodded.

After two hours, Emily's muscles relaxed when the *Torvatta* reached a depth where light began to illuminate the area. The dark depths were depressing. She eased up even more when the *Torvatta* broke out of the ocean and flew toward low orbit. It was good to see air around. She studied Acrolis as she went over to talk with Evaran and Sivaran. Emily wondered what they would discuss. Most topics would probably be gagged under Evaran's rules, assuming Acrolis had met the group in the past, which it seemed like she had.

After two hours, the *Torvatta* landed outside Acrolis's base. Ten minutes later and they had assembled in the main room inside.

Emily gazed as the place came alive. Various entities with differing compositions appeared to come out of the ground and walls to greet Acrolis. Some were like Grozelgug and seemed to be wormlike as they popped out from the walls, ground, and ceiling. Others were humanoid, while others appeared crab-like. Emily's skin crawled, but she knew she was in no danger.

Acrolis extended her arms off to the sides. "I'm back!" She gestured at Kassikel. "Retrieve the information that Evaran and the others seek."

Kassikel entered the place she had initially entered from, and exited a moment later with a fist-sized cube. She walked over and handed it to Evaran.

Emily realized that Kassikel already knew of the Zayt information, but she had not mentioned it earlier. She probably knew that Acrolis would have come back. In that regard, Kassikel was sort of like a living security key. Her presence aboard the *Torvatta* would have signified to Acrolis that it was time to give the Zayt information.

Acrolis gestured at the cube. "I have everything that I've gathered on the Zayt on that cube. The algorithms to decode it are on the faces."

"Thank you," said Evaran. "It would seem we put in a request to have this ready for when we visited."

Acrolis nodded. "I'm no stranger to time travel and its rules, and yours by extension." She walked over to Dr. Snowden and put a hand on his shoulder. "Be wise in how you use the information, and stay strong."

Emily narrowed her eyes. She was not sure why Dr. Snowden had been singled out, but it seemed deliberate. Perhaps it was nothing, but Emily found the smallest actions by a powerful being oftentimes had hidden meanings. If that was the case here, then Acrolis was telling Dr. Snowden to stay strong ... for something.

"I hope we're wise with it," said Dr. Snowden.

"I know you will be," said Acrolis. She studied Sivaran. "I'm sorry to hear about the *Karus*."

"I haven't told you about it…"

"Yet." Acrolis focused on the group. "The Zayt are rapidly expanding. Nothing has been able to stand in their way. Not even my fellow matter mages, what few of us there are."

"It seems like you could fight them," said Lord Vygon. "You're a very powerful being."

"Sadly, we can't," said Acrolis. "As Evaran and Sivaran are unique, so is Wardax. He has already killed one of my kind."

"Does he have cosmic energy?" asked Dr. Snowden.

"I don't know," she said. "I can't sense him, so he has something."

Lord Vygon sighed. "Does the information you retrieved contain Wardax's location?"

"It has a list of possible places. I couldn't get too close."

Sivaran nodded. "Some is better than none. We appreciate you getting this information. I guess we'll ask you to do that in the past."

"I can't say."

"Of course not. Our rules," said Sivaran, waving a finger between him and Evaran.

"It is clear, then, that our next step is to study the information and determine a plan," said Evaran.

"I wish you the best of luck," said Acrolis. "We will meet again ... in one way or another."

Emily followed the others as they began to leave. She peeked back and watched as Acrolis gazed at the group. The

Zayt information would help, but Emily could not help feeling like there was something else not being mentioned. It could be that she was always looking for potential threats. She was sure that if she felt it, then Evaran and Sivaran probably did too.

A dark thought ran through Emily's mind that maybe Acrolis and Wardax were related somehow. Emily sighed. She hated this feeling of uneasiness, but she had no doubts the group could handle anything tossed at them. This group configuration was one of the more powerful ones, right alongside when Dalton Kingston traveled with them. She watched Acrolis wave goodbye, then focused on the steps ahead.

11

Dr. Snowden stared at his breakfast burrito. It was 8:30 a.m. and the conference room was empty. Evaran had called for a meeting, and Dr. Snowden had no doubt that Evaran had probably spent the night dissecting the Zayt information. Sivaran, V, and Q had most likely assisted Evaran. Emily had been in the holo room working out, and Dr. Snowden was not sure where Lord Vygon was.

Something about meeting Acrolis seemed off. She had apparently met the group before, and her touching his shoulder and saying to stay strong had seemed ominous. He had learned never to discount even the slightest action by someone of her caliber. It was similar to Evaran choosing somebody to escort a new guest to their living quarters.

Dr. Snowden bit into his burrito. Although it tasted good, it reminded him of eating breakfast with Kess. He frowned. If she was there, maybe things would seem lighter. The situation was rough. Lord Vygon witnessing his planet's destruction and Sivaran losing the *Karus* were not minor events to start an adventure off with. Still, Dr. Snowden appreciated the opportunity to meet another version of Evaran and Lord Vygon.

After ten minutes, Emily and Lord Vygon arrived.

They were joking around, not something Dr. Snowden had expected.

"Someone missed training this morning," said Emily, slapping him on the back as she went to the matter replicator.

"Yeah, I was, uhh … training my mind," said Dr. Snowden.

"To sleep, maybe," said Emily.

Lord Vygon plopped down next to Dr. Snowden with a glass of blood. "Emily is quite the workout machine."

Emily sat across from them. "You're tough yourself!"

"So you joined her in a morning workout," said Dr. Snowden.

Lord Vygon nodded. "It helps relieve me."

"I get it," said Dr. Snowden.

After five minutes and some light conversation, Evaran, Sivaran, V, and Q entered and took their seats.

Evaran swept his gaze around. "I hope everyone had a good sleep."

Everybody indicated they had.

"Excellent. As expected, I worked through the night with Sivaran, Q, and V on the new Zayt information. This is what we found," said Evaran. He interacted with the table console.

A projection shot up of the galaxy with a tiny portion of the southeast quadrant colored red.

"This was before the Zayt expanded."

The colored area expanded to ten times its initial size, covering a third of the quadrant.

"This is where the Zayt expansion stands now. With no significant adversary, they will consume the galaxy in time."

Dr. Snowden adjusted his glasses. "They expanded fast."

Sivaran frowned. "Too fast. Wardax is their edge. When matter mages flee from him, that's not a good sign."

"Yeah, definitely not," said Emily.

Evaran interacted with the table console, and a blue dot appeared in the northern part of the Zayt's domain. "We need to capture a guardian to determine the Zayt control and communication structure. While the scans from our first trip helped, some areas were impenetrable. We need a physical examination. To that extent, the blue dot represents a prison that has low security per Acrolis."

"So we're going to bust in and grab the warden?" asked Lord Vygon.

Evaran nodded. "We are. While there, we will take a specimen to see if the infection can be reversed. Also, we can free any prisoners there."

Sivaran motioned at the projection. "The Zayt usually don't take prisoners, but these have exotic energy of some type. They're held until they can be transferred elsewhere."

Lord Vygon eyed Evaran and Sivaran. "Low security or not, that'll be a rough fight, not to mention if the prisoners get ideas."

Q gestured around the room. "Per V's and my assessment, this group is more than capable of accomplishing this."

Evaran half smiled. "I concur that we can handle it."

"So what's the plan, then?" asked Dr. Snowden.

Evaran interacted with the table console.

Dr. Snowden studied the projection that shot up of the prison layout sitting on a moon. The atmosphere was harsh, so even if a prisoner escaped, they would be held in by the nasty environment. The prison had weak shielding, and per Acrolis, there was not a lot of security, probably due to it being deep inside Zayt territory.

Evaran motioned at the layout. "There is a spaceport some distance away that connects to the prison via an underground tunnel. We will infiltrate the spaceport, then access the tunnel. Once we are at the prison, we can locate the warden, then capture him and one of the infected along with any data while there. The prisoners will be released, and together, we will all leave. The *Torvatta* will provide portals to the prison transports."

"A bold plan," said Lord Vygon. "I wouldn't underestimate Wardax, though. Knowing him, he has some type of backup plan for this situation. Well, not this attack in general, but more of an 'if the prison were captured.'"

"Perhaps, but he has never faced two Evarans at the same time before," said Evaran. His and Sivaran's eyes glowed.

Dr. Snowden felt better about the plan. Evaran was right in that Wardax most likely would have never faced off against such a powerful group before.

"Will the prisoners have a safe place to go?" asked Emily.

"Analysis. There is a large empire known as the Crostsheen. They have held against the Zayt expansion and had relations with some of the fallen civilizations per Acrolis. The transports can go there."

Emily nodded. "Makes sense. I guess they'll be able to find their way from there. It's not like they can go back to their home planets."

"The Crostsheen are one of the most powerful groups in this quadrant, but I suspect even they will fall in time," said Lord Vygon.

"That is Acrolis's assessment as well," said Q.

Lord Vygon sighed. "I'm ready to deal a blow to Wardax."

Evaran shut off the projection. "Very well. V, activate scan profile one and stealth mode, then take us to the spaceport. Everyone else, be prepared to go when we get there. Handle any business you need to now."

Dr. Snowden swallowed hard as he stood. Although he had no doubt they would probably succeed, Wardax having some type of plan could be an issue. Dr. Snowden hoped it would be a quick in and out. The uneasiness of the situation still kicked around inside him. He went to his living quarters and made sure he had no business to deal with. The last thing he needed to happen was for him to want to use the restroom in the middle of the prison.

Ten minutes later, he assembled with the others in the command center.

The *Torvatta* hovered over the spaceport on the prison moon.

Dr. Snowden surveyed the layout, which matched Acrolis's data. The landing area was relatively simple compared to the ones he had seen traveling with Evaran. There was a grid system with sixty-four cells. A bubble shield of some type covered the base, and a large domed building sat in the middle. All the ships seemed to be of the same design, and the *Torvatta* identified them as transports.

There was movement from a new type of Zayt member that the *Torvatta* categorized as an enforcer. It led what appeared to be a group of prisoners who all wore blue clothing. The enforcer stood nine feet tall with a husky build, and it probably could do some major damage. Large tusks shot out of its boar-like face, and a suit of heavy green armor rounded out the profile. Dr. Snowden never wanted to meet that in a back alley. It seemed the enforcers were not all standard.

"It's interesting that the prison itself is a bit away and underground," said Emily. "I guess one way in and all that."

Dr. Snowden pointed at the sun in the distance. "I suspect the closeness of this planet to the sun is a factor as well. Look at the temperature."

Emily shuddered. "Yeah, I don't think anything wants to be on the surface."

Dr. Snowden gulped when the *Torvatta* breached the spaceport shielding. Several drones had come to investigate the crossing, but they would not find anything. It was the next part that would be challenging. He gripped his PSD. Hopefully, they would get everything they had come for.

Emily's heart pumped as the *Torvatta* landed in a cell close to the main building. She, along with the others, stood on the ramp. The only visible security was the drones and a few guard patrols. The current plan was to reach the open doorway that allowed cargo and people in. From there, V would disable the system, then they would access the tunnel and head to the prison itself.

It surprised her that the *Torvatta* had given Q limited ability to pilot it. Although Q would not be able to open a portal or jump through time, he could activate the shield's heat modulator if necessary to rescue them. Q appeared to have no issues with that.

As for the others, Evaran had on his usual suit, while Dr. Snowden wore his survival one with helmet up. V was in body mode and fully shielded, while Lord Vygon had on a custom suit designed by Sivaran and Evaran that the *Torvatta* had replicated. It was spaceworthy and consisted of a strong armor with medium kinetic shielding. His dual blades could still pop out.

Emily focused on the situation. Her suit made her feel safe. When she focused, it was like power strands shot through her body. Her nanobots tingled in anticipation of combat. All of the sensations caused her to be amped up.

Evaran waved forward. "Let us go."

The group advanced with Evaran and Sivaran in the lead. V and Emily had the rear, while Lord Vygon and Dr. Snowden were in the middle.

The first drones that flew over crashed after a bombardment of stun blasts. Several of the large boar-like enforcers rushed out, but like the drones, they succumbed to a blizzard of blue beams.

Emily was thankful that stun worked. She recalled fighting enemies where she had to get close inside their shielding in order for it to be effective.

The group burst through the large hangar entrance.

Emily studied the massive vines that canvassed the walls. They spanned the entirety of the area, including the ceiling and floor to some degree. Branches snaked off the vines, which seemed to avoid the pulsing yellow light structures on the side panels. The overall theme was a mishmash of plants and technology.

"More plant stuff," said Dr. Snowden. "I think we can safely say that the Zayt have some form of plant focus."

Evaran nodded and then pointed at a console off to the side. "V, access that and shut off the alarm. We will cover you."

"Acknowledged," said V. He hustled off and then connected.

Evaran and Emily stood at forty-five degrees to each other and provided an energy shield barrier. Dr. Snowden fired stun blasts and Lord Vygon and Sivaran knocked away any enforcer that got too close.

Emily's heart thumped. They were in the middle of a battle, yet it seemed relatively easy to this point. Granted, they had the advantage of a sneak attack, but this group was powerful compared to what they had faced so far.

The pulsing light shut off.

"Analysis. The alarm system has been disabled, as well as the main administrative functions for the spaceport."

Evaran nodded. "Good. That means the prison will not be able to override anything." He pointed at a massive descending ramp ahead of them. "We can enter the main transportation tunnel there and breach the prison from that. Perhaps it is time for the Emily wagon."

Emily laughed. "I got it!"

She loved that her PSD could create things. After selecting the pattern from her builder application, she formed the wagon. It had four wheels and, per Dr. Snowden, resembled a red one he had had as a kid, except this one had no handle up front to pull it. To her, it resembled the back of a pickup truck, complete with a rear door that converted to a pull-down ramp. She pulled the ramp down.

Everyone boarded.

She went to the front and extended her right arm ahead to provide an energy barrier. Dr. Snowden got the left side, while Evaran had the right. V sat in the back, in effect providing coverage from all angles except the top.

They began to move.

"Your PSD is more powerful than I was led to believe," said Lord Vygon. "It's like Sivaran's armor, except in a small rod form factor."

Sivaran slapped the side. "I love the Emily wagon!"

Emily smiled at him. She loved his enthusiasm. Driving while also providing an energy shield required her concentration. Prisoners who had been escorted were openly fighting the enforcers. It seemed the gang's presence had already caused a stir.

They descended down the ramp and entered the main tunnel.

Emily was thankful the ground was flat, and that the wagon had decent speed. As expected, the walls had massive vines on them with smaller ones striking out. There were even some unusual treelike structures on the ground that butted up against the wall.

The few enforcers they ran into were easily dispatched by Dr. Snowden and Evaran with stun blasts. One group of guards tried to ram the side of the wagon but were swept away by Lord Vygon's blades and a steel bar that formed from Sivaran's right arm.

About halfway through the bright tunnel, Evaran raised a hand. "A large group approaches."

Emily focused but did not sense anything. She stopped the wagon.

"I sense them too," said Sivaran.

"I don't," said Lord Vygon.

"Me either," said Dr. Snowden.

Evaran nodded. "Everybody off and prepare to fight."

Emily waited until everyone was off the wagon before pulling it back into her PSD. She could now detect the tip of what seemed like a mass of something coming their way.

"It's a swarm," said Lord Vygon. He looked around. "And in a cramped tunnel. It's about to get serious."

Evaran motioned at Emily. "Face forward and form an energy shield and cover the right side. I will get the left. Sivaran, Dr. Snowden, Lord Vygon, V, and Q will be behind us and deal with any that breach our shields."

She formed her shield to match the size of what Evaran had. She had expanded her shield to the eight-by-ten-foot size before, and with her standing next to Evaran, it presented an effective energy barrier.

"Here they come!" said Dr. Snowden, pointing forward.

Emily swallowed hard as she studied the advancing swarm. It was packed with infected leading the charge, and they seemed like they could not wait to slaughter the group. A small army of enforcers backed the infected humanoids. Most enforcers were like the boar-like ones she had seen before, but some were of the rhinoceros style. The spherical infectors and their spindly legs bounced around, making the group seem like it was all over the place. She spotted a few controllers, who seemed to hang back.

The enforcers fired at the group, but the energy shields held.

Dr. Snowden unleashed a mist beam, which Emily ignited. It slowed the swarm down.

She braced as the enemy finally made contact. The initial surge pushed her back some, but Evaran held his ground. The infected that slipped through were handled by the others.

Sivaran's suit spawned metal rods that ended in a block of steel and were effective at hitting the attackers. The rods would retract into his suit after every hit. They were like missiles firing off his body. His stun beam barrage from both wrist-mounted devices impressed Emily.

Evaran used his free hand to wield his baton and crushed any that got near him. V stood strong as he batted away both infected and infectors that came within his grasp.

Lord Vygon danced around with his dual blunted blades. He moved in a blur and fought like a cornered tiger. Dr. Snowden took his time and fired precision shots at any that made it past the others.

The infectors were something Emily thought might be an issue if they tried to infect, but the group did a good job of disabling them first. That strategy had not even been discussed, but the group naturally adapted.

They continued to march forward. Once the controllers were down after ten minutes, silence reigned.

Emily observed some of the smaller vines from the side of the wall, reaching out to snag the Zayt that had fallen. "What's all that about?"

"It would seem they are trying to resuscitate the fallen," said Sivaran. "I had heard of it, but never seen it."

Emily shook her head. "So we might run into these again when we come back."

"It's possible," said Sivaran. "Perhaps we will find a counter to the vines when we reach the control center."

She nodded.

"Wow," said Dr. Snowden, catching his breath. "That was intense."

"And a small swarm," said Lord Vygon.

Dr. Snowden grimaced. "I can't even fathom fighting a large one, especially if they heal up afterward."

"We must remain vigilant," said Evaran. "I suspect they only had one swarm to protect this tunnel. There may be another inside the prison. We should walk from here."

"Great," said Dr. Snowden.

Emily gestured at Sivaran. "I loved your suit. It formed those blocks and rods quickly."

"While it's powerful, I may need to look at changing the blocks to an energy shield like what you have. I also wish I had V's shielding," he said.

V high-fived him.

The group continued forward.

"I'd settle for any of that," said Lord Vygon. He examined his blunted blades. "These have proven to be quite effective, though."

"I can't imagine you without them," said Dr. Snowden.

Lord Vygon nodded. "Now imagine me with V's shield, Sivaran's morphable metal suit, Evaran's energy shield, and your PSDs."

Emily swatted his arm. "You would be an unstoppable force."

"I'd like to think that."

The group chuckled.

Emily's muscles relaxed as they walked. They had performed as expected, and Sivaran's suit had surprised her with its effectiveness. The fact that he moved with power and grace was what she would have expected of an Evaran. Lord Vygon fought like the one she knew back on her Earth. V, as always, was a bulwark against those who tried to harm the group, and she loved that he was with them. Dr. Snowden predictably sat in the rear and used precision to shoot at range.

The trip so far had been smooth. If the swarm was all Wardax could muster for a defense, then the prison was ripe for capture. She understood that she should not get complacent, but with a group as powerful as this, it was hard not to.

Lord Vygon walked in silence as the group approached the prison. What he had seen so far had been impressive. Evaran had been a wall against a rampaging swarm. Any that got close were dealt with quickly. It surprised Lord Vygon how fast Evaran was. Sivaran had performed as expected, something Lord Vygon was familiar with.

V had been a surprise. His shielding was far tougher than advertised. Lord Vygon could not imagine Q with V's shield, but Lord Vygon suspected Q would want that. V had seemed to focus a bit more on those that came close to Emily, probably due to their close relationship.

Emily had fought well, and her energy shield had held against tremendous numbers of the swarm. Lord Vygon wondered if he could get a shield like hers. She also moved fast, and her free hand whipped around like a blender as it knocked away Zayt minions. Dr. Snowden had been no slouch, either. His shots were exact, and it appeared as a light show at times.

Overall, the group astounded Lord Vygon. No wonder Evaran and the gang fared so well on their adventures. For the first time in a long while, Lord Vygon felt hopeful about their chances of taking down Wardax. If anything could fight him, it would be this group. Lord Vygon raised his head a bit. He would avenge his race in the process.

The group paused before a massive sealed door.

Evaran motioned off to a side console. "V, open this."

"Acknowledged," said V as he lumbered over.

Lord Vygon watched in fascination as V extended a finger that shot out small tendrils into the console interface. Having a powerful AI like V definitely had its benefits. Lord Vygon had seen Q do something similar, but not in a hostile environment.

The doors whooshed and slid apart.

Evaran waved forward. "Let us go."

Lord Vygon admired Evaran's fearlessness. Usually Lord Vygon would be with Sivaran, who led the way. It seemed even he deferred to Evaran in terms of leading the group. That was not too surprising since, from what Lord Vygon had seen so far, Evaran was a powerful force to be reckoned with.

The short tunnel they entered led to a large circular hub with other tunnels running off in other directions. Two turrets fired on the group, but the reflected beams made quick work of the turrets.

The vines from the tunnel extended into the room. They were everywhere, and Lord Vygon suspected they were some sort of support system. Thankfully, they were not aggressive. The last thing they needed to fight was the tunnel and prison.

"Which way?" asked Dr. Snowden, looking around.

Evaran pointed to the left. "Per the layout from V's interaction, this will take us to the control center. I suspect the guardian we seek is there."

Lord Vygon followed the others as Evaran took off. He had reflected the turrets' beams as if they were a mere annoyance. Lord Vygon once again appreciated the efficiency of the group. He was anxious to see the guardian get dismantled.

The tunnels had given way to hallways with a metallic-paneled floor and featureless walls. On the ceiling were occasional light fixtures of some type that illuminated the area. Every now and then on the wall was a screen, but there were also holographic displays that appeared an inch or two off the sides every ten feet or so. The lack of vines stood in stark contrast to the previous areas.

The scattered groups of guards they ran into stood no chance. They had a mix of enforcer types. Although Lord Vygon understood that the prison was considered one of the less secured areas relative to other places in the Zayt empire, it still amazed him how effortlessly the group moved through the area. His senses went wild as they approached the control center. There was exotic energy everywhere. He did not recognize most of the energies and wondered if they had been extracted from the prisoners during their imprisonment.

The group reached a four-way intersection.

Evaran raised a hand. "Something approaches."

Lord Vygon growled when a ten-foot humanoid robot appeared at the end of the hallway ahead of them. Its metallic body was covered in what appeared to be bolt heads, and its head was an orb with an indented glowing red line dividing it in half horizontally. Two turrets sat on the upper arms, while the massive hands ended in eight spindly talons.

Lord Vygon focused on the noise around them. He could now sense a tremendous amount of something coming from the sides and behind them. It reminded him of when they had fought the swarm earlier.

"I am Wardax," said the robot, taking a step forward. "This attack is surprising, but it will be dealt with. Your first fight on the transport gave me a good insight into what I was fighting. This unit has not been upgraded yet, but it should still be able to handle you."

Evaran and Sivaran's eyes glowed. Evaran pointed at Wardax. "I would not be so sure of that. You have sent another swarm to pin us down here."

"Of course," said Wardax.

Evaran faced the group. "I will deal with Wardax. Sivaran will hold the left hallway, Emily the right, and Lord Vygon behind us. V and Dr. Snowden will be in the middle and provide assistance to any side that needs help."

Sivaran forearm-shook with Evaran, and their eyes glowed again. "We'll be fine here."

Evaran rushed toward Wardax.

Lord Vygon extended his blunted blades and faced the hallway they had come from. The swarm was moving fast, and he could now see them. As expected, the infected led the charge, and they were backed by a horde of enforcers and infectors. A controller appeared in the rear.

Emily and Sivaran had already advanced deeper into their hallways and now began firing. Dr. Snowden shot a mist and stun beam at the ones approaching Lord Vygon, while V waited to determine which side to go to.

Lord Vygon burst down the hallway and into action when the first infected reached him. He moved faster than an individual infected, and with his superior strength, he easily overpowered it. The problem was that the swarm now filled the hallway. Even with Dr. Snowden's assistance, they kept coming. Lord Vygon got pushed back some due to sheer numbers. He took a quick look around to make an assessment of the others.

V entered the fray and began to disable infected that reached Lord Vygon. Evaran seemed to be holding his own against Wardax, while Sivaran and Emily dealt with a weaker swarm on their sides.

Lord Vygon reentered his hallway and focused on trying to beat back the swarm, but they kept pushing. After making some progress, a sizable portion of the swarm had bypassed him and had reached the intersection, where they fought V.

Dr. Snowden cried out.

Lord Vygon was not sure what he was seeing. The infected had picked up Dr. Snowden and were moving him away. They passed by Lord Vygon in the blink of an eye and handed Dr. Snowden off to enforcers, who bolted.

"Uncle Albert!" said Emily.

"Go!" said Sivaran. "V and I will hold the center."

Emily joined Lord Vygon as they chased the retreating enforcers. As fast as Emily and Lord Vygon were, the enforcers used some of their rear guard to cause a slowdown. Dr. Snowden fired several stun beams before his PSD was ripped out of his hand. Emily picked it up along the way.

Lord Vygon had never seen such unusual behavior from a swarm. They did not kill Dr. Snowden— they wanted him alive for some reason.

Emily and Lord Vygon rushed into an octagonal room. In the center resided a large tree-trunk-like object that had a reddish doorway carved into it. The doorway interior shimmered, and the enforcers wasted no time in rushing Dr. Snowden into it. The shimmering faded and left no trace of its presence.

Emily screamed as she charged into battle, dismantling any enforcer that got in her way. Her bladed staff proved lethal, and between her and Lord Vygon, they cleared the room in record time. Emily frantically searched around and called out Dr. Snowden's name several times.

Lord Vygon studied the floor, which was littered with downed infected and enforcers. The controller in the room had been slammed against the wall by Emily's repulsion blast.

"Emily, what is going on?" asked Evaran over comms.

"Uncle Albert is gone! The swarm took him through some portal or something!"

"We are on our way," said Evaran. "Wardax's guardian has been captured, and Sivaran and V have dealt with the remaining swarm."

Lord Vygon sighed as he studied the doorframe. He was not sure how a portal could exist. The room they were in was far enough away from the entrance that the portal would not be easily detectable. Emily kicked the Zayt minions out of the way as she searched the room for any piece of information. Lord Vygon no longer sensed Dr. Snowden. His icon was also grayed out.

Evaran and others arrived. He examined the area. "Dr. Snowden is not here." He scanned the trunk. "This is where he went through?"

Emily nodded.

Sivaran surveyed the scene. "I sense the rapidly disappearing signature of something dimensional."

"It is similar to the dimensional presence in the guardian," said Evaran. "That is unexpected. V, see if you can find anything in the systems related to this."

"Acknowledged."

Emily lowered her helmet. Her frown indicated the general mood of everyone. "He was … right there," she said, pointing at the trunk.

Evaran walked over and put his arm around her. "We will find him."

She rubbed her misted eyes and laid her head on Evaran's chest. "We couldn't get to him."

"The swarm passed him along," said Lord Vygon. "I've never seen them do that before."

"It appears it is a new tactic," said Evaran. "The captured guardian may give us some insight. Sivaran will coordinate the prisoner release while V continues searching the system. I will bring the guardian and infected specimen to the *Torvatta*."

"I'm gonna stay here for a bit with V," said Emily.

Lord Vygon stood next to her. "I will as well."

She sniffled and nodded at him.

He felt guilty that he had been unable to reach Dr. Snowden before he had disappeared. The swarm capturing people was not unknown. The prison stood as a testament to that. A portal in the base was new, however, especially one carved into a trunk. Acrolis had never mentioned it. Then again, she could not detect dimensional or exotic energies. With so many energies present, a portal would be easy to disguise.

A sinking feeling in his stomach arose at the thought that maybe Wardax had planned for this. Lord Vygon hoped that it was just a spur-of-the-moment decision, but why Dr. Snowden had been chosen remained a mystery. Although the gang's goals for the prison raid had been achieved, Dr. Snowden's abduction had been unexpected. Lord Vygon was not sure what their next step would be, but getting Dr. Snowden back was a high priority.

12

r. Snowden grunted as he rubbed his eyes. The last thing he remembered was being carried away by the infected and pushed through a portal in a tree trunk. Everything was blank after that. Now, he stood at the end of a driveway of a street familiar to him. It was where he had grown up. His throat constricted. The place brought back a lot of memories.

He peeked down and noticed his survival suit was gone. In its place was what he used to wear before he got the suit. His brown pants and jacket, along with a vest and a bow tie, felt real to him. He ran his hands over his head, but it was still balding with two major tufts.

His attention focused on Evaran approaching. "Evaran?"

"Not quite. I'm Wardax, and I've come to learn about you, and by extension, the group you're a member of."

Dr. Snowden's breathing increased. "Why?"

Wardax gestured around. "This is your mind, and this is one memory. You have many memories, and I seek to know what you are, who you are, where you came from, and why you're here."

"No. I won't let you! And why do you look like Evaran?"

"I chose a form that relaxes you," said Wardax. He studied Dr. Snowden. "You have cosmic energy in you. Your nanobots do too. They put up quite a fight, even killed a few infected that hooked you in, but against a greater cosmic entity, your nanobots eventually acknowledged me."

Dr. Snowden's eyes narrowed. "You have cosmic energy, then."

Wardax nodded. "Oh yes. Much more than you, although you having *any* is quite a surprise. Don't worry, no physical harm will come to you. However, I'll also be around in your dreams."

Dr. Snowden found it difficult to believe he was in some type of mental torture scenario. He wondered if the thoughts he had now were somewhere else in his mind, or if Wardax could even hear them. Everything felt real to Dr. Snowden, and he was not sure how he could escape this.

"How did I get here?" he asked.

"Palisin energy knocked you out," said Wardax, examining his hand. "Then it was a matter of strapping you to a slab, hooking up an interface, and here we are. As I mentioned before, the first few infected that tried to interface with you got a nasty surprise. Your nanobots demolished them and even the slab you were on. That was a good lesson, and now you're on a much sturdier slab and surrounded by a palisin energy mist to neutralize you."

"I'm not going to help you learn anything!"

Wardax smiled. "That's going to be your choice. We're about to embark on a long journey together. I don't normally do this … but you're unique and work with powerful forces out to kill me. I don't think it's unreasonable to want to understand why."

Dr. Snowden gritted his teeth. Everything in him told him to fight, but he wasn't sure how to. He did not have his PSD or survival suit, and his physical form was no match for Wardax. Perhaps since this was all mental, he could morph into something more powerful. He closed his eyes and focused on changing his form to Evaran's. When he opened his eyes, nothing happened.

Wardax sneered. "I bet you're wondering what you can and can't do in here. Don't worry, I thought about that and put in some blockers. You're locked to this form, as I am to this one. That will minimize the damage to your mind."

"Fine, then I'm not moving."

Wardax studied the house. "This was one of your earliest memories with your parents." He pointed at a window. "There you are looking out."

"And?" asked Dr. Snowden.

"As I said, you have a choice. If you cooperate and give context as needed, then you retain the memory. If not, it's gone forever, then we move on to the next one. It's up to you if you wish to be riddled with lost memories. I'm being attacked by not one, but five cosmic beings with a powerful ship. I need to know why."

Dr. Snowden breathed heavier. "You can't mess with my memories like that!"

Wardax walked over and put his hand on Dr. Snowden's shoulder. "When my life is at stake, I *will* do that. As there is no meaning here for this memory, let's go to the next one."

Everything went black.

Dr. Snowden sighed as he scrutinized the backyard, where his dad had just brought out a new telescope. Dan, Dr. Snowden's brother, joked around. Dr. Snowden remembered the day clearly because it was when he had decided he wanted to be an astronomer.

"Now, tell me, what do you remember of the last memory we were in?" asked Wardax.

Dr. Snowden focused. "We were in front of my childhood home." He shuddered as it became harder to recall.

"That memory was going to be deleted, and you sensed it fading. I've decided to retain it for you. If I hadn't, you would not be able to recall it," said Wardax. He raised a finger. "You value your mind. What happens when you have no memories to value? As for me, I have the memory being recorded, so I'll remember it, but you won't. If you resist me, I'll be more *you* than you are at some point. So the choice is yours. Cooperate and keep your memories, or fight me and lose them."

Dr. Snowden cringed at the thought of losing his memories. If they were all gone, he knew he would lose what made him who he was. His greatest fear was losing his mind, and Wardax seemed to understand that.

Dr. Snowden scowled. "You're a monster. Fine, so I just give you context, and that's it?"

"Yes. I could take your brain out of your body, slice it up and scan it and then pull the data that way, but then I'd lose the opportunity to discuss the memory with you. Besides, I don't like to take life if I can avoid it."

"What're you talking about? You destroyed Lord Vygon's planet!"

"We'll go over that later so you understand my reasoning. Your conclusion is without context."

Dr. Snowden gulped. Scanning a brain, then mining it digitally was something he had discussed with Dr. James Bryson, a colleague, long ago. Wardax seemed advanced enough that he could pull it off. Although Dr. Snowden did not want to die, he did not want to help either.

"I'll give you context, but I'd be careful about what you wish for," he said.

"There we go. That's what I like to hear," said Wardax. He motioned at the telescope. "This a big memory for you, it seems. Why is that?"

It irked Dr. Snowden that Wardax took Evaran's form. Wardax even seemed to be enjoying the memories. All Dr. Snowden could do now was misdirect and delay until the others found him. He hoped it was soon as there was no guarantee that Wardax would honor his side of the deal and not destroy every memory after getting context.

Emily stared out across the *Torvatta*'s roof guardrails as several prisoner transports flew through the *Torvatta*-generated portal to Crostsheen space. Sivaran had found a Crostsheen regional representative that arranged for a place the ships could go to, then coordinated the release.

Evaran had brought the guardian and an infected aboard, and the *Torvatta* would soon be leaving. Thankfully, he had downloaded everything from the prison, and information from the guardian and specimen might help locate Dr. Snowden.

She struggled to come to grips with his absence. It seemed unfathomable to her. Her throat constricted. She could only imagine what torture he might undergo, and she felt helpless to do anything about it, a position she hated being in. Perhaps she could have moved faster, or even dived in after him. As fast as she had been, though, the swarm had been faster.

Sivaran joined her on the roof. "Are you all right?"

She shook her head.

He eyed her. "Know that we'll do everything in our power to get him back."

"I know. I just hate this feeling."

"Understandable," said Sivaran, squeezing her arm. "We're about to begin our analysis of the specimens if you're interested. Evaran has split out various parts, and there are some strange readings. We think we might be able to communicate with Wardax and find out about your uncle."

Emily perked up. "Really? Let's go!"

They hustled down to the medical lab.

Emily inspected the setup. Evaran had separated the arms, legs, and head of the guardian's robot body. Each part rested on nearby slabs. However, it was the coconut-shaped object with what had been identified as a nervous system underneath it that caught her eye. It made her skin crawl. Data windows hovered over everything.

On another slab was the infected humanoid specimen. It appeared to be unconscious, but Emily suspected Evaran would return it to the spaceport once the analysis was done. Above the infected were several holographic body layers. She was used to seeing that when Evaran diagnosed a condition.

Q and V pored over the specimen, while Lord Vygon and Evaran studied the coconut-shaped object with the nervous system underneath it. Sivaran and Emily joined Evaran and Lord Vygon.

She gestured at the nervous system. "How is that a nervous system?"

"It is apparently a plant-based nervous system. When fitted into a guardian body, it allows for total control of the robot," said Evaran. He motioned at the object up top. "That is a shell that exists in this reality, and also in another dimension."

Lord Vygon shook his head. "That means that something in the other dimension could control something here. Like Wardax."

"That's the idea," said Sivaran. He shook a finger in the air. "The dimensional connection is hampered at the moment, but we think if we loosen it some, we can talk to Wardax."

"Let's do that," said Emily. She was not sure what to expect, but if there was a chance to learn more about Dr. Snowden, they had to take it.

"Very well," said Evaran. He grabbed the helmet and placed it over the shell, then connected a few wires. "This should allow us to communicate."

After he interacted with his ARI, the red horizontal slit on the helmet glowed.

"You figured out how to dampen my connection. Impressive."

"Wardax," said Evaran.

"Yes ... and you're Evaran. I also see Sivaran, Lord Vygon, Emily, V, and Q. The whole gang is here."

Emily stepped forward with balled fists. "Where's Uncle Albert?"

"Oh ... he's here. His memories are difficult to access, but they are accessible."

Evaran raised a finger. "That would suggest you possess cosmic energy."

"I do," said Wardax. "Although it seems I have less than you or Sivaran, but definitely more than Dr. Snowden."

"What are you doing to him?" asked Emily.

"Do you want to talk to him?"

Emily glanced at Evaran, then back at Wardax. "Yes."

Her heart thumped when Wardax played a recording of Dr. Snowden screaming out in pain. His anguished cries were unlike anything she had heard before. She scowled.

"Stop this," said Sivaran.

"Of course," said Wardax. The playback stopped. "I'm sorry he couldn't talk. He's more conversant in his mind, so I crushed his right knee so you could hear him. Loud, isn't he?"

"We're coming for you!" said Emily.

"I know, and that's to be expected. Your uncle will give me some valuable insight into what to expect."

Lord Vygon growled. "Why did you destroy my planet?"

"Ahh, you again," said Wardax. "Thanks to Dr. Snowden, I now know the exotic energy you possess is called Daedrould. It seems it is not compatible with my extraction method. I have a long history with Drydris, and it deserved what it got."

"You killed so many."

Wardax snickered. "A minor number relative to what's to come."

"Why are you causing this chaos?" asked Evaran.

"To survive, of course. I know I'm meant to be more than I am, but this reality seems determined to wipe me from existence before I learn what that is. Dr. Snowden may have some insight there, unless you're willing to volunteer any information…"

"We will not," said Evaran.

"I see," said Wardax. "I will then continue to mine Dr. Snowden's mind and sweep across civilization after civilization until I find what I'm looking for."

"You don't need to destroy them," said Sivaran.

Wardax sighed. "I thought that at first as well. Unfortunately, civilizations and various groups harassed me with their primitive justice systems. I find it to be more effective to remove such distractions."

"Know this. You have been made a priority." Evaran glanced at Sivaran and their eyes glowed.

"I understand, and I look forward to capturing and studying you all," said Wardax.

The helmet's eye slit dimmed until it stopped glowing.

Emily gulped. "He's hurting Uncle Albert."

"We don't know that," said Lord Vygon. "It could be a trick."

"Analysis. I calculate that Wardax wants to leave the plane."

Q nodded. "An astute determination. I would add that as he is a cosmic entity, he may have a main form in the Cosmic Medium that he can't reach."

Evaran rubbed his chin. "There is a lot to think about. For now, we can focus on studying the physical aspects of the guardian and the infected specimen. We can also determine how the infected's virus works and see if there is a counter." He walked over and placed an arm around Emily. "We will find Dr. Snowden, and Wardax will answer for his transgressions."

Emily swallowed hard. "Uncle Albert sounded in so much pain."

"I know," said Evaran. "Get some rest as we research this and determine our next steps."

Emily sighed. "I'd rather hit something."

"Holo room?" asked Lord Vygon.

She nodded.

"Okay. Let's go."

13

V cruised with Q along the digital pathways of the infected's virus. The fact that the infected had a technological system intrigued V. It was not as advanced as what he or Q had, but there was enough of it to spread throughout the body. It resembled the nervous system that the guardian had. In the case of the infected, it was not quite as detailed, but the network reached every part of the body, and it had a primitive operating system that could be accessed.

V had assumed a humanoid form, as had Q. They had entered via a strange structure in the brain, which seemed to be where the largest amount of foreign material was. Once jacked in, they could assume their digital forms. There was no virtual or artificial intelligence to stop them, and it was easy to dive into the infected's systems.

Several tests showed that they could activate a system, and the infected would respond, such as by moving a leg, arm, or finger. V had understood the virus to essentially make a living organism into a mindless robot. What he had not expected was how advanced the virus was. It had not only some plantlike components but also an inorganic part. The virus would expand its tendrils throughout the body, and V determined that basic control would be established shortly after infection.

V enjoyed having Q along. He was chatty and liked to ask a lot of questions, which V appreciated. There was a bond between them due to both having traveled with an Evaran, and V understood the significance of that. V suspected that Q must have felt out of place on the *Torvatta*, as much as an AI could, so V made sure to include Q where possible. Understanding a techno-organic virus was one such situation.

They paused to study the virus's backup feature. It was able to replicate a copy of itself once a host had been fully compromised. The resulting hard-shelled object was tiny but had everything needed to recreate the digital aspect of the host's system.

"This is an interesting backup strategy," said Q.

V nodded. "Based on the instructions we found, it seems this object is offloaded at regular intervals and a new one formed." He peered over at Q. "Did you have a backup system on the *Karus*?"

Q frowned. "I did, but now I don't. I have had to contemplate my existence, something I had done before Sivaran rescued me."

"The *Torvatta* has backup systems if you want to use them while you are here."

"Would it allow me to?" asked Q.

V smiled. "I believe it would."

"My system may be too complex."

"It should not matter. The backup system uses dimensional mechanics. While you back up locally, it sends your backup through to dimensional storage."

The shimmering light around Q became brighter. "I'd like that, then. Although I may not join the others in battle, or even be in danger while aboard the *Torvatta*, it would be good to know I can be brought back. The downside is I'll have a loss of knowledge between backups."

"Yes, but it is better than not having any backup," said V.

"Point taken," said Q. He studied V. "You have seen much traveling with Evaran through your various forms. I'm impressed you've lived through many forms."

"I am glad to be alive."

"I'm glad you are too," said Q.

V had ran simulations to determine what it would be like to have Sivaran and Q as permanent members of the gang. Two Evarans would enhance the gang's power significantly, and Q could add to that as well, especially if the *Torvatta* let him pilot. It would be a bigger group, and the cookouts would be more interesting.

"You were processing something," said Q.

"I was. I ran a simulation of you and Sivaran joining us back in our universe."

Q gazed off in the distance. "I would like that, but Sivaran was clear on not interfering with another plane form unless absolutely necessary, such as now. When this is over, I suspect we will be staying here."

"I understand," said V. "My simulation showed that we would be a much stronger group."

"My calculations show that as well."

V continued to analyze the rudimentary backup system of the virus. It seemed in order for the backup object to be created, it needed nutrients not native to the host. A deeper dive showed there to be a crude file system of some type that had instructions on how to assemble it, and what ingredients were needed. This went along with the host body performing actions to keep it healthy.

As he and Q perused the system, they uploaded what they found into a secured digital space in the *Torvatta*. V had no worries about the virus infecting the *Torvatta*. Its system was far too advanced for that. As powerful as a host's brain might be, it did not have a dimension powering it to protect it, or Syrilus in some form for that matter.

"This virus is well designed," said Q. "It is not natural."

"I have reached the same conclusion," said V.

Q waved a finger around. "It does require some maintenance, and in order to reduce the effort needed, I have determined that Wardax can only infect a certain percentage of any given population, and even then, only those with the required health level."

V nodded. "Perhaps more are taken over the threshold as a buffer. I did not see any system regarding reproduction. It seems that function is suppressed."

"The urge to reproduce can be powerful, so I understand the efficiency in that decision."

V pointed at another area inside the digital space. "The waste system has also been changed. All waste is reused."

"Also efficient," said Q.

"I think Emily would say 'eww' to know that."

"She most likely would."

While V enjoyed being around Emily and Dr. Snowden, as well as Evaran, having another AI to share experiences with had proven to be illuminating. There were other AIs that he had interacted with, but usually not on this level. Solia, his android girlfriend from an alternate timeline, was the closest he had been to another AI, but she was gone forever. He liked the idea of having an AI girlfriend travel with the gang, but an AI buddy would work too.

There were other systems in the virus that needed to be checked still, and V relished doing so with what he was beginning to view as a close friend.

Lord Vygon waited in the conference room with Emily. It had been a day since they had talked to Wardax, and Evaran had called for a 9:00 a.m. meeting.

Emily had worked herself into a frenzy in the training room the previous day. Lord Vygon suspected that Wardax would have a bad day when the gang found Dr. Snowden. After four hours of an exhausting workout, he had sat with her and talked about the situation. It did him good to see her feel better when he had left her.

Now, sitting in the conference room with her after a strong morning session, he sensed she was agitated still. She had devoured a hefty breakfast and already slammed down two glasses of orange juice.

"We'll find him," said Lord Vygon.

Emily sighed. "I know. I just hope we're not too late. Uncle Albert values his mind, and to be violated like that ... it's the worst thing you can do to him."

Lord Vygon nodded. "He's strong, though. I wouldn't count him out yet."

"Here I am going on about this, and you just lost your whole planet. Did you have family there?"

"It's okay," he said. "There will be a time to mourn, and I can do so once Wardax is defeated. I did not have family in the way that Halkins, and humans from what I read, did. However, I did have a clan of thousands, with hundreds turned by me. I felt their deaths."

Emily grimaced. "I feel like we've had setback after setback since we came out here."

"True, but there's now at least some semblance of hope."

Evaran, Sivaran, V, and Q entered the room.

Evaran squeezed Emily's arm as he passed and took his seat. "I hope you got some rest."

She shrugged. "Some."

"I understand," said Evaran. After the others sat, he interacted with the table console. "We have some topics to go over based on our research from yesterday. The first deals with the virus."

A projection displayed.

Lord Vygon thought the virus resembled a plant cell. The difference was the technological components on it.

"The lining is similar to that of a plant cell," said Evaran. He gestured at the thin tendrils that shot out of the cell. "However, those filaments are technology-based and are used to infect. The virus can adapt to any organic system and carries instructions on how to transform the host into a mindless drone."

"Is it airborne or contact only?" asked Emily.

"Thankfully for us, it's not airborne. It has to be injected," said Sivaran.

"Analysis. That is the sole purpose of the infectors, which have a similar appearance to the virus, only at a macro level."

Lord Vygon shook his head. "Giant viruses. I'm sure the transformation is painful."

Q raised a finger. "Actually, the virus disables pain while it transforms. It moves very fast."

The projection changed to show another cell type.

Evaran pointed at the cell. "This is a custom virus that Q and V created. It is purely technological in nature and is designed to attack the control structure that the virus creates in the host's brain. It essentially disables the virus and frees the host."

"Analysis. The countervirus also moves the dead cells to the host's waste system before leaving as well. The countervirus can be deployed on droplets that saturate an environment."

Lord Vygon drew his head back. "So the countervirus can be airborne. If we had a decent deployment system, that would wreak havoc."

V nodded. "It can also use its filaments to move around and seek out infected hosts."

"A truly amazing design," said Lord Vygon.

"Of course, we designed it," said Q, high-fiving V.

Lord Vygon laughed. "Right, what else could it be?"

The projection displayed a space station.

Evaran gestured at the display. "To that end, we are going to go there to test it. However, there is a second reason for traveling there. Acrolis has highlighted this as a regional control center for five systems. It orbits a star, and I suspect the station has detailed information on the dimensional network we discovered. More importantly, it may help us find Dr. Snowden."

Emily perked up. "I'm ready to go."

"I understand your eagerness, but this is much more heavily defended than the prison," said Evaran. "One thing to note is that the defensive forces appear to be mostly robotic. While there are some infected and infectors, the enforcers are robotic."

"They can convert the sun's energy into matter, so replenishing the ranks would be fairly easy," said Sivaran.

"Doesn't matter what they have," said Emily, scowling.

Sivaran glanced at her. "This one will be much tougher to take. Now that we're aware of the ability of the infected to grab someone and portal them away, we'll need to take that into consideration."

"It won't happen again," said Emily.

Lord Vygon raised a finger. "I'd like to use a PSD if you have a spare one. While I'm confident in my blunted blades and melee combat, I don't have any ranged ability. I'm a fast learner."

"I can train you on the spare one," said Emily, looking at Lord Vygon, then Evaran.

Evaran nodded. "That is fine. Take a few hours, then, to learn it, then we may go."

"I'm ready to begin training now," said Lord Vygon.

Evaran half smiled. "I suspect you are. The assault on the regional control center will require several steps. The landing area needs to be cleared first. Q will stay aboard the *Torvatta* and help provide data from its scanning."

The projection showed a layout of the station with green dots and a blue line connecting them.

Evaran motioned at the projection. "This is the layout when Acrolis probed it. The first green dot is the landing area. The blue line is the path we will follow to where a guardian should be. Once there, V will interact with the station's systems and we will defend him while he does so. Sivaran and Emily will then go to the other green dots and release the countervirus canisters. If everything goes as planned, we all meet up back at the *Torvatta*, and the station should be purged of Wardax's control. We can then monitor in stealth mode and scan profile one safely from the *Torvatta*."

Lord Vygon's eyes narrowed. "An ambitious plan, but I like it. I'm still curious as to how Acrolis had this much detail."

Sivaran slapped him on the back. "Probably part of the out-of-sync thing. We'll most likely meet her in the past, then tell her to get this information, and in particular, more detailed versions on specific areas."

"If you say so," said Lord Vygon. "It sounds like we could just give the countervirus to Acrolis and she could have stopped Wardax before he began."

Emily shook her head. "That didn't happen, though. If it did, we wouldn't be here."

Lord Vygon sighed. "Time travel gives me headaches."

"Analysis. A soothing tea might help."

"I appreciate the thought. One other problem is you know Wardax will have adapted to our last few encounters. I would expect something palisin-based," said Lord Vygon.

Sivaran nodded. "We have a counter for that. Evaran has some containers that spray a mist that neutralizes it."

"That'll be awkward to use, it sounds like," said Lord Vygon.

"We'll manage."

Emily's eyes narrowed. "I'm just glad we have a plan and that we might find where Uncle Albert is. I can't imagine what he's going through right now."

Evaran raised his head a bit. "If Wardax tries to access specific memories with Levaran in them, he may be in for a surprise."

"How so?"

"Although she is gone, a part of her still lingers in you and Dr. Snowden. She will manifest to protect crucial memories."

Emily nodded. "I hope she does, then."

Evaran looked around. "Okay, then. Lord Vygon, you train with Emily on the PSD. Once that is done, we will head to the regional control center."

"I'd like to sit in on the training," said Q.

"Analysis. I would as well."

Emily stood. "The more, the merrier."

Sivaran gestured at Lord Vygon. "We'll look at adding some type of energy shield that extends past your blunted blades."

"I'd love that," said Lord Vygon.

He stood with the others. The plan sounded great, and he looked forward to learning about the PSD. It was a powerful device. The energy shield would also be nice to have. Emily's spirits seemed to have been lifted, and it hit Lord Vygon how Evaran brought hope wherever he went. That was a feeling that seemed to be in short supply as of late, but now, they had a chance to find out where Dr. Snowden was and also strike a massive blow against Wardax. Lord Vygon bared his fangs. Vengeance would be his.

Dr. Snowden frowned as he scrutinized the chemistry lab at the college where he taught. The difference between the lab he knew versus this one in the memory was that his younger self was there with Susan Kilten, his first girlfriend. The last thing he wanted to do was discuss his love life with Wardax, but the alternative was forgetting the first time he had met her.

To this point, Dr. Snowden had gone through a ton of memories with Wardax. They were not every waking moment but ones that had significance, per Wardax. It seemed strange that he could not infer his own context, but Dr. Snowden had provided commentary on each memory. He dreaded the upcoming ones since they were more powerful than the ones he had had so far. The memory selection had been focused on some of the more recent adventures, but they were now back to a chronological perspective.

There had been a brief moment of pain, and Wardax had informed him that he had talked to Evaran and the others. Unfortunately, Dr. Snowden's knee had been crushed so that his physical form would make noises. It angered him that he was so helpless.

Although he hated what was happening, Wardax had been a persistent fountain of questions and listened as Dr. Snowden discussed each memory. A part of Dr. Snowden had come to enjoy discussing memories that brought joy. Wardax treated Dr. Snowden as an equal, and for brief moments, he forgot that Wardax was the enemy.

"This is a powerful memory for you," said Wardax. "Why is that?"

"It was my first time talking to Susan, my first girlfriend."

Wardax steepled his fingers. "Ahh, young love. I've noticed that you haven't had many memories up to this point with that emotion."

Dr. Snowden shrugged. "I was a quiet person, and I liked to study and read. Those weren't exactly appealing traits to have."

"I see," said Wardax. He pointed at Dr. Snowden's younger face. "I see your face turning slightly red. It makes you wonder what she was thinking, doesn't it?"

"I guess. She probably thought, 'Why is this weird guy talking to me?'"

Wardax chuckled. "I don't know about that. Observe her actions."

Dr. Snowden complied.

"Notice that she moves her hair off to the side. She also touched your arm several times. More noticeable, though, is that she laughed at your last joke."

Dr. Snowden grinned. "I thought it was funny."

He gritted his teeth and scowled. He was trying to avoid showing any sign of enjoyment, but the memory was powerful, and seeing it from an outsider perspective allowed him to evaluate it differently. Wardax seemed to play on the fact that people like to talk about themselves. Given the intimate nature of memories, it was hard to avoid.

"Stop trying to pretend like you care about this. What does this have to do with anything?" asked Dr. Snowden.

Wardax nodded. "I understand your confusion. As we're going through your memories, barely any time is passing outside your body. These memories give me an idea of who you are. That's the current focus. I see that you're a caring being. You loved Dan, Sarah, and Emily, as well as your parents. You've formed strong bonds with others, and you like to learn. These things help you survive. You're not the type of person I would associate with assassination, yet that seems to be the end goal for you with regard to me."

"Well, yeah, but you're a murderer on an epic scale."

Wardax sighed. "We'll move on to your more recent memories, but before we do, I think you deserve to see some of my memories to understand where I came from. Would you like that?"

"Sure," said Dr. Snowden.

He saw an opportunity to gather intel, although what he would be shown would probably be propaganda. He focused on the new memory that he entered. Hovering above a luscious valley gave a good view of it.

In the center was a large plant that had a bulb at the bottom. Vines snaked out like spokes on a wheel, and along the vines were smaller ones that branched out. Whatever they touched, life seemed to bloom. Strange animal types roamed around, but he studied the green humanoids that bustled about. It struck him as odd that there were buildings, and the beings seemed peaceful.

"What is this?" he asked.

Wardax pointed at the large plant. "That's my original form, at least in this reality. A part of me exists in another dimension, and through me, a portal exists. The green beings you see moving around and protected by me are known as the Hanginoi. They embraced life and were very intelligent. They appreciated art, music, and dancing. They were also eager learners of science and how the world worked. I suspect in time they would have become an advanced society. I defended them since the world outside my reach at the time was brutal and unforgiving."

Dr. Snowden's eyes widened at the sight of the thick and scary-looking forest beyond Wardax's grasp. The trees had many sharp branches, and there were a multitude of animals that appeared as predators.

"As long as the Hanginoi stayed near me, they were safe. I continued to grow over time, and as their knowledge increased, they learned to tame the outside wilderness."

Everything went black before they entered a new memory.

Wardax frowned. "This is my first memory of the Kapak, a vicious and brutal doglike alien race."

Dr. Snowden noted the stark contrast between the alien ship bristling with weapons and a group of Hanginoi near a small tree who were enjoying being out in the sun. When the Kapak opened fire, they slaughtered the Hanginoi. Dr. Snowden could sense Wardax's pain. He truly loved them. Dr. Snowden was not sure if the senses he felt were real or not, but this was a sad memory for Wardax.

The next few memories displayed the Hanginoi being slaughtered everywhere that Wardax could see. He had tried to fight, but as powerful as his large vines were, they could not reach into the sky. The Kapak attacked from range and did so without mercy. Dr. Snowden swallowed hard when they came to another memory that showed the same perspective as the first memory, but instead of a green valley, it was a charred and burning wasteland. Nothing moved around.

"This is what the Kapak left me. I was able to go underground, then snake a vine up to see the aftermath," said Wardax. He lowered his head. "I tried to save the Hanginoi, but

I couldn't. They couldn't use my portal since my dimensional environment was hostile to them. I failed them." He raised his head. "I don't consider myself a vengeful being, and even at this point, I tried to hide."

A new memory materialized with Wardax's plant form huddled in a dark cave.

"This was where my form in this dimension died. The Kapak had begun to establish bases and terraform the planet. They knew of me and had been hunting me for six years at this point. Their war machines dug nonstop, and their snakelike burrowers destroyed all life they encountered, even plant life. The part of me in another dimension would continue on, but the part in this reality would be destroyed."

Dr. Snowden cringed when he watched Wardax's form get sliced to shreds with energy beams and explosions. He stood no chance against advanced technology. The feeling of death was not new to Dr. Snowden, and he felt it creeping around.

"However … a miracle happened much later."

A new memory formed, showing a strange environment made of vines, thorns, and trees. There did not seem to be a ground, and everything hung in space. It reminded him of a connection dimension he had visited a while back.

"What is this place?"

"The dimensional part of me," said Wardax. "All this is me."

Dr. Snowden shielded his eyes as a bright yellow glow appeared and infused itself everywhere. He flinched when a voice bellowed out for Wardax to survive.

"You received cosmic energy?" asked Dr. Snowden.

"You understand," said Wardax. "Yes. I have no idea why I got it, and at this point, I didn't know what it was. What

I did know was that I now had knowledge that wasn't there before. I felt raw power coursing through me. Although the cosmic energy did not stay in my dimension, it exited into a new form in your reality. My new form was resilient against energy and fire, and I could now split off parts of me and keep control via a dimensional network. That allowed me to interact with things far away."

"What was that voice?"

"I don't know. It remains a mystery to me, but I did what it asked of me. I survived," said Wardax.

The new memory that appeared showed Wardax reestablishing himself in this reality and using vines to take over a base.

"This was the first installation I attacked," said Wardax. "I learned a lot here about technology and was able to craft a virus that would incapacitate the Kapak without killing them. It took some time, but I evolved the process. Eventually, I removed the Kapak from the surface, but they kept coming." He faced Dr. Snowden. "Tell me. What do you do when you want to exist in peace, but something tries to kill you every moment that you're alive?"

Dr. Snowden adjusted his glasses. "You'd have to take the fight to them, or it would never be over."

"And that's what I did. Using the new knowledge I gained, I built ships based on the Kapak design and fought them. They were the first civilization to be incapacitated."

"So their individual mind is still intact, then?"

Wardax nodded. "They live in a peaceful dream state. I overlay that on top of the real world so they exist in bliss as they perform whatever needs to be done."

"That sounds like slavery, just through mental means."

"The alternative is they eventually kill me. I prefer not to die. Also, this … cosmic energy in me … it seems to want to go somewhere, but I don't know where or why."

"Okay, but why're you doing this to other civilizations?" asked Dr. Snowden.

"With the fall of the Kapak, other races came and attacked. In self-defense, I expanded. It seemed no matter how many I defeated, more and more arrived to attack me. I did negotiate peace settlements several times. In one instance, a coalition of societies, including the one from Drydris, used it as an opportunity to try to kill me on another world. There was no civilization there, but they didn't care. One thing I learned from those incapacitated was the attackers' true intent. The overall sentiment was that they wouldn't rest until I was dead as they feared I would take over the galaxy, and they were interested in my dimensional abilities. I just wanted to survive in peace."

Dr. Snowden gulped. Wardax had a rough past, assuming it was all real. Perhaps it was not, but the overall picture being painted was that Wardax was being hunted because he possessed an ability that would be powerful in certain hands, but he refused to die. The attackers had taken everything from him, and being given a second chance with something telling him to survive, it was not hard for Dr. Snowden to see why Wardax did what he did.

Dr. Snowden still did not like all the death involved, but it showed Wardax in a different light. Even if Evaran brokered a treaty, there would be elements continually trying to capture or kill Wardax. The communication aspect via dimensional means alone would be game changing. Dr. Snowden could see humanity trying to take advantage of that.

He shook his head. The scientist in him wanted to dismiss the background story of Wardax, but it did provide some insight into Wardax's current actions. Dr. Snowden sensed that the memories he had been shown were real, and Wardax's pain was almost overwhelming at points. Everything seemed confusing. This was definitely not what Dr. Snowden had expected.

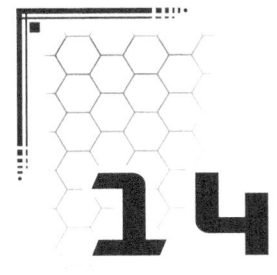

14

Emily's nanobots tingled as the *Torvatta* approached the Zayt regional control space station. The gang had a plan and she was ready to let loose. Although her body always revved up before a fight, this time it was more so than usual. The place to find out information on the dimensional network and locating Dr. Snowden was in front of her. She frowned as she thought of the pain he was probably going through.

The ring-shaped station was broken up into segments, with smaller rings appearing wherever two parts met. Six of the segments had a large thruster-like design, while others were mainly smooth. The station orbited a star, and solar collecting material seemed to be everywhere. A large sphere with a flat surface pointed toward the sun resided in the middle of the station ring.

Emily thought the station resembled a bicycle wheel to some degree. The segment they were approaching appeared to be a docking port of some type with a light green shield covering the entrance. What surprised her was the strange moss that seemed to thrive on the outside. She was not sure how it survived in space. Thick vines wound themselves around the segments, and the overall design was one of the oddest she had ever seen.

Next to her was Lord Vygon, who stood ready with his PSD in hand. He had learned it quick and was prepared for battle. V was in body mode and stood silent next to Q, who would be staying behind in the *Torvatta*. Evaran and Sivaran were front and center with their hands behind their backs. Emily had no doubt they were going over the plan. The group had several containers that fit on their belts, with some holding the countervirus, others the palisin counter.

The *Torvatta* flew through the light shielding and landed.

Emily had seen many docking bays while traveling with Evaran, and this one was not unusual. There were a hodge-podge of ships parked around, and their varying designs suggested they were probably from different civilizations. The one unique thing about the bay was the thick vines that ran in and out of the walls. Illumination was provided by large circular dots spread out over the ceiling.

The small treelike branches that covered parts of the walls and ceiling made the place look diseased. Across from where they landed was a massive hallway entrance. Their path led into that area, so she expected that would also be where reinforcements came from.

Emily had thought there would be some type of response to the *Torvatta* slipping through the shields, but all that occurred was several robots going to investigate. Although the type of robot enforcers had not been detailed, she could see these were humanoid with four arms. Their sleek green armor was segmented into various sections, but the large pauldrons stood out.

Some larger enforcers had metallic shields and wielded a melee weapon. Smaller ones had a two-handed assault weapon. One thing common to both types was they had a half-spherical helmet with an embedded gold line that went around the middle. Along with the enforcers were small drones that hovered in the area and performed scans. They reminded her of large bees.

"This is new," said Lord Vygon, studying the robots.

Emily twirled her baton. "We got this. Use mist on those with shields, stun on those with a mist present or without a shield, repulsion on any that get too close, and sticky globules as a last resort. If they have heavy kinetic shielding, we'll need to get near them."

Lord Vygon nodded. "Just like we practiced, then, although these are robots and not infected or organic enforcers."

Evaran examined the group. "Are we ready?"

"Let's do this!" said Emily as she activated her energy shield. She had already focused on the robots sent over to investigate the disturbance.

Evaran strode out with his enlarged shield facing the large hallway entrance across the room. Sivaran and V followed him.

Emily shot a mist beam at the small group near the shielding, who had now focused on the gang.

Lord Vygon ignited the cloud, and the smaller enforcers fell, along with the drones. The larger enforcers' shielding lit up as they charged.

Sivaran ran and jumped through the air. He landed in the middle of the enforcer group, and multiple rods shot out of his suit, knocking away each enforcer.

Emily took that as her cue and whirled into the enemies. She had re-formed her baton into a staff and used it to tap each enforcer she spun past.

After a moment, they lay still.

Evaran motioned ahead. "A new wave approaches. Let us go."

Emily's breathing increased. She loved fighting which was something she had never thought she would enjoy. Every second was important as long as Dr. Snowden was in danger, but she enjoyed doling out what she felt was punishment.

The group marched on. Various enforcer groups tried to stop the gang but were unsuccessful.

Emily admired Evaran's speed as he shrunk his energy shield and shredded a path through the enforcers. His raw strength was also on display as he knocked away several large defenders like they were paperweights. Sivaran resembled a tornado that blasted steel rods all over the place. Anything near him was knocked back and subsequently shot with a stun beam from his forearm-mounted devices.

V was his usual juggernaut self in body mode. He took several energy beams but marched through them to rip apart the robots he could reach. Lord Vygon was a dervish as he wielded his dual blunted blades with precision. His quick adaptation to using an energy shield and PSD surprised Emily somewhat, and he had no problems with showcasing his ability. Sivaran and Lord Vygon would have been a terrifying team to fight against.

After ten minutes, the gang paused at the hallway entrance.

Evaran pointed at a console on the side. "V, see what you can do there."

"Acknowledged," said V. He hustled over and connected.

"I can feel a stronger response coming," said Sivaran.

Evaran nodded. "Our sneak attack gave us an advantage in the docking bay. The upcoming fights will not be as easy."

Lord Vygon spun his PSD around. "With this group, easy is relative. We went through that enforcer defense like they weren't even there."

"Let us not get complacent," said Evaran, raising a finger. "I do not want to lose anyone else."

Emily got goose bumps when Evaran's eyes glowed. She could feel his cosmic energy, and it fluctuated wildly. That meant he was angry despite his face outwardly showing calmness. Even Sivaran's energy was in flux, and his scowl indicated his mood. She wondered if Evaran would scowl if he could.

Although she was feeling confident about the group's chances, she had felt that way last time when Dr. Snowden had been captured. It bothered her how fast the infected had pulled him away. He had his strength, suit, and PSD, but they had effectively neutralized them. Her eyes narrowed as she peered down the hallway they would be going down. Dr. Snowden's whereabouts were potentially here, and all it would take was dismantling a space station. She could do that.

Lord Vygon had to exert himself to keep up with the frantic pace of the group. He was no stranger to fighting robots, but the group moved effortlessly. V had attempted to disable the station's systems, but there was a secondary organic one, as if the station had a central nervous system. One system would be disabled, only to come back up, then V was locked out.

It was determined they would proceed to the control center and deal with any lockdowns as they went.

The strange mix of vines and other plantlike life mixed with metallic panels resembled a typical Zayt environment. Lord Vygon thought he saw some of the smaller vines pulse as the group marched on. It made him think the station was alive and they were traveling through its body.

Lord Vygon kept an eye on Emily. She was full of seething rage, and he watched as she took several hits to the head, which she shrugged off. Her response was to tear off the robots' heads with her bare hands. Her speed was much more noticeable now compared to what it was in the training session he had done with her. Her staff spun around like a hurricane. When she did shoot beams, her shots were precise and tactical.

Evaran and Sivaran moved as if they were one. Evaran would grapple beam an enforcer and reel it in halfway, then Sivaran would disable it as he flipped over. Their movements were fluid, and between Evaran swinging what was known as a grappling block around and Sivaran's suit shooting out metal rods everywhere, most of the enforcer groups they ran into did not last long.

V had proven himself to be sturdy. He took many a hit and shrugged it off, only to march over and dismantle whatever had shot at him. Lord Vygon was not sure what type of shielding V had, but it was apparently strong enough to take some serious damage. It made Lord Vygon wonder why the others did not have that level of shielding. Perhaps due to the size and energy costs. Then again, if dimensional mechanics were at work, that would not be an issue. Maybe they were being used, and the end result was a robot body that seemed like an invincible juggernaut.

The group paused at a T-junction.

Lord Vygon's eyes narrowed when doors sealed behind them, then to the left and right. They were trapped.

"What's going on?" asked Emily.

"I do not know," said Evaran. He studied the strange mist that began to shoot out from small holes on the walls. "They are attempting to flood the area with a palisin mist of some sort. We must break through a door."

Sivaran grabbed a container off his belt and activated it. "This should weaken the mist."

The group rushed to the right and stood before the sealed door.

"I got this one," said Sivaran.

He extended his arms and formed two large piercing blades. They poked effortlessly through the door, and after several cutting motions, he had cut out a doorway. His blades morphed back into his suit.

"Your suit is awesome," said Emily.

Sivaran nodded as he grimaced. "We should go. I'm already feeling the effects of the mist, and that's with our counter in place. We'll need to use the countermist containers sparingly."

The group rushed through.

Evaran pointed his utility handle back through the opening and released a repulsion beam. The mist swept away. "We are close to the control center. The mist was not on any of the system layouts or Acrolis's scans. Wardax is adapting as we go."

"Great," said Lord Vygon. "And of course, palisin energy doesn't affect the station. They could have flooded the whole place with it. I feel like we're being herded somewhat."

Evaran nodded. "Perhaps. We should not stay here longer than we need to. Q, how is the docking bay?"

"It remains clear so far, but they have begun to pump a similar mist into the area," said Q over comms.

"Won't that affect the *Torvatta*'s shielding?" asked Lord Vygon.

"It will not, as the shielding is a planar void. However, it will make any traversal to the *Torvatta* more dangerous. Wardax may have other means at his disposal that I am unaware of," said Evaran. "Q, take the *Torvatta* outside the station."

"Moving it now," said Q.

Lord Vygon's eyes narrowed. Although the mist was not everywhere, it was in the two places the group had been. The palisin mist was new, and he could see it as an anti-Evaran tactic, although the amount needed to generate a cloud seemed absurd. Wardax must have been busier than Lord Vygon realized. What bothered him was he had not sensed the palisin energy in the mist until it had begun to be secreted. It was as if the source was not on the station. Although the group had a counter, it was meant for the guardian if it had palisin energy. Getting them to use the canisters before then might be Wardax's ploy.

Emily shook her head. "I didn't even sense the palisin energy until the mist."

"Analysis. My simulations have determined that the palisin mist may come from the dimensional network, similar to the one that Dr. Snowden entered. The mist is then pumped where it needs to go. The alternative is that it came from a magnetically shielded source."

"That's just what we need right now," said Emily.

"We will deal with it. As Wardax is a cosmic being, and potentially using a dimensional network for control, a palisin mist there would disrupt that. Nonetheless, let us focus," said Evaran.

The group marched on.

It did not bode well that both Evarans seemed to have been caught somewhat off guard by the palisin mist. The thought of the *Torvatta* being held in place, preventing escape, crossed Lord Vygon's mind. He understood why Evaran had moved it out of reach. If they needed to make a quick retreat, the *Torvatta* would need to come back in somehow.

After fifteen minutes, they stopped at the large hallway before the control center.

Evaran tilted his head. "A swarm approaches."

Lord Vygon readied his energy shield, blunted blades, and PSD. He could now sense the oncoming enemy. Robots always had a buzz, but whatever was coming also had an organic component.

His eyes widened at the strange group that rushed forward. They reminded him of an upright log with robot arms and legs. The head was simply an orb with a slit around the middle. The fingers resembled knives while the blocky feet had four claws at each corner.

Although one could easily be handled, the hallway was now filled with a horde of them. They were not just coming on the ground but running on the walls and ceiling as well. The green sheen of the metal parts indicated these were enforcers, but unlike any Lord Vygon had seen to this point.

Emily shot a mist beam at the swarm, which Evaran ignited. It slowed the swarm down, but others surged ahead.

Sivaran ran forward and jumped into the mass of enforcers, then shot rods in every direction from his suit.

The enforcers went tumbling off to the sides.

Emily used a mist beam on the left side, and Evaran got the right.

Lord Vygon wasted no time in igniting both areas.

The effect was immediate as the remnants of the swarm struggled to fight V, who had burst into action and worked to disable anything still moving. After a few minutes, the hallway was littered with fritzing enforcers.

Emily bent over. "I'm feeling weaker."

"I am as well," said Evaran. "It seems there is a trace of the mist here. We should not be here longer than we need to. Let us go."

Lord Vygon had not had to exert himself, but he could see that Evaran, Sivaran, Emily, and even V were moving a tad slower. Hopefully, there were no palisin mist elements in the control center room that was coming up.

There was still a guardian to deal with, and the few controllers he had seen had already fled the area. He did not think there would be another swarm, but if the guardian was tough and there was a palisin mist present, it could be rougher than anything the group had fought before. It was time to find out.

15

Emily grimaced as she entered the space station's control center. The palisin mist seemed to be heavy, and it was like the station had spewed it everywhere. Although it was not enough to knock her out, it had a definite effect on her. Evaran, Sivaran, and V were also affected. The anticosmic approach by Wardax was proving to be effective. The thirty minutes it had taken to arrive had not been a picnic either.

The control center had a central cylinder with vines and metallic wires running over its surface. There seemed to be more plantlike material on the walls, floor, and ceiling compared to the rest of the station. There were several workstations in cubbyholes that were embedded into the walls. Along the base at several points were small holes spewing the palisin mist. The room was well lit, and the rustling sounds of something moving filled the air.

Her focus was drawn to the ten-foot wooden humanoid with metallic plating. It was like a stick man, except with vines and metal plates for skin. Next to him were some of the unusual enforcers from before. It was not a true swarm, but there were plenty that could create an issue, especially with the mist causing problems. Evaran and Sivaran released the last of their countermist, and she and Lord Vygon had shot sticky globules on the areas releasing the mist. Hopefully, it would be enough.

Evaran pointed at the nearest workstation. "V, begin your infiltration. For the rest of us, we will defend you."

The robot in the room stepped toward the group. In a digitized voice, it said, "There you are. Your performance to get here has been exemplary."

They formed a protective arc around V as he operated.

"I assume I am speaking to Wardax," said Evaran.

"Of course, but you already knew that."

Evaran tilted his head. "Your transgression against Dr. Snowden cannot stand. We will find him."

"I have no doubt you will try. The real question is … what state will he be in? The palisin mist was his idea. Well, to be clear, he provided the basis for it."

Emily gripped her staff as she stood next to Evaran. "He wouldn't help you!"

Wardax scoffed. "You're right. However, if his nanobots can cause a mist-like entity that devours everything, why can't there be one made of palisin energy that counters it?"

"Your arrogance is misplaced," said Sivaran. "While a palisin mist may be effective in slowing down cosmic beings, it would have no effect on planar beings like Lord Vygon."

Wardax nodded. "This is true, but he would be the only one in your group."

"You underestimate my wrath," said Lord Vygon, growling.

"That's possible," said Wardax. He gestured at V. "As he is finding out, not everything is as it should be."

A chill swept through Emily. Wardax's statement sounded like something Evaran would say.

Evaran raised a finger. "We are aware that the station is alive to some degree. We also know that it has some form of connection to a dimension. V understands this, but similar to Lord Vygon, I believe you underestimate V's ability."

Wardax grinned. "You're wrong on several counts." He examined Emily. "Your uncle has proven to be quite resilient. He also understands the situation, and if he knew what you were doing here, he would disapprove. Once again, I'm under attack and have to defend myself. Yes, I think your actions here would disappoint him."

Emily rushed forward and swung at Wardax with her staff.

He grabbed it and tossed her off to the side. The swarm activated and began to attack.

"Cover V and release the virus!" said Evaran, looking at Sivaran and pointing at V.

Sivaran complied and threw two canisters at Wardax's feet. When the canisters stopped, they spewed a green mist.

Lord Vygon cleaved his way through the swarm. When he reached Wardax, he jabbed him in the sides with his forearm blades.

Wardax batted him away.

Evaran leapt into the air and, using his staff, came down hard on Wardax, sending him stumbling back.

Emily shook off the momentary confusion as she stood. The palisin mist dulled her senses even with the counter one working on it, and the swarm was on her. She noted that, as weakened as she was, some of the swarm seemed to hold position, as if they were awaiting orders. The countervirus must be working. She took the moment to break through the ones near her and dash toward Wardax.

Lord Vygon jumped over several enforcers and leg-swept Wardax, who fell.

Evaran tried to punch through Wardax's chest, but he rolled out of the way and kicked Emily back into the wall.

She was tired of being batted around. The virus was not working as fast as she had expected it to. She hopped up and gritted her teeth. Wardax was going to pay, and no palisin mist would stand in her way. She focused, causing her suit to respond. An enforcer tried to stab her, but she picked it up and tossed it at Wardax.

Wardax knocked the enforcer down, but his attention was on Evaran, who spun around Wardax like a tornado and unleashed a hailstorm of hits, kicks, and jabs.

Emily checked on Sivaran and verified that he was able to protect V, who had taken a few strikes. Sivaran moved slower, but his suit responded with brutal efficiency to anything that came near. His fighting moves also helped keep the area clear. She ducked as Evaran went flying past her.

Lord Vygon shot sticky globules on Wardax's face.

Wardax tried to remove the globule, but his hands got stuck.

Emily took advantage of the situation and yelled as she charged with her bladed staff out front. It pierced through Wardax.

He stepped back and kicked Emily away. The hole she had formed healed up. Not only was he strong, but he also had a high regeneration factor.

She rushed over to Sivaran and grabbed the remaining virus containers.

"New plan!" she said. She tossed several at Lord Vygon. "Go distribute these! I'll get the other half of the station."

Lord Vygon nodded and took off.

"No!" said Wardax as he focused on him.

Emily went in the other direction and shot a stun beam at Wardax, who chased her out of the room. She had initially thought that Wardax would stay and disrupt Sivaran and V, but the virus seemed to be his highest priority at the moment, which was good for her. Thankfully, Evaran followed and harassed Wardax, but the main thing was to clear the room.

Several enforcers tried to get in her way, but she bulldozed through them. When she reached what showed as the power room on her ARI, she tossed a canister in.

The enforcers there initially went to attack her, then paused.

"Stop this!" said Wardax, bursting in after her.

Evaran kicked Wardax in the back, sending him flying. "Keep going!"

Emily found herself enjoying the worry in Wardax's voice. She was not sure how they would stop Wardax as he seemed unstoppable. He had no cosmic energy in this guardian form, and she suspected the real one was much tougher. Perhaps his dimensional network gave him strength.

After several more areas were hit, Q contacted her. "I have an idea. Similar to what you did with the ancient vampires and Sivaran's rescue. I've marked a room. If you can get Wardax there, the *Torvatta* will melt him."

"Got it," said Emily.

She hustled to the room that Q had marked. Wardax's berating of her and Evaran was constant, and as weakened as she knew Evaran and she were, they still slowed Wardax down.

Evaran and Emily lined up against the wall and faced an angry Wardax as he burst in.

"Enough of this!" said Wardax. "You've earned my ire. All I want to do is exist, and now I have to deal with yet another threat. I will learn from this virus you're deploying and adapt. Please stop this."

"We will not," said Evaran.

He and Emily fired grappling beams at Wardax and reeled him in. When he was close, they released the grappling beam and rolled forward, then spun around and fired sticky globules, which pinned Wardax against the wall.

Wardax gargled some before the *Torvatta* melted through both him and the wall.

Emily closed her eyes for a moment and relaxed. This fight had been tougher than she had expected, and the cumulative effect of the palisin mist made her nauseous.

"Your plan worked," said Evaran, laying a hand on her shoulder.

"Thankfully, but it was Q's idea to melt Wardax. This mist is killing me."

Evaran tilted his head.

"Not literally."

Evaran nodded. "You should board the *Torvatta*. I will rendezvous with the others and clean up."

Emily hugged Evaran, then joined Q in the command center. She lowered her helmet and took some deep breaths. Everything already felt better, but she attributed that to being out of the mist. There would need to be new countermeasures to handle that since the containers had been used up quick. They would also need to deal with Wardax, who kept devising tougher and tougher scenarios.

"As Evaran said, your plan was effective," said Q, looking at her.

"I liked your 'melt Wardax' plan too," she said.

Q smiled. "I did as well."

She relaxed in her chair and focused on the windows showing the view from Evaran's suit.

Lord Vygon liked Emily's spur-of-the-moment plan. It was obvious that Wardax was not concerned with V accessing the system. That might be due to the secondary organic aspect of it, which V would not be able to deal with. That left the virus containers as a major threat, and Emily had figured that out and let Wardax chase her. With Evaran going after both, Lord Vygon was confident that they would deal with Wardax.

As Lord Vygon rushed out of the room, he asked over comms, "Where am I going?"

"I have marked several places for you on the map inside your helmet," said Q. "I've also marked where Emily is going, or rather, where she will be going and leading Wardax."

"Got it," said Lord Vygon.

He studied the three locations he needed to reach. One seemed like a gathering center of some type, another was cargo storage, and the last was a large hallway that seemed to serve as a hub. His adrenaline pumped through him, and his heart still beat furiously. Wardax had been a fight and a half, but the virus incapacitating the swarm gave Lord Vygon hope. When he had left, Sivaran had been in the process of dealing with the last of the swarm while protecting V.

Lord Vygon reached the gathering center with minimal interaction. Although a few enforcers had tried to stop him, they were no match for him with his energy shield out and his PSD shooting all sorts of beams. The energy shield prevented him from getting hit, and everything fell that came within range of his blunted forearm blades.

He had expected there would be chairs or something in the gathering center, but there were posts instead. A harness of some type was on each post, and he surmised that the enforcers or infected hooked into those as needed. It seemed strange to have a gathering center, and Wardax giving speeches to those he already controlled would be an odd sight. Lord Vygon suspected the room was meant more for mass actions or updates without the need for a controller.

There were only a few enforcers in the room, and Lord Vygon happily tossed the virus container in, then burst away. He could hear the enforcers moving, but they did not pursue him. It made him wonder if the virus was traveling along the organic pathways created by the vines. Perhaps the station's organic system itself was compromised. Either way, he took advantage of the situation.

The cargo storage took fifteen minutes to reach, and while going there, he observed enforcers moving much slower. From listening in on Evaran and Q talk, it seemed Wardax's guardian body had been melted by the *Torvatta*. Lord Vygon tossed the virus container into the room, then listened to V over comms.

"Analysis. The virus seems to affect the plant material on the station. I took control of the digital system, but the station's organic component was the backup. I could not affect that. However, I have connected with Q and downloaded all available information to the *Torvatta*."

Evaran spoke next. "You are correct that the virus is affecting the station's organic components. We should not be here when it comes completely undone. The organic system was in part controlled by the digital system. Without that link, I suspect the station will have some problems. Lord Vygon, what is your status?"

"Only one more place to go, then I'm on my way to the *Torvatta*."

A red dot appeared a few rooms away from the hallway.

"Meet us there afterward instead," said Evaran. "The *Torvatta* will pick you up from there."

"Sounds good," said Lord Vygon. "It seems the *Torvatta* melting objects and beings is a common thing."

"That was Q's plan, and it worked well," said Evaran.

"He's good like that," said Sivaran.

"Thank you," said Q.

Lord Vygon chuckled. Even in the midst of a dangerous operation, there was some humor. He liked this group and saw the power of what could be done. It made him wish they had been around for Drydris, but even with time travel, it could not be saved as it was a part of events now. His blood raged as he thought of all those lost, and he took it out on the few enforcers he ran across.

He wrinkled his brow when he reached the large hallway. Several controllers stood still as they looked around, seemingly in confusion. He tossed the virus container, then watched them flee. Without any instructions from Wardax, or the ability to control the now free enforcers, they were in panic mode, it seemed. A part of him felt bad since he did not know the controllers' species, but from their perspective, they had probably woken up on a space station that was rapidly becoming chaotic.

He entered the room that Q had marked. "I'm here."

"Seal the door and stand against the opposite wall the *Torvatta* will be coming through," said Q.

Lord Vygon complied. He grinned as the *Torvatta* melted through the wall. Its shielding ensured nothing got sucked out, but he figured it would be a bad day for anything that tried to enter the room. Once the *Torvatta* stopped, Lord Vygon rushed on board. He joined the others in the command center.

V had taken the front console back over, and Evaran sat in his command chair. Sivaran and Q were in the left U-shaped seating area, so Lord Vygon joined Emily on the right. He took a quick survey of the mood. Emily had her helmet down and seemed to be in some pain. Sivaran scowled as he rubbed his forearms. Even Evaran with his usual stoic face had lips that turned down slightly. The palisin mist had unfortunately been effective.

"V, keep us in scan profile one and stealth mode and perform deep scans of the station for the rest of the day. We can observe the virus's impact," said Evaran.

"Acknowledged."

Lord Vygon marveled at being able to stay right outside such a space station and remain undetected. "I hope there was information on the dimensional network on that station."

"Analysis. There was."

"Enough to find Uncle Albert?" asked Emily.

V nodded. "It will take some time."

Sivaran gestured at the station. "We'll also find out how effective the virus was and its spread capability. I would say this mission was a success, although we have some lessons learned." He pointed at Emily. "An excellent idea to lead Wardax away."

Emily nodded. "Wardax underestimated V and the virus's impact on the station's systems."

"He did," said V, high-fiving Emily.

Lord Vygon grunted. "We still took a beating. I'm hurting all over."

"We will rest up," said Evaran. "The palisin mist's effects will take some time to disperse. If you or Emily require medical assistance outside of that, we can treat you in the medical lab."

Emily stood. "I'm okay, I just need to go lay down some."

Evaran squeezed her arm as she passed. He was sort of like Emily's father figure from everything that Lord Vygon had observed. Evaran's tender action made her smile briefly, and Lord Vygon understood the power of family. His stomach churned as he once again thought of Drydris.

He stood. "I guess I'll get in some blood, then some rest as well. I'm looking forward to seeing the analysis on everything soon."

"We'll get it," said Sivaran. "Rest well."

Lord Vygon nodded at everyone and walked away. Although they had obtained everything they had come for, his overall mood had not changed much. There was still work to be done, but he did feel confident that, between Evaran, Sivaran, V, and Q, they would analyze the new data and find solutions.

16

Dr. Snowden sighed as he studied the memory of his graduation from college. Wardax had been thorough up to this point in going through memories.

Dr. Snowden was not sure how long he had been away, but it seemed like he had lived a lifetime since being captured. Given some perspective on Wardax's past, Dr. Snowden tried not to feel sympathetic, especially with what had transpired, but Wardax was logical, and it was hard to refute his points sometimes.

Wardax frowned as they entered a new memory. It showed Evaran and the others fighting in a bare room outside a central cylinder and some workstations embedded in the sides.

"Your friends have attacked me again," he said.

"Well, yeah. You kidnapped me and are mentally torturing me. Oh, and you broke my knee. What did you expect?" asked Dr. Snowden.

Wardax scowled. "The *Torvatta* is very powerful to have traveled the distance it did to get there and be completely undetected."

Dr. Snowden shrugged. "If you don't want to be attacked, have you tried fleeing?"

"Of course I have, but even then, I'm discovered and assaulted. Should I just lie down and die? If someone came into your house and killed Emily, Dan, and Sarah, then pursued and hunted you, would you stop, sit down, and let them kill you?"

"No."

"Would you try to talk to your attackers? I have … several times, and each time ended up with them attacking. To survive, you either fight, or you die. It's that simple."

Dr. Snowden could see how the assault by the rest of the gang would be construed as an attack. They were simply looking for information, something Dr. Snowden recognized as a part of trying to understand the enemy. He also understood Wardax's position. After hundreds of years of being hunted and attacked, on top of watching the race he had tried to protect become a victim of genocide, he just wanted to live. Events between Wardax and Evaran and the others had probably escalated too far for reconciliation.

"If you gave me back, I'm sure Evaran would talk with you," said Dr. Snowden.

Wardax eyed him. "I'd like to believe that, but at this point, what's done is done. They will find you in time, I'm sure, and once again, I'll have to flee for my life. Evaran and Sivaran are cosmic beings, like me, and they're powerful. Everything in me tells me that they will not stop until I no longer exist or my cosmic energy is taken."

Dr. Snowden's eyes narrowed. Wardax was right that Evaran and Sivaran would most likely either outright banish Wardax to his dimension by killing his form here or strip him of his cosmic energy somehow. Evaran had almost sacrificed himself to remove a cosmic shard. That was how dedicated he had been to ensuring that cosmic energy, outside of the gang, the chosen, and the *Torvatta*, was removed.

They entered a new memory that showed the *Torvatta* melting the guardian body.

Wardax's eyes narrowed. "And as expected, I lost against two cosmic beings. They unleashed a virus of some type. Every infected on the station will now have to deal with the chaos that will unfold. Without maintenance, the station will fail, and they will all die."

"Evaran and Sivaran wouldn't allow that."

"Sadly, they've left, and there is no sign of them. They've condemned hundreds of innocents to their death. Of course, a part of me is on that station, and it too will die. That is the price for being so bold as to declare that I live."

Dr. Snowden shook his head. "Then maybe you shouldn't have put those innocents there in the first place. Evaran would save them if he could."

"Then where is he?" asked Wardax, gesturing around

Dr. Snowden surveyed the environment. He had a unique insight into the station and could see the vines dying as they decoupled from the life-nourishing technological network. The matter conversion part of the station was disabled, and the station's orbit had deteriorated.

"I want you to feel something," said Wardax. He closed his eyes.

Dr. Snowden fell to his knees as hundreds of confused and scared feelings assaulted him. He felt when some died. His heartbeat pulsed wildly as he struggled to breathe.

"Please ... stop," he said.

Wardax opened his eyes. "Done. I let you sample what I feel right now. I want to help them, but I can't."

"As I said before, they shouldn't have been where they were to begin with," said Dr. Snowden.

He struggled to stand. The helplessness and sheer fright unnerved him. It was no wonder Wardax fought as hard as he did, even if he was guilty of putting them there, and now he was going against arguably the strongest group he had ever fought. Everything in Dr. Snowden knew that Wardax would probably end up losing, and although the wave of feelings came from the station, some were from Wardax himself. He was scared. That was a sharp contrast to what he expected those around Evaran to feel.

"So what do I do?" asked Wardax. "We've yet to dive deeper into your memories with Evaran and the *Torvatta*, but that's next. I suspect that it will only confirm what I know: they want to take my cosmic energy and leave me at the mercy of others. Am I wrong?"

Dr. Snowden sighed. "Probably not. I don't know why you have cosmic energy, but yes, it will probably be removed somehow."

"Now imagine if you were being hunted by powerful beings and their friends who wanted to leave you at the mercy of other enemies."

Dr. Snowden had to refer to thoughts of being captured to keep his anger up. Wardax's situation seemed hopeless, and despite his efforts, he would most likely lose. If his cosmic energy was removed, Dr. Snowden had no doubt that Wardax would be killed in short order. Maybe Evaran could transport Wardax someplace safe, but that assumed the removal of cosmic energy did not kill him outright.

"I'm not going to die without a fight," said Wardax. "My drive to exist is strong, and I suspect I'm meant for more than this. Otherwise, why would I be the recipient of cosmic energy?"

"I don't know."

They entered a memory of the Krotovore virtual simulation, the first time Dr. Snowden had met Evaran.

"Then I want to know what is trying to kill me in detail," said Wardax. He looked around. "Although we've seen snippets of your more recent memories so I could understand names, places, and technology, this appears to be your first memory of meeting Evaran. We can start here."

Dr. Snowden grimaced as he remembered peeking out through the door hole and seeing Evaran for the first time. Little had Dr. Snowden known how much his life would be changed from that event. He settled in for yet another discussion.

⸻

Q exited the research lab, where he, Evaran, Sivaran, and V had pored over the data retrieved from the space station. There was a lot of information, and the group focused on categorization first.

Q could multitask and decided to check on Emily. He liked her plan on the station, and she seemed sad. Dr. Snowden's absence probably played a large part in that, and Q's instinct as a medical support AI kicked in.

He checked the *Torvatta*'s systems and saw that Emily was on the roof. After verifying that he could still analyze and move around, he went there. Emily studied various statistics and data windows on the interior shielding. She appeared less sad. He understood that Halkins, and humans it seemed, could be distracted.

"Q," she said, turning her head.

"Your senses are finely tuned," he said as he joined her.

She nodded. "What's up?"

He ran a query and determined this was slang. After another lookup, he defined her question as asking him the status of the situation. "We're currently analyzing the data from the station."

"And yet you're here," she said, looking him over. "Multitasking thing, right?"

"That's correct."

Emily smiled. "V does that sometimes. He can be in multiple places at once."

Q nodded. "It's a useful ability. Are you feeling okay, relative to the situation?"

She shrugged. "As good as I can be, I guess. I miss Uncle Albert, and I know we're doing everything to find him. It's just … I wish I could do more."

"I understand," said Q. "We're classifying the types of data, and there is information on the dimensional network. If we can discover its topology, I'm sure we can determine where your uncle is."

"I hope so," said Emily. She eyed him. "Speaking of helping, the *Torvatta* must like you if it let you pilot it. That's a rare honor."

"I agree. It has been more than accommodating to my access requests," said Q.

The *Torvatta*'s systems were strange and Q had never encountered such an odd setup. There was a digital component, but also organic, energy, and dimensional ones. Although he could only traverse the digital, everything was connected. When he had tried to access the others, he had been denied, and he was not even sure how the interface between the various parts worked.

The *Torvatta*'s allowed-pilots list was a short one. Q found it efficient to be there as he was not a combatant. Although he could defend himself, every calculation showed that he would have slowed the group down if he had entered the field. His observations classified Emily as a fierce fighter similar to Sivaran. Q had thought Sivaran was the only cosmic being in existence, but that assumption had been blown apart since he had met the gang.

"So how does this compare to what you and Sivaran have experienced?" she asked.

"It's very different," said Q. "The *Torvatta* adds a new level of powerful abilities that opens options. In addition to that, Evaran is the most powerful being I have ever observed, even more so than Sivaran."

Emily grinned. "Yeah, Evaran's on another level for sure."

Q raised a finger. "In addition to all that, you and your uncle are formidable in your own right, and V is quite versatile."

"We're the gang."

"I like that term. It fits."

Emily sighed. "Yeah. It just eats me that we couldn't stop Uncle Albert from being pulled away."

"I understand," said Q. "Wardax is not to be underestimated."

"I can't believe he has cosmic energy. I wonder where it came from."

Q ran over various possibilities. "I'm not sure. Now that I'm aware there are other plane forms, it could be that this is a rogue one."

Emily shuddered. "A corrupted Evaran. Yeah, I don't like to think of that."

"It could also be the plane form's cosmic energy without the plane form."

"You mean like pulled out of a plane form?"

Q nodded.

She frowned. "We saw that with the Overlord. He absorbed some of Levaran, and he gained the ability to re-form upon death."

"Is that an Evaran trait? To re-form upon death?"

Emily gazed out. "It's complex. It depends on several factors. If the plane form is too damaged, the cosmic energy is absorbed by the plane. If it's strong enough, it's ejected out of the plane. There is a moment during re-formation, though, where Evaran has plane-wide powers. I suspect if Wardax was a re-formed Evaran, Wardax would have done a lot more than what he's doing now, so I don't think he is that."

"I didn't know that," said Q.

"Yeah, and we also know that cosmic energy can be siphoned away. Maybe Wardax siphoned cosmic energy from something, although he would have to be very powerful to pull that off."

Q realized how much more Emily knew about Evaran, in any plane form, than he did. Perhaps that was a benefit of traveling with Evaran. Sivaran usually kept information on a need-to-know basis and rarely covered topics like the ones Q and Emily talked about. Q inferred that Emily was of special importance to Evaran and Sivaran, and that Dr. Snowden was regarded in a similar manner.

"I appreciate these discussions," said Q. "It adds some information I was missing."

"I'm surprised Sivaran never discussed these with you," said Emily.

"Perhaps he feared I would be compromised and give away his secrets. I'm only an AI, but that is a valid concern."

Emily squeezed his arm. "I think you're much more than just an AI. The fact Sivaran chose you means you're special."

"Thank you."

Although Q did not experience emotions, he had a simulation running at all times, and Emily's embrace of him made him feel good, or so his programming told him. She was kind yet tough and held a significant position with both Evarans.

He glanced at her. "I would like to learn more about Evaran if you don't mind."

"All we have is time. Fire away."

Q created a list of questions that would help fill in the gaps. In addition to making him more knowledgeable in order to have better data points, the discussion would also create a distraction for Emily. He processed what it must be like to have an inner container similar to V's and experience pseudoemotions. His medical programming told him he was helping Emily, but his general programming viewed her as a friend.

17

Emily's heartbeat quickened when Evaran called everyone to the research lab. She had had dinner earlier and thought that maybe they would have a conference room meeting the next day. It was 6:30 p.m. and she was glad she did not have to wait. A nap had danced through her mind, and the bed in her living quarters enticed her, but now she was amped up.

On her way to the lab, she spotted Q coming from the command center. She had enjoyed their talk on the roof. Although he was an AI with simulated emotions, he came off as genuine and caring. His friendliness and devotion to helping find Dr. Snowden endeared him to her. It would be fun to have both Sivaran and Q join the crew, but she understood they probably would not.

When she reached the research lab, she surveyed the setup. Evaran and the others stood around a ring on the floor that projected various holographic displays. It was like a cylinder of the holo room had been cut out and pasted into the lab.

She was used to having these types of meetings in the conference room, but maybe this one required Evaran to move about or interact on a display that was wider than normal. The holo room seemed like it would be a better fit, but she figured Evaran had something physical he was working on.

V high-fived her. "It is good to see you."

She returned the high five. "You too. Now, what's going on?"

"I'm with her," said Lord Vygon. "My curiosity is piqued."

Sivaran smiled. "Good news finally. We think we've figured out where your uncle is."

Emily licked her lips. "I'm expecting a but…"

"You are correct to assume so," said Evaran. "Observe."

The holographic display changed to show a flat galactic map. Various green dots appeared.

"This is where portals, similar to the one Dr. Snowden went through, exist in our reality," said Evaran.

The projection showed another rectangular layer underneath that had blue dotted lines connecting the portals to an orange sphere at the bottom.

"The orange object is a dimension. The blue lines represent the dimensional network."

"No rift energy was detected, though," said Emily.

Evaran nodded. "Yes, and that is because whatever is in the dimension can maintain these connections. That requires some type of multidimensional mechanism."

"The plant life," said Lord Vygon.

Sivaran pointed at him. "Very observant. Our current hypothesis is that whatever is in the dimension is plant-based and multidimensional, and it extends its reach to our reality.

This should be rare … but we suspect that cosmic energy is involved, which is far more powerful than rift energy."

"I didn't sense cosmic energy on the portal, though," said Emily.

Evaran raised a finger. "That is because the dimensional network is powered by cosmic energy, but the portal is just a dimensional endpoint on the network."

Lord Vygon shook his head. "I didn't even know there was cosmic energy out and about and able to do things like this."

"There usually isn't," said Sivaran. "The cosmic energy involvement is troublesome. The only positive is we think it's in our reality, most likely in whatever form Wardax is in, and he's using it to expand his multidimensional ability. Outside everyone here, Dr. Snowden, Dalton Kingston, our other plane forms, and any rogue cosmic entity, cosmic energy should be nonexistent. It had to come from somewhere, though. The current thought is that this is a cosmic entity from the Cosmic Medium outside the plane."

Emily played with her ponytail. "Then the solution is simple. Find a portal, toss in a quantum beacon, and we'll fly in and scour the network and figure out which portal in our reality is being used to enhance the dimensional network."

Sivaran chuckled. "That's a good plan, but the portal would most likely collapse before a beacon could get through. It was able to sense you and Lord Vygon chasing Dr. Snowden, so we know it has some form of awareness, or rather, whoever is powering it does."

"It makes you wonder why they kept the data on the portals in our reality on board the space station," said Emily. "This could be a trap."

Evaran nodded. "Possibly. However, even if another civilization got this information and understood that there was a dimensional network with endpoints in places Wardax already controlled, there is not much they could do with that knowledge. I suspect it was kept more for controllers to work with."

"So … the portals collapse at the presence of cosmic energy, or if Wardax is aware," said Emily. "If we could sneak someone in with a quantum beacon, they could toss it through, and we'd have at least some idea of the dimensional network."

Everyone stared at Lord Vygon and Q.

Lord Vygon laughed. "Why do I suspect we were just volunteered?"

"I would be too slow," said Q.

Lord Vygon shook his head. "But I'm not, so I'd be the natural candidate. We don't even know if the portal can sense exotic energy in general."

"You are correct," said Evaran. He pointed at one of the dots. "However, there is a generic record of items going in and out of the portals. One entry noted that there was cosmic energy present. I suspect that is where Dr. Snowden is."

"So we know where he is? What're we waiting for, then?" asked Emily.

Evaran half smiled. "I understand the desire to rush in, but we need a plan, which I am working on. We can achieve two goals at the same time. We need to get Lord Vygon in to drop the quantum beacon in so we can learn more about the dimensional network, then we rescue Dr. Snowden. The countervirus works, so that requires deployment as well. I would also expect to fight an enhanced guardian. Caution should be observed."

"I know," said Emily, frowning.

He walked and put his arm around her. "I am as troubled as you are that Dr. Snowden is not among us. Know this We will rescue him and be one step closer to stopping Warcax."

"I'm ready to go whenever," said Lord Vygon. "Sneaking on and getting close to a portal is going to be tough."

Q nodded at him. "We'll figure something out. The countervirus design is proof that we understand how the Zayt sense the world. It may be possible to obscure you from their senses."

"All right."

Evaran looked around. "Although we do not have a full plan yet, I am glad you all are here to be brought up to speed on what we had learned up to this point." He peered down at Emily. "It should help you sleep better."

She hugged him from the side. He always seemed to know how to make her feel good, and he was right that with a plan being devised and knowledge of the portals, she did feel more relaxed. Her heart warmed when everyone squeezed her arm or tapped her back. This was what families did in times of crisis: pull together for the common good.

Dr. Snowden sighed as he watched the memory where Levaran re-formed from an old man to a woman. Outside of Evaran, she had been the first plane form Dr. Snowden had met. She was also the first plane form re-formation he had seen. Although the Overlord, a Hadryn spawn, from a previous adventure had re-formed, he was not a plane form. Dr. Snowden's heart sagged as Levaran strode out of the re-forming room in the *Torvatta*'s maintenance hub.

"This is interesting," said Wardax.

Another copy of Levaran appeared next to Wardax. "You don't belong here." She reached out and grabbed Wardax's neck and lifted him off the ground.

"What is this?" he asked before fading away.

Dr. Snowden wrinkled his brow. "Levaran?"

She walked over and put her arm around him. "This memory is protected. Know that I'll always be here for you."

He slumped against her and struggled to breathe. Tears ran down his cheeks as he relaxed. The constant memory hopping he had done up to this point had been fueled by fear and adrenaline. The thought of losing even one memory stressed him, and after hundreds, he was tired.

"You're okay while here," said Levaran.

Dr. Snowden stepped back and wiped his eyes. "How is this possible?"

"I am a part of you, at least in these memories. I can manifest and protect specific ones that involve me."

"Can you be in all of them?" he asked.

"Unfortunately not, but I understand what's going on. This Wardax is poisoning your mind. He will not get all the memories he wants, though."

Dr. Snowden adjusted his glasses. "I miss the others."

"I'm sure you do," she said. "Trust that Evaran and the others are doing everything they can to retrieve you."

He sighed. "Yeah, I'm sure they are. I also understand things run slower in the real world compared to the time spent going over all these memories."

It bothered him that even if he came out of this, he would have tainted memories with Wardax in them. As if that was not enough, he used Evaran's form, which created a repelling factor that Dr. Snowden knew he would need to deal with.

Levaran paused for a moment and her eyes glowed. "Ahh, Sivaran. I accessed some of your more current memories. You've met yet another plane form. I recall seeing his form among others when I initially arrived."

"Yeah, and I like him," said Dr. Snowden. "Sorta reminds me of you."

She nodded. "I can see that. Two plane forms working together again."

"Three with you around," he said, grinning.

His headache had disappeared, and he realized how nice it was to have someone other than Wardax to speak to. Dr. Snowden felt bad about Levaran's eventual fate, but she had played a pivotal role in banishing the Overlord. Everything was somewhat normal with her around.

"Your time here is limited," said Levaran. "Wardax will pull you into another memory soon."

Dr. Snowden swallowed hard. "I hate this. And he has the audacity to take on Evaran's form."

"I understand, but remember this: you're special," said Levaran. "Not many could handle what's happening now without breaking down, but you've done well. Your mind is strong. You will survive this."

He appreciated her vote of confidence, but the thought of continuing on instilled dread in him. "I wish you could come with me to the other memories."

"Know that I exist in some capacity, and those memories with me will give you some respite."

His stomach churned as the memory faded and a new one formed around him. In it, he talked with Emily.

Wardax was back. "Well, that was interesting."

Dr. Snowden shook his head. "I tire of this."

"There is much more to go," said Wardax. "While your physical body may weaken, your mind is more resilient."

Dr. Snowden did not want to lose any memories, and that thought alone kept him going. He was a prisoner, and it irked him that he could not fight Wardax.

"This Levaran, as you call her, intrigues me. It seems Evaran has other forms, yet they're different," said Wardax. "Evaran, Levaran, Sivaran. The same being, but not."

Dr. Snowden snorted. "And you'll get to deal with them. You said that you're attacked and hunted, yet you decide to fight against the most powerful being in the plane. How do you think that will end up?"

Wardax shrugged. "Perhaps, then, this has always been fated to be my last battle."

"Despite what happens to me, I'd count on it. You've experienced an angry Evaran already, and when he catches up to you, I would not expect him to be lenient."

"I understand that I may not survive this, but I must try. Being here, in your mind, has shown me a great deal about what I'm dealing with. Evaran is no common opponent, but I'll adjust. I now know his weaknesses."

"Palisin anything can be countered."

Wardax smiled. "No. That's a weakness, but a minor one. It's you, your niece, and those he cares about. He goes out of his way to protect you all, and that can be used against him. Your capture shows me this, and your memories verify it. Your value as a hostage is the most potent weapon I have."

"Then I guess you'll find out what happens when you truly anger the most powerful cosmic being in the plane."

Wardax frowned, and Dr. Snowden sensed a hint of fear in him. While he might be tied into Dr. Snowden's memories, Dr. Snowden was also tied to Wardax's senses at some level.

When Evaran was angry, he was a force to behold. Although Dr. Snowden was confident he would be rescued, he was not sure what state he would be in. He hoped for the best, but he saw that Wardax was beginning to understand that he had stepped into a fight that he might not come back from.

* * *

V surveyed the conference room. It was 9:30 a.m., and the previous day had yielded a wealth of information. Evaran sat at the head of the table with Lord Vygon and Emily to the right and Sivaran and Q on the left. V was in projected mode and sat next to Q.

These meetings provided V with observational data, which helped him understand how others acted based on what they said, and he enjoyed adding to his organic interaction library.

Emily's flaring nostrils and slightly widened eyes indicated her excitement. Today would be the day that Dr. Snowden was hopefully rescued. She also fidgeted in her seat, but she appeared ready to fight at a moment's notice. Lord Vygon was cool as always, and V detected an elevated heartbeat. That could possibly be due to his role in the upcoming mission.

Sivaran was all smiles, and V appreciated the opportunity to compare two Evarans and map their expressions. It would help V understand Evaran better. Q was his usual rigid self, and V suspected that Q was performing a similar observation of others. That would not be unexpected.

"I hope everyone is rested up," said Evaran. "We can begin." He interacted with the table console.

A holographic projection shot up of a base layout inside a mountain.

"This research facility is on a hostile planet. As the record from the data we analyzed showed something with cosmic energy exiting, we believe that is where Dr. Snowden is, which means there is also a portal there. The facility is embedded in a mountain, and the native species is some type of insectoid. The planet's atmosphere is hostile to human life, and the insectoids' tunnels form a sprawling network. There are no constructed landing spots, and entry to the tunnel system is via caves."

"Nasty place," said Emily.

Evaran nodded. "Thankfully, we will not need to be exposed to the atmosphere for long. The tunnels will lead us to the base, and security is mostly in the form of the insectoids. They will most likely be infected. There may be some enforcers, and of course a guardian, but those can be dealt with when we get there. This will require multiple steps."

Lord Vygon studied the projection. "I'm guessing these detailed layouts came from Acrolis again."

"It did," said Evaran. "It would be easy for her to gather this information, and also bear in mind, these are from when she surveyed the area. The layout might have changed since then."

"Analysis. We will adapt."

"That's the idea," said Sivaran. "Another aspect we'll probably need to watch for is a palisin mist. However, we designed an outer layer for our suits with the counter. That should nullify the mist for a while before it erodes. It may not protect against a palisin beam, but we've always had that issue."

Evaran raised a finger. "Yes, and we will need to be alert for any new surprises from Wardax." He pointed at a series of rooms on the left side. "With that said, this is where we figure Dr. Snowden is. These rooms are meant for holding prisoners, but per Acrolis, they could also be some type of research rooms." He gestured at the center of the base. "Power generation comes from there. We can deploy the countervirus at that location. However, we need to locate the portal before we do anything."

"And that's where I come in," said Lord Vygon.

"Yes. The palisin mist does not affect you, and your suit has a camouflage aspect. We are not familiar with the insectoids' abilities, so we will assume they have enhanced senses. To that end, your suit must eliminate sound, and staying out of line of sight is advisable. A scan of the insectoids will help us replicate their general smell. That should provide you with an advantage."

Lord Vygon grinned. "I like it."

V noticed that Lord Vygon's heartbeat had slowed. This must mean he was more confident. V wanted to do the reconnaissance of the portal, but his cosmic energy would give him away. In orb mode, he would stand little chance if one of the insectoids got a hold of him.

"So the plan is as follows," said Evaran. He motioned at Lord Vygon. "Once we have him ready to go, he will infiltrate the facility. After finding the portal, he will toss in the quantum beacon. Note that we have enhanced the beacon with additional abilities to hopefully glean information once it goes through. Once that is done, the rest of us will travel to the power generation room and release the virus. Sivaran and Emily will rendezvous with Lord Vygon while V and I head to Dr. Snowden's location. Once Sivaran and Emily have retrieved Lord Vygon, they will group up with me and V. Hopefully, we will have found the location by then."

"Analysis. I will need to be in body mode."

Evaran nodded. "I suspect that we will find Dr. Snowden and engage Wardax before the others arrive."

"We'll come quick," said Emily.

Q tilted his head. "Once the infected become themselves, they'll probably attack anything near them."

Sivaran motioned at Emily. "That's why she's coming with me."

"Ready when you are!" she said.

V noticed the friendly relationship between them. They had bonded, and he wondered if Emily viewed Sivaran as Evaran or something completely different. It was a data point he would like to have defined.

Lord Vygon cleared his throat. "What if we find Dr. Snowden, and he has some sort of mental breakdown? We know Wardax is mentally torturing him."

"I do not know," said Evaran. "We will discover that when we find him, but yes, that is a possibility."

"Just hold Wardax until I get there," said Emily, scowling.

Evaran nodded. "I suspect we will still be fighting when you arrive." He looked around. "Let us do the suit upgrades, then head to the planet. Everyone deal with what they need to before then."

V stood with the others. The upcoming assault would make use of his body mode. He preferred to be in orb mode, but that would make him too fragile for battle. Emily had already bounced out of the room while Lord Vygon still sat. He was probably thinking about his role with the quantum beacon. Evaran and Sivaran talked off to the side, and Q was on his way out. V was ready to fight alongside the gang again.

18

Lord Vygon's adrenaline coursed through him as the *Torvatta* descended into a murky greenish mist. The ground was highlighted and the mountain they approached had several openings obscured by the mist.

The planet's harsh atmosphere was as advertised and strange reptilian-like creatures had been spotted flying about. Emily referred to them as bat-like, but he told her he did not know what a bat was. She seemed to find that funny and mentioned something about vampires and bats.

The infiltration plan made sense, and Lord Vygon was ready for it. He hoped the portal would not close if it sensed his Daedrould energy, but he suspected it would only be impacted by those with cosmic energy. Once he had his smell altered, he would be going into some pitch-black tunnels. His helmet would protect him from the mist and also guide him.

He had a backpack that would carry the quantum beacon, and with his blunted blades and PSD, he would be set. The camouflage aspect of his suit added to the sneaking ability, and if things got hairy, the PSD would be used.

"This place sucks," said Emily.

"In what way?" asked Q.

"Analysis. She means it is not a pleasant place."

"Oh."

Emily chuckled. "Yeah, what V said. It's like a really hot day with a mist hanging around. The gravity is lighter here, too, compared to Earth." She glanced at Lord Vygon. "You might be able to super jump here."

Lord Vygon nodded at her and noted that her mood had changed. She seemed almost giddy. They were finally going to retrieve Dr. Snowden, so Lord Vygon understood her enthusiasm. However, he remained uncertain about what he would encounter. Acrolis's scan was old, and now that Wardax had Dr. Snowden, the facility would surely have been enhanced to detect and defend against what was coming. Wardax was no fool, and he had shown the ability to upgrade.

The *Torvatta* came within range of one of the caves and highlighted several insectoids scurrying around.

"Eww," said Emily, pointing at one of the zoomed windows. "Those are some big bugs."

"Sure are," said Lord Vygon.

He shared her sentiment. The mostly green insectoids stood almost six feet tall and scurried around on four legs. The body was a curved back shell, and inside it were a multitude of brown appendages of varying lengths. The face was a mess of mandibles and eyes. The bugs were essentially a shell on legs.

"They look like giant crabs sorta," said Emily.

Evaran nodded. "V, scan them so we can determine their odor properties."

"Acknowledged."

The *Torvatta* hovered over one of the insectoids that clung to the surface outside the cave.

Lord Vygon studied the readings. The insectoid was infected and pulsing circuitry-like lines covered the body and legs. He could now see four arms with claws at the end, and four smaller ones that ended in sharp bony points. The legs were strong, and both they and the shell were covered with a chitin-like armor.

"These creatures look like they could put up quite a fight," said Lord Vygon.

Sivaran pointed at the torso that was exposed inside the shell. "Yes, but they are vulnerable to stun. As long as you can keep them at range, you should be okay."

"Let's hope I don't need to fight any," said Lord Vygon.

Evaran stood and gestured at the research lab. "We have the odor properties, as well as a sample of the environment. We can replicate that aspect on your suit."

Lord Vygon followed everyone to the lab. There was a lot of pressure on him to infiltrate and toss the quantum beacon through the portal. He appreciated everything that Evaran and the others had done to this point, and the thought of figuring out where Wardax was made Lord Vygon salivate. Drydris would be avenged and then some when that time came.

He stood next to a table that Evaran had gestured at.

Evaran and Sivaran each grabbed a pen-like device and tapped at various points on Lord Vygon's suit.

"The suit will generate a small amount of the insectoids' odor once your helmet is up," said Evaran.

Sivaran grabbed a quantum beacon from the back and placed it in Lord Vygon's backpack. "Once you find the portal, all you need to do is toss this through, then we'll begin our march to the power generation room to unleash the countervirus. After that, Emily and I will come get you, or we can meet up someplace while Evaran and V retrieve Dr. Snowden." He laid a hand on Lord Vygon's shoulder. "You ready for this?"

Lord Vygon raised his head. "Just like old times." He gazed at Emily. "We'll get your uncle back, shut down this base, and find out more about Wardax's dimensional network."

Emily shook her fist. "That's what I want to hear!"

Lord Vygon loved her enthusiasm.

"Okay, to the ramp," said Evaran.

Lord Vygon followed the others, and once he arrived, he realized that the *Torvatta* was now in the cave. It was pitch black out, but he could see in the dark naturally. The insectoids scurried along the walls, ceiling, and ground. He raised his helmet.

Emily grimaced. "Wow. That's horrible."

"I take it I don't smell too good."

She ran inside the *Torvatta*.

"Be safe, and if you run into danger or need extraction, let us know," said Evaran. "A light palisin mist has been detected, but you should be okay."

Lord Vygon nodded, then activated his camouflage shielding. His breathing increased when he stepped through the *Torvatta*'s shielding and onto the rocky ground. When he peeked behind him, he saw nothing but darkness even though he knew the *Torvatta* was there. Its stealth was truly amazing.

"Can you hear us?" asked Evaran.

"Sure can," said Lord Vygon. He checked the mini-map inside his helmet. "Moving out."

He took a few steps and made sure he did not leave any tracks. When he stood still, he could hear clicking sounds reverberate. It dawned on him that the insectoids might have echolocation. That would not be good for him.

He hustled farther into the cave until it narrowed down to a large tunnel. It was rounded except for the flat ground. He wondered how the tunnels were created. Large vines came in and out along the wall, and a maze of smaller vines covered parts of the ground, ceiling, and walls.

He stuck to a side wall and entered. There were fewer infected roaming around, and thankfully, he had not been detected yet. That meant they probably did not use echolocation. He did get an up-close view of some of the insectoids as a few crossed his path. They moved aimlessly, or if there was a pattern, he did not know what it was.

After fifteen minutes, he reached what appeared to be a ring-shaped doorway. He thought that he would see some type of advanced base, but it was more of what he had come through. The difference showed itself when he passed through. Several openings led to rooms, and that was where he saw some sign of technology.

One room had strange equipment in it that he had never seen before. He recognized that it was some form of advanced tech based on the workers interacting with it. Instead of display screens, there were round bubbles that coursed with various colors. He was not sure what that was about, but it seemed to draw the insectoids' gaze.

Other rooms had infected lowered to the ground so only their shell showed. Those were probably living quarters of some type. It made him wonder what they ate. While he continued his trip, he tried to sense the portal. Its dimensional signature would be easy to detect, and as an ancient vampire lord, he had a larger detection radius than other ancient vampires.

The layout of the base from Acrolis did not line up exactly with what he was traversing, but it still had the general design right. After ten more minutes of navigating the various tunnels, he paused.

"I'm detecting the portal," he said.

"Good. Be cautious," said Evaran.

Lord Vygon sighed. "Yeah, and along the way, I also saw a larger version of these insectoids."

"We'll deal with them when we get moving," said Sivaran.

Lord Vygon appreciated their confidence. This place was a nightmare, and he would be glad to have the assistance of the others. He reached the room where the portal was. Unlike most of what he had seen up to this point, it was relatively bright due to the portal. A wooden structure ringed the portal, and vines secured it to the ground and ceiling. Several infected walked around, but they kept to the edges of the room. The portal appeared to aggravate them some.

He took out the quantum beacon and lined up in front of the portal. Although he was still far away from it, he hoped his proximity did not trigger a response.

"I'm going to throw it now," he said.

"Good luck," said Emily.

Lord Vygon focused on the portal and determined the force and trajectory. Lighter gravity was also a factor. After concentrating for a minute, he threw the quantum beacon.

It sailed through the portal.

The infected became active and roamed around when the portal briefly lit up.

He slid out of the room and ran into an unoccupied one. "It's done!"

"We have the location where it went. We can study it when Dr. Snowden is retrieved," said Evaran. "It is time to introduce ourselves. Stay safe until Sivaran and Emily meet up with you."

"Sounds good," said Lord Vygon.

His breathing increased as he watched the tunnel outside his room fill up with activity. If Wardax did not know they were there, he would now. Lord Vygon just needed to stay out of the way until Evaran and the others became the focus. Fighting in an enclosed room against a horde of fast-moving tanks was not what Lord Vygon wanted. He moved to the back of the dark room and waited. Something he was familiar with as an ancient vampire lord.

Emily's heartbeat surged as she stood on the *Torvatta* ramp. Lord Vygon had completed his part, and now the cave was bustling with activity. The insectoids ran around like they were on fire. Wardax surely knew that the base was under assault, and she suspected he would be ready for them. What form that would take remained unknown.

Evaran was calm as always and had his energy shield and utility handle out. Sivaran had his wrist-mounted blasters in place and stood alert. V was in body mode, and she thought she saw his lights flicker red for a moment while they waited.

She was confident in the group and had no doubt about what they could do. Everyone had two countervirus containers on them, as well as some palisin mist counteragent canisters, and the first goal was to reach the power generation system. Thankfully their suits also had a thin layer of a palisin repellant, but it would only last so long.

"Let us go," said Evaran, motioning forward. He charged with his shield raised. His utility handle had morphed into a staff.

Emily narrowed her eyes as she exited the protection of the *Torvatta*'s shielding.

The response to them was immediate. Insectoids began to flow toward them.

Emily repulsed a group coming from the right, while Evaran did the same on the left. Sivaran formed a metallic shield connected via rods a few feet away from his body. It smacked away the infected, and any that slipped past were tossed around by V.

They reached and entered the main tunnel.

Evaran laid a countervirus container near one of the large vines. "This should begin the process."

From what Emily had seen before, the countervirus dissemination process would take a while, but the power generation room would speed it up. She focused on the new formation that the group had adopted. Evaran led in front, while she had the rear. Sivaran had the left, and V the right. The diamond formation worked well, and they kept the infected at bay.

After fighting through several groups, they paused at a larger tunnel that slanted down. A massive insectoid, flanked by smaller ones, charged.

Its shell seemed thicker, and its claws were her size. It could do some serious damage if it grabbed a hold of anyone. She shot a repulsion beam, which swept away the smaller ones, but the larger one continued on.

Evaran ran shield-first into it and knocked the large insectoid back.

It tumbled down the hallway.

He fired a mist beam, which Emily ignited.

The large creature seized up, then stopped moving.

She was glad that the stun worked because the only other option was to go lethal. It was not the creatures' fault that they battled. They were under Wardax's control, although she figured they would fight even if in control when they saw four humanoids invading their tunnel system.

The group hustled down and swept through several more groups until they reached the power generation room.

She eyed the mass of vines that blanketed the walls. Per her helmet's interface, the vines went all through the facility. They had digital wires and bendable pipes on some, and that was probably the technical component. The center of the room had a fusion reactor that reminded her of a domed gazebo. It was covered in vines, and she thought she saw some pulse.

"Place the countervirus canisters around the reactor," said Evaran.

She wasted no time in deploying hers.

"Lord Vygon, we have placed the countervirus containers. Between the one at the entrance and the ones here, they should permeate the base here shortly. Sivaran and Emily are on their way to you now," said Evaran over comms.

"Got it," said Lord Vygon.

Sivaran tapped Emily's arm. "You ready?"

"Always," she said. She focused on Evaran and V. "You two be safe and get Uncle Albert. Save some of Wardax for me."

"Analysis. We shall," said V. He high-fived her.

She returned the high five, then nodded at Sivaran. "Let's get Lord Vygon."

They hustled out of the room.

Emily peered back and saw Evaran and V take off. They could handle themselves, but a part of her wanted to be there during the initial fight with Wardax. She gritted her teeth.

"Are you all right?" asked Sivaran as they entered another tunnel.

She sighed. "Yeah. Just a lot of pent-up anger is all."

"I understand," said Sivaran. He pointed at a swarm of insectoids massing their way. "Looks like some of the infected are no longer under Wardax's control, and they seem angry, at least from what I can tell."

Emily aimed forward. "Unfortunately for them, they're in our way." She fired a repulsion beam and dashed ahead.

Sivaran followed behind her with rods popping out of his suit, slapping away smaller insectoids.

She liked the progress they were making. Between her shield and repulsion, mixed in with stun beams, and Sivaran's rods from his suit, they cleared a path with ease. Lord Vygon had taken advantage of the chaos and moved to meet them. After ten minutes, they rendezvoused.

"Glad to see you both," said Lord Vygon, knocking away a large bug. "These things are everywhere and they seemed agitated."

"I'm just glad you're safe," said Emily.

He nodded. "Let's get your uncle."

They took off.

After another ten minutes, Evaran contacted them. "V and I have reached where Dr. Snowden is. There was a large force of enforcers initially, but they fought us, the newly released insectoids, and some of their own as the countervirus took hold."

"How is Uncle Albert?" asked Emily.

"His knee is still repairing. It seems the palisin mist has slowed down his healing ability. However, he appears to be okay, but he is unconscious."

"We're not too far away," said Sivaran.

Evaran nodded. "Be careful. I have not sensed Wardax, and I do not believe he would leave Dr. Snowden unattended. However, I have detected magnetic shielding."

Emily nodded and took off with Lord Vygon and Sivaran in tow.

After a bit, they reached where Evaran was. The room was large and contained a variety of slabs. All were empty except the one Dr. Snowden was on. Cabinets sat in the back, and vines snaked their way across the ceiling, walls, and ground. Several light strips above provided illumination. It was a stark contrast to the dark tunnels.

Emily rushed over to where Dr. Snowden lay on the slab. She grabbed his hand.

"Analysis. We removed a device that was attached to his head. It appeared to be some form of memory manipulator."

"Did it cause any damage?" asked Emily.

Evaran raised a finger. "His memories still appear to be there. However, I do not know what state they are in."

Emily laid her head on Dr. Snowden's chest. She could hear his heart.

A hologram appeared opposite them.

Emily was not sure what she was seeing, but it resembled a walnut shell suspended in the air by an army of vines.

"So ... you did come. And you tossed something into my portal before I could shut it down, which I did," said the hologram. "I believe it was a quantum beacon per Dr. Snowden's memories. Congratulations, Lord Vygon, on a job well done."

Lord Vygon growled.

"Wardax," said Evaran.

"Yes, it is I. It's no surprise you're here. I planned for this, and Dr. Snowden has been most helpful in giving me information."

Emily stepped forward, brandishing her staff. "You better not have done something to his mind!"

"Ahh, yes. Emily. Your uncle cares for you deeply, and I understand your relationship much better now," said Wardax. "Actually, I understand the overall situation. You're cosmic beings bent on removing my cosmic energy."

"It is apparent you are using it for nefarious purposes," said Evaran.

"From my perspective, I was gifted it and told to survive, and I will. You all represent the greatest threat to me at this point, but I now understand your weaknesses and tactics. If you leave now, I will consider this a misunderstanding. I left Dr. Snowden here as a sign of my goodwill. If you choose to continue your fight against me, harsher measures will be taken."

Sivaran's eyes glowed. "You've crossed a line that you can't go back over. Know that you are now a priority."

Wardax scoffed. "Yes, I know of your priorities. Very well, then. You've made your choice. On another note, your countervirus is quite effective. I haven't made a counter to it yet, but I'm working on it. However, I think it's time you met the full wrath of an Enclavian hive."

A panel in the back room slid open, showing a large purple Enclavian strapped to a vertical slab. It had smaller claws, but more legs. The shell on the back resembled the top half of a submarine sandwich.

Emily sensed the magnetic shielding surrounding the queen. That was why it hadn't been detected before.

"This is an Enclavian queen, and I suspect she's not happy," said Wardax. "You might have noticed there's no guardian here, and the area was only defended by one controller and a small enforcer group. I wanted to use magnetic shielding to trap you, like Vice Inspector Tarkaric did on your last outing. However, I didn't have time or resources to build that here. I did have time to wrap the queen in shielding and also build this…"

Another panel in the back opened up. A tray slid out with a device on it. A light magnetic shield around the device dissipated.

"Palisin bomb!" said Evaran. He rushed toward it with his energy shield out.

V and Lord Vygon grabbed Dr. Snowden and moved to a corner on the other side of the room. Sivaran rushed after Evaran.

Emily faced the bomb with her shield out while backpedaling toward V and Dr. Snowden.

A bright flash enveloped the room.

The Enclavian queen shrieked as her shield dissipated.

Emily swallowed hard when she saw Evaran and Sivaran on the ground. Evaran had taken the brunt of the blast, and even though his shield prevented some of it, the palisin energy had knocked him out. Sivaran rolled around on the ground and struggled to move. V had stopped moving, but Lord Vygon seemed to be okay. She felt the palisin energy sapping her strength. Although she was not knocked out, she had difficulty moving.

This had been Wardax's plan. He did not need to fight them directly; instead, the queen would now call upon her newly freed army to decimate a greatly weakened group. If the queen could get loose, Emily suspected she would do a lot of damage. She checked on V, whose lights flickered, but he began to move.

"We're in no position to handle what's coming to this room," said Lord Vygon. "I sense a horde approaching. Their queen is calling them."

Emily nodded. "Q, bring the *Torvatta* to here."

"Are you sure?" he asked over comms.

"Yes! Evaran, Sivaran, and V are down, and I'm greatly weakened. Uncle Albert is incapacitated, and Lord Vygon is the only one capable of fighting. There's also a swarm of angry Enclavians headed our way."

"On my way," said Q.

She struggled to stand.

Lord Vygon helped her up. "You're in no condition to fight."

"Neither are they," said Emily, gesturing at Evaran and Sivaran.

Lord Vygon stood at the entrance with his energy shield facing forward and both dual blunted blades out. "It falls to me to defend the area until the *Torvatta* arrives, then."

She admired his determination. It angered her that she could barely support herself. Dr. Snowden was already hurt, and now he would be weakened even more. At least she had sensed that he was still alive. V was coming back online, and he struggled to move. She tried to help Lord Vygon, who had already engaged a few Enclavians, but she fell down.

While she had hope that the *Torvatta* would arrive soon and that Lord Vygon could hold his own, Wardax had instilled a sense of dread. Not only had he disabled the group, but he had also mentally attacked Dr. Snowden. The situation was grim, but she knew they would pull out of this. Then it would be licking wounds time. She did not know what state Dr. Snowden would be in, and her heart sagged to think of what he had gone through.

Using immense effort, she crawled over to Lord Vygon and used her PSD to shoot repulsion beams. Although she could not contribute to the melee aspects of the fight, two PSDs were better than one. Lord Vygon seemed to appreciate the help as he almost got swarmed a few times, but he shook them each time, and his energy shield kept the bulk from surging past.

The Enclavians wanted their queen and were probably confused as to what was going on. All they knew was that their queen was in danger, and a group was preventing them from accessing her. Emily sighed as she focused on the next wave.

Lord Vygon breathed easier when Emily crawled over and helped out. He had been using repulsion beams mixed with mist and stun ones to hold back the Enclavians, but they were determined. His energy shield had proved effective, but sometimes he felt like it slowed him down. With Emily's assistance, the line was being held. She had begun to fire sticky globules, which gummed up the hallway and acted as a natural barrier.

"I think we got this," said Lord Vygon.

Emily nodded and continued firing.

Her will amazed him. She had fight in her, and then some. Despite being greatly weakened, she fought on without hesitation.

"Q! Where are you?" asked Lord Vygon over comms.

"I'm fifteen seconds away. I'll be coming in from the side of the hallway entrance."

"Hurry!" said Lord Vygon.

He was beginning to feel somewhat better about the situation, but if the queen broke out or the Enclavians found another route into the room, the others would be stationary targets. Wardax had played an almost perfect hand and had dealt the group a big blow. He now possessed the group's knowledge on tactics and weaknesses. Some of that had been utilized to get everyone to one spot, then detonate a palisin bomb. Lord Vygon was not sure who Vice Inspector Tarkaric was, but it seemed that was the tactic's origin.

The intense shrieking and claws hacking away at the glued bodies made Lord Vygon snap back to the battle. He relaxed when the *Torvatta* melted through the hallway entrance area, making the Enclavians back off. The *Torvatta* now plugged up the entrance.

Q rushed out. "I'm here."

Lord Vygon pointed at Evaran and Sivaran. "Get them!"

Q complied.

Lord Vygon helped Emily to the ramp.

"Just put me here. Get the others!" she said.

Lord Vygon hustled off and grabbed Dr. Snowden.

Q had grabbed Sivaran and met Lord Vygon at the ramp. They both went to the medical lab and laid Sivaran and Dr. Snowden on slabs. After a few minutes, Evaran, V, and Emily had been taken to the lab.

"Get us out of here!" said Lord Vygon.

Q nodded and took off.

Lord Vygon slumped against the wall. He frowned as he examined the five occupied slabs. The impact of the fight hit him hard. If this had been any other group, he would be looking at corpses, assuming he survived at all. He walked over to Emily's slab.

She grabbed his hand. "You did good."

He squeezed back. "You weren't so bad yourself, although I think you were lying around on that last part."

She laughed, then grimaced.

"Relax," said Lord Vygon. "Q is taking us somewhere safe, then I'll assist him with the others. I think you just need some time to recover from the palisin bomb."

Emily nodded. "Hopefully not too long. If Q is taking us where I think he is, we'll have time to heal, then we can come back a second after we left. To a new place, that is."

"Yeah. Is there anything I can get you?"

"Some water would be nice."

Lord Vygon patted her arm. "Say no more."

He went over the matter replicator and got a glass of water initially but saw there was a holder of some type with a straw in it. He used that and returned to Emily.

She guzzled the water.

Q entered the room. "The *Torvatta* has allowed me to use portals and time travel functionality. We are in a safe spot now outside the galaxy and in the past." He surveyed the others. "We need to secure them so they don't roll off."

Lord Vygon smiled at Emily, then followed Q.

Dr. Snowden was the first to be secured. Lord Vygon frowned at seeing the emotionless look on Dr. Snowden's face. He had been mentally tortured and blasted by the palisin bomb. He most likely would wake sore, weak, and confused, which was usually not a good combo. The crushed knee seemed to be healing based on the holographic overlay.

After Dr. Snowden was secured, they went to V. Lord Vygon had no idea what to do, but Q moved with purpose and hooked several wires up to some ports on V's body. V had jumped in front of the blast and provided a barrier that split the blast up some. Lord Vygon had not known V could move that fast, but with so much on the line, Dr. Snowden might not be here if V had not done what he had.

Evaran was next. He had taken the brunt of the blast, and seeing him lie motionless was disturbing. Q motioned at some straps, and Lord Vygon got to work. Evaran could easily break the restraints if needed, but they would at least serve to stop him from casually rolling off. Lord Vygon was not sure how to heal Evaran but suspected that, like Sivaran before, it would take time for the cosmic energy to surface again.

Sivaran was conscious and stared at the ceiling. He eyed Lord Vygon and Q when they walked over. "I hope this isn't a new habit."

Lord Vygon laid a hand on his shoulder. "I'm just glad you're okay, old friend."

"Okay and weak," he said. He eyed Q. "You're becoming quite the *Torvatta* pilot. It seems to have fully accepted you."

"It's a good ship," said Q. He peeked over at Evaran, then back at Sivaran. "You need time to rest, similar to Evaran."

Sivaran nodded. "I'm not going anywhere. At least we now have Dr. Snowden."

Lord Vygon peered over at him. "Yeah, but Wardax now has a lot of information on us."

"As expected," said Sivaran. "Wardax is not to be underestimated. He is a cosmic being and thinks like one. The fact that he used a tactic from Evaran's past was a sign of that. I suspect if he had more time, there might have been casualties."

"When we find him, he will not go quietly," said Lord Vygon.

"Probably not. I feel like we're fighting another plane form."

Q raised a finger. "My simulations show that Wardax is probably not one your plane forms."

Sivaran frowned. "I know. I'm saying he thinks like one. The palisin bomb, Enclavian Queen, and expectation we would use the virus were good defensive tactics." He stared at Lord Vygon. "He failed to factor you in, though. You got a quantum beacon through and secured the room while Q brought the *Torvatta*. I doubt any of us would be here if it weren't for you."

Lord Vygon's throat constricted. That was high praise from Sivaran. "I was just doing my part. Wardax won't make that same mistake next time we see him."

Q tilted his head. "You may become a focal point of revenge since you disrupted his plan."

"Great," said Lord Vygon. He chuckled when Sivaran returned a thumbs-up to Emily. "I guess, then, we take some time for everyone to recover."

"That's the idea," said Sivaran.

Lord Vygon furrowed his brow. "I'm still surprised that Wardax gave Dr. Snowden up."

Sivaran nodded. "I suspect that Wardax has everything he needed from Dr. Snowden. This might sound strange ... but I think Dr. Snowden was a peace offering."

"After all Wardax has done?"

Sivaran smiled. "I think Dr. Snowden may have convinced Wardax."

"Misdirection," said Lord Vygon, looking over at Dr. Snowden.

"That's my thought."

Lord Vygon nodded and spotted a chair near the front of the room. It would allow him to see both Sivaran and Emily as well as the others. The adrenaline that had pumped through him earlier was beginning to subside, and aches and pains that he had ignored to that point made themselves known. Rest time sounded blissful, along with a nice cup of blood.

The *Torvatta* made him feel safe, not something he was used to feeling on a ship. In the past, he would have been checking places to run to if spotted, but not with the *Torvatta*. He eased back into the chair he had selected and closed his eyes. Perhaps a quick nap was in order.

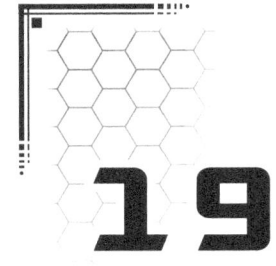

19

Dr. Snowden was not sure what was happening. One moment he was in a memory, with Wardax poking around for information on junction dimensions, the next, everything was black. Something was different. While in the memories, he always felt somewhat disconnected, but the sensations swarming him seemed real. He heard familiar voices and smelled comforting odors. More importantly, he sensed himself breathing.

"Analysis. He is waking up."

Dr. Snowden recognized V's voice. Several hands on Dr. Snowden's arm registered as new sensations. However, it was his knee pain that shot through him like a lightning bolt. He recalled Wardax crushing his knee, but the pain had been blocked after the initial feeling. Now it ran rampant. Everything suggested that Dr. Snowden was exiting the mental hell he had endured.

He focused and opened his eyes. This could be another layer of deception by Wardax. It would not be beyond what Dr. Snowden knew Wardax was capable of. A quick check of his environment showed he was on a slab. To his left were V in body mode, Sivaran, and Q, and to his right were Emily, Evaran, and Lord Vygon. The familiar feel of the *Torvatta* surrounded Dr. Snowden. A thought flashed through his mind that maybe he had really been rescued.

"You are safe now," said Evaran.

Dr. Snowden's heart pulsed as he rolled to the left and fell, although Sivaran caught Dr. Snowden's torso. He tried to move away from Evaran, who might still be Wardax.

"Whoa there," said Sivaran. "Relax, you're safe."

Emily rushed around and helped ease Dr. Snowden to the ground. "Uncle Albert! What's wrong?"

He gulped as he stared at Evaran. "How do I know this isn't some trick?"

Wardax had created some false memories where the gang had saved Dr. Snowden. He had thought they were real, but they had ended up being another deceptive ploy. This one felt different, but he would not put it past Wardax.

"It is not," said Evaran. "You talk to me as if I am Wardax." His eyes narrowed. "He used my form in your memories."

"Yeah, he did, or you did," said Dr. Snowden as his pulse quickened. He was tired of these games, and a headache rampaged through his mind.

"I assure you I am Evaran. Wardax has conditioned you to view me as him," said Evaran. He motioned at the others. "To aid in his recovery, I will leave."

Emily nodded at Evaran, then squeezed Dr. Snowden's arm. "It's okay. We're here now."

Dr. Snowden's gaze followed Evaran until he left the room.

"Wardax had you on some slab when we found you," said Emily. She hugged him.

If this was a false memory, it was well constructed, but he sensed he was back in the real world. The full weight of having so many memories altered crashed down on him. He whimpered as tears rolled down his face.

Emily hugged him tighter and in a weak voice said, "We got you."

He was confident now that the torture was over, and the new realization that his mind was messed up ate at him.

V knelt and comforted Dr. Snowden. "We will assist you in your recovery."

"Thanks, V," whispered Dr. Snowden. He took several deep breaths to normalize his breathing.

"Let's get him up," said Sivaran.

After getting back on the slab, Dr. Snowden took a moment to reflect on his situation. Now back in reality, he would need to get up to speed on everything. Although there were moments where he felt sorry for Wardax, that was no excuse for his assault. What Wardax had done was wrong, and Dr. Snowden's blood began to boil.

"I'm sure this is confusing," said Emily. "I can't believe Wardax used Evaran's form."

Dr. Snowden wiped his face. "It's not just that. He inserted himself in almost every memory I have, teasing, taunting. The only ones he didn't reach were those with Levaran and when we left the universe."

Sivaran perked up. "We suspected as much. How did it go?"

"She protected me," said Dr. Snowden. "It gave a reprieve, but only for a short time. Then it was back to giving context to my memories." He grimaced. "Wardax knows everything I know almost."

"That doesn't sound good," said Lord Vygon. "Wardax had a nasty trap waiting for us when we retrieved you."

"We might not be here if it wasn't for Lord Vygon," said Emily.

Lord Vygon nodded.

"I agree. Lord Vygon is the reason we're here now instead of being eaten by the Enclavians. Evaran and V also jumped in front of a blast that would've probably ended you." Sivaran rubbed his chin. "In regard to Levaran, she left a part of herself to guard your memories with her. No small feat, and now we are facing a cosmic opponent who knows us."

Q tilted his head. "That will need to be factored in going forward." He faced Dr. Snowden. "We can get you up to speed, but you have some concern with seeing Evaran."

"It's not him, it's just … subconsciously, I see him as the enemy, but consciously, I know he isn't," said Dr. Snowden.

"Analysis. He can interface with you to clear your mind of Wardax's interaction."

Dr. Snowden frowned. "As if we have time for that."

Emily raised her brow. "Did you forget we're on the *Torvatta*?"

"No … but I don't know how long it would take to do all that."

Sivaran studied Dr. Snowden. "I can scan and determine what's needed, and then with Evaran's help, we'll get you back to your old self."

Dr. Snowden's throat constricted. "I'd like that."

"Analysis. Then it will be done. Are you hungry?"

"I am, actually."

"Perhaps a delicious burger and some fries will cheer you up."

Dr. Snowden smiled. "Yeah, that sounds great." He glanced at Sivaran. "Please let Evaran know I'm not angry with him. I just need some time to adjust."

"He knows," said Sivaran. "You get some food and drink in you, and I'll consult with Evaran on our next step."

Dr. Snowden nodded. "Thank you. I'm glad you're here." He looked around. "All of you."

Emily and V helped him stand while the others left the room.

"I'm so glad you're back," said Emily.

"Yeah, me too," said Dr. Snowden.

He shuddered as he exited and saw Evaran and Sivaran talking. It angered Dr. Snowden that his body had reacted the way it had. Evaran was the same person he had always known. It would take time, and Dr. Snowden was not familiar with the process to reverse what Wardax had done. Why memories of Evaran and Sivaran did not have the same resistance as the Levaran memories was a mystery—hopefully one that could be resolved.

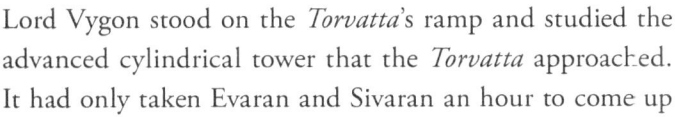

Lord Vygon stood on the *Torvatta*'s ramp and studied the advanced cylindrical tower that the *Torvatta* approached. It had only taken Evaran and Sivaran an hour to come up with a solid plan.

Dr. Snowden would be taken to a safe place outside the *Torvatta* and they would work on cleaning up memories. The *Torvatta* would then jump forward two months and pick them up. During that time, they would analyze the data gleaned from the quantum beacon as well as planning the next step. It amazed Lord Vygon the options that opened when time traveling was as easy as taking a walk.

Dr. Snowden stood front and center on the *Torvatta*'s ramp, with Sivaran and Emily helping him stand. Lord Vygon, Q, and V stood behind Dr. Snowden. Evaran was in the command center, and his absence did not go unnoticed. It must be a strange feeling to know you trusted someone, but your body said otherwise.

According to Evaran, they were on Earth in AD 514,723 in the universe the gang came from. They were to meet someone named Kess, who was Dr. Snowden's girlfriend. The fact she resided half a million years ahead of Dr. Snowden's time period intrigued Lord Vygon. Surprise was a constant state when on the *Torvatta*. This was also his first excursion to another universe. Evaran had already contacted Kess, and in the communication window, Lord Vygon watched her move like she was on fire before the call had ended. She and Dr. Snowden must have a very strong relationship.

The *Torvatta* landed on a landing pad that sat outside an expansive apartment.

"We're here," said Emily. She and Sivaran escorted Dr. Snowden off.

Lord Vygon's eyes narrowed when he saw what must be Kess streaking toward Dr. Snowden. She had tan skin and was about five foot eight. Her advanced suit stood out, and he sensed several exotic energies on her. She was probably very powerful. He exited with the others.

Kess hugged Dr. Snowden. "Albert! Are you okay?"

"Not really," he said, frowning.

She pecked him on the cheek and then stood back. "So he had some sort of mind invasion thing?"

Emily nodded. "Some cosmic being named Wardax. Thankfully, we think there's a way to reverse it. Uncle Albert just needs a comfortable place to do it, so here we are."

"It's so odd not to think of the *Torvatta* as a safe place to heal up. Nonetheless, you came to the right place, then," said Kess. She went up and hugged a startled Lord Vygon. "Glad to see you again."

He hugged her back. "I think you met another version of me specific to this universe."

"Oh," said Kess, drawing her head back some. "Evaran didn't mention that."

"There's a lot going on."

"Apparently," said Kess. She eyed Sivaran. "And you feel like Evaran but don't look like him. How much did I miss exactly?"

Emily gestured at her. "You remember Evaran had eight plane forms that entered the plane initially?"

"Yeah," said Kess.

"Sivaran is the sixth. I'm surprised Evaran didn't mention that."

Kess flung her arm in the air and snapped at Sivaran. "Well, get over here for a hug, then. All Evarans are welcome here."

Sivaran returned her hug. "It's good to meet you. I suspect we'll get to know each other well over the next two months." He motioned at Q. "This is Q, an AI that travels with me."

Kess laughed when Q offered a high five. She returned it, then did the same with V. "I'm glad to meet Q, and always happy to see V again." She faced Lord Vygon. "And you're not staying, right?"

"I'm not," said Lord Vygon. "From my perspective, I'll board the *Torvatta*, fly up, jump forward two months, then come back down. V and Q will be joining me. It will only take the amount of time to get to orbit, time travel, and fly back."

Kess nodded. "I see. I know Evaran will come out once we're settled, then." She faced the others. "Let's get Albert situated, then I can get fully up to speed."

Lord Vygon continued to study her as she led Emily, Sivaran, and Dr. Snowden away. Kess was full of life, and Lord Vygon could see why Dr. Snowden was attracted to her. She had an aura of authority about her, which made sense given her position. Lord Vygon suspected she would catch up on everything quickly.

Although he wanted to stay, he understood that the focus was on Dr. Snowden being healed. The fewer distractions, the better. Another thought was that maybe Evaran and Sivaran had an ulterior motive for him staying away. It might be due to there already being a Lord Vygon in this universe, and Evaran and Sivaran wanted to minimize potential conflicts. He continued to ponder it as he walked to the *Torvatta* with V and Q.

Evaran waited on the ramp with a hover slab packed with equipment.

"Looks like it's your turn to disembark," said Lord Vygon.

"It is," said Evaran.

Lord Vygon was fascinated by Evaran's seemingly emotionless face. However, the quick solution and jump to this place and point in time showed how serious he was about resolving the problem. It boggled Lord Vygon's mind that they could even stop everything indefinitely to do whatever.

He laid a hand on Evaran's shoulder. "I hope you can restore Dr. Snowden's mind. You mean a lot to him despite what his body might be showing."

Evaran nodded. "It will take some effort, but the plan is sound. Once this is done, Wardax will be dealt with."

"Looking forward to it," said Lord Vygon.

He watched Evaran head out. From what little Lord Vygon understood, Dr. Snowden's recovery involved going in and manually removing Wardax from every memory he infected. That sounded impossible to Lord Vygon, but that word was losing its meaning the more he was on the *Torvatta*. He popped into the command center, where V and Q stood at the front console.

"Analysis. It is time for us to go."

Q nodded.

After twenty minutes, they were in low orbit.

Lord Vygon shuddered when everything outside disappeared, then eased back in. Although he had seen it when they had traveled to Drydris in the past, it still unsettled him.

The *Torvatta* descended, and another twenty minutes later, it had landed on Kess's landing pad.

Seeing Dr. Snowden joking and laughing with Evaran, Sivaran, Emily, Kess, and some doglike alien seemed like a good sign. Lord Vygon joined V and Q as they departed the *Torvatta*.

"Lord Vygon! V! Q!" said Dr. Snowden.

"Analysis. You seem much better."

Dr. Snowden tapped his chest. "Oh yeah. I think I got a mental cleanse on top of the purge. I feel great."

Q tilted his head. "So all the memories Wardax infected are cleaned now?"

"All of them."

Evaran raised a finger. "There was no memory loss either. The more memories were cleaned, the easier it became to undo the later ones."

"He's strong like that," said Kess, winking. She gestured at the doglike alien. "Oh, this is Ambassador Jago, a good friend of the gang."

Ambassador Jago shook hands with Lord Vygon and Q, then high-fived V. "I was wondering where my high-fiving friend was."

"He is here," said V, smiling.

"I'm just glad Uncle Albert is back to his old self," said Emily.

Lord Vygon embraced Dr. Snowden. "As am I. It pained me to see you in that previous state."

He nodded. "As much as I would like to stay here, we still have Wardax to capture." He faced Kess. "I wish you could come with."

"You know I would if I wasn't in the middle of some delicate negotiations. And, yes, I know you could hop forward to the end of the negotiations and pick me up, but I don't know if there would be other things to consider. You might be hopping for a bit."

"I know," said Dr. Snowden, frowning.

Kess glanced at Lord Vygon. "I got to know Sivaran quite well, but I wish I had more time to know you and Q."

"Likewise," said Lord Vygon.

"Perhaps when this is over, we can visit," said Q.

Kess stared at Evaran.

"I cannot promise anything until the situation is resolved," he said.

"I'm teasing you." Kess looked around. "I'm going to miss having you all here for two months."

"As am I," said Ambassador Jago. "Another Evaran … just when I thought I'd seen it all."

The group chuckled.

"We can board the *Torvatta*," said Evaran. "I'm sure Dr. Snowden and Kess would like a moment."

Lord Vygon watched as everyone moved to the *Torvatta*'s ramp except for Dr. Snowden and Kess. They kissed and held each other. Ambassador Jago had come along with the others to the ramp and talked animatedly with Evaran and Sivaran. Lord Vygon wished he had two months of uninterrupted chaos to relax, but he would not stop until Wardax was gone.

Thankfully, Dr. Snowden seemed to be okay now, and the mission could continue. It impressed Lord Vygon that Evaran had friends where he could drop in for two months unannounced. Although Lord Vygon had traveled some with Sivaran, those experiences were far different than traveling with Evaran. Lord Vygon enjoyed the calm and peaceful moment.

A thought went through his mind about him, Sivaran, and Q maybe coming to this timeline. Lord Vygon was not sure what the rules were for two Evarans or moving timelines, but events like Wardax's ascension could be dealt with before they destroyed planets. For now, Lord Vygon soaked everything in.

20

Emily smiled before downing some orange juice in the conference room. She had gotten in an excellent workout, and it was 9:15 a.m., fifteen minutes before a meeting. The past day had been great. Dr. Snowden was back, and he had caught up on everything. It did her heart good to see him interact with Evaran as if nothing had happened. If anything, they seemed closer now.

The previous two months had been a drastic change of pace. It was not normal that they would stop in the middle of dealing with something to do that. It showed Evaran's commitment to protecting one of the gang, no matter how long it took. Sivaran had been fun as he and Kess had talked and gotten to know each other. Emily had enjoyed spending time with them both.

Kess had been a fireball of energy as she doted over Dr. Snowden. When Evaran and Sivaran did their memory cleanup thing, Emily hung with Kess and learned more about her. Emily appreciated being taken everywhere. Even Ambassador Jago had come out, and Emily enjoyed seeing his face when he learned of the situation, especially about Sivaran.

Unfortunately, now they had to deal with Wardax. Her eyes flared just thinking of him. He was the craftiest opponent the gang had faced yet, and he seemed to have no problem violating Dr. Snowden's mind. It did not help that Wardax had cosmic energy, and they had not seen his true form to this point unless it was that vine hologram thing. She chomped down on her sausage and egg burrito.

Dr. Snowden entered and went to the matter replicator. "Hey!"

"Hey right back at ya," she said.

He got his coffee and sat across from her. "So glad to have my mind back."

"I bet. How're you feeling today?" asked Emily.

"Great! Although … I do miss waking up to Kess," said Dr. Snowden.

Emily flashed her hands off to the side. "Who wouldn't, right? That's what she would say."

"Yeah, you're right about that," said Dr. Snowden. He sipped his coffee.

Evaran, Sivaran, Q, V, and Lord Vygon arrived. While they took their seats, Lord Vygon picked up a glass of blood, then sat.

"I hope everyone is rested," said Evaran, glancing at Dr. Snowden.

"I'm one hundred percent ready to go," he said.

Lord Vygon nodded at him. "It's good to have you back."

"Analysis. I am glad Evaran does not repulse you anymore."

Dr. Snowden grinned. "Yeah, he can do that sometimes."

Evaran eyed him. "It seems we are in a good mood as well." He raised a finger. "As you all know, Sivaran and I had two months to discuss our next steps."

"I missed this," said Dr. Snowden.

"And you were missed," said Sivaran.

Dr. Snowden gestured at Evaran. "Sorry. Continue."

"It is okay," said Evaran with a half smile. He interacted with the table console.

A projection shot up a galactic map with dots.

"Acrolis had a good mapping of the Zayt Empire as she came across installations. However, these were done as fast as she could travel, so some of this data may be out of date. We know our countervirus works, and Wardax has no response to it that we know of at this point in time. The next step is to travel to the past and place the virus in a container that will release it in this time period. The container will be buried deep in the ground, then bore up into the Zayt facility at a later date."

"What about the dimensional network? Can that be used?" asked Lord Vygon.

"Unfortunately not," said Evaran. "However, the quantum beacon confirmed that there is a trace of cosmic energy running through the network. We suspect that is how Wardax is able to sustain it, thus providing gateways to move around and extend his control to guardians. Without that cosmic energy, the network collapses. It also confirms that our hypothesis about Wardax sending a palisin mist via the network was incorrect. It would not be able to exist there. Per Dr. Snowden,

ADAIR HART

he was shown the space station after our assault. Wardax had the palisin energy behind magnetic shielding furthest away from the docking bays, then unleashed it when we arrived. That is why we did not detect it."

Lord Vygon growled. "Wardax is so devious. He needs to lose that cosmic energy."

"Oh, he will," said Sivaran.

Emily tilted her head. "So this is a test run, basically?"

"Yes," said Evaran. "If this works, then we can place these on all the locations in the past so that, when we return to the present, every facility will be freed simultaneously."

"*Then* we focus on Wardax," said Lord Vygon. "He'll be without the Zayt Empire and all he'll have left is the dimensional network with nothing to connect to. I love it."

Evaran nodded.

"Umm ... not to be a downer here, but there are thousands of dots," said Dr. Snowden.

Sivaran pointed at him. "Noticed that, did you? The solution is that Evaran and I, along with Q and V, will deploy them. It may take months, but from yours and the others' perspective, it should only be the amount of time it takes to leave and come back from Acrolis's home base."

"Makes sense," said Dr. Snowden. "I'd prefer to stay on the *Torvatta* in that time, though."

"It's your choice," said Sivaran. He glanced at Emily and Lord Vygon. "You two as well. This was an attempt to avoid what may be a somewhat tedious task."

Emily nodded at Dr. Snowden. "I go where he goes."

"Same here," said Lord Vygon.

"I can just feel the love," said Dr. Snowden.

The group laughed.

"Very well," said Evaran. "Sivaran can retrieve the device that will bury itself, then head to the ramp. The rest of us can go to the command center and begin our trial run."

"Let's do this!" said Emily as she stood.

It felt good to be back to work and have a solid plan. She imagined Wardax's face when the full weight of the countervirus attack from the past hit him. There were still a lot of unknown variables, though. The devices could be detected and destroyed or even fail to start up. Wardax might even already have a counter.

She joined the others in the command area and took her seat next to Dr. Snowden in the left U-shaped seating area. Q and V stood at the console, while Lord Vygon sat on the other side. Evaran was in his large command chair, and she caught a glimpse of Sivaran wheeling out a cylindrical device on wheels.

"V, take us to the planet I have marked. We will assess its current state," said Evaran.

"Acknowledged," said V.

The *Torvatta* opened a portal and flew through.

Emily frowned at the stations she saw in orbit. There should have been ships, but it seemed still, with just the stations floating around. A closer scan revealed the stations in structural disarray. After twenty minutes, the *Torvatta* cruised over an apocalyptic wasteland. Although the native species were present, they were focused on factories of some kind that spewed a noxious-looking gas.

"What is all this?" asked Dr. Snowden.

Lord Vygon sighed. "This is what Wardax does. Once a civilization is infected and under his control, they turn into slaves, essentially, assuming he decides not to destroy the place."

"It's horrible," said Emily. She pointed at a city in the distance. "That looks empty, yet the area around the factory seems to be slums of some sort."

Lord Vygon nodded. "While infected, the natives have no concern about their surroundings. I suspect conditions are worse than we know for them."

Evaran interacted with his chair console. "They will have a chance to be free." He pointed at a location a few miles away from the outskirts of the factory town. "That is where the beacon needs to be buried. V, take us up, then back a hundred years."

"Acknowledged," said V.

The *Torvatta* reached low orbit.

Emily watched the familiar fade out and in of everything outside the *Torvatta*. She grimaced at the advanced ships and orbital structures that now appeared to be bustling with activity. The civilization had no idea what was to happen.

"How is the virus going to be deployed?" she asked. "It worked on a station and base, but this is a whole planet."

Evaran nodded. "The canister will deploy the countervirus in aerosol form."

"Airborne," said Lord Vygon. "That makes sense."

Q raised a finger. "Due to the design of the virus, the effect should cover the world in less than a week."

"That's efficient," said Lord Vygon.

The *Torvatta* descended, and after another twenty minutes, it hovered over the designated spot Evaran had selected in the future.

"Deploying now," said Sivaran over comms.

Emily's eyes were glued to the window showing him pushing the canister off the ramp. Once the canister hit the ground, it burrowed in. The strange foam it released caught her eye.

"What's that?" she asked.

Evaran half smiled. "It is a nano swarm foam that will create a structure to fill in the hole. The surrounding dirt will be pulled in, and as it goes down, it ensures that the hole is plugged. Once the canister is ready to surface, the nano swarm loosens the path."

"That's a good idea," said Dr. Snowden. "It sucks knowing what's going to happen to this civilization."

"I concur," said Evaran. "V, take us to this location a moment before the canister deploys its payload."

"Acknowledged."

The *Torvatta* reached low orbit after twenty minutes, jumped forward one hundred years, then flew down.

Emily motioned at the data window. "Look, there's the canister!"

The canister paused when it broke the surface. It whirred and clicked, then spewed the countervirus.

Emily was thankful that the *Torvatta* highlighted the countervirus since it was colorless and too small to see otherwise.

"V, take us two weeks into the future," said Evaran.

"Acknowledged."

After the *Torvatta* did so, Emily studied the chaotic factory town they hovered over. The buildings were half demolished, and the slums were a war zone.

"Getting their free will back was not a smooth transition, it seems," said Dr. Snowden.

Evaran rubbed his chin. "Yes. It will take time for this civilization to heal. The months ahead will be rough, and this species' resiliency will be tested." He raised a finger.

"However, they are free now to choose their path instead of letting Wardax do so."

Dr. Snowden shook his head. "I hope they come out of it. I guess we know the process works with the countervirus burrowing up. Back to the past?"

"That is the plan," said Evaran. "V, take us back one hundred years and we can begin the process of seeding these canisters."

"Acknowledged."

Emily frowned as she continued to watch the chaos unfold. They were leaving to do this in all the places where the Zayt Empire had been, and she suspected the body count would be tremendous. Wardax had brought this on those civilizations, and she hoped that after he was gone, they could heal. Looking at all the fighting below, she did not think it would be a quick process.

———

Lord Vygon found the first few deployments to be routine. The *Torvatta* would portal to a location, descend, drop the canister, and wait until it reached its destination, then it was on to the next planet. Each stop was a minimum of forty minutes, and it was now 2:00 p.m. per the clock showing on the front wall. There were thousands to do, and tedious was an apt description of what was to come.

He had enjoyed lunch with Emily, Dr. Snowden, and Q. Evaran, Sivaran, and V stayed in the command center, but Lord Vygon knew he would have plenty of time with them. Sivaran handled the drops, while V controlled the piloting.

Evaran watched over it all. Lord Vygon was impressed by their almost robot-like precision.

Lunch on the other hand had been animated. It was good to see Dr. Snowden joking around, and even Q got into the mood. Dr. Snowden's zeal for life was infectious. It paid to have friends like Evaran, especially when your mind was violated.

Lord Vygon was now back in the command center with everyone else and reflected on how unique it was to be where he was. The planets they had visited already had advanced civilizations. Each one would succumb to Wardax and the Zayt, and it reminded him of Drydris. He wished it could have been spared, but it was what it was.

All he could do was try to figure out a new path for the last remaining ancient vampires. One advantage they had was they could create members much easier as lords. An alert beeped as he studied the planet they orbited.

A screen popped up showing a large exotic energy signature on the ground.

"Analysis. Alkarin exotic energy detected."

"Alkarin energy? Never heard of that," said Emily.

"Lightmires," said Dr. Snowden.

Emily shrugged. "And that is…"

Dr. Snowden raised a finger. "They're like the opposite of vampires on Earth. Not many of them, and they congregate in specific locations. They use advanced technology on par with the Helians, and instead of drinking blood, they eat diseases and heal others."

Lord Vygon tilted his head. "That's an interesting type of being. You said they're our opposites? Assuming, that is, that the vampires you know are like us."

"Well, from what I understand, vampires draw life, lightmires give it."

"Your planet is even stranger than I imagined." Lord Vygon gestured at the signature. "Do lightmires appear like that?"

"They do not," said Evaran. "This must be a pure Alkarin entity. Lightmires are the product of the bonding between Alkarin energy and an organic host. However, I am certain that whatever is on the planet is unique."

"What we do we do?" asked Emily.

"We investigate. V, take us down for a deeper scan," said Evaran.

"Acknowledged."

After twenty minutes, the *Torvatta* approached a ten-foot tall, semitransparent cube with a red glow around it. Barren and scorched land surrounded the cube for miles. A window zoomed in and showed something inside, but it did not move.

"What is all this?" asked Dr. Snowden.

"Burnt land around the cube and the local civilization avoiding the area makes it seem like the cube isn't friendly," said Lord Vygon.

"I agree. I have no record of this energy type," said Q.

Sivaran nodded. "I didn't until I synced with Evaran."

Dr. Snowden glanced at Evaran. "So ... friendly or not?"

He half smiled. "Like many things in life, it may or may not be. Whatever it is, it might be an ally against Wardax."

"I guess we'll find out," said Emily.

The *Torvatta* landed outside the cube.

Evaran and Sivaran stood.

"Wait here," said Evaran. They exited the *Torvatta*.

Lord Vygon sat up as he peered out the transparent front wall. He appreciated that he saw with clarity. There had to be some type of audio enhancement because he could hear their footsteps. That probably meant they could talk and be heard in the command center.

Evaran scanned the cube with his ring. He tilted his head. "Acrolis is inside this structure."

"Acrolis?" asked Dr. Snowden. "What the heck is she doing in there?"

"I do not know," said Evaran.

He and Sivaran stepped back as a red tendril formed a diamond-shaped swirling mass of red energy that hovered off the ground.

"What are you?" it asked in a slow, deep voice.

"I am Evaran, and with me is Sivaran. Who are you?"

"I am a sentry of Kingartochores."

"I am not familiar with that name. Why is Acrolis inside this structure?" asked Evaran.

The sentry pulsed. "She is a prisoner."

"She is our friend."

"Then your presence is unwelcome," said the sentry. It washed over Evaran and Sivaran but dissipated along with the cube.

"What just happened?" asked Lord Vygon.

"Cosmic energy is more powerful than Alkarin," said Q.

Evaran and Sivaran walked over and picked up a slumped-over Acrolis.

Lord Vygon found it hard to believe that someone as powerful as Acrolis could not only appear weakened but also be captured and held. She squinted around in confusion as if she was trying to figure out what was going on.

"What ... how?" asked Acrolis.

Evaran offered her his hand. "Allow us to take you from here."

She accepted his support and struggled to stand. "I don't understand. How'd you defeat the sentry?"

Evaran and Sivaran began to escort her to the *Torvatta*.

"It is a long story," said Evaran. "However, the sentry attacked us and failed in its attempt."

A large bolt of red energy struck the ground before them. It re-formed into a swirling mass.

They laid Acrolis down and then stood in front of her.

"I am Kingartochores, god of this world. What are you doing?"

Evaran nodded. "We are taking Acrolis from this place. Do not be foolish, as we will not be lenient in a second altercation."

"I make the rules here. You have no authority over me."

"I disagree with that assessment," said Evaran.

Sivaran crooked a thumb at Evaran. "What he said."

"You may have destroyed my sentry, but it was just that, a sentry. You now face me!"

"For a god, you talk a lot," said Sivaran. "As Evaran said, don't do something you'll regret. Just go. This is our last warning."

Kingartochores extended a hand and shot a red beam at Evaran.

He reflected it back with his energy shield.

Kingartochores streaked toward Evaran.

When Kingartochores came within ten feet of him, he solidified into a humanoid form. "What ... what is this?"

"A consequence being realized," said Evaran.

His and Sivaran's eyes and hands glowed as they touched Kingartochores's shoulders.

Kingartochores shuddered, then cried out as glowing yellow lines coursed over his body before he exploded into a mist, which dissipated.

Lord Vygon stood. "Now what happened?"

Dr. Snowden drew a circle in the air. "Any energy being solidifies when entering Evaran's aura. After that, well, king whatever just got vaporized."

"He is correct," said Evaran, picking up Acrolis with Sivaran's help. "Normally, with a lesser energy being, I can do that. With someone as powerful as Kingartochores, I cannot."

"With two Evarans, though, not a problem," said Sivaran. "I wish it hadn't gone that far, but he was warned."

"Huh," said Emily. "I guess if Sivaran had been with us when we faced Chuuldragra, he coulda been vaporized too."

Evaran nodded. "As it was only me, the *Torvatta*'s tractor beam worked well in that situation."

"These names are cracking me up. I can't even fathom how anything other than two Evarans would have fought that king guy," said Lord Vygon.

"Not successfully is how," said Q.

Lord Vygon shrugged. "I guess so."

Evaran and Sivaran returned with Acrolis and went to the medical lab. The others joined them.

Acrolis relaxed on a slab. "I'm regaining my sense of self, but something is interfering with my abilities still."

Evaran gestured around. "It is the *Torvatta*, my ship, that is dampening you. However, we have a beam that should revitalize you. It may take a while."

"Why are you helping me? I've been a prisoner of King-artochores for so long, I've lost track of time."

"Rest for now," said Evaran. "When you are fully healed, we can discuss this in some detail. There is a lot to discuss, and our meeting, while seeming coincidental, is most likely not. Do not be startled by the planar beam."

She lay back and stared at the ceiling as a light blue beam began to wash over her. "I didn't catch your names."

"I am Evaran, and with me is Sivaran. As for the others, we can go over that when you're fully back to yourself."

Acrolis sighed. "Thank you for my rescue. This whole thing is strange, but I trust you for some reason."

Lord Vygon's mind raced as he thought about the meeting with Acrolis in the future. She seemed to know them, and this must be the event that had caused that. It made sense when looking at a timeline from an objective perspective, but definitely confusing when viewed from his personal one. He wondered how often that occurred when traveling with Evaran, because Dr. Snowden, Emily, and V acted like this was nothing new. What a strange, yet exciting, group to be with.

Dr. Snowden enjoyed his pork chop dinner with mashed potatoes. The discussion of Acrolis had him intrigued. She had been regenerating via the planar beam for the last three hours, and per V, she was almost back to full health. The dinner discussion covered what exactly a matter mage was and how it could control matter within a range.

Per Evaran, a matter mage was a subatomic entity that could re-form matter. Planar beings resided in various levels of existence, and Dr. Snowden recalled beings like Bob and Sam from a previous adventure who could mimic anything. Dr. Snowden had met a few matter mages, so he was aware of their limitations and weaknesses. He would add Alkarin energy as a weakness.

Lord Vygon had a lot of questions about Alkarin energy and lightmires. Dr. Snowden figured that mentioning them as opposites must have intrigued Lord Vygon. The fact that the *Torvatta* kept Lord Vygon from the knowledge base remained a mystery as all his questions could easily be answered there. Emily was also curious about lightmires. Dr. Snowden only knew of them because he had met another professor at a conference who was one.

Q had gotten up to speed and appreciated the exotic energy database the *Torvatta* maintained. Like Lord Vygon, Q asked a lot of questions, mainly about other exotic energies. V was able to answer most, as were Evaran and Sivaran. Dr. Snowden appreciated Q's curiosity, and he could see where Q would be a valuable resource with Sivaran.

Everyone dispersed after dinner, and Dr. Snowden retreated to his living quarters. After cleaning up, he relaxed in his recliner. It was the site of many a great nap, and with good food and discussion in him, he closed his eyes.

His PSD buzzed.

He sighed as he spawned a holographic screen from it. It seemed Acrolis was fully healed and eager to chat. Dr. Snowden now wished he had maybe held off on dinner. He wanted to learn more about Acrolis's situation and its bearing on the current state of events, but his mind begged for a quick nap. He stood and stretched. A cup of coffee was needed.

He got one after going to the conference room. A quick check around the room showed everyone to be there. Evaran sat at the head of the table as always, and Acrolis was opposite him. To his left were Sivaran and Q, and to the right were Emily and Lord Vygon. Dr. Snowden took his seat next to Q.

Evaran gestured at Acrolis. "I am sure you have a lot of questions. However, before we begin, let me describe the current situation to you."

Acrolis nodded. "Please do."

"We are from a hundred years in the future where a cosmic being named Wardax and his Zayt Empire have been conquering system after system. The only planet to truly stand against them was razed," said Evaran.

Lord Vygon sighed.

Acrolis studied him, then faced Evaran. "You're time travelers. That was unexpected, but not too surprising."

"Really?" asked Dr. Snowden.

Acrolis waved around. "You all freed me from arguably one of the most powerful beings I've ever met, fed me a planar beam of some type, and this ship … being able to time travel is the least surprising."

"You are wise," said Evaran. He gestured at Acrolis. "As for our effort to learn more about Wardax, Sivaran suggested we meet with you, and we did. You provided us with critical information on the Zayt Empire."

"This meeting would have an impact on that meeting in the future," said Acrolis.

"It did, but you did not mention this meeting. We most likely told you not to say anything."

Dr. Snowden motioned at her. "I think you're told about my capture by Wardax and his assault on my mind. You told me to be strong, and I think it was in reference to that."

"As I now know that, that sounds like me," said Acrolis. "So what did I give you all in our first meeting?"

"A galactic map with every planet and stellar object that the Zayt were in control of. Some of it is outdated, but that is mostly due to the distances involved," said Evaran. "I think we were meant to find you so you can go create the map that you will give us in the future."

Acrolis shook her head. "A predestination paradox. You were always meant to come here to free me so I would do this. If you gave me the map, that would add an information paradox, so I suspect your not giving me the map is to keep the paradoxes to a minimum."

"Quite right." Sivaran waved a hand around. "Not that hard to run into these types of situations when you have a ship that can time travel."

"I guess not."

Dr. Snowden rubbed his chin. "Well … I would suggest that if Acrolis is going to do this, why not deploy the canisters too? Assuming that she is planning on doing this."

Acrolis grinned. "You all saved me, and I'm in your debt. If this will help you in the future, I have no problem with it. What's in the canisters?"

"A countervirus to the one Wardax uses to infect civilizations and control them," said Evaran.

Acrolis leaned back in her chair. "So Wardax is going around and infecting everything?"

"Yes. Observe," said Evaran. He interacted with the table console.

A projection shot up of a planet being infected and its aftermath.

"Why don't we just stop it before it happens?" asked Acrolis, eying Evaran.

"It's because we're a part of events, and that's not what happened," said Emily.

Acrolis steepled her fingers. "How interesting. So in order to maintain timeline integrity, a certain set of events needs to occur. If they don't … then I suspect the future changes."

"Yeah, and we try to avoid that," said Sivaran. He glanced at Acrolis. "I've known you for some time, in the future that is, but I didn't know you knew all this at the time. You keep secrets well."

"Of course. I may be a matter mage, but I like to think of myself as a knowledge mage. Secrets are a part of that."

Dr. Snowden found Acrolis's acceptance of the situation to be what he had expected. He had to stop sometimes and take a step back to take everything in. Evaran was by far the most powerful entity Dr. Snowden had ever met. Sivaran was another version of Evaran. Lord Vygon was a powerful ancient vampire lord. As a matter mage, Acrolis added another power player. Then there were V and Q, two strong AIs. Tack on Emily, and the room exuded raw power. Wardax's mental violation made Dr. Snowden look at things in a fresh light, and he loved being back in the thick of things.

"There is one last thing before we break," said Evaran. He half smiled at Acrolis. "You need a safe home base."

A projection shot up of a planet.

"Are you aware of this place?" asked Evaran.

"No, but I'm guessing this is my home base in the future." Acrolis studied the projection. "It's isolated enough."

Sivaran nodded. "The planet has natural defenses against being detected, and there are many lava tubes underneath in which to form a home base."

"So then we go there, you give me your canister blueprints as well as the countervirus specifics, and I'll begin my exploration," said Acrolis.

Dr. Snowden had wondered how they were going to fit thousands of containers at Acrolis's home base, but it was another example of a matter mage's power. Acrolis would just create what was needed when she got to the planet. That way she would not need to travel with anything. That assumed the materials were readily available, though.

"It will be done, and we appreciate you assisting us," said Evaran.

"I'm just glad to be free. Exploring is something I *need* to do. I've been imprisoned for too long," said Acrolis.

"Very well," said Evaran. "V, take us to Acrolis's home base."

"Acknowledged."

Everyone stood.

Dr. Snowden appreciated the plan. If everything worked as expected, then when they went to the future, Wardax would lose his empire in one fell swoop. That would leave him vulnerable. The depths of his crime needed to be dealt with, and Dr. Snowden anxiously awaited Wardax receiving judgment.

21

Emily studied Acrolis as she wandered around a lava tube in what would be her eventual home base. Everyone had gathered outside the *Torvatta*, and they stood in a massive tunnel. To even get there required going through lava, something that seemed to thrill Acrolis. She had been a nonstop chatterbox the whole way.

Emily understood her reaction. She had been imprisoned for an unknown amount of time, and her captor no longer existed. Now she had a home base that had natural defenses, such as being hard to reach and detect. She bounced around and spouted off ideas on how to fix up the place.

Emily went over the fight with Kingartochores. It had given her goose bumps to see both Evaran and Sivaran completely destroy him. She had never seen that before, and it was hard to surprise her anymore. Even if they were to have spared him, she was not sure he would have sat back and let things pass.

He most likely would have come after them in some capacity, or even become another Wardax in time or possibly his ally.

Dr. Snowden bumped her and gestured at Acrolis. "Reminds me of when you graduated high school."

Emily wrapped her arm around his. "Yeah, I can see how being in a lava tube is similar."

He eyed her, then they laughed.

Dr. Snowden's return made everything seem all right, even if they were deep underground with searing lava nearby. V was flying around and scanning while Evaran, Sivaran, Lord Vygon, and Q took the brunt of Acrolis's discussions. It sounded like a one-way discussion. Acrolis had the canister and countervirus design and replicated a few with ease. A scan showed them to be identical to the test one that had already been deployed.

The plan that had been designed to take out the Zayt Empire took some time to figure out, but she liked it. From their perspective, they would hop back to the future, and Acrolis would have all the canisters deployed. Although that had not been known by the gang during their first meeting with her, she had known. Meeting her in the future again would be interesting.

Acrolis waved at a large rocky wall and opened a tunnel into it. "Yes, this place will do nicely." She faced the group. "Once I'm done here, I'll begin my trip across the stars."

Evaran nodded. "Very well. We shall meet again, of course."

"I look forward to it."

Everyone except Acrolis assembled in the command center.

"V, take us to orbit, then jump forward a hundred years. We can check out a few worlds."

"Acknowledged."

As the *Torvatta* took off, Acrolis waved goodbye.

"I know we're going back to the future, but when were the canisters to activate?" asked Emily.

Evaran raised a finger. "A good question. The time index I have given V is to the point when they should have activated."

"This'll be exciting," said Lord Vygon. "However, we still need to find which world has Wardax's main form. Maybe Acrolis already found it but couldn't say anything until this event occurred."

"It's possible," said Sivaran.

Q tilted his head. "Acrolis can't detect cosmic energy and doesn't know what form Wardax would take, so it would be unlikely that she would locate him."

"Analysis. A pattern can be detected in assimilation dates. If the premise is that the Zayt Empire spread out from a central point, then locations, along with assimilation dates, can be used to determine a source."

Dr. Snowden wagged a finger. "I like that. I guess finding the assimilation dates will be difficult."

"Not quite," said Sivaran. "We thought of that. The canister deploys a small nanoprobe to check the environment occasionally, and that information is relayed to the canister's database. It will record when the world is assimilated."

"Ahh, so we just need to check the canister, then."

"You got it," said Sivaran.

Emily eased into her chair. Evaran and Sivaran seemed to think of everything, but it made sense to have some way of checking the date of when a world was infected. A nanoprobe was small enough that it would not be detected, and if it was, it could destroy itself. Due to its size, the canister could hold one for every day for a hundred years and still have space to spare.

The *Torvatta* reached orbit and jumped a hundred years forward.

"V, take us to the first planet I have selected," said Evaran. "Acknowledged."

Emily studied Q. He seemed intent on watching the interaction between Evaran and V. Q's relationship with Sivaran was probably similar, but she suspected their relationship was much different. Another aspect that caught her eye was that Q studied Lord Vygon and the others. Traveling with companions may have been a rare thing on the *Karus* but common on the *Torvatta*.

She inspected the planet the *Torvatta* appeared over after it flew through a portal. Large beams shot from the planet and there was ship debris in orbit.

"Uhh ... is the planet shooting at the ships?" asked Dr. Snowden.

Evaran studied his chair console. "It would seem so. The countervirus would not reach those in ships. Those freed on the ground may not be receptive to the infected who control ships."

Lord Vygon shook his head. "This means that for planets without a planetary defense system, they'll be prey to an assault by the infected."

"For a short while," said Sivaran. "In time, the virus spread will reach everywhere as civilizations begin to recover."

The *Torvatta* descended until it detected a signal from the canister. A moment later, the container shot a stream of data to the *Torvatta*. It took some scans of the chaotic cities below, then ascended to orbit and flew through a portal.

Emily wrinkled her brow at the lack of anything in orbit. Per the *Torvatta*'s initial scans, the second planet was somewhat primitive. It did not seem like a place Wardax would want to infect.

The *Torvatta* descended.

"What's the story here?" she asked.

"Per Acrolis's scans a long while back, there was a civilization preparing to make the technological leap to put things in orbit," said Evaran.

Emily's eyes were glued to the transparent front wall as the *Torvatta* approached cities that reminded her of a setting in the 1800s. The big difference was the natives resembled three-foot cat humanoids. While most seemed to be helping each other, others were involved in vicious catfights. Her heart sank. It must be confusing to wake up and not know what was going on, then realize no one else did either. Some might take advantage of that, and she figured that depended on the range of personalities a society had.

Dr. Snowden scrunched his face. "This is probably happening everywhere." He glanced at Evaran. "There's going to be a lot of casualties."

"I concur," said Evaran. "However, I think we can conclude that the canisters have done what they were intended to do. V, get the canister information from this world. Afterward, the next step is to sync up with Acrolis and determine if she has located Wardax's world. If not, we will continue checking the planets until a pattern is revealed."

Lord Vygon's eyes narrowed. "I hope she found it. It would save us a lot of effort."

"I'm with him," said Emily, gesturing at him.

He nodded. "I feel like we're getting closer, but I can't help think that Wardax has some contingency for this exact situation."

"He's a cosmic being," said Sivaran. "I'd count on it."

Dr. Snowden sighed. "I'm really looking forward to capturing him and ending this." He waved a finger between Lord Vygon, Q, and Sivaran. "There'll be a lot to deal with after that."

Lord Vygon raised his head. "Assuming we survive, I can live with that."

"I would like to survive," said Q.

"And we will," said Sivaran. "Let's go check on Acrolis, who I'm sure has been waiting for us at this point in time."

After reaching Acrolis's world, V verified that the *Torvatta* had the correct path laid into her home base underground. Over the last hour, he had been observing the others. His organic interaction library could always use new information, and with Sivaran around, there was an incentive to be more observant than usual. V was glad he could multitask as he piloted the *Torvatta* and used its internal video feed to study everyone.

Evaran appeared calm as expected. His face showed subtle movement that indicated his mood. V could also detect his energy state. It seemed the canisters working made him happy, but the chaos on the planets dismayed him. As a check, V compared it to Sivaran's face, which showed a smile, then a frown. When put side by side, there was a relationship that was easy to map between Evaran's state and Sivaran's face.

Emily was more neutral than anything else. She always seemed to be studying something, and when visiting the newly freed planets, she had been focused on that. V had noticed a slight smile when she had seen the cat humanoids. Perhaps she recalled Evot, a previous traveling companion who could shape-shift into a cat form. A planet of those would be interesting and full of excitement.

Dr. Snowden had made several faces that flashed between anger and worry. His accelerated heartbeat suggested that anything to do with Wardax still troubled him physically. V had run simulations of how Dr. Snowden would respond to situations after the treatment administered by Evaran and Sivaran. It seemed Dr. Snowden had been jovial at first, but encountering anything related to Wardax, even on a newly freed world, evoked a strong negative response.

Lord Vygon's constant eye movement suggested he was observing others, like V was. With Lord Vygon's planet gone, it made sense that he would not relax until Wardax was captured. V wished there had been more the gang could have done to save Drydris, but it was a part of events now.

V monitored Q's interaction with the ship. He spent an inordinate amount of effort studying everyone, even more so than V. That was to be expected as Q did not have an inner container. V would relay his observations to Q before he left the *Torvatta*. He had been an interesting case study so far, and while V had an organic interaction library, he had a chance to add to his AI ones. He had met quite a few AIs and understood that their simulated emotions and general processing state could vary wildly.

After a while, the *Torvatta* landed outside Acrolis's home base.

The mood was a mix of cautiousness and excitement. V calculated that they were hoping she had found Wardax's home planet, but that they were prepared to spend a considerable amount of time looking for it if not.

The group assembled outside the *Torvatta*, where Acrolis met them. She ushered them inside, and after a brief walk, they stood in her grand chamber.

"So ... we meet again," said Acrolis. "Did you forget something?"

Evaran shook his head. "Our meeting in the past has occurred, and the canisters you placed have activated."

"Finally. We can be in sync now."

"That's the idea," said Sivaran. "You knew about me during all those times we met in the past."

"It was hard not to say anything," said Acrolis. She gestured at Evaran and the others. "Even harder when they came. But I stayed true to my word."

Evaran nodded. "You did."

"And I mentioned my mental assault back then, then you told me to be strong in our first meeting, which I didn't understand at the time," said Dr. Snowden.

Acrolis sighed. "I wish I could have said more but ... I kept silent. I'm sorry."

V observed Dr. Snowden's body temperature rise.

"But we're in sync now. No more time-hopping out-of-sync madness," she said. She snapped her fingers. "Kassikel, bring out the information they need."

Kassikel appeared in her humanoid rock form out of a nearby cave wall with a box in her hand. She walked over and handed it to Evaran.

"Everything you require to update the original data I gave you is there," said Acrolis. "But what I suspect you really want to know is ... did I find Wardax's world?"

V timed the awkward silence at 1.6 seconds.

"Yes, we would like to know," said Evaran.

"I think I did. Well, I found three worlds that were unusual. I can't detect exotic energy, but I can detect when matter should have properties. If it comes up blank, that usually means there is exotic energy there, but I don't know what type. The three worlds in question each have that. One is a world filled with high pressure and lava. Another is a water world. The third is a barren world filled with dust and dirt, but there is a strange structure in the desert. If I had to guess, Wardax's world would be the barren one, but as I said earlier, there was matter I could not detect, despite seeing it visually."

Evaran rubbed his chin. "This is good. We can check that out, and if it does not bear out, then we will continue with our original approach to use location and assimilation date to narrow down a point of origin."

"I wish I could be of more help," said Acrolis.

"You've done a lot for us already," said Sivaran.

"I hope Sivaran and I can see you again after Wardax is captured and the others have left, assuming we survive," said Q.

V noted the unusual look Q gave Kassikel. It was only for a few microseconds, but it showed some type of interest. Kassikel's smile indicated a positive response to the idea of seeing Sivaran and Q again.

Acrolis swept her gaze across everyone. "I expect to see everyone before they take off to do whatever. I don't know what your future holds, but I hope it's good."

"We do too," said Evaran. He looked around. "I believe we are ready to begin our next step. As it is close to 11:30 p.m. Earth time, we can leave in the morning. Let us go."

As everyone began to walk away, V observed Sivaran and Q staying behind. What they discussed remained a mystery, but V suspected they were planning on meeting up later. V had no concern that there was anything malicious at play, as Evaran would have detected that. Acrolis's perspective to this point must be illuminating to her. V hoped he could talk about it with her later.

The next step was to scout out a planet that Wardax potentially resided on. V was not sure what to expect, and there were many variables to consider. A barren world with a structure possibly containing cosmic energy evoked several composite images in his processing. The big concern would be if there was also palisin energy. He faced Emily when she put her hand on his shoulder.

"You coming?" she asked.

V looked around, then smiled at her. "Acknowledged."

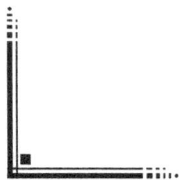

22

Lord Vygon enjoyed a good night's rest. It was now 10:00 a.m. and everyone had assembled in the command center. He loved having a nice blood drink for breakfast, and he tried a bacon, egg, and cheese biscuit sandwich per Dr. Snowden's recommendation. It was delicious regardless of what it was made of.

Evaran and Sivaran did not seem to sleep, and V and Q had been in low power mode, although it was hard to distinguish how powered up they were. Emily and Dr. Snowden were excellent breakfast companions, and they seemed eager to get going.

Lord Vygon tensed up when the *Torvatta* flew through a portal and arrived outside a brown planet with a few small pockets of blue. Per the data labels, the planet had an interesting atmosphere that closely resembled the one on Drydris. Dr. Snowden pointed out that the planet was Earth-like, but a little hotter.

The syncing up with Acrolis intrigued Lord Vygon. As powerful as she was, even she had needed help. How it had been provided was beyond anything he had expected. They were nearer the goal now thanks to her, and he would be forever in her debt.

"Only a few stations out here," said Dr. Snowden.

"Yeah, I would have expected an armada of ships or something," said Emily.

Sivaran shrugged. "Perhaps that is by design. Given that there appears to be nothing on the surface, most would assume the stations are for monitoring or research."

Lord Vygon sighed. "It wouldn't surprise me."

Lord Vygon now understood just how difficult Wardax was to deal with. It would be a Wardax move to have the planet look as natural as possible to deter invaders. Lord Vygon wondered if there would be any civilization at all.

"Analysis. Magnetic shielding detected."

Lord Vygon studied the unusual spot that a data window had zoomed into. A massive ring sat partially submerged in the ground. Inside it was a jungle of some sort. A huge pillar rose up from the middle, and a semitransparent bubble shield covered the area.

"That's a pretty big shield," said Emily.

Evaran rubbed his chin. "It is, and we shall investigate. V, take us down."

"Acknowledged."

The *Torvatta* descended through the atmosphere until it hovered over the structure.

Lord Vygon's eyes narrowed. It appeared small from orbit, but up close, the ring covered a lot of ground. Per the *Torvatta*'s readings, it had a radius of thirty miles. Although the *Torvatta* had difficulty piercing the shielding, it was able to get some readings.

Inside the ring were reddish trees and a mass of vines. Smaller ones branched out, and they appeared to weave through the trees. The high number of life-forms also stood out. Although it was difficult for the *Torvatta* to zoom in, he saw a variety of types of beings, including tall, thin humanoids who resembled stick figures.

"Lot of life here," said Dr. Snowden.

"There also appears to be something under the area. The ringed segment extends underground, as does the pillar, and they are connected by both metallic-covered tunnels and ones that appear to be natural. A high number of life-form signs have been registered underground," said Q.

Lord Vygon shook his head. "This is strange. Nothing alive anywhere but here, an oasis of life powered by something massive underground."

"That would make penetration by the *Torvatta* dangerous," said Sivaran. "Probably what Wardax expected. He's using life-forms as shields since he knows we won't sacrifice them. I suspect he is in that underground facility, or at least the part of him that resides in this reality is."

"I wish the *Torvatta* could scan through magnetic shielding better." Dr. Snowden adjusted his glasses. "Anyways, how are we going to get in there? Wardax has seen everything I know."

Evaran eyed him. "He does not know that the planar beam can penetrate magnetic shielding."

"I didn't know it could do that. Well, he saw it work against the Time Warden's shielding when we retrieved Levaran."

"Yes, but that was not magnetic. The fact you did not know means Wardax would not."

Emily wrinkled her brow. "We coulda used it on our last summons."

Evaran shook his head. "The magnetic shielding in the last summons was a thin layer over the facility infrastructure, unlike this, which is a large dome."

"Ahh."

Q tilted his head. "What is the plan for removing cosmic energy from Wardax? We don't know his true form."

"I may have an idea on that," said Sivaran. He faced Q. "Before I extracted you to the *Karus*, I worked on a solution to remove cosmic energy from a being."

"You did?"

Sivaran nodded. "I wasn't expecting Wardax, but the general idea of a cosmic being, like a Hadryn spawn, arriving. The one Evaran fought could be banished due to the low level, but Wardax requires more. The approach should work, although I'm missing a component for the actual extraction. However, after syncing with Evaran, I think the cosmic storage boxes from the re-formation room, along with technology from the Rift Guardians, can create something that would suck the cosmic energy right out of Wardax."

Emily perked up. "Sounds interesting. We should visit Jelton."

Dr. Snowden eyed her.

"What? It makes sense."

"Analysis. He was teasing you."

"I know," said Emily, pointing at Dr. Snowden.

Lord Vygon did not fully understand the discussion between Dr. Snowden and Emily, but it seemed she was interested in this Jelton person.

"Analysis. I can perform reconnaissance inside the underground tunnels and facility."

"Perhaps," said Evaran. "However, you have cosmic energy, so Wardax would be able to detect you."

"My calculations show that we would have a higher chance of survival if the environment and adversaries are known. Wardax will not catch me. I also have a PSD, which will help if I am attacked."

Evaran studied him. "Okay. We will need to determine an entry point."

Dr. Snowden sighed and looked at V. "Thanks to me, Wardax will know all about your reconnaissance abilities. I wish there was a way to mask your cosmic signature."

"V's cosmic energy cannot be masked," said Evaran. "However, he does have stealth mode, which should render him undetectable by anything less than Wardax. V can also fly fast."

V nodded. "I am also quite nimble."

Dr. Snowden grinned. "Yeah, you are. Still, there could be some mist that tracks you by turbulence. Hopefully not. You would think there would be at least *one* exotic energy that can hide cosmic energy."

Lord Vygon appreciated Dr. Snowden's furious curiosity about everything.

"There are thousands of exotic energies. Their interactions can be explosive as we saw with Kingartochores," said Evaran. "If Alkarin energy were more powerful, it could mask a cosmic energy signature similar to how it makes lightmires appear human to nonhumans."

Dr. Snowden shrugged. "I guess V will just have to be careful."

"Analysis. That is the plan."

Sivaran glanced at V. "I have no doubt you can do it."

He smiled.

"We will observe him from the holo room," said Evaran. He studied the magnetic shielding. "The planar beam generator can be fired somewhere near the top. That should minimize contact with the area, and the *Torvatta* will fly in through the hole generated. While we do surface scans, V can survey the underground system." He interacted with his chair console. "V, take us to the spot I have marked."

"Acknowledged."

Lord Vygon admired V's fearlessness. In the face of potentially being captured, he was willing to put it on the line to give the group better odds. Although Lord Vygon could attribute that to an unfeeling AI, he knew V was anything but that. His family was going into battle, and V planned to make sure they had the best intel possible.

The *Torvatta* flew off to the side and top of the shielding, then positioned itself so the ramp pointed toward an area right below the top.

"We are in position," said Evaran as he stood. He gestured at V. "I will get the planar beam generator and meet you on the ramp."

Lord Vygon followed the others out. The planar beam generator that Evaran brought was odd-looking and had a cable hooked up that led to somewhere else. Lord Vygon was not sure what was so special about this device, or why it required such an effort to use.

The generator anchored itself.

V flew over and hovered.

"Are you ready?" asked Evaran.

"I am," said V.

Evaran interacted with the generator, which fired a beam in a pattern that allowed the *Torvatta* to fly through. The hole closed after they entered.

V faded away and flew forward. A moment later, he said, "I am going to the underground system once I find an entry point."

Evaran nodded. "We will scan the surface and wait for your return."

Lord Vygon noted Dr. Snowden and Emily's concerned faces. Hopefully, V would come back safe and sound, and there would be a lot of information to sift through. Lord Vygon was impressed that this level of reconnaissance could be done with V. Whatever plan was devised, it would need to account for many variables, but some would slip through just because Wardax was involved. It was interesting to watch what was essentially a cosmic chess match.

Dr. Snowden relaxed in the holo room. While V scoured the central pillar's base for an entry point, the *Torvatta* flew around and scanned the surface. The environment surrounding them was from the *Torvatta*'s vantage point. Everything outside the shielding seemed blurry.

He surveyed the room. Emily sat to his left, while Lord Vygon was to the right. Evaran, Sivaran, and Q stood a bit away opposite the others. Dr. Snowden loved the fact that comfortable settings could be created.

Evaran interacted with an interface. "We can switch to V's perspective now while continuing our surface scan."

Dr. Snowden gripped his chair when the environment showed V poking about the central pillar. It rose high into the sky, and small drones flitted about. Strange snakelike creatures also flew above and reminded Dr. Snowden of miniature dragons. The holo room made everything seem real, and although he knew it was just visual holograms, he jumped when one of the creatures flew through him.

After he settled down, he studied the area around the pillar. The jungle seemed vast and provided a stark contrast to the high-tech nature of the ring and pillar. There was a lot of movement between the reddish jungle trees. Strange noises permeated the air, and a slight mist of some type resided as a thin layer on top of the trees.

V dove through the mist a bit away from the pillar and toward a large gaping hole in the ground.

Dr. Snowden gulped when he saw thick vines slinking between trees. Tall, thin wooden humanoids with no faces roamed aimlessly, while a group of humanoids with oversized heads and stick bodies darted about. There were sightings of denizens that had tulip-like petals as a dress and elliptical green heads that contained a massive mouth. Another large beastly being plodded around and reminded Dr. Snowden of a gorilla, except this one was made of rock and dirt.

"Analysis. These creatures do not appear to be native to this planet."

Dr. Snowden scrutinized the data labels. V was right. Each creature had some dimensional energy about them per the *Torvatta*'s scans. The planet was dry for the most part, and the beings inside the ring appeared to be specific to the ringed structure.

Emily shuddered. "This does not look like a place you want to get lost in."

"I concur," said Evaran. "Perhaps these are denizens of Wardax's dimension."

Lord Vygon scowled. "Strange and creepy, so probably true."

V arrived at the hole in the ground.

Dr. Snowden pointed at it. "Reminds me of a subway street entrance, minus the stairs."

"I could see that," said Emily.

V flew in.

"Not much light," said Sivaran, surveying the environment. "Then again, there seems to be no technology present. Just dirt walls."

Q gestured at a dim light in the distance. "It appears there is some."

The massive tunnel surprised Dr. Snowden. It resembled the aftermath of something huge burrowing through the ground. The sides were smooth for the most part, but the ground was flat. Although there was low light due to glowing moss, V had detected creatures, similar to the ones above, moving around listlessly in the tunnel. Dr. Snowden's neck hairs rose upon hearing the strange and deep groaning noises.

V continued on.

Dr. Snowden appreciated the map window that popped up and showed everything V had mapped up to that point. The tunnels crossed each other, and some went up, some down, while others extended. V had detected movement on the walls, and that turned out to be the mosslike thing. It generated a dim light when moving, which gave off an eerie feel.

"This place just gets worse and worse," said Emily. She gestured at the map window. "Look how far V's gone so far. It's endless."

"Analysis. I can replicate the smells if you wish, but it has an odor consistent with rotting garbage."

Lord Vygon raised his brow. "I think we can avoid that experience."

After another hour, V reached a new part of the tunnel that had a semitransparent light blue shield covering the entrance to an advanced-looking hallway with metallic panels.

"I think it's safe to say that's definitely a part of the pillar," said Dr. Snowden.

Q nodded. "Matching up V's and the *Torvatta*'s scans indicates that this structure continues down and has several entrances similar to this."

Emily narrowed her eyes. "Almost seems like Wardax dropped this place onto this world, and inside the ring, he brought a part of his dimension through."

"Definitely possible," said Sivaran.

V flew up to the shield and scanned it, then went through.

"Huh, I woulda thought it would be solid," said Emily.

"Analysis. It is a filter of some type."

"Ahh."

Dr. Snowden examined the hallways as V cruised along. If Dr. Snowden did not know better, he would say the pillar was a ship. Treelike humanoids with green armor and biotic weapons patrolled the area. Definitely enforcers. The lack of anything other than tunnels and side rooms packed with advanced technology gave him the impression that it was not built to house others. The enforcers would probably need a place to rest or recharge, and it hit him that he had no idea what they did when not doing something for Wardax.

V found a wall interface in a side room and was able to connect. There was no AI present, and he began to download the structure's system information.

Dr. Snowden watched with rapture as data windows showed a dizzying amount of information. Everything from layouts to material design appeared. Although V was efficient, a part of Dr. Snowden wondered if Wardax had expected this to occur and planned accordingly. No system AI was to be expected. He would not suffer anything that might challenge him.

After a bit, V disconnected and flew away to a colossal room.

Dr. Snowden's eyes widened at the sheer size of the place. The area was well lit with pillars made of glowing bubbles encased in purple oil. Vines slithered on high-tech walls and wrapped around the pillars. In the back sat a massive rectangular device that had thick cables leading off into the walls. Per V's scans, it was a power conduit of some type with connections to the wall.

However, it was the large egg-shaped object in the center that caught Dr. Snowden's eye. The object was held in place by a series of vines that reached from the ceiling to the ground. The bottom half of the vines were much thicker and resembled a tree stump. A dim golden glow surrounded it and highlighted the part of the structure that was semitransparent. Its organic nature was a sharp contrast to everything else.

Dr. Snowden jumped when a large voice boomed out.

"V. I ... sense ... you."

V hovered and scanned the area.

"Ahh, there you are."

V flew back a bit.

"I knew this time would come, and Dr. Snowden showed me how it might happen."

"Yeah, that's definitely Wardax," said Dr. Snowden. "Not liking the disembodied voice thing."

"Why don't you come to me?" asked Wardax.

The place became active. Vines stretched out, looking for something to grab.

"Get out of there!" said Emily.

"Acknowledged." V flew away.

Dr. Snowden's pulse quickened when the egg structure popped out of the area that held it. A massive vine from behind powered it, and smaller vines seemed to serve as legs, antennae, and wildly flailing hair. It reminded him of a large house centipede. The egg part cracked like a clam shell, revealing a mouth packed with sharp teeth.

"What the heck is that?"

"Wardax's form in this reality," said Sivaran, narrowing his eyes.

V flew out of the cavern and back into the hallways.

Dr. Snowden rubbed the goose bumps on his arm as V's rear view showed Wardax rampaging forward.

Enforcers in the front of V shot in his general area. He had tried to use the enforcers to block Wardax's path, but Wardax swept them to the sides like they were not even there. V was faster, and he kept Wardax at length until the dirt tunnels. As V flew out of the structure, sticklike creatures from before swarmed the area and randomly reached into the air as if trying to snag V.

Dr. Snowden's heartbeat shot up when a large treelike humanoid grabbed one of V's arms.

"Oh no!" said Emily.

V shot a repulsion beam, which did not faze the creature. Another one came over and hit V, while vines snaked up the treelike humanoid and reinforced its grip on V's arm.

Emily jumped up. "We have to help him!"

"It is too dangerous," said V. "I will escape."

Dr. Snowden swallowed hard as he heard Wardax saying V's name in a singsong manner. Wardax's movement sounded like he was crashing through the place, and the thud of each heavy footstep made Dr. Snowden's skin crawl.

V severed his arm and continued on. He kept close to the ceiling and, after a while, reached the surface with Wardax hot on his tail.

Dr. Snowden gripped his chair when V burst free.

Wardax made one last final chomp attempt. He was big and fast and apparently strong enough to propel himself into the air like an alligator launching from water.

A swarm of reptilian-like creatures chased after V, and after he reached the *Torvatta*, Evaran used the planar beam generator to open a hole in the magnetic shielding. The *Torvatta* flew out.

Emily rushed out of the holo room.

Dr. Snowden figured that V would go to the medical lab. An arm could be replaced, V could not. Thankfully, it was not worse than that. Dr. Snowden joined the others and assembled around V on a slab.

Emily held one of V's arms, while Evaran worked on attaching a new arm and cleaning V's orb.

"That was some journey," said Lord Vygon. "It's like a completely different world in there."

"Analysis. The creatures seemed to respond to Wardax, but they were not infected."

"I noticed that as well," said Q. "Perhaps there is some type of bond in the other dimension we aren't seeing."

"It is possible," said Evaran. "Now that we know what we are up against, we will need to create the device to remove cosmic energy. We also have to formulate a plan to get to Wardax. As V's scouting has shown, that will not be an easy task. Once the device design is completed, we will visit Jelton."

Everyone nodded.

Emily smiled at V. "I'm glad you're safe."

"It was a rough experience, but the information gathered shall assist us," he said.

She patted his orb. "There. There."

His lights glowed. "You are teasing me."

"Yep!"

Dr. Snowden figured that since V was safe, Emily felt more at ease. It could also be that her good mood was tied to seeing Jelton soon. Dr. Snowden's heart still raced when he thought of the ring structure. It was out of place, filled with strange creatures, and had Wardax behind it. Nothing good would come from that. At least now, they had an idea of what Wardax's main form was, and they knew where he was. Everything seemed to be coming together.

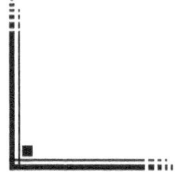

23

Emily bounced out of bed. The previous day had been interesting, and V had made his reconnaissance run without too much issue. She loved that she could watch it in the holo room, and after he had been patched up, he had joined her on the roof, and they had discussed life in general.

V was her best friend, and she could not imagine life without him. Now that Evaran and Sivaran had time to design a cosmic energy extracting device, the gang was ready to take the next step.

She got cleaned up in record time. V and Lord Vygon, and even Q, were meeting her for a workout in the holo room. Although Q was not meant for battle, he said he could wield ranged weaponry with high accuracy. She would find out.

An hour later and after a good workout, she was in the conference room with them. Q's ability in the workout had surprised her. He was an efficient marksman and used a heavy stun gun with wide and narrow beams against waves of Zayt enforcers. Although not as handy in close-quarters combat, he was able to use his raw strength to some effect. Lord Vygon had been a whirlwind of devastation, and she sometimes found it hard to distinguish him from the one she knew back on Earth.

Dr. Snowden arrived and retrieved his cup of coffee as well as a plate of bacon and eggs. He sat and nodded at her. "Somebody looks like they got a workout in this morning."

"Sure did," she said. "You're always welcome to join us. Even Q was there!"

"I enjoyed our training simulation," said Q.

Dr. Snowden shrugged. "Maybe one day. I'd just slow everyone down, I think."

"Emily said you would sleep in, then get coffee and a hearty breakfast," said Lord Vygon.

Dr. Snowden eyed her, then wolfed down some bacon.

"Careful, you still need to breathe," said Lord Vygon, laughing.

Dr. Snowden swallowed his bite and scrutinized him.

"Did I say something wrong?"

"That's what the Lord Vygon I know said to me the morning before we left."

Lord Vygon wrinkled his brow. "He's stealing my lines now."

The group chuckled.

Evaran and Sivaran arrived and took their seats.

"It appears everyone is up and ready to go," said Evaran. He examined Emily. "Some more so than others. Nonetheless, we can begin." He tapped at the table console.

A hologram popped up showing a gold sphere with silver dots on the outside. A cutout showed a green crystal of some type sitting on top of a box. Surrounding it was a nano swarm.

"This sphere contains the same box used in re-formation to hold cosmic energy. The crystal is a rift one and is similar to what the Rift Guardians used to drain energy. The nano swarm exits the sphere in the form of strands. The idea is to get the sphere near Wardax, then the sphere will bind itself to him while draining him."

"Seems easy enough," said Dr. Snowden. "We can just shoot it at him."

Sivaran raised a finger. "I wouldn't underestimate Wardax. He's aware of the ability of the Rift Guardians to drain energy and also would know about the box. He may not know about the nano swarm wires that will emerge, but I suspect he will be ready for some type of draining attack. What his counter might be remains unknown."

Evaran nodded. "Once we have this device, we will proceed into Wardax's domain and drain his cosmic energy."

"What do we do with him once he's powered down?" asked Lord Vygon.

"We do not plan to kill him," said Evaran. "However, without his cosmic energy, he will not be able to control the guardians that sustain the Zayt Empire. With his virus countered and no means of control, he will be left to his own devices."

Lord Vygon growled. "Or we could kill him."

"Or banish him," said Dr. Snowden. His eyes narrowed. "Wouldn't bother me at all."

Emily had seen that look before on the Lord Vygon she knew. It was the same face as when her Lord Vygon had helped Evaran banish another cosmic being, known as the Overlord. Dr. Snowden's reaction caught her by surprise. He hated death in general, but it seemed with Wardax, that was not an issue.

"Once we leave and Sivaran and Q are back to where they should be, whatever occurs was meant to happen."

Lord Vygon eased back into his chair. "All right."

Emily suspected that, once the gang left and Sivaran and Q went their way, Lord Vygon would hunt down and kill Wardax. Perhaps that was the way it was always meant to be, and she understood his desire to short-circuit the process. Evaran would give Wardax a second chance, but she did not think he would make use of it, unless he won, which she did not want to happen. She pushed the thought out of her mind.

Evaran looked around. "We are now ready to collect the energy-draining component of the device, and to do so, we will visit Jelton. I have already contacted him via our rift door, and he has given us a time to be there. Let us go."

Emily hopped out of her chair, then followed the others to the command area. Evaran took his usual seat, while Sivaran and Dr. Snowden sat in he left U-shaped seating area. Lord Vygon joined Emily on the right side, and V and Q stood at the front console. Emily smiled as the *Torvatta* opened a portal and flew through.

Her heart raced at the sight of the familiar landing spot on the large chunk of rock that seemed to float in darkness. The massive green crystal overhead illuminated the area. She jumped up after the *Torvatta* landed.

"Watch out! Don't get in Emily's way," said Dr. Snowden with an arm across Sivaran.

She gave him an amused look, then burst out of the command center. It did not take her long to spot Jelton and Gowldin Khull, the supreme leader of the Rift Guardians. She rushed up and hugged Jelton and gave him a quick kiss, then she hugged a surprised Gowldin.

"I didn't mean to startle you," said Emily.

Gowldin nodded and, in a deep voice, said, "It's okay. I know you're excited to see Jelton."

"And you too!"

He nodded and then focused on Evaran and the others approaching. "I see you have some new companions."

Evaran arrived and forearm-shook with Jelton and Gowldin. "We do indeed."

Jelton walked over and forearm-shook with Lord Vygon while slapping him on the back with his free hand. "It's good to see you again."

"We haven't met yet," said Lord Vygon.

Jelton wrinkled his brow, then glanced at Evaran. "This an out-of-sync thing again?"

Evaran raised a finger. "Not quite. This Lord Vygon is from another universe."

"No surprise there," said Gowldin.

"And this is Sivaran, another one of my plane forms. As I was the first, he is the sixth."

Gowldin's eyes widened. "Okay. Surprise there."

Emily laughed.

Sivaran shook Gowldin's hand, then Jelton's. "I've synced with Evaran, so I know what he knows. You sacrificed yourself to save him when he tried to eject a cosmic shard."

"Well, I did die from that," said Jelton.

"Yes, you did. It's good to meet another cosmic being." He nodded at Gowldin. "And you too, of course."

"Of course," said Gowldin. "Two Evarans. I know Jelton mentioned something about plane forms, but I never expected to see two." He shook Lord Vygon's hand. "I believe this is our first time meeting, regardless of version."

"That it is," said Lord Vygon.

V high-fived Jelton and Gowldin.

"It's good to see you again, my friend," said Jelton. He extended a hand toward Q. "You're new as well. I'm going to guess you travel with Sivaran."

Q returned the handshake. "You're correct. I appreciate this opportunity to meet you."

"No need to be so formal here. Any friend of the gang is a friend of mine." Jelton glanced at Evaran. "We've disassembled one of our siphon tanks for you to work on."

"Excellent," said Evaran. "We can take the *Torvatta* to the prison planet."

"I'm curious to see this device you mentioned in your earlier communication," said Gowldin.

"It's cool," said Emily. "Uses rift and cosmic tech with a nano swarm."

Dr. Snowden smiled. "Not something you leave lying around, that's for sure."

Jelton scrutinized him. "Are you all right?"

"I think so."

"Your cosmic energy is in flux."

Dr. Snowden sighed. "We ran into another cosmic being, who captured me, then violated my mind. I was recently rescued and spent some time at Kess's while Sivaran and Evaran removed the remnants of the other being."

Jelton frowned. "I'm sorry to hear that, my friend." He eyed Evaran. "You could've come and gotten us if you needed help."

"It was a search effort for the most part," said Evaran.

Emily loved the genuine concern that Jelton showed Dr. Snowden. She knew Jelton would put everything on the line if it helped. That was just who he was. Everything was better with him around, and she knew it would take some time to assemble the device. Per Evaran, they would stay the night, and she looked forward to spending it alone with Jelton.

Lord Vygon studied Jelton and Gowldin as they conversed in the command center. They were no strangers to the *Torvatta*. Jelton had cosmic energy in him like Emily and Dr. Snowden, and Lord Vygon wondered how big the difference was.

He also understood how powerful it was to have a head-quarters hidden away in a dimension. That was something he wished the ancient vampires had done. If he ever got a second chance, he would repopulate them by turning new members and finding a home dimension secure from threats.

Gowldin appeared confident and his demeanor was that of a leader. He was friendly, yet spoke with an authoritative voice. The fact he led a powerful group but took the time to meet with Evaran showcased the respect he had for him. That went for Jelton too. He must have been good friends with the other Lord Vygon. It was becoming an itch to meet him.

Like Sivaran and Q, this was Lord Vygon's first introduction to the Rift Guardians. After having met Kess, another powerful friend, it was easy to see the advantages of having a ship that could fly through not only time but also other realities. Lord Vygon wished that Sivaran had contacted Evaran earlier, but Lord Vygon understood it was a last-resort thing.

The *Torvatta* ascended and flew through a portal. A space station sat in orbit over a planet.

"Welcome to a prison planet," said Emily, gesturing out.

Lord Vygon tilted his head. "I heard that before, but how is this that?"

Gowldin nodded. "This is where we keep prisoners. They have a spacious outdoor environment with matter replicators and other amenities."

"That's very humane," said Lord Vygon. "How do you handle powerful beings?"

Jelton grinned. "A good question. We have siphon tanks that make ascended mortal."

"Ascended?"

"Oh," said Jelton. "Those with exotic energy, like yourself. You're ascended due to possessing Daedrould energy."

Lord Vygon ran a hand over his mouth. Being mortal again was not something he thought of often. There was no way that he would give up being an ancient vampire lord. He enjoyed the long life and enhanced abilities. Even the taste of blood did not bother him.

After a bit, the *Torvatta* approached a large facility planetside.

"Is this some type of warden's office?" asked Q.

"In a way," said Jelton. "This is a processing facility and the only place where ships can land, so it functions as a spaceport, but also a hub for the planet. The siphon tanks are here."

"Interesting. You're not worried the prisoners will escape?" asked Lord Vygon.

Jelton shook his head. "We're at the end of time, when the last planets exist. There would be nowhere for them to go. Even if they got to the space station, it would be evacuated and the portal shut down."

"Very efficient."

"We like to think so," said Gowldin.

The *Torvatta* landed outside the massive processing facility and everyone exited.

Lord Vygon examined the immediate area. The landing pad was metallic, and gray dirt surrounded it. A concrete-like pathway led to the facility. As he walked with the others, he peered off into the distance and recognized some type of shimmering effect. Perhaps those were force fields of some type that acted as cell walls. To have a planet as a prison was an intriguing idea.

Evaran pushed a slab that had the golden sphere with silver dots next to a dark gray box.

They reached the facility and entered it.

Lord Vygon observed the various guards that the group passed. The Rift Guardians were an elite civilization. No wonder they were friends of Evaran. There was no doubt in Lord Vygon's mind that if the ancient vampires had such allies, there would be more of his kind alive. He sighed.

After twenty minutes, the group reached a large research lab. Various personnel moved around a variety of work areas separated by light shielding.

Jelton led them to the back.

The area they arrived at had a big octagonal cell border outlined on the ground. A green crystal with tendrils sat on a table in the middle. The design that Evaran and Sivaran had created would hopefully work well. Lord Vygon's main concern was being able to get close enough to deploy it. The cosmic energy draining part was one of those things that he would need to see to believe. The thought that this device could make someone mortal was both fascinating and terrifying.

"Here we are," said Jelton. "One energy-draining crystal."

"Analysis. Assembly will take some time."

Jelton nodded. "We have a lounge with an Earth-like design."

"I want to see this device being built," said Lord Vygon.

"I'd be curious too." Jelton gestured for a researcher to come over. "Bring out seating arrangements and dock it to this work area."

"Yes, sir," said the researcher.

"Thank you," said Lord Vygon.

Evaran pushed the hover slab inside the cell. Sivaran, V, and Q followed him in, and a light blue semitransparent shield was erected around the cell. Lord Vygon appreciated the long couch-like structure that the researcher brought. It covered almost half the length of the octagonal cell, so there was plenty of space to sit.

Emily and Jelton had cozied up on one side, while Dr. Snowden and Gowldin sat a bit away from them.

Lord Vygon took his seat. Gowldin was the nearest person, and he seemed entranced by what Evaran and the others were doing inside the cell. To be fair, so was Lord Vygon. The various holograms made the area look busier than it probably was. The hookup of the crystal to the box took some precise movements, not something that would slow Evaran down.

"So Evaran is new to you," said Gowldin, looking over.

Lord Vygon eased back into the couch. "This Evaran is, but then again, all of this is. I did know Sivaran and Q from before, though."

Gowldin shook the couch with his laughter. "I understand. Most Rift Guardians view Evaran as a god and Jelton as a demigod."

"I could see that," said Lord Vygon. "I wish he would have arrived before my planet was destroyed."

"Who would do such a thing?" asked Gowldin.

Lord Vygon scowled. "Wardax, another cosmic being. He will pay for what he has done."

Gowldin nodded. "I'd offer the Rift Guardians service if it helped, but Evaran would refuse it. He doesn't like to ask for help in that regard."

"I understand," said Lord Vygon.

Although he said he did, it did not make much sense to turn down such strong assistance. There might be other factors that Lord Vygon was not aware of, and the loss of his home planet might be clouding his judgment. Still, he felt safe where he was, and if this device could be built, it would be a game changer.

Over the next five hours, Lord Vygon sat riveted as Evaran and Sivaran masterfully moved nano swarm lines between the crystal's tendrils and the box. How the box could contain cosmic energy was not immediately obvious. Dr. Snowden and Emily said they had seen the box release cosmic energy before to form another *Torvatta*. The process seemed delicate but when a tendril had connected to the box, it had formed a solid connection. Lord Vygon took it that not just anything could do that.

Once the crystal was fully attached, the nano swarm formed a bubble around the whole device. Evaran held half the golden sphere shell in place around the bubble while Sivaran got the other side. After the two sides connected, V and Q fired an energy beam of some type that fused the two halves together in such a way that there was no evidence left that they were separate. As a test, they stood back as several nano swarm tendrils emerged from the silver dots on the circle.

Evaran and Sivaran faced the group while V and Q continued to test the device.

"It is ready," said Evaran. "There is one last test. I will let it pull some cosmic energy from me."

"Are you sure that's wise?" asked Dr. Snowden.

Evaran nodded. "It is only a minuscule amount. While everything seems to be in place, we do not want to deploy this against Wardax and not have it work."

Dr. Snowden shrugged. "All right. Just be careful it doesn't sap you dry."

Sivaran smiled. "I'll pull him away before that happens."

Lord Vygon grimaced as Evaran extended his hand toward the sphere. V interacted with a holo screen nearby, which Lord Vygon figured was some sort of interface.

Evaran's lips turned down slightly when the tendrils touched his hand. A moment later, he moved it away. "The device works. However, once it is deployed, it will be at full sapping strength. We can discuss the plan to reach Wardax over dinner."

"You're welcome to use one of our conference rooms," said Gowldin. "Even if we can't go with you, I'd still like to hear the plan and what you're up against."

Evaran nodded. "Very well. We have a few hours until the meeting. Everyone rest until then."

Lord Vygon's adrenaline pumped through him. They now had a device that would remove Wardax's cosmic energy. He would become his normal monstrous-looking self. More importantly, all his guardians would fall along with his communication ability. Lord Vygon could not wait to see Wardax's buggy face as he realized that he was at the mercy of those he had wronged.

24

Dr. Snowden had enjoyed talking with Jelton, Gowldin, and the others after the device had been created. The conference room where they had eaten was impressive. It reminded him of a movie theater, but instead of rows of seats, there were crescent-shaped booths scattered throughout with the inside facing the front. There had been a variety of food such as pizzas, including a pineapple one, Jelton's favorite. Dr. Snowden cracked up when Lord Vygon poked and prodded his slice before eating it.

Jelton made sure these type of conference rooms existed on the off chance that the gang might visit. Everyone could have met in the *Torvatta*, although the room would be packed. This one was spacious, and with Evaran and Sivaran up front, there was plenty of space for others to sit.

The stage Evaran and Sivaran were on was essentially a raised platform with a ringed border embedded in the floor. Dr. Snowden figured that was for holographic displays. The mood overall seemed comfortable. Jelton and Emily sat next to each other in one booth, while V and Q were in another. Gowldin and Lord Vygon joined Dr. Snowden in his booth.

He liked the spread-out style, and everyone was at ease. It might be that they were in a place Wardax could never reach, although that could also be said of the *Torvatta*. Dr. Snowden eased back into his chair and laced his fingers.

A hologram appeared to the side of Evaran that showed a three-dimensional cutout of Wardax's structure.

Dr. Snowden studied the path V had mapped. The main room that Wardax appeared in had some type of power conduit that seemed to be part of a bigger system deeper in the facility. Wardax had vines tapping into it, so he must have fed off it to some degree. Dr. Snowden took a moment to realize how much power might be flowing through. Trivial for a cosmic being to design.

The topside of the projection had a side view of the jungle and the strange creatures that had been detected. The central hole that led to the tunnels seemed like an easy place to defend, and it made Dr. Snowden wonder if there were any other surface entrances outside the shielding.

"Let us begin," said Evaran, looking around. He pointed at the magnetic shielding. "We can fly the *Torvatta* through, similar to how we did on our initial reconnaissance, then land at the entrance to the tunnel system. That will block it off, and hopefully prevent any of Wardax's reinforcements arriving."

"The *Torvatta*'s shields will expand to cover the full entrance," said Q. "The *Torvatta* by itself is not large enough."

"That is correct," said Evaran. He gestured at a blue line that navigated through the tunnels. "Per the layout information V secured, that is our path." He pointed at a ramp area. "We split up there. One group goes to turn off the power to the room, the other will put the device on Wardax. Once the cosmic energy has been extracted, both groups reunite, and then we leave."

"We're going to split up?" asked Lord Vygon.

Evaran nodded. "If we shut off the power generator as one group, it would most likely be turned on again when we left. The group there has to defend the area."

"It could just be destroyed," said Lord Vygon.

Evaran raised a finger. "There appear to be redundancies for that situation that would route control to a generator in another room. By shutting it down, the control is kept in place. Q will ensure that it stays down, but we need to prevent the manual override from being used."

Jelton perked up. "We could assist in that step."

Evaran shook his head. "I appreciate you offering the Ravaw. They have proven themselves in battle already, and they are needed for your current campaign."

"They would follow you anywhere," said Gowldin.

"Perhaps, but their fate should be tied to Rift Guardian affairs and this timeline."

Gowldin shrugged. "Well, we were more than happy to assist you in fighting the Mortani."

Lord Vygon studied him. "Mortani?"

"Cosmic refugees who had a bad habit of ensnaring ascended in portals, then feasting on their energy."

Lord Vygon's eyes narrowed. "Like cosmic spiders."

Gowldin nodded.

Dr. Snowden recalled taking down the Mortani. Afterward, they had come to the same facility everyone was in now, and their cosmic energy had been taken away. Although most were still there, some had been released per a deal with Evaran. They told him of a corrupted cosmic energy source they had discovered in another universe. It made Dr. Snowden wonder if that was Wardax, but the amounts did not match. That meant there was still something out there even more powerful than Wardax. Thankfully, they did not need to mess with that for the moment.

Evaran slightly bowed. "I appreciate the offer of help, but the siphon crystal is more than enough."

"All right," said Gowldin, glancing at Jelton.

"Once we are in the tunnels, we will most likely fight," said Evaran. "Wardax has had time to prepare, and he knows everything about our tactics from Dr. Snowden."

"Yeah, not by choice," said Dr. Snowden.

"We just need to use unconventional ones, then," said Sivaran. "The countervirus deployment should disable any enforcers, but I suspect we'll run into creatures that we did not see during V's reconnaissance. However, they should be vulnerable to stun and close quarter combat."

Dr. Snowden sighed. "And I bet Wardax knew we would get information from the system. How can we be certain how accurate it is?"

"A good point," said Evaran. "The *Torvatta* has confirmed the layout. The purpose may be different, but the rooms do exist."

"Hopefully there isn't too much fighting," said Gowldin. "I didn't see Wardax's appearance, but heard he was some big bug or something?"

The holographic display projected Wardax.

Gowldin's eyes widened. "Okay, that's disturbing."

"What are the groups?" asked Emily.

Evaran motioned at V, Dr. Snowden, and Lord Vygon. "They will come with me to put the siphoning device on Wardax." He glanced at Emily. "You and Sivaran shall shut down the power generator and hold the area. Q is on standby on the *Torvatta*."

Emily smiled at Sivaran. "We can hold that area."

"Of that, I have no doubt," said Sivaran.

"I just hope there isn't a lot of that palisin mist."

Evaran nodded. "The countermist should negate that, and we can carry more than we did last time. Wardax will most likely expect it."

Emily scowled. "So we might counter his mist, then he could have a counter to that. This is like some fourth-dimensional chess."

"I understand." Evaran moved his hand in an arc. "We can spend the remaining part of the day here. Enjoy the lull and then get some rest. We will enact our plan when everyone is refreshed."

Lord Vygon double-checked his armor and weapons. They were fully powered, and over the last day, his mind had gone over every aspect of the plan. Evaran and Sivaran's plan seemed well designed, but Lord Vygon still felt uncertain about it due to Wardax's craftiness. There were so many ways that Wardax could break the plan, but Lord Vygon was confident in the group he was with.

Going into battle was not new to him. However, he had never gone into one with the stakes as high as this. If they failed, Wardax would be able to continue to expand unchecked. Whatever the cost, he had to be stopped.

Lord Vygon studied his living quarters. They had been his refuge while traveling with the gang, and he wondered for a moment if he would ever see them again. It was almost 10:00 a.m., which was when they had planned to meet, so he got up and left.

He assembled with the others on the *Torvatta* ramp. Evaran and Sivaran never seemed to don anything outside of what they normally wore. V was in full body mode, while Dr. Snowden and Emily had on their survival suits with helmets down. Although Lord Vygon could not sense Evaran's or Sivaran's mood, Dr. Snowden's and Emily's were easy to assess. They were anxious like Lord Vygon was.

Q stood at attention next to the planar beam generator. The *Torvatta* had left the Rift Guardian headquarters, opened a portal to Wardax's planet, and hopped through, and now it hovered inside Wardax's magnetic shield bubble. They would be at the entrance shortly.

"Is everyone ready and clear on the plan?" asked Evaran.

"Yep," said Emily.

"Ready as we can be," said Dr. Snowden.

Lord Vygon shared Emily's enthusiasm, but also Dr. Snowden's cautiousness. "I'm ready for battle."

"Analysis. We will be successful."

"That's the idea," said Sivaran. "The first step is to plug up the entrance, then we proceed to the split off point inside the pillar facility." He looked at the others. "Your grapple hammer won't be effective in there, but repulsion for weaker foes and stun for stronger ones should suffice. If that doesn't work, glue them to the ground or knock them away in close-quarters combat."

Evaran nodded. "We may encounter new creatures, or even obstacles in the layout. As long as we stay focused, we can deal with it. For this first step, we will move in a diamond formation. I will serve as the forward point, and behind me will be Emily to my left and V to my right. Sivaran will serve as the rear point, and ahead of him will be Dr. Snowden to his left, and Lord Vygon to his right. That should provide us with ample coverage and also allow us to re-form as the situation calls for it."

The *Torvatta* arrived at the entrance and landed inside the mouth.

"We are here," said Evaran. "Q, expand the shields. For the rest of us, let us go."

"Let's do this!" said Emily.

Like Emily, Lord Vygon's anxiousness had given way to excitement. Adrenaline raced through him, and he was ready to fight. Although he would cover the rear right, he suspected he would see his fair share of fighting.

The group exited.

Lord Vygon spawned a smaller version of his energy shield and extended his dual blunted forearm blades while keeping his PSD out. His ancient vampire senses were on full alert, even if the tunnel they entered was clear of hostiles.

The first group of tall, thin treelike humanoids announced their arrival with a cacophony of groans and moans.

Evaran and Emily fired a repulsion blast, which knocked them down. A mist and stun beam combo later, the creatures were out.

Lord Vygon's confidence began to rise. Although the humanoids were probably an advance scouting group, they went down quick. Hopefully, the rest of the trip was like that.

After ten minutes, they encountered another group.

Lord Vygon's eyes widened. The tunnel ahead of them had enlarged, and a swarm of enemies marched toward the group. In addition to the attackers the group had fought before, there were new monsters. One type seemed like a walking tree and filled the full height of the tunnel. Other types were smaller, around three foot, but had oversized heads and carried primitive weapons. Another creature resembled a daisy flower head, except with fangs and petals for legs. A snakelike beast slithered along the ground and its large, elongated head seemed out of place compared to the rest of its body.

"I guess they know we're here," said Dr. Snowden.

Evaran pointed to each side. "Form a line."

Lord Vygon appreciated Evaran's knowledge on tactics. There was room for a horizontal formation, and as they had cleared everything behind them and there were no side tunnels to this point, the line formation made sense.

"Repulsion," said Evaran.

Evaran, Emily, Dr. Snowden, and Lord Vygon fired repulsion beams.

The smaller enemies were swept away, but the tree humanoids sank their rootlike feet into the ground, holding them in place. They extended their hands and joined together to form a living wall. The next set of repulsion blasts did not move them or those behind.

"That's new," said Emily. She fired a stun beam.

The tree humanoids marched on.

"Well, that sucks," she said.

"Continue to fire mist beams. We can spark it and it should get those behind," said Evaran.

"I'll deal with any left standing," said Sivaran.

The group fired mist beams, then ignited them.

After those behind the living wall stopped moving, Sivaran burst forward. He spun like a tornado and his suit extended rods of varying lengths that broke up the wall.

Evaran charged in and knocked the tree humanoids to the wall, where Emily, Dr. Snowden, and Lord Vygon glued them to it. Once a path ahead had been cleared, the group moved through.

Lord Vygon did not recall seeing the tree humanoids gripping the ground earlier, so that was a new tactic. He still did not think the group had experienced a full assault yet. This seemed more like Wardax was testing them.

They fought smaller groups until they reached the filtered entrance to the pillar structure. Upon arriving, a small group of enforcers took position just inside. They fired energy beams which were reflected back.

Lord Vygon grimaced when one of the enforcers shot a repulsion blast. It was powerful enough to send him, Dr. Snowden and Emily scooting back. Lord Vygon loved his energy shield.

"They're using our own tactics against us!" said Dr. Snowden.

The group fired repulsion beams and swept back the mist to the enforcers. Once ignited, they fell.

"Interesting," said Evaran as he walked past the downed enforcers. He picked up one of their weapons and studied it. "No dimensional mechanics to handle recoil, but it was still functional."

"I'm just glad there's no palisin mist to weaken us. I would not want to deal with all this in a weakened state," said Dr. Snowden.

Evaran nodded. "We are close to the splitting point. Let us go."

Lord Vygon examined the downed enforcers as he stepped through them. He was not sure what species they were or if they were created. They were susceptible to stun, which was good. The fact that only enforcers had been found inside the facility so far stood out to him. It made him wonder if the filter shielding at the entrance kept the tree humanoids and the like out.

After a few minor skirmishes, they reached the splitting point.

"Given what we've fought so far, I'm not anticipating a lot of issues," said Sivaran.

"Yeah, we got this," said Emily.

Evaran nodded. "The rest of us will continue on to Wardax's main room. Hopefully, you two can shut down the power generator before we arrive."

"We should be able to," said Sivaran. "Our trip is much shorter than yours."

"Okay. Good luck, and we will see you soon," said Evaran.

Sivaran and Emily rushed down a side hallway.

They seemed fearless in all this, and Lord Vygon knew they made a formidable pair. His group was no slouch either. Evaran was a force unto himself, and V had a juggernaut robot mode. Dr. Snowden was a marksman with his PSD, and Lord Vygon was confident in the group's combat abilities.

With Evaran's utility handle and two PSDs in play, there was plenty of support and ranged options available.

Evaran waved forward.

Lord Vygon focused on reaching Wardax's room. It was almost twice as far as Sivaran and Emily had to go, and Lord Vygon had no doubt there would be fighting along the way. He had not had to use his blunted blades yet, but with a smaller group, he suspected he would. So far the incursion had been successful, but he knew better than to get complacent.

25

Emily's heartbeat raced as she and Sivaran moved down a side hallway toward the power generator control room. It was one of many and seemed to be built to regulate power distribution for various sites. The one they were going to would disable the conduit in Wardax's room. Their mission was simple: shut down the power and defend the area until they could leave.

She was confident in her ability, and with Sivaran, she had no doubt they could handle whatever came their way. She preferred not to split up, but Evaran's group was powerful as well. Hopefully, they did not run into any major issues. Sivaran was Evaran with a different form, and she felt that bond even though she had only known Sivaran for this adventure.

They rushed headlong into a group of medium-sized enforcers that appeared. They fired energy beams, which Emily reflected.

Sivaran ran through them after most had gone down and stunned those still left standing.

"Nice work," he said. "Your timing in order to reflect is impressive."

"I'm okay with it," she said.

"Modest. I like it."

They reached a T-junction and went right.

"Not too bad so far," said Emily. "Now watch something pop out."

Sivaran raised a hand. "You may get your wish."

She sensed the heavier footsteps as well. The hallway was spacious, and whatever was coming was either very dense or just big.

A large quadruped with a humanoid torso appeared. It wore green enforcer armor and had a device on its back. The weapon it held was attached to the device by several thick cables. The weapon whirred to life.

Emily expanded her shield and set it in front of her while Sivaran adopted a defensive stance.

The weapon fired and sent a repulsion blast that sent Emily sprawling.

She had not expected that. As she jumped up, Sivaran rushed forward and slid into the creature, knocking out its front two legs.

It crashed to the ground.

Sivaran grabbed the weapon and broke it in half, then stunned the enforcer with two quick shots.

Emily joined him. "Wardax is playing games by using our own tactics against us."

"They're effective," said Sivaran. He motioned forward. "C'mon, let's go."

It bothered her that she had been literally blown away. To compensate for that, she would change her stance up so she had more leverage. She could have also just shot a mist and stun combo. If anything, she was now aware of that type of threat. Her stomach churned to think about what would have happened if they had to fight through sticky globules.

The next few skirmishes were light, and she was glad they used regular energy beams. Wardax was crafty, and she was sure the easy fights so far were like a status update for him.

After twenty minutes, they reached the power generator control room.

Sivaran's eyes narrowed. "The layout said there were two entrances." He walked across the spacious area and to the right. "Interesting. This door is welded shut."

"So we have a choke point, then," said Emily. She shook her head. "And something tells me Wardax planned for that."

"My thoughts exactly," said Sivaran. He moved over to the far-left corner, where a section of the wall jutted out, creating a small space that had a console and various screens on the walls. After placing a connection device, he contacted Q. "We're connected."

"I'm in, but there's an AI here," said Q over comms. "The system and V's information showed no signs of one earlier."

Sivaran sighed. "Then it's there on purpose. Can you overcome it?"

"Definitely, but it will take some time."

Sivaran glanced at Emily. "Until then, we defend the area."

She coughed. "I'm sensing palisin energy."

"Over there," said Sivaran, pointing at several grills along the bottom part of a wall.

Emily marched over and covered the slats with sticky globules, then used her heat beam to solidify it. "No more palisin mist, but there's still some here."

"Not much, just enough to be irritating," said Sivaran as he deployed a canister that spewed a white mist to counter the palisin one. "That will deal with that." He rubbed his chin.

"You're trying to figure out if he planned for this too."

"I am. For all we know, we're doing exactly what he wants us to be doing."

Emily perked up. "Something's coming!" She faced the hallway they came in from and adopted a defensive stance.

Sivaran joined her. "I sense them too. Enforcers, although these are heavies."

"Last one had a repulsion blaster," she said.

Her heart raced when three heavies, each similar to the one before, arrived. She expanded her shield and leaned forward more than she normally would. A repulsion blast would not knock her away a second time.

The left and right enforcer shot a stream of sticky globules at Emily.

Although her shield caught the mess, it obscured her view. She deactivated her shield, causing the goop to fall to the ground.

The middle enforcer hit her with a repulsion blast, sending her tumbling into the wall.

"Damn it!" she said as she struggled to get up.

Sivaran had extended rods behind him that prevented him from being tossed. He retracted them and charged forward, yanking the weapon out of the middle enforcer's hands. Rods shot off to the sides, piercing and disabling the left and right enforcer's weapons. He kicked the middle heavy back, then positioned his arms in a downward V formation and shot stun blasts from his wrist-mounted weapons. After ensuring the side attackers were down, he lined up both arms in front of him and fired a dual stun blast at the one he kicked away.

Emily joined him and huffed. "I think they're out to see who can blow me away."

"Their focus on you, though, allowed me to get in close," said Sivaran.

She swatted his arm. "Okay, next time you be the distraction." She scowled as she activated her energy shield and faced forward. "Next round."

Sivaran squeezed her arm and stood beside her.

She appreciated having him there. It was hard to distinguish him from Evaran at times, but then Sivaran would crack a smile or laugh. In battle, Sivaran was just as fierce and elegant as Evaran was.

Several presences were detected at the entrance, but she did not see anything. She fired a repulsion blast.

Three enforcers appeared out of stealth and were blown away.

"That's new," said Emily. "Wardax had to know we'd sense that." She tilted her head. "They're carrying palisin-coated knives."

"Yes, and I suspect that was to test our senses. I bet he's—"

A horde of small spheres with tentacles surged into the entrance.

"Infectors!" said Emily. Her senses went wild. "And more of those infiltrators, but hard to distinguish them from the infectors."

"And the plan is revealed," said Sivaran. "Keep the right side clear, I'm going to the left."

She focused on firing repulsion beams. As Sivaran ripped through the left side, he tossed them into her repulsion blast arc. She liked his strategy. It kept the attackers from forming a massive group and attacking at once, and allowed him to handle smaller groups while she kept them at bay. At some point, they would just pile up, but the idea was to keep them backed up and in a continual state of chaos.

Sivaran moved like a ninja as he flipped around everywhere. His suit emitted rods of varying lengths and thickness that knocked away anything close to him. His rapid firing of his wrist-mounted stun weapons kept fast foes from blowing past him.

Emily was beginning to feel like they were getting pinned in. Although she was sure they could fight their way out, they were essentially hemmed in by the constant stream of enemies. That would ensure that Evaran's group would be alone in their fight, but she trusted they could handle themselves. She wished that she and Sivaran could join them, and hopefully they soon could.

She would make sure that Wardax could not regenerate or draw power from the conduit in the main room. All she needed was the okay to move out. For now, there were enforcers to repulse.

***

Dr. Snowden's heart thumped as Evaran led their small group. Lord Vygon seemed like he was ready to fight to the death, and Evaran and V were their usual stoic selves. Dr. Snowden was not sure he was ready to face Wardax, and the current situation brought up a lot of painful memories. Although

Wardax had been purged, Dr. Snowden still remembered being captured. The thin vines that wove in and out of the hallway they advanced down did not help things.

Emily and Sivaran would have no problem getting to the power generator room. Emily was a fighter, and Sivaran was an Evaran. Although Wardax might use palisin energy in some form, it would be limited unless he wanted to risk having it used back on him. Dr. Snowden wondered if Wardax had planned for the group to split up. Knowing him, he probably had.

Evaran paused to study Dr. Snowden. "Are you okay?"

"Yeah, yeah, I'm good."

"Analysis. You are stressed."

Dr. Snowden chuckled. "Well, we are on our way to fight Wardax, so yeah, maybe a bit."

V placed a hand on his shoulder. "We are with you this time."

"Yeah," said Dr. Snowden.

He appreciated Evaran and V's confidence. Lord Vygon was probably driven by rage, so he had no time to feel anxiety. Wardax being some huge bug and plant hybrid did not put Dr. Snowden at ease. Regardless, he would stick with the plan and contribute.

The group paused after a few minutes. Several small enforcers had arrived and opened fire. They did not survive the reflected beams. Several more popped up behind the group, but Dr. Snowden got those.

Lord Vygon shook his head. "Save some for me."

"I am sure that an opportunity will arise for you to engage in combat," said Evaran. He motioned forward. "Let us go."

Dr. Snowden studied the fallen enforcers. They had treelike bodies with green armor. The attack felt like a probe, and Wardax would know this assault would be futile. Dr. Snowden's stomach knotted up more. Wardax was planning something—he had to be.

The group continued on until they came across two heavily armored quadruped enforcers with humanoid torsos. A device sat on their backs that linked up to a weapon. The enforcers raised their weapons.

"Repulsion blast!" said Evaran as he expanded his shielding to cover the group.

The enforcers shot a repulsion blast, which pushed Evaran back but did not knock him down.

Dr. Snowden, Lord Vygon, and Evaran took the time between blasts to fire a mist beam, then ignite it, downing both enforcers.

"Your shield is truly amazing," said Lord Vygon.

Evaran nodded. "Let us hope these types of enforcers are not more common. If we do run across them, make sure you are behind me."

"Yeah, no argument from me," said Dr. Snowden. "I woulda probably gotten tossed back."

He stepped around the downed enforcers as the group marched on. It was almost like Wardax was testing units out by sending them piecemeal like this. Dr. Snowden now understood how annoying the PSD must be to enemies. If it did not stun or immobilize you, it would blow you away or trap you with sticky globules.

About halfway to the main room, Sivaran contacted them to let them know that he and Emily had arrived at their destination.

"Now that they are in position and Q is working on the surprise AI, our goal will be to stall Wardax until his power conduit is down," said Evaran.

"How are we going to do that?" asked Lord Vygon.

Dr. Snowden gestured at Evaran. "Wardax will talk to Evaran, cosmic being to cosmic being. Wardax wants to survive, and he knows what Evaran is capable of." He motioned at Lord Vygon. "He also knows the other version of you and how powerful you can be, in particular when you and Evaran took down the Overlord, who had some cosmic energy. I suspect Wardax will weigh his options."

"He could have just reached out to discuss all this from the beginning."

Dr. Snowden shrugged. "I'm not trying to defend him, believe me, but I do understand his fear."

"I concur," said Evaran. "We will use parlay tactics until we can move." He pointed at the backpack on V. "The primary goal is to get the energy siphoning device on Wardax."

"Got it," said Dr. Snowden.

They proceeded on, and after a few light skirmishes, they reached the main room, where Wardax was.

Dr. Snowden's pulse quickened as he stepped into the room. It was just as V had scanned it. The strange egg-shaped structure in the middle of the room was held in place by vines but was not what it appeared to be. Thankfully, he knew it was Wardax in some type of energy recharging phase.

The power conduit in the back was as V had shown it. Its thick cables ran from its rectangular structure and into the walls, and it seemed the vines had partially merged into it. Dr. Snowden had not figured out how Wardax used the power since it would have no impact on his cosmic ability. Evaran seemed to think it was to help maintain all the connections and to also tie Wardax into a control system. There might also be regenerative effects.

"Evaran … you've finally arrived," said Wardax via the egg-shaped object.

"I have," said Evaran.

Dr. Snowden's breathing became haphazard. Although the voice was different, he could sense Wardax. Lord Vygon had extended both his dual blades and fidgeted with his PSD. V stood next to Evaran and seemed ready to dash over to Wardax at a moment's notice.

"I knew you would come, thanks to Dr. Snowden," said Wardax. "'To fight you is foolish' is a phrase I saw uttered more than once. The foes you fought were powerful. You also appear to be a being of reason. There's no need to fight."

Evaran raised a finger. "Unfortunately, you have caused much mayhem, and you do it with cosmic energy aiding you. I cannot allow that to stand. You have not been a good steward of it. If you had been, I would not be here."

"And if you take it … what then? I'd be at the mercy of a galaxy that wants me dead."

"That is of your doing, and the natural order of events," said Evaran. "I understand that you were almost killed, and it was cosmic energy that saved you." He glanced at Lord Vygon. "However, you razed some worlds, killing untold numbers."

"They had to be stopped."

"Genocide is never the answer," said Evaran. He cast a sidelong glance at Dr. Snowden, then faced Wardax with glowing eyes. "You also assaulted Dr. Snowden's mind. That is unforgivable."

Wardax sighed. "I see that my fate, then, has already been determined by you. I wanted to work this out with you, but I see that you cannot see past minor issues from the past."

"The destruction of my planet is not a minor issue!" said Lord Vygon.

"In the grand scheme of things, it is," said Wardax. "You live, so you can carry on your race. Also, I sense Dr. Snowden seems to be okay."

Dr. Snowden scowled. "You violated me!"

"A small price to know what's coming."

Evaran shook his head. "And that is why you are not fit to carry cosmic energy. Your complete lack of concern for other life makes you dangerous. You could have stayed in your dimension."

"Why? There is so much to learn in this reality. Why should I be the one to retreat? Why can't those who attacked me pay for their crimes?"

"I understand wanting revenge, but your actions have gone beyond what I would normally tolerate."

"So what now?" asked Wardax.

Evaran gestured at V. "We have a device that will remove your cosmic energy. Accept it, and we will leave."

"You've already somehow deployed your countervirus to everyplace I have control. I suspect time travel is involved, although I don't know the specifics. My dimensional network is still active, but I can't communicate with any of my guardians. And now you want to take away the very thing that allows me to defend myself? No. That's not going to happen. I've seen what you fought in the past, but they didn't have the knowledge that I have now. I'm saddened that you've come to the conclusion you have."

Evaran activated his energy shield and studied his surroundings.

"I thought we could come to an understanding. Apparently not," said Wardax.

Dr. Snowden's skin crawled as he sensed the movement on the edge of his senses. A lot of something was coming.

Lord Vygon and V adopted an offensive stance.

"You will release your cosmic energy, willingly or not," said Evaran.

The power conduit powered down.

"As expected," said Wardax.

Dr. Snowden gulped. It seemed maybe Wardax did not need the power conduit at all and had used it to split up the group. There was no doubt this fight would go much easier with Sivaran and Emily present. Dr. Snowden knew one thing for sure: Wardax was not going to go without a fight and a carefully crafted plan. So far his plan seemed to be working.

26

Lord Vygon whirled around to face what appeared to be a swarm of small plantlike creatures. They had square cushion-shaped bodies with plantlike stalks at each corner and a mouth on the underside filled with razor-sharp teeth. Behind them were enforcers, who unleashed a barrage of energy beams. Evaran had called Emily and Sivaran for assistance, but Lord Vygon wondered if they would arrive in time. He faced forward with his shield out.

Evaran jumped up front and expanded his energy shield, but the swarmers went by and over it.

Lord Vygon's skin crawled when a large noise erupted from behind him. He spun around.

Wardax popped out of the central structure he was in and charged right for Evaran, who turned to fight.

"Dr. Snowden, we could use your shield!" said Lord Vygon as he knocked away swarmer after swarmer. He braced himself as the swarmers launched himself at his shield.

ADAIR HART

Dr. Snowden took Evaran's place and used his free hand to shoot anything that got by, but there were too many. Some had attacked his arms and legs.

Lord Vygon and V rushed over and cleared Dr. Snowden of any attacker.

Although V had the cosmic energy siphoning device, he went around the shields and targeted the enforcers. He got mobbed but tossed swarmers around. His chest light had turned red, and when he reached the enforcers, he grabbed one of their guns and used it on the swarmers. With his other hand, he flung enforcers around like rag dolls.

Lord Vygon had never seen V in this mode before, but it seemed to be one with no problems of creating casualties. Then again, this was not a situation where trying not to kill could lead to problems. The swarmers that V punched through were not coming back from that. Nor were the ones he shot a hole through. Confident that Dr. Snowden and V had slowed the frontal assault enough for them to handle, Lord Vygon grabbed the backpack from V and turned to help Evaran.

Wardax was massive and filled up nearly half the back room. Evaran's speed and raw strength were on display as he moved like a lightning bolt around Wardax while using his staff to keep any of Wardax's many vines from touching him. Two cosmic beings squaring off in physical combat was something Lord Vygon knew was extremely rare. Without Evaran there, Lord Vygon suspected Wardax would have run over everyone in the room with ease.

Lord Vygon rushed forward and dodged a swipe attempt by one of Wardax's vines, then used his blunt blades to chop off the vine. He pulled out the device which Wardax knocked away toward the entrance.

"Damn!" said Lord Vygon.

Wardax roared and then curled up. He shot out all his vines at once, hitting both Lord Vygon and Evaran and sending them sprawling back.

Lord Vygon grimaced. Although he was able to get his shield up, the vine still hit him hard. If he did not have the shield, he expected his chest would be caved in. Wardax had pure power, and Lord Vygon was sure that the cosmic energy was boosting that. The siphoning device rolled around on the ground. He needed to make sure it did not directly touch Dr. Snowden, V, or Evaran.

Evaran jumped back up and shot a mist beam and then ignited it.

Wardax unfurled and charged Evaran, who blocked a few vine strikes.

Lord Vygon focused on Dr. Snowden when he cried out in pain. A heavy enforcer had charged forward into his shield and crushed him against the wall. V had gone to assist and gotten sidelined by another big enforcer. Lord Vygon burst over to the one on Dr. Snowden and jumped over it. As he did, he unleashed a point-blank stun.

The enforcer growled and stepped back.

Dr. Snowden breathed hard and fired a mist beam.

Lord Vygon lit it up and the enforcer crashed to the ground.

Dr. Snowden took a moment to catch his breath. "Thanks." He pointed at the siphoning device, which an enforcer had picked up and turned to run away with. "They're trying to get away with it. You got to get it."

"All right," said Lord Vygon. "Hopefully Evaran can keep Wardax busy and you and V can hold this front. I'm going."

"Be careful," said Dr. Snowden, gesturing at the swarm, which had fully entered the room. Some were even fighting Evaran.

"I will. Help Evaran!" said Lord Vygon.

He raised his energy shield and charged into the mass of enforcers, helping to give V some breathing space. Once done, Lord Vygon burst into the hallway leading out. The siphoning device was not hard to detect, and the enforcer who had initially grabbed it had passed it on.

He did not waste time trying to fight everything but instead used them against each other. Although he had his energy shield, it was awkward in close-quarters combat when surrounded. Instead, he would grab a smaller enforcer and use it in front to absorb any energy beams.

Wardax's growls and roars could be heard even as far away as Lord Vygon was. He was not sure where the siphoning device was being taken, but it needed to be retrieved.

After five minutes of frantically chasing the device, he arrived at a four-way intersection. The device was held to the chest of a smaller enforcer who crouched under an array of heavy ones. Swarmers came from all directions, and he was not sure how he was going to get it out, but he had to try.

He fired a repulsion beam that swept away the swarmers, who just came right back. A mist beam followed by a stun beam seemed to shake some loose, but he was also dodging energy beams at the same time. He raised his shield and expanded it some.

"The enforcers and swarmers are guarding the device," said Lord Vygon over comms. "I'm not sure I can reach it."

"I'm almost to your location," said Emily. "Sivaran is going to the main room."

Lord Vygon relaxed some at hearing Emily's voice. As hectic as it was, she made it seem like everything was under control. He peeked out and saw the smaller enforcer run in the opposite direction. It could not be allowed to escape.

He charged into the room and jumped onto the back of one of the large enforcers. As he went to go past it, one of the heavies grabbed him and threw him against the wall. He tasted blood as he struggled to move. The other heavies had turned to face him and the swarmers approached from all sides, even above him. He fired a repulsion beam and rolled to the side. As he rushed into the corridor where the siphon device had been taken, he got hit by a repulsion beam.

Several swarmers jumped on him and bit.

He growled as he shook them off. These things were playing for keeps. He ducked into a side hallway and took a moment to assess his situation. The siphon device was not too far away, but he was going deeper into enemy territory and the attacks were getting tougher. He was not sure how Evaran, Dr. Snowden, and V were faring, but the longer it took to retrieve the device, the more danger they were in. Lord Vygon drank two blood vials. That device was coming back.

* * *

Emily's heart sank when they had turned off the power generator, which seemed to be something Wardax had planned for. It became obvious that it was a ruse to split up the group. While the power he siphoned could heal him or give him a boost, he might not even need it to fight Evaran and the others.

She and Sivaran had taken off per Evaran's request, but then Lord Vygon had mentioned the device was being taken away. The plan was then for her to help Lord Vygon, while Sivaran would assist Evaran and the others. Sivaran had already left, and she went down a side hallway toward Lord Vygon. It killed her to hear the frantic discussion of the others, and Lord Vygon's vitals seemed to be all over the place.

She narrowed her eyes and focused. Dr. Snowden's vitals had dipped a bit when he had been crushed against the wall, per the chatter. Lord Vygon had selflessly charged into enemy territory by himself to retrieve the device. Evaran was holding his own against Wardax, but even he struggled some. The fact that this had occurred suggested Wardax's true strength. V did all he could to keep Evaran and Dr. Snowden from getting swarmed. Her suit responded to her rising anger and provided clarity for her.

The first group of enforcers and swarmers she met were no match for her. It was like they moved in molasses, and she swept them away or stunned them with her staff. It was a massing of heavies in the next hallway that gave her some issues. She had to use her shield, and she braced herself this time. Once she survived that, she hurtled toward them like a heat-seeking missile and knocked their legs out from under them.

They crumpled to the ground and shrieked when she hit each one in sequence with her staff and stunned them.

She could see Lord Vygon on her map, and he was quite a bit away from both her and the main room, which Sivaran had almost reached. His fighting on the way had alleviated the pressure put on Dr. Snowden and V, based on what she heard. She wanted to join them as soon as possible, but Lord Vygon was by himself. She admired his tenacity and fearlessness and did not plan on letting him down.

When she reached a T-junction, she jumped back into the perpendicular hallway as a repulsion blast shot from left to right. She had sensed the heavy enforcer, but also a swarm coming from behind and another heavy enforcer in the right hallway. It seemed odd to her that the left heavy would fire since, if it missed, it would hit the right one. A quick peek verified that was exactly what had happened.

She focused and blazed around the corner, barely stopping to touch the enforcer in the head with her staff and unleash a shock. Lord Vygon was only a few hallways away, and it seemed he had retrieved the siphoning device but was under a sustained assault. She heard him growling when she got close. It reminded her of when the Lord Vygon she knew had fought the Overlord.

After reaching Lord Vygon's position via the north entrance in a room with two entry points, she surveyed the scene. He had his shield out and fired repulsion and stun beams nonstop. He was bloody, probably due to the swarmers taking a few bites. She hustled over and helped shoot beams.

"Emily! I'm glad to see you," he said, taking a moment to relax.

She figured he had been under constant duress her whole way over.

"We need to get this device to Wardax, now!" he said.

Emily nodded. After a final barrage of mist and stun beams, they were on their way. Although she wanted to carry the device, she understood it would try to sap her cosmic energy if she held it. It had no effect on Lord Vygon, though. She had thought the siphoning aspect would operate on any energy, but apparently it had been tuned to only cosmic energy. She would have to personally thank Jelton again for that later.

The journey to the main room was much easier. Lord Vygon had already cleared a path when he had gone after the device, and Sivaran had mopped up anything left on his way over. Her eyes widened as they stepped in. Evaran and Sivaran had massive vines wrapped around them. V and Dr. Snowden dodged vine attacks while trying to free Evaran and Sivaran.

"How are we going to get near Wardax?" asked Emily.

Lord Vygon studied the battle. "My last attempt had the device knocked away. That's not going to happen this time. Can you provide a distraction?"

She nodded. "I'll help Dr. Snowden and V."

"I'll need V," said Lord Vygon. "V, can you open Wardax's mouth?"

"Yes," he said over comms.

Lord Vygon's voice cracked. "Good. Emily is going to provide a distraction and take your place. You get Wardax's mouth open, I'll get this device in."

"Acknowledged."

Emily eyed Lord Vygon. Something was off. She had never heard his voice crack before. "You all right?"

He cleared his throat. "Yeah. Create the distraction."

She looked him over, then charged in with her staff. Her first goal would be to free Evaran and her bladed staff should work there. As she rushed over and sliced and diced any vine that got too close, Wardax focused on her.

V advanced and jumped into Wardax's large mouth. He used both hands to keep the lips apart, then climbed in and wedged himself.

Emily whacked away at the vines but kept an eye on things. She watched as Lord Vygon moved like a bolt toward

Wardax. It would be like playing basketball at this point, and Wardax's mouth was the hoop.

"For Drydris!" said Lord Vygon before he shot into Wardax's mouth like a missile.

Emily did a double take. That was not what she had been expecting.

The vines around Evaran and Sivaran weakened, and they burst free.

V tried to grab Lord Vygon's ankles before he disappeared into Wardax's snakelike body.

Wardax wrapped his vines around V, then flung him across the room. "How rude. I guess Lord Vygon—" He convulsed.

Evaran grabbed Emily's arm and pulled her back. "Everyone back!"

She watched in rapture as tiny dots appeared on Wardax's skin. His gnashing and snarling indicated that the device was siphoning off his energy. A bright glow formed around Wardax before dimming into nothingness.

Wardax trembled as he paused for a moment. He faced Evaran. "I can feel the cosmic energy leaving. As you have taken from me, I have taken from you."

"Get him out!" said Evaran as his and Sivaran's eyes glowed.

Even powered down, Wardax still put up a good fight. His vines swirled around like whips, keeping Sivaran and Evaran at bay. V had rejoined the fight but got slapped away again. It seemed Wardax did not want a repeat of his mouth being forced open.

She snapped her head toward Dr. Snowden, whose breathing had become erratic.

He charged like a crazy man at Wardax's midsection, then rubbed his hands on the side.

She knew what he had done, and the cosmic nanobots went to work dissolving Wardax. The only problem was that Lord Vygon would be at risk too.

Wardax slowed down, and Evaran and Sivaran were able to hold down his vines.

The cosmic nanobots turned black as the device absorbed their energy, but they had opened a hole and Lord Vygon's arm was visible.

Emily hustled over and helped pull Lord Vygon out. Her heart sank. Half his body had been crushed, and although she sensed his Daedrould energy, it was weakening. She did not sense his breath or heartbeat.

Dr. Snowden dropped to his knees and cradled Lord Vygon. "No! Wake up!"

Wardax slowed down, then stopped.

She sensed that the damage from the device and nanobots was too much.

Evaran, Sivaran, and V rushed over to Lord Vygon. Evaran scanned Lord Vygon, then moved his lips down slightly. Sivaran scowled as his eyes misted.

Emily's heart hurt. Lord Vygon had sacrificed himself to stop Wardax. That was nothing less than what she would expect from Lord Vygon. She realized that he had known all along what the play was, and he was going to trade his life for Wardax's to end the threat. His tactic removed any possibility that Wardax would knock the device away again, or even worse, grab one of the others and use the device on them. Evaran's cosmic energy was fluctuating wildly, which showed the depth of his pain at Lord Vygon's loss, even if he was an alternate version.

Evaran sighed. "Wardax's form in this reality is destroyed, but he still lives on in his dimension."

"What do we do now?" asked Dr. Snowden, wiping his eyes.

"We get Lord Vygon back," said Sivaran. "The Daedrculd stone. He gave that to you for a reason. We can use the siphoned cosmic energy to power it." He glanced at V. "Let's get the device into the backpack, then get to the *Torvatta*."

"I thought that cosmic energy was for your *Torvatta*?" asked Emily.

Sivaran shook his head. "Not when a friend is in need."

Emily's throat constricted. Sivaran had shown no hesitation about helping someone in distress, definitely an Evaran trait.

V grabbed his torn backpack and fetched the siphoning device, holding it like a hot potato as he placed it in.

"Let us go," said Evaran. "With Wardax's control broken, the enforcers will not fight as a unified enemy. However, they may still be a threat."

Sivaran picked up Lord Vygon. "They won't be a problem. Let's go."

Emily put her arm around Dr. Snowden. A frown was etched on his face. There was no guarantee that the Daedrould stone would work, but they had to try. There was a small glimmer of hope that maybe this was the Lord Vygon they knew, and the stones might resurrect him. She did not think it worked like that, but for now, any hope was better than none.

27

Dr. Snowden fumbled around the small nightstand next to his bed, where he had put the Daedrould stone. His breath was still ragged from having fought nonstop on the way back to the *Torvatta*. Evaran and Emily had been hurricanes as they had whirled through enemies and tossed them away. V had dealt with any that came from behind while Sivaran had carried Lord Vygon. Dr. Snowden recalled how everything had seemed orderly as they had mopped up enemies.

It had not taken long to reach the *Torvatta*, and Lord Vygon's lifeless body now lay on a slab in the medical lab. It was strange to still sense Daedrould energy on him but not hear or see anything indicating he was alive. Dr. Snowden focused on the present and relaxed some when he found the Daedrould stone. A quick burst later and he was in the lab with the others. He handed the stone to Evaran.

"So how does this work exactly?" asked Dr. Snowden.

Evaran put Dr. Snowden's half of the Daedrould stone together with Emily's. "I believe we place the two halves together, then place it on him."

"I don't see how that will do anything," said Emily.

"I am not sure either, but we can try," said Evaran. He placed the complete stone on Lord Vygon's chest.

A black mist formed around his body.

Everyone stood back.

Dr. Snowden's skin crawled as the mist seemed to be sucked into the stone. It was like someone opening a window in a smoky room. He flinched when a silver glow emanated from the stone's underside. It pained him to have to be dealing with this, and Lord Vygon deserved more. He had given his life to end the threat, which was exactly what Dr. Snowden would have expected the Lord Vygon he knew to do.

"What is that glow?" asked Emily.

"I am unsure," said Evaran. "Let the stone complete what it needs to do, then we can investigate it."

Emily walked over and intertwined her left arm with Dr. Snowden's. V patted her back.

Although she was tough, Dr. Snowden suspected she hurt as bad as he did. Sivaran's grimace indicated how he felt about the situation, which was a far cry from the emotionless face of Evaran. However, Dr. Snowden sensed the flux in Evaran and knew he was agitated.

The dark mist dissipated and the glow around the stone faded.

"I believe it is safe to check it out," said Evaran. He scanned the stone, then picked it up. Upon studying the underside, he handed it to Sivaran.

"Well, now that's interesting," said Sivaran. He passed the stone to Dr. Snowden.

He studied the strange symbols and lines. "What is all this?"

"A set of *Torvatta* coordinates," said Sivaran. "It points to a specific point in time, space, and reality."

V peered over Dr. Snowden's shoulder. "Analysis. It points to Dr. Snowden and Emily's Earth around 10,100 BC."

"What do you think that means?" asked Dr. Snowden, glancing at Evaran.

He half smiled. "I believe it means that is where he will be resurrected. That is why he does not have the universal signature of this universe. He will get a new one in ours."

"Okay, but what about Lord Noskov, Lord Skar, and Lord Cyrus?"

Evaran nodded. "Their signatures will fade over time and adjust to our universe. It is why, when we encountered them on Earth in the past, their universal signature from Sivaran's universe had already been replaced."

"So this *is* the Lord Vygon we know!" said Emily.

"It would seem so," said Sivaran, smiling. "This all assumes the cosmic energy the siphoning device expels will work."

"Let's go!" said Emily.

The group hustled to the command center.

"V, take us to the coordinates," said Evaran.

"Acknowledged."

Dr. Snowden took a measured breath. Everything seemed to be looking up, although even if this did work, Lord Vygon would be alone on a world alien to him with no friends. Dr. Snowden had been somewhat skeptical that the stone would work, but he was a believer now.

That led to an information paradox. The stone had the coordinates but had been broken up to give to Dr. Snowden and Emily so they could have it in order for it to work in the future. The question was, when had the coordinates gotten etched on there? Another question was why the stone had been split in half.

The *Torvatta* opened a portal and flew through, exiting into low orbit over Earth.

Dr. Snowden relaxed. Per the data windows, this was his Earth. It felt strange to be back, and even if it was almost twelve thousand years in the past, he would take it.

After twenty minutes, the *Torvatta* hovered over a cave entrance.

Dr. Snowden's eyes narrowed. "That's odd. This is where Lord Vygon took us after our first meeting in 2610 BC."

"Yeah, not coincidental at all," said Emily.

Evaran stood. "Let us go."

After fifteen minutes, Lord Vygon had been moved out via hover slab, and the siphoning device sat next to him. Its tendrils were out and wrapped around the Daedrould stone.

"I believe we are ready," said Evaran. He glanced at Dr. Snowden and Emily. "Raise your helmets."

They complied and everyone stood back.

Evaran interacted with his ARI.

The siphoning device glowed as cosmic energy rushed out along the tendrils and exited the stone.

Dr. Snowden's eyes narrowed when the stone lit up like the sun. The dark mist he had seen enter before was now even thicker when expelled. It surrounded Lord Vygon's body. Dr. Snowden did not fully understand how it would revive Lord Vygon, but he thought he saw a finger move.

The mist continued to enter Lord Vygon, and after a minute, it dissipated and the stone cracked in half and began to crumble into a fine ash. The cosmic energy stopped being transmitted and the siphoning device shut off.

Dr. Snowden's heart raced when he sensed Lord Vygon's faint heartbeat. "He's alive!" He lowered his helmet.

"Yes!" said Emily.

Evaran scanned Lord Vygon. "He is weak, but with blood, he should heal up." He raised a finger. "However, we do not know what mental state he is in. There is still the possibility that this is not the Lord Vygon we are familiar with."

"Definitely true," said Sivaran.

"Analysis. That would be highly unlikely."

Q nodded. "I agree with V's assessment."

Dr. Snowden wagged a finger. "Yeah. Aren't you saying we should never ignore coincidences?"

"I am," said Evaran. "But there are a host of situations that would still give us the Lord Vygon we met in 2610 BC, who is different than the one coming back now from death."

Emily sighed. "You're right. Maybe it takes eight thousand years for him to remember everything."

"As V mentioned, it is probably unlikely, but we must be prepared for that," said Evaran. He pushed the hover slab onto the *Torvatta*.

"I guess it's a waiting game, then," said Dr. Snowden.

Sivaran rubbed his hands together. "Yes, and we'll need a strategy for the other ancient vampires when they wake up."

Dr. Snowden adjusted his glasses as he surveyed the forest outside the cave. He remembered coming there before. Once was when he had first met Lord Vygon; the second was in an alternate timeline. Now this was a third time, and he had witnessed Lord Vygon's resurrection. Sometimes it seemed like death was just a phase, as Levaran had said before.

***

Lord Vygon surveyed the desolate wasteland of jagged black crystallized structures. Pools of red liquid bubbled everywhere while vats of a black substance appeared to torment those caught inside. He knew he was in the domain of the Daedrould prince Druulkahn the Destroyer, a being of pure Daedrould energy that was also the creator of the ancient vampires. If Lord Vygon was there, then he was dead.

Druulkahn was easy to spot. He sat on a throne comprised of bones and held court before strange and unusual creatures of varying shapes and sizes. His dark red skin and black armor, the bone spikes extending from his shoulders, and the cape behind him made him look fierce.

Lord Vygon had talked with Druulkahn before. It was something an ancient vampire lord could do. Anything less required the vessel to be in full bloodlust, but then Druulkahn could control the body.

"Approach," said Druulkahn in a deep, grizzled voice.

Lord Vygon complied. He was not sure what would happen to him, but he hoped it was not the vat of black liquid. His footsteps crunched on the crusted ground and it seemed louder than it should be. The misshapen creatures behind the throne stood silent and stared at him with a multitude of eyes. He stood before Druulkahn.

"I guess I'm dead," he said.

"Not quite," said Druulkahn. "A Daedrould stone has been used."

"Even so, it requires a lot of power to be used for resurrection."

Druulkahn scoffed. "You traveled with Evaran. *Two* of them! Do you think power is an issue?" He stood and gazed off into the distance. "I lost a world that represented my strength, and to a cosmic being no less. They play with life and death, and even someone as powerful as I am can only watch."

"Drydris," said Lord Vygon, scowling. "If it matters, Wardax is dead. I put a device in him that extracted his cosmic energy."

Druulkahn nodded. "I know. And here you are, being pulled back to life by another faction of cosmic beings. No, your destiny doesn't end here. You have more work to do."

"You're not going to fight to keep me here?"

Druulkahn glared at Lord Vygon. "Do you think me a fool? If cosmic beings are involved in any way, you leave the situation. However … it may be useful to have good relations with some cosmic beings."

"You mean Evaran and Sivaran."

"Yes. When cosmic beings war, we all lose. It's wise to be on the winning side," said Druulkahn. He sniffed the air. "More importantly, you're now in another universe. A new opportunity presents itself. Gather the last of the ancient vampires and rebuild. Stay in Evaran and Sivaran's grace. Now go … there is much for you to do."

The environment shook, then faded away.

Lord Vygon grimaced as pain wracked him. There was blood being infused into him, and he sensed he was on a slab. A headache thumped away. He tried to swallow, but his throat and mouth were as dry as a desert. Even trying to move sent pangs everywhere. With new blood swirling around in him, his advanced regeneration should take him to a stabilized state. All he had to do was wait.

As he lay there, he heard Evaran and Sivaran talking. It seemed strange that Druulkahn, who Lord Vygon thought was almost godlike, was afraid of them. Although Druulkahn did not outright say it, his actions did. Lord Vygon understood that fear. It had only taken one cosmic being to almost eradicate all ancient vampires. Thankfully, another faction of cosmic beings had stepped in.

He would close his eyes and sleep, but his eyes were already shut. Still, he concentrated and cleared his mind. He could deal with everything when he was in better shape.

After a while, he stirred. His eyes instinctively tried to open, but it hurt to do so. His regeneration was still going full speed ahead, and he felt strong enough to awaken. He opened his eyes with some focus. Thankfully, the light above the slab had been dimmed.

"Easy," said Evaran. "Your body is still undergoing regeneration."

Lord Vygon grinned when he saw him and the others assembled around the slab. "I'm back."

"Yeah, you are," said Emily, squeezing his hand.

"I guess Wardax had some indigestion."

Sivaran chuckled. "He sure did."

"What's the situation?"

"Wardax is dead, you're not. We're on Dr. Snowden and Emily's Earth and you now have a universal signature tied to this universe, not the one we came from."

Lord Vygon propped himself up with some effort. "Earth. Why are we here?"

Dr. Snowden pointed at Lord Vygon's chest. "The Daedrould stone lit up when it held your Daedrould energy. On the underside were *Torvatta* coordinates to this location, which is well known to us."

"I didn't add coordinates to it," said Lord Vygon. He examined the stone granules on his chest. "I'm guessing it's gone."

"Yeah, and in the future, you'll create a new one and put the coordinates on it, it'll get split somehow, and then you'll give Emily and me each half."

Lord Vygon wrinkled his brow. "I guess so. That means this event always happened, and I was the Lord Vygon you knew all along."

Emily's eyes softened. "You're stuck with us, mister."

"I don't mind that at all." Lord Vygon glanced at Evaran and Sivaran. "Druulkahn seems to know you both."

Evaran half smiled. "I would expect so. I suspect that is why he let you go."

Lord Vygon shrugged. "He wants me to be here."

"I know."

It fascinated Lord Vygon to see the interaction between such epic beings, and he got a front-row seat to it all. A Daedrould stone took a lot of time to make. He had lost his on Drydris, but it seemed he would be making a new one and putting coordinates on it. The two halves did not make much sense to him, but since it was a part of this event, that meant it would occur sometime in the future for him. Time travel was strange.

"What about the other lords?" he asked.

"Their status is stable, and they will awake with you inside the cave we are in," said Evaran. "There are already some powerful Outsiders here, known as Helians. You will be a new threat to them, but we can give you some information to help with that."

"Sounds good." Lord Vygon eyed Q. "I bet you didn't expect to see all this."

"It has been informative."

"Sure has," said Lord Vygon. "Okay, I guess I wait until I'm strong enough to move, then we begin a new chapter."

Emily studied the large cave area the group had assembled in as V and Q moved various pieces of advanced equipment in. It had been about three hours since Lord Vygon had woken and it was now 7:00 p.m. He talked with Evaran and Sivaran, while Dr. Snowden had taken off to survey the cave system. Although she had not seen it firsthand, he apparently had, and she suspected he wanted to see how it compared to what he knew.

This was to be the ancient vampires' base of operations until they got settled in. She only remembered the entrance where she had been teleported away to Egypt, then to a prison planet. Lord Vygon had met them in 2610 BC in a spot not too far away. He had a long future ahead of him. She joined Evaran, Lord Vygon, and Sivaran.

"This must bring back some memories," said Sivaran, smiling at Emily.

"Not fun ones," she said.

Lord Vygon shook his head. "There is so much I don't know, but will in time."

"As it should be," said Evaran.

Everyone focused on Dr. Snowden arriving.

"Yeah, place is a little different, but the layout is similar to what I remember," he said.

Evaran studied him. "You checked out the room you slept in after Emily was teleported."

Dr. Snowden sighed. "Yeah."

V and Q entered, pushing a hover slab with several devices on it.

Emily thought the first device resembled half a metallic ball with several tentacles underneath. Another was a small matter replicator while the third one's purpose, like the first one, remained unknown.

Evaran pointed at the ball device. "This fusion device will provide power for the other devices that V and Q are bringing. Once it is placed on the ground, the tentacles will anchor it. V and Q will connect the matter replicator to it. The other device obscures this location from surveillance."

"From these Helians, right?" asked Lord Vygon.

Evaran nodded. "They are the strongest nonhuman power on this planet, outside the Ollikrin Nation, but the Helians are advanced. Humanity is still evolving from a technological perspective. They are similar to the Halkins you knew, and their blood is compatible."

"I see." Lord Vygon motioned at a tunnel that led outside. "What about the other ancient vampire lords?"

"You can release them after we have gone. You will need to feign ignorance when they ask how they got to where they are, but you can reveal information on these events at a future meeting we will have on August 4, 2013, at 8:00 p.m."

Lord Vygon's eyes widened. "That's ... a long time from now."

"Indeed. From our perspective, we will leave here and go right there, so you have approximately twelve thousand years to keep this information secret."

"These are strange times," said Lord Vygon. "I'm glad to have a second chance. There's a lot of work to do and a new world to explore. I can already sense this planet is full of fresh experiences."

Dr. Snowden nodded. "Definitely some interesting ones for sure. The tables are turned this time. When we first met you here, we had no idea who you were, but you knew us. This time we knew you, and you didn't know us."

"That's how the *Torvatta* knew my favorite drink," said Lord Vygon.

"Yep."

"Analysis. We are bringing in the stasis capsules for the other lords now."

Evaran nodded.

Emily studied the area where Lord Vygon had chosen to place the energy device. Its tentacles came alive as they pulled the device into the wall a bit. The ancient vampires would have some time to get things going while they adjusted to the world. It excited her to think about meeting them in the future when they all understood the situation.

After ten minutes of light chat, V and Q arrived with Lord Noskov and Lord Skar's capsules.

Evaran pointed to a side room. "They can be unloaded there. They are under sedation and should wake in an hour or so."

"I'll have to pretend I don't know how we got here," said Lord Vygon. "They're going to have a lot of questions, but ... I think we'll be okay."

Emily followed V and Q into the side room. Four wooden cots with some blankets on them were scattered around the room. V released the capsule lock for Lord Noskov's capsule, then laid him on one of the cots. Q got Lord Skar. Lord Cyrus would be next, and then Lord Vygon would be on his cot and have to hide a secret for a long time. She rejoined the group in the main room.

"I wish I had more time to spend with you all," said Lord Vygon.

Sivaran sighed. "The feeling's mutual, but you *will* see us again." He crooked a thumb at Evaran. "Well, you'll see him a lot more than me, but you'll see me at this meeting we're going to."

"I look forward to it," said Lord Vygon. He scrutinized Evaran. "Any tips on how to deal with the nonhumans on this planet?"

"That is a part of your learning experience. However, I would suggest caution with the Helians. Delia Everoak of the Ollikrin Nation would be a good person to meet. However, it would be wise not to mention us or how you arrived."

Dr. Snowden adjusted his glasses. "Wow, I didn't know she was that old."

Evaran nodded.

"I guess then I don't need to worry about someone like Wardax coming and destroying this planet," said Lord Vygon.

"No need to worry about that here," said Emily.

Lord Vygon nodded at her. "That's great, although it would be nice to have our own dimension at some point."

"You can add that to the list of many things to do, then," said Emily, swatting his arm.

Everyone watched V and Q arrive and then unload Lord Cyrus onto a cot.

"It is time for us to go," said Evaran.

Lord Vygon looked down. "It's hard to believe all that's happened, but we're alive, and we have a second chance." He raised his head and extended a hand toward Evaran. "We owe you everything."

He returned the handshake. "You will be fine."

Lord Vygon went around the room to say goodbye.

Emily hugged him when he came to her. She sensed his sadness that the group was leaving, but there was also a sense of excitement at starting anew. Although she knew Lord Vygon was tough, his softened eyes approximated misty ones. He had formed a strong bond with everyone, and it now made sense why he had been so excited to see them in 2610 BC. It made her wonder if he had met other Evaran versions before then.

Dr. Snowden had pulled Lord Vygon in for a half hug and slap on the back.

Emily recalled that was how they met in the future, and Lord Vygon had remembered it. She peered back as the group boarded the *Torvatta*. Lord Vygon frowned as he watched them go. It made her want to rush out and hug him to let him know everything would be fine. She was excited that she would get to see him soon in the future meeting.

28

A lump formed in Dr. Snowden's throat as the *Torvatta* ascended. Lord Vygon stood below at the cave entrance and waved goodbye to them. He had proven himself to be the same Lord Vygon that Dr. Snowden already knew. In time, Lord Vygon would also become Dr. Snowden and Emily's best friend. Dr. Snowden frowned when Emily did. Although they were going to meet Lord Vygon in the future, it felt like they were abandoning him, but Dr. Snowden knew this had to happen.

After twenty minutes, the *Torvatta* reached low orbit, jumped forward in time to 7:30 p.m. on the day they had initially left for Sivaran's universe, then descended. After another twenty minutes, they hovered over Lord Noskov's base.

"We are early, so if you have any business to handle, do so now," said Evaran.

Dr. Snowden made a quick pit stop to relieve himself and clean up some. His suit had the same self-cleaning aspect that Evaran's had, but his hands and face still needed to be washed up. After ensuring he was presentable, he joined the others on the ramp. Emily had also freshened up, but she had done a quick wash of her hair, a technique she had mastered in her early college years.

Evaran and Sivaran stood tall, front and center, with V and Q flanking them.

It was what awaited them on Lord Noskov's platform that made Dr. Snowden get goose bumps. The four ancient vampire lords had on what appeared to be dark gray ceremonial robes, with large collars that expanded out and above their heads. An elegant golden design resided on the back of their black capes with silver interior. The design seemed to be unique for each lord. A silver belt sat on each of their waists. Dr. Snowden could not recall ever seeing the outfit before.

"Those outfits are cool," said Emily.

Q nodded. "The air flow in the design would seem to indicate that."

"Analysis. She meant she liked them."

"Oh."

Dr. Snowden recalled a time when V had thought that someone calling Emily "hot pants" implied that her pants were literally hot.

The *Torvatta* landed.

"Let us go," said Evaran.

Dr. Snowden marched behind him as they approached the lords.

They kneeled and bowed their heads.

"There is no need for that," said Evaran.

The lords stood. Lord Vygon embraced Evaran, and then the others. The other lords did as well.

"You all must have just come from leaving me behind at the cave," said Lord Vygon.

"We did," said Evaran.

Lord Noskov shook his head. "This morning, Lord Vygon informed us of how we really came to Earth."

Lord Skar laughed. "He kept it to himself for almost twelve thousand years. I'm not surprised."

"It does make you wonder what else he hasn't said," said Lord Cyrus, smirking.

Dr. Snowden had not interacted much with Lord Cyrus and Lord Skar in the past, but he knew by their actions that their hearts were in the right place. They were not as visible as Lord Vygon or Lord Noskov when it came to Earth Ward politics or interacting with other factions. However, their presence was felt when they did work on the ancient vampires' behalf, and they filled in when needed. They seemed to like being left alone for the most part.

"Did you tell them about how you stopped Wardax?" asked Dr. Snowden.

"I sure did." Lord Vygon laid a hand on V's shoulder. "He opened Wardax's mouth and I jumped right in."

"We were a good team," said V.

"That we were." Lord Vygon grinned at Emily. "It was a hell of a fight to reach Wardax, though. Thanks for being my partner in crime."

She hugged him. "No biggie."

Lord Vygon stood before Sivaran and placed both hands on Sivaran's shoulders. "It's been a long time since these eyes have seen you. I've been looking forward to this for a while now."

Sivaran bowed his head slightly. "It's good to see you again, old friend. I'm glad everything worked out."

"Are you planning on staying?" asked Lord Vygon with hopeful eyes.

"Unfortunately not," said Sivaran. "However, I have a chance to see Evaran's world firsthand before I go back. This meeting is a treat."

Lord Vygon embraced him.

Dr. Snowden's eyes misted. These had been two old friends even before the gang had gone to the other universe, and here they were, reunited again. It boggled his mind that Lord Vygon had known of this adventure when Dr. Snowden had first met him.

Lord Vygon moved on and pulled Q into a hug. "Get over here and get some hugging."

A startled Q returned the hug.

"It's good to see you again as well," said Lord Vygon.

"The feeling is mutual," said Q.

Lord Noskov gestured at a grill near the base's entrance, where Mikhail, Jake Melkins, and Robert Melkins awaited. "As per our usual tradition, we have food and drinks to celebrate the occasion."

Dr. Snowden's mouth watered. Although replicated food was good, nothing beat a freshly grilled burger. As he joined the lords on the walk over, he noticed Lord Vygon stayed behind with Evaran and Sivaran. Dr. Snowden figured they were probably going to discuss things that the rest of the group was not privy to. That was fine as he was curious to hear what the other lords had been told of the situation.

The trip to Sivaran's universe put into context the close relationship that Lord Vygon had with Evaran of any form. Although not chosen by Evaran or the *Torvatta*, Lord Vygon was just as important in Evaran's life.

Lord Vygon watched the others head to the grill. It felt good to have everyone together, and this meeting had been a long time coming. Although it might have seemed like just hours ago that they had left him at the cave entrance, it had been over twelve thousand years for him. It was hard to keep the secret, but he knew he had to until this meeting.

"You are deep in thought," said Evaran.

Lord Vygon furrowed his brow. "I was just thinking of things from your point of view. One minute you're reviving me and setting me up here, the next, you're twelve thousand years or so in the future here. From my perspective, this has been a long time coming."

Evaran nodded. "I understand."

Sivaran gazed over at the grill, where the others had clustered around. "I'm enjoying a live tour of Evaran's side of things. This is a bit different than the universe we knew."

"Definitely," said Lord Vygon. "We've done well here and risen to the top in the nonhuman world, and the human one to some extent. With the Earth Ward, we have a voice at least"

"How many ancient vampires are there now?"

Lord Vygon nodded. "Several thousand, although most are from Lord Noskov. I have a few hundred myself, but they are spread out through the world. Lord Skar and Lord Cyrus also have a few hundred that they keep close, but they prefer to stay in isolation somewhat."

"That sounds about right given your personalities," said Sivaran. "How did the other lords take to learning about how they came from Drydris? From their perspective, they tried to escape and ended up here."

"I played dumb as expected, and the matter replicator helped those first few months," said Lord Vygon. "Human blood was far more delicious than either of you let on."

Evaran eyed him.

"No, we didn't kill anyone who didn't deserve it, but after we established communications with the Helians and met Delia Everoak, we went our separate ways to rebuild. I stayed here in North America, Lord Noskov visited Asia, Lord Skar went to Europe, and Lord Cyrus traveled to South America."

Evaran rubbed his chin. "There were already other vampire strains present. I assume they did not care for your presence."

Lord Vygon snickered. "Initially, no. However, we proved ourselves in a short amount of time. Yes, there were fights, but as the Blooded and other strains learned, they were not a physical match for us."

He remembered the early days on this Earth. Challenges had come from everywhere, from vicious animals to tough human groups. Most nonhumans had given ancient vampires space, but others had tried to either kill or enslave them. That had not worked out for them.

"I'm sure your blunted blades were put to use," said Sivaran.

"You could say that. It would have been nice to have an advanced suit, energy shield and PSD."

Evaran eyed him.

Lord Vygon grinned.

Evaran peered over at the grill. "I understand now how you came to know so much, although the *Torvatta* did not allow you information access. Yet you have information beyond this trip you went on with us."

Lord Vygon gazed off in the distance. "I can't speak to that."

"Sounds like you met a different Evaran or two, and they were future versions of this one," said Sivaran, gesturing at Evaran.

Lord Vygon shrugged. "At this point, I'm quite familiar with Evaran, in *any* form."

"I would expect that," said Evaran. He studied him. "When we had completed the purification event, you were going to say something to me. Whatever it was had some impact on you. Was it in regard to Drydris?"

Lord Vygon sighed. "No, and that's all I can say on that until later. I will say ... I'm partial to the two forms before me."

"You're a box of mysteries," said Sivaran.

"Don't I know it. It drives Lord Noskov crazy."

Lord Vygon and Sivaran cracked up while Evaran half smiled.

Lord Vygon found it interesting to compare what he figured a reaction to a situation would be, then see the reaction on two different versions of Evaran side by side. While Lord Vygon knew other incarnations, he had a soft spot for the two versions in front of him. Sivaran had been his friend from before he had come to this universe, and Evaran was from this one. Lord Vygon's fate was intertwined with theirs.

"What are your plans now?" asked Lord Vygon.

Sivaran nodded. "I go back after this tour. Only one Evaran should be in a timeline. In the end, we both will merge with our main form, assuming we're in a state to do so."

"Who knows, then? I may see you yet again," said Lord Vygon.

Evaran and Sivaran stared at him.

"You know I have to say that, even if I knew."

Sivaran laid a hand on his shoulder. "I know, old friend."

Lord Vygon cleared his throat. "You gave up having a *Torvatta* for me."

"I did, but you're worth it."

"I don't think I am," said Lord Vygon. "I mean … the *Torvatta* is a one-of-a-kind thing."

"As are you. Besides, there is some cosmic energy left over. I can use it for shielding and to give Q an inner container," said Sivaran.

"He'll love that."

Evaran nodded. "Jelton also has technology to enter and exit a time stream. With those additions, the *Karus* can live again with the ability to time travel and use advanced shielding."

"The downside is I won't be able to travel anywhere outside the timeline, so there are some restrictions, but it'll do," said Sivaran. "Q is quite excited about the changes."

"You'll have a fixed point with Wardax and Evaran visiting," said Lord Vygon. "You'll probably need to stay away from that."

Sivaran chuckled. "Yep, but that's a small price to pay for the upgrades. Also of note, I'll have a means of communication with Evaran. We may be in different universes, but we'll keep in touch."

Lord Vygon wrinkled his brow. "How will you do that?"

"The quantum beacon that was used to notify Evaran of my position initially. With some tweaking using leftover cosmic energy, it can allow for two-way communication. Obviously, we will only do so in an extreme emergency."

"I wish you both could stay here, but I know that's not how it works," said Lord Vygon, frowning.

"We understand," said Evaran.

Lord Vygon glanced at Sivaran while motioning at the grill area. "Let me introduce you to a freshly grilled burger.

After things wind down, I can give you a tour of the base and update you on the current state of things and what we've been up to. I know you don't sleep, and I'm between rests, so we should be good."

Sivaran slapped Lord Vygon on the back. "Lead on, brother."

Lord Vygon understood how rare this moment was. There were only a handful of times when he would meet more than one Evaran at the same time. Lord Vygon had wanted to mention Sivaran before in the past, but until now, he had not been able to.

It stuck out that Evaran recalled Lord Vygon wanting to say something at the end of the purification event. He had, but the time when he could speak about it had not come. He sighed. There would be a time when he did speak of it, but it would be after an event that was drawing close, one that made his heart hurt just to think of it. For now, he would relish the opportunity before him and enjoy both Evarans.

29

V had enjoyed the previous night. Everyone had a good time, and he had been able to add more information on Lord Skar and Lord Cyrus, the two ancient vampires V did not have much interaction with. They seemed to know him well, though.

Sivaran had talked with everybody, and after Dr. Snowden, Emily, Jake, and Robert had gone to sleep, anyone still up had talked well into the morning about a variety of topics. V appreciated these opportunities to study and learn how others interacted.

It was now around 12:30 p.m. the next day, and Inspector Dalton Kingston and his team were on their way. Jake had gone to pick them up and was due any minute. Sivaran had been interested in meeting who the *Torvatta* had chosen. V understood that although Sivaran knew Dalton from syncing with Evaran, meeting the person was another matter. V could relate to that. He had vast amounts of information on people, and when he met them, he updated his interaction library.

Emily was full of sunshine as she joked around with Evaran and Sivaran. She had formed a close bond with Sivaran and it showed. Her playful taps on his arm indicated she was very comfortable with him.

Dr. Snowden talked with Lord Skar and Lord Cyrus. V had determined a pattern in which, anytime they were around, Dr. Snowden made a point of talking to them. They seemed to be delighted to return the favor.

Lord Vygon, Lord Noskov, Mikhail, and Robert conversed with Q. He was most likely updating his organic interaction library and comparing notes against the ancient vampires from his universe compared to this one. His perspective was unique, and his recollections of Drydris entranced Lord Vygon and Lord Noskov. Mikhail and Robert appeared to be excited to learn more about ancient vampire history.

V faced the landing pad as Jake's ship landed.

Dalton emerged with four individuals who V knew quite well.

Dalton had traveled with the gang on the last adventure, and the *Torvatta* had chosen him. He was unique and had a sliver of cosmic energy, the largest amount outside of Evaran and Sivaran yet. His nanosuit was always on, and he had it configured in default mode, which was what he used in casual situations. His black boots, jeans, and loose dark gray T-shirt fit well over his fair skin. Although his hair was slicked back some, it had semishaved sides similar to Evaran's style.

Everyone went to greet Dalton's group.

"Quite a few people here to meet us for lunch," said Dalton, grinning. His eyes glowed when he forearm-shook with Evaran.

Evaran motioned at Sivaran while looking at Dalton. "This is Sivaran, the sixth plane form to enter the plane after I did. We synced earlier, so he is aware of everything I knew after your trip with us."

Dalton shook Sivaran's hand and their eyes glowed.

"Oh yeah, you're an Evaran," said Dalton.

"I like to think so," said Sivaran with a smile. He gestured to the side. "This is Q, a ship AI transferred to a body and my traveling companion."

Dalton shook Q's hand. "AI's everywhere."

Q tilted his head. "You have an AI in you."

"Sure do, and I'll get to that." Dalton motioned at his team. "I guess introductions are in order. Let's start with Brad Washington, who is a Wildborn and can talk to technology."

Brad raised a hand and nodded.

V updated his image library for Brad. His dark skin and shaved head were as expected, as was what he wore: black boots, shirt, and pants. V had enjoyed discussing topics with him in the past, and they had even met in cyberspace several times when perusing around. He had come from an alternate cyberpunk Earth where AIs hunted him.

"Next up is Valerie Simmons, the only Outsider I know of who is also a vampire. Her race is Zikarian," said Dalton.

She smiled at everyone.

V had placed Valerie in a fighter category. She had a sharp sense of humor and did not seem to fear death. As a former assassin, that was to be expected. She and Mikhail seemed to have formed a bond, and by his big grin, V suspected he was more than happy to see her again. Her skin was unusually pale, and it stood in stark contrast to Brad's. She seemed reserved this time around. Perhaps it was due to being in the presence of ancient vampire lords.

"Then there's Todd Armani. He's only human," said Dalton.

"Yeah, just human," said Todd with a dip of his hat.

The group laughed.

V had only talked to Todd a few times. He had light tan skin and wore camouflage-patterned pants with a loose T-shirt and ball cap. His easy-going personality made it easy to talk to him, and his past as slayer had trained him to be a fierce combatant. Slayers were the foot soldiers of the Faith Militia, a group dedicated to the eradication of all nonhumans.

Dalton squeezed Evot's arm. "And of course, the lovely Evot. She's the AI shackled to me, but she controls two servbots that control a nanoswarm she can morph. This is one with her humanoid form."

She waved excitedly at everyone, drawing a few chuckles.

V enjoyed being around her. She had been an enhanced virtual intelligence for over seventy years before Dalton had been infused with cosmic energy. That event had destabilized her, and in order to save her, Evaran and V had transformed her into an AI.

Her zeal for life was infectious, and even now, she seemed beyond excited to meet everyone. This was an environment where she did not need to run security protocols and could allocate resources to organic interaction, something she loved and also had goals for in her programming.

"And that's my new team," said Dalton. He extended a hand toward Lord Skar and Lord Cyrus. "I know we haven't talked much, so I'm looking forward to doing so while here."

They nodded and returned the handshake.

"Lunch is on the grill, so everyone grab a plate and some drinks, and enjoy the afternoon," said Lord Noskov.

"Don't need to tell me twice," said Todd. "That food smells good."

As the group broke apart, V studied how the smaller groups formed. Evot, Brad, and Q had broken off to talk. V had expected that. Dr. Snowden, Emily, Jake, Robert, and Todd went to the grill. Valerie and Mikhail had joined up, and together, they talked with Lord Skar and Lord Cyrus. V determined that she wanted to meet them, and Mikhail was her safety blanket. Dalton met with Sivaran, Evaran, Lord Vygon, and Lord Noskov.

When V joined them, Dalton high-fived him.

"There he is," said Dalton.

"Acknowledged."

Dalton grinned. "I never tire of hearing you say that." He faced Sivaran. "I know how rare it is to meet two Evarans."

"And for me, someone who the *Torvatta* chose," said Sivaran. He waved a hand out in an arc. "Lot of cosmic beings out today."

"Analysis. A cosmic party."

"Something like that."

"It's so strange to see two versions of Evaran and see different reactions but know the cosmic energy flux is about the same," said Dalton. He faced Evaran. "It gives me some insight." He eyed Sivaran. "I'm sorry, but we're going to have to run you through the full set of emotions so I have a base to work from."

Sivaran nodded. "I think I like you."

They burst into laughter.

V observed the ease with which Sivaran interacted with others. Although Dalton and Sivaran had just met, they joked around as if they were old friends.

Evot joined them and hugged a startled Sivaran.

"Oh! Well, hi there," he said.

"You're Evaran, just in a different form. I owe my existence to him."

Sivaran winked. "We're helpful like that. Your servbot is similar to my nanosuit."

"I've read the specifications on your suit. It's quite impressive," said Evot.

"As are you," said Sivaran.

Evot's eyes lit up.

"So you saw my trip with the gang via the sync with Evaran," said Dalton.

Sivaran nodded. "I did, and it was definitely an adventure."

Evaran raised a finger. "It was Dr. Snowden and Emily's first dual summons."

"I'm just glad the *Torvatta* decided to come out. I was at my end," said Dalton. He gestured at Sivaran. "Were you the target of a summons too?"

"I wasn't," said Sivaran. "I activated a quantum beacon, which the *Torvatta* noticed."

Dalton swatted Evaran's arm. "Okay, he wins the award for the most creative way to get your attention."

Evaran half smiled. "Perhaps so, but your summons did not involve fighting another cosmic being."

"You guys fought another Evaran?"

Evaran shook his head. "It was a being named Wardax who possessed cosmic energy."

"And now doesn't," said Sivaran. "Well, he doesn't possess any form in my timeline either."

Dalton rubbed his chin. "Sounds like a rough case."

"Something like that," said Evaran.

V enjoyed interacting with others, and he liked to sit and observe. Although one might infer that cosmic beings naturally got along with each other, V had met the Mortani, cosmic refugees who were dangerous, and also Wardax. V appreciated being included in the discussion, and even if he did not speak as much, it did not matter when among friends.

After a bit, he met up with Q and Evot. Brad had gone over to talk with Dalton, Evaran, and Sivaran.

"This get-together is fascinating," said Q.

"I love organic interaction," said Evot.

Q nodded. "Unfortunately, I don't experience it like you two do. V has an inner container to help with organic interactions, and you have Dalton's body to assist you. Sivaran said he will create an inner container for me, but I'm unsure of the process."

"You could then experience like us," said Evot with a smile.

V motioned at Sivaran. "Acrolis would give him the planar energy needed for your container."

Evot nodded. "You should build a nano swarm around it. It would be more efficient than a shell and allow you to take on multiple forms."

"One disadvantage is you give up a strong body," said V.

"Why not have both?" asked Evot.

"Good points. I have some things to process," said Q. "I'll check with Sivaran."

Evot danced around.

Q studied her, then focused on V.

"She likes to spontaneously dance," said V.

"I see," said Q.

"It's cat dance time," said Evot, morphing into a gray cat.

V followed suit, but as an orange cat. He hopped up on his hind legs and followed Evot as she danced around and played music while swatting at the air. Their actions drew laughter from everyone. He enjoyed doing things with her, and if Q got an inner container, he would understand the organic interaction aspect better.

"Go, Evot! Go, V!" said Emily, pumping her fist in the air.

V knew how rare moments like these were, and he cherished them. Everyone had their own schedules, and as this recent outing showed, life was precious.

***

Emily frowned as she surveyed the hangar where the *Karus* had been rebuilt. It had been a week since the group had left her universe, and now they were in Sivaran's. Acrolis had been kind enough to meet with them on a habitable planet and create a bay to work from. She had also repaired the *Karus* after Evaran had found it. They had just finished a good lunch, and Emily wished it had been longer.

She loved the design of the *Karus*. Now that it was not damaged, it shined and hummed. It was larger than the

Torvatta and easily filled up the small hangar where everything was hooked up. Acrolis had not been able to work with the cosmic or rift energy components, so she had made all the parts that needed to be assembled. It had been a busy week doing just that.

Sivaran had given them a tour of the *Karus*, but she recalled a lot of it from when they had first investigated it. There were several dimensional rooms and even a holo one. The command center was redesigned to be similar to the *Torvatta*'s. It had a sleek commander's chair, with seating off to the side and a wraparound console. The ceiling and sides were transparent, and data windows could appear on the inside. The dimensional rooms allowed the *Karus* to stay small, but also pack a lot of features.

One of the big changes was that Sivaran had created an inner container for Q. It used a sliver of the remaining cosmic energy, and Acrolis provided planar energy. V contributed his interpretation algorithms, and Q had been a nonstop smiling machine. Everything he had ever calculated or determined had a new dimension added to it.

Unfortunately, the moment had come. It was time to go, and although she tried to put up a brave front, it killed her to leave Sivaran and Q behind. She had formed a strong bond with Sivaran and saw him as Evaran with a different wrapper, but it was still him. It was apparent in his actions, the way he did things, and what he said. Q had also grown on her. His quirkiness and desire to learn endeared him to her.

She was glad that Lord Vygon had come along. Evaran had allowed him to visit Drydris and record its current state. It was still a boiling cauldron. She had thought Lord Vygon might be sad, but he seemed indifferent. Maybe twelve thousand years was what it took to put something behind you. It was yet another special moment to fly above Drydris with him, and like Evaran, she held Lord Vygon as one of the few she trusted with her life.

Everyone had gathered outside and stood between the *Torvatta* and the *Karus*.

"Well, here we are," said Sivaran. He glanced at Evaran. "I really enjoyed getting to see your world in person."

"And I, yours," said Evaran. "You have the quantum beacon should you need me."

"I know. At the end, we'll meet in our main form when we merge."

"That we will," said Evaran. He raised a hand and held his palm flat against Sivaran's. Their eyes glowed for a moment.

Emily wished Levaran had a quantum beacon. They could have swooped in and helped her out, although Emily knew her death was already a part of their past.

Sivaran walked over to Lord Vygon. "It's been a long and unusual trip."

Lord Vygon sighed. "I hope we get to meet again."

"Wait a minute ... you know the future, though. Something you want to tell me?" asked Sivaran, smiling.

"I only know the future to some extent," said Lord Vygon. "You've been a true friend to me and the ancient vampires. We'll never forget you."

Sivaran's smile lowered. "Maybe I can pop in and visit from time to time."

Emily knew that probably would not happen due to Evaran's plane forms staying out of each other's way. It sounded good, but by Sivaran's facial expression, she understood that he understood that.

"We'd like that," said Lord Vygon, shaking Sivaran's hand and then pulling him into a quick hug.

Sivaran walked over to Dr. Snowden. "It's been great to meet who travels with Evaran." He looked over at Emily and V. "All of you. A cosmic crew. I can definitely see the benefits in that."

"And now we are a cosmic crew," said Q, smiling.

"Yes, we are."

Dr. Snowden extended his hand to Sivaran. "It's going to be like meeting Q all over again for you. Plus, you can travel in time now thanks to the Rift Guardians, and with cosmic shielding and an advanced condensed space drive, you can go anywhere within the timeline."

"Absolutely," said Sivaran.

Sivaran chortled when Dr. Snowden did his famous shake and slap on the back hug.

Emily's throat constricted when Sivaran visited her.

"We made quite the duo," he said.

"Yeah," she said, frowning.

"Hey, bring it in," said Sivaran with outstretched arms. They hugged.

She realized why his departure hit hard. This was goodbye. To an Evaran. It was one of the worst things she could imagine, and although it was not the one she traveled with, it was still an Evaran. Her eyes misted.

"I wish you could travel with us," she said in a soft voice.

He stepped back and squeezed her shoulders. "Never say never, right?"

She nodded and wiped her eyes.

Evaran walked over and put his arm around her.

Emily leaned into him.

Sivaran high-fived V. "It's been a pleasure getting to know you. Our child, sort of."

"Analysis. You will be missed."

"That goes both ways," said Sivaran.

Q walked around and high-fived everyone. "V has shown me the way to greet others. There may be an issue for races that don't have arms, though. I now understand why he does it."

V nodded. "Learn. Adapt. Evolve."

Dr. Snowden pointed at him. "What he said."

"I have accepted your family motto," said Q. "Hopefully, this is not our last meeting."

Dr. Snowden shrugged. "You never know."

Emily enjoyed the brief moment of laughter, but her heart still sagged. Sivaran and Q had fit naturally on the *Torvatta*. It did not surprise her that it allowed Q to be a pilot. It must have known that he would get an inner container and have cosmic energy at some point.

"What are your immediate steps after we leave?" asked Dr. Snowden.

Sivaran gazed out of the hangar. "There's a lot of chaos with Wardax's influence gone. Q and I will do our best to help stabilize things."

"That's a lot of work," said Lord Vygon. "It's been so long since I heard some of the names of civilizations you'll be visiting."

"A good challenge," said Sivaran. "I also plan to check out Earth at various points. It's a bit away from here, but with the upgraded *Karus*, not a problem anymore. Nonetheless, it's time Q and I headed out."

He did a final round of handshakes as did Q, then they boarded the *Karus*.

Everyone else stepped back.

A lump formed in Emily's throat as the *Karus* hummed loudly, then hovered. It moved forward slowly, and once outside the hangar, it streaked toward the sky. She frowned at a holographic display showing the word goodbye that the Karus projected before exiting out of sight.

Lord Vygon looked down. "He brought out a lot of old feelings. I'm going to miss both of them. And Q now experiencing emotions? I wish I could see that journey."

"We all do," said Emily.

He nodded and sighed.

"See how you make us feel?" she asked, playfully swatting Evaran's arm. She did the same to V. "You too."

"I know the impact an Evaran, in any form, can have," he said.

"Analysis. I also understand how my presence can uplift others."

She gave them both a quick hug, then faced the *Torvatta*. "I guess it's time for us to go home."

"Sounds good," said Dr. Snowden.

Emily smiled as V rubbed her back on the way to the *Torvatta*. She observed that he seemed down too, at least as much as he could show. Sivaran and Q had made an impact, and she would never forget them. Like Evaran, Sivaran stood larger than life.

She lamented that she would not get to see Q's journey with an inner container. He was the perfect offset to Sivaran, and now Q had his own adventure to look forward to.

She took a final look at the empty hangar. At least Sivaran was not alone, and if need be, he could always contact them.

Although he was only supposed to do it in emergencies, she hoped he did it just to visit.

Dr. Snowden peered out over the *Torvatta*'s guardrail on the roof. Lord Vygon had been dropped off and the gang had assembled. They were flying back to Dr. Snowden's house and would be there shortly. He made a lot of observations this time around, and he suspected Emily did too. To his right were Evaran, Emily, and V in sequence.

"So, another mystery finished," said Dr. Snowden.

"An unusual one," said Evaran.

"Tell me about it. Two Evarans. The ancient vampires' origin. Fighting another cosmic being. I didn't care much for the torture part, though."

"You seemed to have adapted," said Evaran. "You are resilient in that regard."

Dr. Snowden shrugged. "There's still some Wardax in my head. He may be gone from my previous memories, but he freaks me out."

"Yeah, he's a big plant bug. I'm glad he got squished," said Emily.

Evaran eyed her.

"Well, I am."

"I understand," said Evaran. "Wardax is an example of what happens when the wrong being gets a hold of cosmic energy. I am unclear as to how he obtained it. He said it was given to him by something, then it told him to survive."

Dr. Snowden nodded. "When I was in that torturous nightmare, I saw it. I don't know if it's real, but he believes it is. What type of being can just hand out cosmic power like that?"

"Analysis. Evaran can, between his plane form death and ejection from the plane."

Dr. Snowden and Emily stared at Evaran.

He half smiled. "Yes, that is correct. However, I do not think I would send my cosmic energy back to cause genocide."

"Maybe it isn't your cosmic energy that gets sent or even you that does it," said Dr. Snowden.

"Definitely a possibility."

Dr. Snowden adjusted his glasses. "On another note, meeting Lord Vygon before he came to our universe was interesting."

"Yeah, and it gives a whole new perspective on him," said Emily.

Evaran nodded. "He is resilient, and it is no surprise that he has survived as long as he has. However, he had the help of two Evarans. That is not coincidental."

"What do you think it means?" she asked.

"I am not sure, but I suspect like Jake Melkins, Lord Vygon is an anchor for me."

Dr. Snowden found Lord Vygon's journey to be fascinating. While he had had some basic knowledge of the future when dropped off, he had picked up additional knowledge from somewhere else. It must have come from further in Evaran's personal timeline, or another version in the future. Dr. Snowden was not sure he would ever know, but it boggled his mind that Lord Vygon had kept a secret for almost twelve thousand years.

"I guess Lord Vygon had to create the Daedrould stone. I wonder how he did that," said Dr. Snowden.

Emily chuckled. "I don't think he'll tell, but I'm glad he did. He had to make it in order for the event to bring him to our universe to occur." She glanced at Evaran. "If the stone hadn't turned to ash, it could be reused and that would lead to an information paradox. That didn't happen, so this is just a predestination paradox, right?"

Evaran examined her. "You have been studying."

"I figured with all the craziness that goes on, I might as well read up on the different paradoxes and theories," she said. "I experienced the information paradox when we dealt with Ziekah. That took a bit to wrap my head around."

"I understand," said Evaran. He scrutinized Dr. Snowden. "I know you have adapted since the purge of Wardax from your memories, but have there been any side effects?"

Dr. Snowden licked his lips as he looked down. "I've had nightmares. Wardax is just outright scary to me. Even though he's gone, I feel like he could pop up any moment to mess with me."

Evaran nodded. "Know that I am here if he should appear."

"I appreciate that," said Dr. Snowden. "I'm just angry he messed with my head is all. I mean, we have had some wild runs, but this one shook me, and I hate that feeling of uncertainty. Even now when I look at you, I sometimes flinch since you were his face for a lot of the torture."

Evaran's lips moved down slightly. "I am displeased he did so."

"He's still out there in whatever dimension," said Emily. "I hope he doesn't find his way out."

"He was a multidimensional being, but now he is a normal denizen of his dimension. It would take external involvement to bring him back."

"Yeah, just need to stop mysterious beings from giving him cosmic power for another run," said Emily, grinning.

"Indeed."

"Analysis. We know his home dimension based on the quantum beacon we put in his dimensional network, and he is aware that we know. Based on the outcome of our last encounter, I do not think he desires a second altercation."

Emily slapped V on the back. "That's what I'm talking about!"

"Yes, I believe so."

Dr. Snowden and Emily laughed. Although V was getting better at responding to certain phrases, sometimes he took things literally, which provided a comedic context. Dr. Snowden appreciated having V lighten up moments, even when he was not trying to.

"I wonder what Sivaran will do first," said Emily. "He said he would help stabilize things, but that seems like such a massive effort would be needed there."

Evaran rubbed his chin. "He will do a survey of the aftermath, then formulate a plan on how he can best assist."

"He tell you that?" asked Dr. Snowden.

"No, but it is what I would do."

"That makes sense. With the upgraded *Karus*, he'll be able to do a lot more."

"I would hope so," said Evaran. "It is still weak to pal-isin-based technology as the *Karus* uses cosmic shielding.

However, he and Q are aware of this, and they will need to use tactical awareness not to be in that position."

"Easier said than done," said Dr. Snowden. "I'm really going to miss them." He cast a sidelong glance at Evaran. "Sivaran gave Emily and me and others some insight into your emotional states."

Evaran nodded. "As expected. We are not too far off in terms of emotions. His were easily shown via facial cues, but our energy flux would have been similar."

"I sensed that," said Dr. Snowden. "You were the control, and he was the variable. Fun times."

Evaran eyed him.

"It's not a bad thing. I think everyone enjoyed that aspect." Dr. Snowden placed a hand on his chest. "Well, I know *I* did."

"Understood."

"I think Q's happy," said Emily.

"Analysis. I hope my interpretation algorithms work for him."

Emily smirked. "He's Sivaran and Acrolis's love child."

V studied her. "I have determined that Sivaran did it out of the strong bond he has for Q."

"I think so too," said Dr. Snowden. His house came into view. "Back to the routine."

"Works for me," said Emily.

V smiled. "Me too."

Dr. Snowden was ready to get back to some normalcy. Although he enjoyed traveling with Evaran, this particular adventure had been more dangerous than he expected. Dr. Snowden's mind was free of Wardax's tampering, but Dr. Snowden still felt like Wardax might pop up and cause havoc. Whatever had given him that cosmic energy might do it again.

"You were thinking," said Evaran.

Dr. Snowden sighed. "Yeah. I'm good. Be nice to be normal again for a change, although I feel like there are still some questions that didn't get answered."

"I know we did not get answers to everything," said Evaran. He gazed off in the distance. "However, everything is as it should be."

THE END

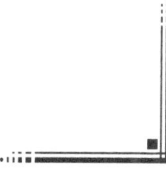

EPILOGUE

Q analyzed the *Karus*'s digital interface. He had a direct connection to it and appreciated the many upgrades the *Karus* had received. His new inner container was full of new sensations, and he spent a considerable amount of time trying to understand it. Like V, it provided an additional parameter to any given input. Whenever Q processed something, he felt it via the inner container, which pulsed with some heat. He interpreted that as feeling good and enjoyed that sensation.

The unexpected sequence of events that had led to him getting an inner container needed to be recorded, and he had already inserted a chunk of information into the *Karus*'s systems. All that was left was his characterization of the individuals involved. Afterward, he planned to talk with Sivaran, who sat silently in his command chair and stared outside the Karus.

Evaran was the first to be entered. Q entered him as Evaran prime. Evaran was the most powerful being Q had ever met. The cosmic energy alone earned him that title.

Q also sensed Evaran's raw power in the hangar, which allowed Q to make comparisons against others. Between Evaran's lightning-fast fighting style and quick thinking, he was a terror on the battlefield. The strange lack of emotions was mostly due to his plane form not displaying many facial or body cues, but Q understood Evaran's energy flux as emotions.

Evaran was also kind, and at times, he was difficult to distinguish from Sivaran in decision making. Q had observed them fight side by side as if they were one being. Both had an aura of confidence around them, and he observed how relaxed it seemed to make others. It was no surprise that Evaran took main command, as Q was used to that with Sivaran.

V had been an interesting case study in AI companions. He was selfless, and due to his special link with his inner container, he understood emotions much better than Q. Although he now had an inner container, he was an AI with one, whereas V was an inner container with an AI interface. It was a subtle difference, and the interpretation algorithms worked differently between them.

V was also loved by the gang. He was family to them, and they treated him like a brother. Q had never had that type of connection with an organic outside of Sivaran, yet with V, he made friends with ease. Q enjoyed their discussions and looked forward to interacting with organics now that he would be able to sense them better.

Dr. Snowden had undergone a harrowing journey. He was a scholar, but when pressed, he could fight right alongside the team. Although not as gifted as Emily in terms of melee, his marksmanship with the PSD was formidable. He also possessed strong tactical thinking. He prided himself on his mind, and what Wardax had done was the worst-case scenario outside of death.

Even with all that had happened to Dr. Snowden, he seemed to have bounced back. There were still times when Q caught him flinching when looking at Evaran. Perhaps that was a subconscious thing. Dr. Snowden was well respected by the others, and Q saw firsthand how devoted the gang had been to retrieving him. They had never faltered.

Emily was a fierce combatant, and she was not shy in showing her emotions. Q had learned she had had a traumatic event in the past when dealing with another cosmic powered being known as the Overlord. This time it was Dr. Snowden who had suffered, but Q saw that she understood Dr. Snowden's pain on a different level. Nonetheless, she was a valued member of the gang, and she seemed to regard Evaran as a father figure. That extended to Sivaran, and Q recorded that they had a very strong bond.

Q had enjoyed her trying to include him in conversations. She also was friendly to him, and although he had had no inner container at the time, the mere processing of images from interacting with her made his inner container hum. He took that to mean he was comfortable with her. When his inner container pulsed slowly, that meant he missed her, and he did.

Lord Vygon's path to where he was now was not something Q could have ever predicted. The Daedrould stone was new, but to go from one universe to another, and also have two Evarans help facilitate that, was not coincidence. It was meant to happen.

Q understood Lord Vygon's grief when he had learned of what had happened on Drydris, and now with Q's inner container fluctuating wildly, it gave another impression of that event. Chaos was not the state he wanted his container to be in, and the goal was to get it to pulse comfortably, like when he was around Sivaran or Emily.

The ancient vampires had rebounded, and they had taken advantage of their second chance under Evaran's protection. Q had run several simulations on their future, and the most probable ones indicated they would expand far beyond where they were now. There would not be another Drydris extermination event if they could help it.

Wardax had been a big threat, and it had taken two Evarans to take him down. His impact on the galactic region he operated in was massive. Q had initially understood Wardax's position from a logical perspective, but the wake of destruction and dismantling of individual will made Q's container pulse erratically. Wardax was a monster, and he had paid the price for his transgressions.

"Thinking hard over there?" asked Sivaran.

Q faced him. "I was entering my research on the events and people involved."

Sivaran nodded. "And now you can understand them better with your inner container."

"Yes," said Q with a smile.

Sivaran laughed. "See, that's what I mean. This is going to be interesting as you learn the various states of your inner container. You can also get a better sense of people."

"I intend to," said Q. "As we do our aftermath analysis, I look forward to interacting with my inner container. We'll have a lot of time in that regard as there is much surveying to be done."

Sivaran sighed. "There sure is. Who knows, though? We may end up expanding our crew during this new journey."

"I'd like that," said Q.

Sivaran eased back into his chair. "Upgraded ship, upgraded you, and we got to meet Evaran prime and see his world. And now, we have our own adventure ahead of us, except this time around, we're better prepared." He grinned big and extended his arms off to the side. "Everything is as it should be."

Evot was a virtual intelligence that allowed Dalton to interact with his nanotech and, by extension, his servbots. Although Evot had had no initial personality, Dalton had given her a female voice and persona for interaction purposes. She also appeared in his ARI. Her processor was embedded inside him, and ever since he had gotten his nanotech, she had been his constant companion.

The servbot morphed into a small drone with a red light and took off into the air.

The alien firing haphazardly into the forest reminded him that he would probably now be pursued. That seemed to be a common theme when hopping around timelines.

His ARI displayed a bird's-eye view of the immediate area. The aliens might shoot down his servbot, but it would self-destruct if needed to avoid capture. It was time to survive.

NOTE FROM
THE AUTHOR

I hope you enjoyed the twelfth book in *The Evaran Chronicles*! Evaran meets another plane form in Sivaran, and the ancient vampire origin is explored. As Emily underwent a traumatic experience in *The Purification*, Book 3 of *The Evaran Chronicles*, Dr. Snowden experiences his own harrowing journey, but he has the gang to support him.

This book is a standalone, but it continues the third series arc. Lord Vygon joins the gang, as do Sivaran and Q, Sivaran's version of V. I enjoyed diving into Lord Vygon's past and showing one reason he was so excited to see the gang in 2610 BC in *The Purification*. This book explores what another corrupt cosmic being would be like, although it is not the one mentioned in *The Time Cube*, Book 11 of *The Evaran Chronicles*.

In terms of cosmology, this book covers multidimensional beings and what happens when they receive cosmic energy. It also delves a bit more into Evaran's entry into the plane.

The idea of a dimensional network powered by cosmic energy is also explored. I spent some time also going over Alxarin energy and what it is. This ties into the lightmires in *Lightville*, Book 2 of *The Inspector Dalton Files*.

If you liked the book, and have the time and inclination, a review would go a long way in helping out this indie author. If you do submit a review, I'll put in a word to Evaran should you find yourself dealing with rogue cosmic entities! Want to be notified about new book releases? If so, you can sign up below.

www.AdairHart.com/MailingList.aspx

I will only send you email about new book releases, major updates, and the occasional newsletter, usually once a month. I dislike getting spammed too, so I will use this sparingly to keep you in the loop.

ABOUT
THE AUTHOR

I have been dreaming about fictional worlds since I was a kid. I devoured anything related to fantasy and science fiction. I developed a setting over the last twenty years and struggled to find a medium I could express it in. Several years ago I discovered I enjoyed writing. It is a passion of mine now, and exploring my setting with it has been an awesome journey.

I work in the information technology field and have my bachelor's and master's degrees in it. It has helped me to shape some of the concepts I write about. I also enjoy keeping up on futurology and science in general.

I live in central Ohio and enjoy walking, reading, gaming, learning, listening to music, and trying to keep up on my never-ending list of TV shows and movies to watch. If you want to contact me, you can do so on my website at

www.AdairHart.com

YOU CAN ALSO REACH ME ON

Facebook............................fb.com/AdairHart
Goodreads.....www.goodreads.com/AdairHart
Email..............Adair.Hart.Author@gmail.com

DEDICATION

To my grandparents, who continue to inspire me.
They may be gone now, but their life lessons and
legacy lives on with me.

ACKNOWLEDGMENTS

This was a great journey for me, but I wouldn't be here without the help of others. I would like to thank, in no particular order,

My editor, Eliza Dee, who continues to help me grow as an author!

My cover artist, Tom Edwards (tomedwardsconcepts@gmail.com), for a great cover! It shows the Torvatta streaking toward something that should not be there.

My family and friends who helped encourage me along the way.

My proofreader, Alexa, for being fast and great to work with!

My formatter and interior designer, Colleen Sheehan (www.ampersandbookinteriors.com/), for once again being the professional she is! She is great to work with and I'm glad she works with me!

BOOKS

You can see all books in the Evaran Chronicles
and the Earthborn at

WWW.ADAIRHART.COM/SERIES/ALLBOOKS.ASPX

www.ingramcontent.com/pod-product-compliance
Lightning Source LLC
Chambersburg PA
CBHW020503260626
47156CB00006B/1838